STRABO: THE UNWILLING LEGIONNAIRE

Preston Holtry

Moonshine Cove Publishing, LLC

Abbeville, South Carolina U.S.A.

First Moonshine Cove Edition December 2021

ISBN: 9781952439223

Library of Congress LCCN: 2021923022

© Copyright 2021 by Preston Holtry

Cover design by Cynthia Guare, interior design by Moonshine Cove staff

For Ruthie in appreciation for her friendship, constructive criticism and support of all my novels.

Acknowledgments

I appreciate the efforts of my wife, Judy, and her sister, Linda Ruth, for the time they spent contributing ideas, needed criticism and trolling for the inevitable typos that often defy discovery before publication although certain to be found by the reader.

I created the map for Celtic Gaul and surrounding provinces and countries from a terrain map obtained off the internet from maps-for-free.com.

Special thanks to Cynthia Guare for the front and back cover design. Once again, I'm grateful to Moonshine Cove for its support and Gene Robinson's willingness to take on another Roman series.

About the Author

Preston Holtry has a BA degree in English from the Virginia Military Institute and a graduate degree from Boston  University. A career army officer, he served twice in Vietnam in addition to a variety of other infantry and intelligence-related assignments in Germany, England, and the United States. Retired from the army with the rank of colonel, he lives with his wife, Judith, and Max, a rescue Retriever in Oro Valley, Arizona. Read more about him and his published books at his website:

http://www.presholtry.webs.com

Preface

In 58 B.C.E. near the end of the Roman Republic, the 41-year-old Gaius Julius Caesar has just vacated his elected term as consul of Rome. On the surface, he is at the apex of a successful military and political career; however, he has incurred the enmity of many political rivals in the Roman Senate who are convinced Caesar has ambitions perceived as a threat to the power of the Senate and future of the Republic. The older Roman senators recall General Gaius Marius, Caesar's uncle who some years before as consul seven times, presided over Rome more as a dictator than a democratic leader of the Senate.

Caesar has been awarded the governorship of two provinces in Near Gaul (see map) consisting of Provincia (Transalpine Gaul), Cisalpine Gaul and the province of Illyricum (modern day Balkans/Dalmatia). He is aware the appointment is a grudging sinecure and awarded primarily to keep him out of Rome. At first, Caesar has no plan to conquer Far Gaul consisting of Aquitania (southwestern France), Celtica (mainly France), and Belgica, (Netherlands and Belgium). He is looking for an opportunity to maintain the attention of Rome and the acclamation of the Roman populace essential to neutralize his many rivals. The opportunity comes when the Helvetii, a tribe located northeast of present-day Geneva, Switzerland, decides to migrate west, away from the stronger, warlike Germanic tribes occupying the tribe's northwestern border. The Helvetii intend to pass through the northern part of Provincia (Provence, southwestern France), which Caesar declares is unacceptable. The situation could not suit Caesar better.

It is Caesar's ambition as much as the Helvetii migration which ensnares Marcellus Strabo in a conflict he has no inclination nor choice to join. He is caught up in circumstances he never envisioned or wanted and resists until he realizes he has no choice but to endure what the gods already decided.

The series unfolds against a backdrop of historical fact and characters both *actual* and those invented to knit together the complicated events and turbulent time frame of the Gallic Wars. Occasionally I fill voids where historical details are absent. In the Author's Notes preceding the Glossary, I indicate where I've strayed a bit from historical truth. The Notes also contain a brief description of how the Romans were organized, equipped, supplied and fought. All tribes cited are identified in the *Commentaries.*

My principal source is Julius Caesar whose *Commentaries* have drawn praise throughout the centuries for its detailed, readable narration of the nearly eight-year conquest of Gaul, including two early incursions into Britannia during the period. I used the Loeb Classical Library version first published by the Harvard University Press in 1917 and republished many times since. Other key sources are Adrian Keith Goldsworthy's *The Roman Army at War 100 BC-AD 200*, and Ramon L. Jimenez's, *Caesar Against the Celts.* Equally helpful to me is Flavius Vegetius Renatus, an early Roman leader who penned *De Ri Militaria*, an influential treatise on the Roman military and widely used by military historians today.

PWH, Oro Valley, Arizona

Principal Characters

The Romans:

Marcellus Strabo, son of General Lucillus Strabo and an Aeduan noble woman

Brecius, *optio*, second century, XI Legion *Claudi*

Flavius Setarius, tribune and former *primus pilus*, X Legion, now assigned to Caesar's staff

†Gaius Julius Caesar, former consul of Rome, now governor of Province (Transalpine Gaul), Cisalpine

Gaius Marinus, centurion and commander, second century, XI Legion *Claudia*

†Publius Crassus, cavalry general and son of Marcus Crassus, friend and benefactor of Caesar

Rufus Valens, *primus pilus* (senior centurion), XI Legion, *Claudia*

Scevola, veteran legionnaire and Strabo's friend and messmate, XI, *Claudia* Legion

Tarquin, a decurion, X Legion, *Equestris*

†Titus Labienus, general, Caesar's Chief of Staff and commander X Legion
Equestris

Tulio, senior optio, XI Legion *Claudia*

Ursinus, a senior cavalryman, X legion, *Equestris* Vinicius, legionnaire and Strabo's friend from Massilia

The Aedui (I due):

†Ariovistus, King of the German Suebi (So a bee) and the other tribes in the German federation northeastern Gaul

Corius, childhood friend of Strabo, leader of the Aeduan scouts

†Diviciacus (Divi she ah coose), clan leader of the Aedui

†Divico, Tribal leader of the Helvetii

†Dumnorix (Doom nor ik), younger brother of Diviciacus

Morgane, wife of Dumnorix

†Liskus, virgobret (chief magistrate) of the Aedui

Raven, sister of Corius

Talos, Aeduan scout

†Historical

CELTICA GAUL 58 B.C.E.

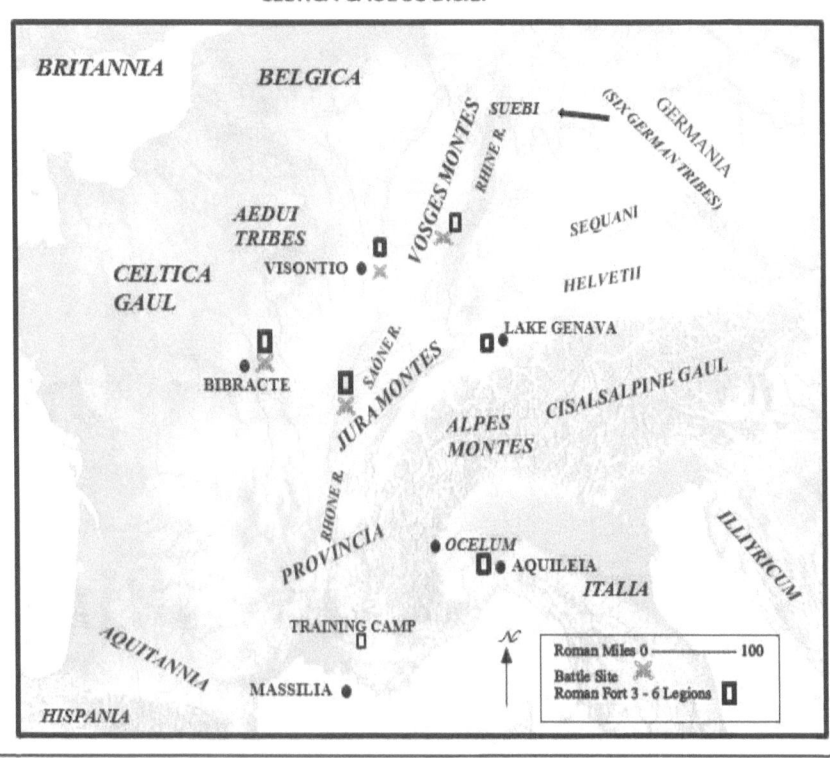

Strabo: the Unwilling Legionnaire

Prologue
Early March, 58 B.C.E., North of Rome in Transalpine Gaul

Otho, Caesar's chief steward and secretary, ushered the aging tribune and younger centurion into the room and waited while Gaius Julius Caesar read the report a decurion had just delivered from General Titus Labienus, commander of the Tenth Legion, *Equestris.* The Tenth Legion was the only legion in Far Gaul and positioned on the northeast frontier of Provincia to put down any unrest among the local tribes to the east and discourage any invasion by the Germanic tribes farther north.

It had been two years since the tribune had last seen Caesar. He was surprised at how much the younger man had aged. In spite of that, he retained the *dignitas* he carefully cultivated over the years. No doubt the thinning hair and lined forehead were a result of his recent political challenges in Rome and now the responsibility of three Roman provinces including command of several legions. Fair-haired with a hint of gray at the temple, Caesar was taller than most men. He was lean, well-built with a square face, high cheekbones, firm jaw and wrinkles at the corner of gray, piercing eyes. He concealed a receding hairline by brushing his naturally curly hair forward. He was dressed in a simple tunic rather than the ornate cuirass or toga he wore in public. Draped across his *curule* chair was the long red cloak Caesar wore on public occasions. Behind the chair stood the *fasces,* the bundle of tied birch rods around an axe symbolizing the *imperium* of a high official. On a nearby table was a gold crown in the design of a wreath of bay leaves recently awarded by the Roman Senate. He was seldom seen without it, both a vanity and a reminder to all he was blessed by the gods. Few would have doubted it.

Caesar finished reading the report and looked up at the three men waiting to see him. His somber expression quickly disappeared, replaced with a warm smile as he greeted the white-haired tribune. "Flavius Setarius, my one-eyed, scar-faced friend, it's good to see you again. I'm glad you're willing to serve me again."

"Caesar, after months of wondering why I left the legions, your letter was like a messenger from Jupiter. You asked me to select two senior centurions to assist me. Centurion Rufus Valens," motioning to the centurion, "will be the primus pilus of the new Eleventh *Claudia* Legion. Centurion Junius Lestus who will join me in a few days will be First Spear of the second legion, the Twelfth *Fulminata*."

"I've heard of you, Centurion. You were the former primus pilus of the Fifth Legion."

The centurion came to attention and saluted. "I was, and I'm honored to serve."

"General Labienus reports the Helvetii are taking active measures to cross the Rhône River into Provincia, which more than suggests it's time to help the Tenth legion. In addition to the three legions, I have wintering in the vicinity of Aquiliea, I need the two new legions at Ocelum in four weeks where they will rendezvous with the three legions now wintering in Aquileia. When you arrive, I'll be there to lead all five legions to Genava to reinforce General Labienus."

Setarius looked at Caesar. "I'm surprised the Senate is supporting the cost of raising two more legions."

"The Senate didn't. I'm bearing the cost. I won't give the money-pinching sycophants in the Senate a reason to complain Caesar is once again robbing Rome's coffers. In truth, Marcus Crassus is providing the resources." He paused and added with a sardonic smile, "With the friendship of the richest man in Rome behind me, I don't need the Senate. In return, I agreed to take on his young son Publius in some position which will give him opportunity to rise in Rome's esteem. It's a small concession for two more legions. I've met him, and he seems bright and willing enough. I'll accord him the title, *dux,* with senior standing. Until I know more of his capabilities, I'll keep him on my personal staff."

"Caesar, I submit the financial support of General Crassus is significant. More critical is the gods' help in getting the legions trained and in the field in half the time normally required."

"This is not a usual time, and with over 300,000 tribesmen prepared to cross into Gaul at any time, there isn't a moment to lose. I do not expect the soon to be Eleventh *Claudia* and Twelfth *Fulminata* Legions to be either fully-trained or close to full-strength. I need two more eagle standards to show the Helvetii. I will not permit any migration west. A cohort from the Eight *Augusta* Legion, one century each from the Seventh and Ninth and the other two legions in Aquileia will provide the cadre you'll need to recruit and train the legions in a fort near Massilia. The equipment and supplies you need are already there. I'm leaving immediately for Genava to consult with General Labienus concerning how the Tenth Legion may best delay the Helvetii advance until I can get the five legions to the border. I'm aware of the demanding task ahead of you. It will be a challenge but it must be accomplished in the time I specified." Hesitating, Caesar frowned before continuing. "I have another matter I invite your counsel. You both know or heard of Lucillus Strabo, former general of the Tenth Legion and eventually Governor of Provincia before retiring to his estates there about three years ago."

Flavius responded, "I had the good fortune of serving General Strabo at different times."

"The name Strabo is well-known," Valens said.

"Strabo is a valued client of mine and one I owe much for supporting both my political and financial interests in Provincia and farther Gaul. His son by the daughter of a senior tribal chieftain of the Aedui Tribe apparently has not lived up to expectations. I gather from the brief description provided he's a young man who seems ready to live on the reputation and bounty of his esteemed father. Strabo knows of my intention to recruit two legions and asked for my help in making something of his son — perhaps an appointment as a centurion or whatever else I deem suitable." Valens happened to glance at Setarius and wondered why the tribune seemed to be suppressing a smile.

"Well, I've no intention of weakening any century by burdening it with a man who's apparently unfit to motivate himself let alone the men he would lead. And unlike Publius Crassus, he doesn't bring anything to me except possibly a problem. General Strabo has given me some latitude concerning what I choose to do, and I would hear what you have to say."

Setarius smiled even broader. "I know something of the boy, or at least he was when the general asked me to find someone to teach him how to use a gladius years ago. He was an apt student, and I thought at the time he would one day serve Rome in the footsteps of his father. With the need for an aggressive recruiting campaign soon to begin, we cannot depend entirely on volunteers; therefore, some conscription will be required. Perhaps General Strabo's son will be among the first conscripts unless he chooses to volunteer which seems unlikely."

"So be it. I'll leave it to you to satisfy General Strabo's wishes, if not his son's. Under the circumstances, it would be best to keep young Strabo's identity known to as few as possible for his own sake. Do what you can to fulfill both the general's wishes and mine, and you'll find me most grateful."

Chapter 1, Near Massilia five days later.

Beyond his large size, there was nothing much to distinguish Marcellus Strabo from the other inebriated patrons of the brothel. He had no idea the evening before when he engaged the services of Helena, a willing and imaginative whore, how his life was about to change in a matter of hours.

The legionnaire looked at the naked man snoring in a drunken stupor with a woman in a similar state draped across him, left hand resting on his crotch. In a dream-like state, Strabo vaguely heard a voice ask, "Are you sure he's the one we've been looking for?"

The optio with the livid scar on his left cheek took a closer look and said, "He has the size, the tattoo on his right upper arm Setarius described and where we would find him. He's the one, and even if he isn't, he'll be a legionnaire in the *Claudia* tomorrow. Whether he'll be a willing recruit is up to him."

The second legionnaire flanking the optio said in unfeigned admiration, "By Jupiter's balls, the bastard is handsome and hung enough the whore might have given it for free."

The optio rolled his eyes in disgust. "Spare me your assessment before I think you're more interested in his parts than the wench. Get him dressed in whatever you can find and into the wagon. It's late, and I've better things to do than this."

With his eyes shut, Strabo reached for the whore in rising tumescent expectation only to receive a vigorous jab prompting him to open his eyes but not too wide. What little light came from the single flickering oil lamp was painful. Dimly, Strabo saw a burly man dressed in the all too familiar uniform of a Roman *optio* and two legionnaires of equal size. The optio jabbed him again with his *hastile*, the long, knobbed wooden staff indicating his rank, and ordered him to get on his feet. Incapable of understanding what he was being told to do much less having the capability of doing it, he took refuge in drifting back into a drunken, dream-like state oblivious to the nightmare soon to follow.

While the two legionnaires lifted the unconscious man by his arms and legs, the optio stared appreciatively at the naked whore.

"Take your time," he called after the legionnaires while removing his belt and pulling down his linen drawers. "I'll be along soon enough."

Strabo woke up with a dry throat, a raging thirst and a head aching so much Jupiter was surely making thunderbolts and using his head as an anvil. Rolling over and reaching for the whore engaged for the night, he felt only cold, rounded bars instead of a warm breast or thigh. Cautiously he opened an eye just enough to realize he was lying on a wagon bed looking at an early morning landscape passing slowly by. The motion was quickly followed by a sudden wave of nausea. He struggled to stand up and only got to his knees before vomiting the wine and whatever he had eaten hours before. Someone cursed, and the next thing he felt was a sharp blow to the side of his head. He fell into a dark void.

Regaining consciousness when a bucket of cold water hit his face, Strabo struggled to stand until he realized his wrists and ankles were tightly bound.

"It seems he may be alive after all. Cut him loose."

Strabo turned his head to see who was talking. A tall, broad-shouldered man with a scarred face, most of his right ear missing and a black eye patch covering his left eye, looked back at him. A cuirass covered with *phalorae* and a helmet with a longitudinal crest identified him as a tribune. Standing next to him were two centurions signified by their transverse helmet crests. Two optiones stood nearby, each holding the long rod distinctive of their rank. The older optio was tall and lean with a seamed face that could have been carved from granite. The second optio was smaller with a livid scar on his left cheek.

Strabo managed to stand and asked in a voice hardly recognizable as his own, "Who are you, and do you have any idea who I am?"

Setarius laughed. "I do, Marcellus Strabo. You may resemble General Lucillus Strabo, but it seems to be all you have in common with your noble and much esteemed father."

The younger centurion's eyes opened wide then quickly narrowed as he looked more closely at the bedraggled young man struggling to stay upright.

Setarius continued, "I'm disappointed you don't remember me. Years ago, I watched you learning how to use a gladius. Time has passed and both of us are older and memories fade. Enough of years gone by, I am Tribune Setarius. I am in charge of forming two new legions. You have now been conscripted into one of them." Gesturing to the older centurion next to him, "Centurion Rufus Valens is in command of the first cohort XI Legion, *Claudia* to which you've been assigned. Tulio," pointing to the second man, "is his senior optio. Centurion Gaius Marinus commands the second century where you're assigned. Optio Brecius is assigned to the second century; you'll come to know him well in the days and weeks to come. There will come a day when your hatred of him will give way to thanks for teaching you how to stay alive in the battles you will soon face."

"I'm a free citizen of Rome, and you've no right to treat me this way."

"Under the circumstances, I have the right to treat you any way I choose. Rome is in imminent danger of invasion and requires the means to resist it."

"I've no intention of remaining here, and my father will see you stripped and broken for treating me this way."

"You've no choice. It's your father who's responsible for you being here."

"I don't believe you."

"It doesn't matter to me if you don't. The fact is you're here, and it will be up to you whether you choose to accept what *Fortuna* has in mind for you and make the best of what you probably feel is a bad bargain. Your father apparently is willing to give you one more chance to be something other than what you have become."

19

"Even if what you say is true, I'll not change my mind. I won't serve."

"The road ahead for you will be troublesome and much more difficult than you can imagine. It may become less difficult should you choose to volunteer and change your status from conscript to volunteer."

"I won't volunteer."

"Very well, conscription it will be. It so happens your father seems to think you're nothing but a wine-soaked wastrel with a stiff cock who spends most of his time riding whores or horses. He thinks your future would be brighter if you were to serve the eagle. I understand you refused the offer to serve as a centurion as your father expected and hoped you would be. It seems you had other ideas. Now you're being given an alternative to make something of yourself."

Strabo recalled the last meeting with his father from whom he had become increasingly estranged over recent years. They rarely saw one another, and when they did, parting was usually strained or even contentious. The last time had been especially heated and ended up with his father warning him to mend his ways, or he would put him on the street without so much as a sesterce to his name. When he left, Strabo didn't believe his aging father would cast out his only son. Now, he wasn't so sure.

"No matter what my father wants or what you do to me, I won't serve."

"What say you, Marinus, does young Strabo need a little persuasion to better understand his situation?"

"I think Brecius can assist in convincing our reluctant volunteer to better understand his present circumstances." Marinus nodded to the optio who stepped forward and without a word rammed the knobbed end of his staff into Strabo's stomach.

Retching and struggling to breathe, Strabo refused to give in and responded with a hoarse voice, "I'll leave at the first opportunity." The bravado earned him a second and even harder blow, and this time Strabo's knees buckled. It took several minutes for him to catch his breath and stop the world from spinning around. Slowly, he pushed himself up and silently faced the three men with a defiant look.

Setarius stepped closer to Strabo and said calmly, "If you leave this camp without permission, you will be considered a deserter, and if caught, as you surely will, the consequence will be painful or much worse. Let me persuade you it's not the best way to leave the legion in which you are now enrolled. You have a chance for a new beginning in a life so far spoiled by privilege. You've no choice but to accommodate or suffer consequences you cannot imagine. The legions are demanding enough without making it even more difficult for anyone who joins, willingly or unwillingly. Centurion Marinus and Optio Brecius will be the means to make something of you. It will be your choice to decide if you're man enough to accept the challenge and the opportunity to make something of yourself as your father expects."

"I curse you and my father for ..." Brecius stepped forward and with another sharp jab stifled whatever else Strabo intended to say.

Setarius looked closely at the young man and said with a combination of resignation and regret, "I think your father is demanding something you're not capable of achieving. I hope I'm wrong, and somehow you have the will to measure up. As for me, I'm doubtful you have the capability. Now, my unwilling legionnaire, listen carefully. Only I and the other four officers know your identity. It will benefit you in the weeks to come if the other seven men in your *contubernium* and the rest of the century don't realize you're General Strabo's son. If they do, you'll suffer for it. They will see you as nothing other than a product of privilege and luxury they've never known or ever will. My advice is to use only the name Marcellus, the name by which you will be entered in the roles of the legion. Brecius, get him outfitted and assigned to a *contubernium*. Marcellus, may the gods favor you in the difficult days ahead for no one else will."

Setarius, Valens and Tulio watched as Marinus and Brecius prodded Strabo in the direction of the supply tent to be outfitted. The tribune said to the centurion, "Rufus, I'm afraid I'll disappoint General Strabo in the outcome."

21

"Possibly, but he has potential. Did you see the way he got back on his feet after Brecius hit him the second time? He has spirit, and his anger of the moment may well lead to a better outcome than you expect." Valens looked across the field and observed the optiones with oaths and knobbed staffs marshalling the latest volunteers assembled into some semblance of order in the field close by. "With the short time we have to ready the two legions, it isn't just Marcellus who needs the favor of the gods."

Setarius said, "We'll do the best we can. You know as well as I do, they'll receive their final training in the field. The reality of screaming Gauls ready to take your head off will inspire them to improve the skills they will learn here."

Valens looked away and asked, "Do you really think the Republic is in danger?"

"From the Gauls, not particularly, possibly from Caesar. Who gives a shit? Most of the politicians sitting on their backsides in Rome care only about their villas on the coast and profiting from patronage and ensuring the plebs and the legions continue to suck hind tit. We accept a laborer's pay with the promise of booty never measuring up to the hardship of long campaigns with little to show for them."

"You almost seem to welcome an end to the Republic," Valens said with a perplexed expression.

"I don't know. I'm always ready for an opportunity to improve what we now have, or better said, what we don't have. Who knows, Caesar's ambition may give us better days ahead."

Centurion Marinus drew Brecius aside as Strabo was being fitted with a tunic, leather *balteus*, minus a *pugio* and *gladius*, and a pair of hobnailed *caligae*. In an undertone, the centurion said, "Put him in the contubernium where Tertious is assigned."

The optio looked at the centurion with upraised eyebrow. "Why Tertious? I've already warned him twice, if he doesn't do more training and less abusing of the recruits, I'll send him back to permanent guard duty and replace him with someone who will do what needs to be done.

The bastard is nothing but trouble. Given the importance of this particular recruit, I'm surprised you would want him anywhere close to that son of a bitch."

"Brecius, you heard Setarius. General Strabo himself is the one who put his son here. He expects us to accomplish what he apparently could not. I think Tertious is exactly the right man to help fulfill the general's expectations. Now do as you're told."

"Yes, Centurion." Stung by the sudden, brusque command, Brecius saluted and watched the centurion walk away. Although he'd only served under the centurion for a short time, until now he had no reason to doubt the officer's judgment. He didn't think it would be too long before Tertious would prove the centurion's order was a mistake.

Chapter 2

To Strabo the past few days had become a blur with each day worse than the one before. His introduction to the other six recruits and Tertious, the one veteran legionnaire assigned to the eight-man contubernium, had not gone well. His taciturn, terse response to the friendly questions concerning his background and why he had volunteered succeeded only in further isolating him. He was dimly aware of the growing hostility of his messmates. The latter was fueled by Tertious, who dominated the microbial world of their leather tent with his constant boasting of his past legionary experience. For the most part, Strabo concentrated on finding a way to escape and ignored the veteran's verbal abuse and petty actions. Tertious ridiculed the new recruits more than helping them acclimate to the harsh training as he was supposed to do. His first open altercation with Tertious occurred when they were released to go to the bathing hut after another strenuous day. Tertious noticed the tattoos on Strabo's arm and drew attention to them.

"Marcellus, I warrant those markings on your arm show you're only a half-Roman with some Gaul making up the rest. Is that the way of it?"

Strabo didn't respond or acknowledge he'd heard and continued to wash. A few of the others paused in what they were doing and looked with a combination of interest and anticipation of a welcome break in routine.

"Did you hear what I said?"

"I heard you. I wasn't interested in anything you have to say to me, now or ever."

"You'd better show me some respect and mind what you say to me. If you think your time here has been hard, I'll make sure in the days to come it will be harder than you can imagine."

"You're a loud-mouthed turd with nothing worthwhile to say; therefore, how could I possibly show you any respect. And further, you're in no position to make my life any worse than it is. Like the rest of us, you're nothing except older and slower."

"No one talks to me like that and—"

"And what? Summon the gods to help you deal with me because it's what you'll need, assuming they will, which I doubt. Now either shut up or come over here and convince me I'm wrong about you."

"What's going on here?" The harsh sound of Brecius' voice was sufficient for all to hear except Strabo.

"Marcellus, are you causing trouble? Because if you are, I'm the last one you want to know about it. Maybe Tertious can't do much to you, but by Jupiter's fire, I can and will. Now all of you finish up here and get back to your tent. Today was bad, tomorrow will be worse."

It wasn't long before the relentless, strenuous training left the recruits too exhausted at the end of the day to do more than dread the next day. Every day they were made to run faster and longer. At first it was without equipment. Tomorrow they would be fully-outfitted. Simple runs became more challenging when they included obstacles or trenches which seemed to grow wider or bigger by the day, taxing their physical capabilities in an ever-increasing tempo. Strabo found the blistering forced marches carrying all their issued equipment strapped to a T-shaped pole slung over the shoulder demanding as the marches became progressively longer. The cadre was merciless in the use of their knobbed staffs in the case of the optiones and the *vitis*, the twisted vine stick carried by the centurions and administered with a welt-raising sting for any real or imagined infraction. The physical demands of the long training days and the brutality of the cadre only increased Strabo's intention to get away. Eventually, he gave up looking for an opportunity to escape when it became apparent the legionnaires from the Tenth Legion were there not only to train the recruits but to prevent anyone who had second thoughts from going over or under the palisade. It took only the seventh day for a young recruit caught soon after escaping the fort to be brought forward and summarily branded on the face. Setarius had not been bluffing about the consequences of desertion. At least for the time being, he would bide his time by remaining faceless and unremarkable.

Tertious continued his unrelenting efforts to impose a dictatorial domination of the contubernium. In time, passive acceptance of his bullying gave way to a growing resentment by the other members of the mess. Circumstances came to a head the night he decided his portion of the evening ration was not enough to satisfy. He eyed what remained in Quintillus' bowl. "Quintillus, you little runt, I'll have some of what you have." Without waiting for a response, Tertious leaned over and spooned a generous portion of the smaller man's porridge into his wooden bowl, prompting Quintillus to jump up and deliver a surprisingly effective kick to the larger man's jaw. More shocked than stunned by the assault, Tertious reached out and pulled Quintillus down by the leg and with one blow knocked him senseless.

Without any conscious thought of the outcome, Strabo said, "Tertious, we've all had enough of your bullying. Give his ration back now, or you'll answer to me."

Tertious leisurely stood. "Sit down, Marcellus, and don't interfere, or you'll get worse than this worthless shit."

Strabo took a step backward as if regretting his intervention. "I won't tell you again. Leave him alone and back away."

Tertious slowly pulled out the small dagger he carried strapped to his left arm and said with a confident, taunting smile, "Your words are bold, but I think all you have are words. I'm going to give you another tattoo as a reminder to never get in my way again."

Strabo did not anticipate Tertious would take the matter far enough to use the dagger. He recalled the training the seasoned centurion his father engaged to instruct him in the use of shield, gladius, spear and dagger, including, if unarmed, how best to disable an armed opponent. Until now, the instruction had seemed theoretical since he never expected he would one day make practical use of the lessons. The larger man's fighting experience and size could easily and quickly decide the issue. Strabo was not certain it would be in his favor. Tertious came slowly toward him with his left hand tightened in a fist. Strabo anticipated what the veteran legionnaire was going to do and ducked under the blow intended for his right jaw and delivered two quick punches to the other man's stomach. Tertious doubled over, and Strabo followed up with an uppercut to the neck that brought his opponent to his knees gasping for air.

Strabo said, "Help me put him on his pallet, and he can sleep it off."

The next morning Tertious lost no time in telling Strabo in a raspy voice, "You'll pay for what you did if it's the last thing I ever do."

"Hear me, when I say there better not be. The next time you try anything with me, or any of the others in this tent, you'll suffer more than a sore throat. If you haven't already learned from what happened to you last night, you'll have more opportunity in the days to come to see you're overmatched." Strabo turned away and left hoping his bluff would dampen the other man's revenge. In the event it didn't, he intended to sleep lightly and count on the others in the contubernium to warn him if Tertious tried anything.

Later in the day there was no longer any concern when Tertious was replaced by another veteran legionary from the Tenth Legion. Scevola was much older and more seasoned than Tertious. The multiple scars on his face and right forearm spoke of his long years of service in the legions. There was none of the braggadocio typical of most experienced legionnaires who embellished their battle experience. Strabo found the older legionnaire a well-spring of practical advice without any of the criticism or bullying Tertious had subjected them to. His seasonal service over the past twenty years provided a wealth of practical advice to the inexperienced legionnaires. Without using ridicule or scathing criticism, he quietly transformed his messmates into a cohesive unit.

From the looseness of his linen drawers, Strabo knew he was losing weight. The cause was the rigorous training and spare rations they were given consisting of thin soup, wheat porridge, hard biscuits and on rare occasions, meat of dubious origin. Following the altercation with Tertious, his relations with his messmates improved. In spite of it, he felt increasingly isolated. He wondered how much longer he could endure both the physical hardships and the reality of being in the company of men with whom he had nothing in common except to get through the next day. He focused on doing whatever was necessary. Brecius expected to be obeyed immediately without question, and failure to do so resulted in a sharp jab from his knobbed staff. There was also the sharp sting of the vine stick Centurion Marinus wielded at the least provocation. At first Strabo thought it was only his imagination the centurion seemed particularly focused on him until it became equally noticeable to his messmates. For now, it was all about appearing to accept his fate until he saw an opportunity to escape.

Strabo thought his chances would be better when training extended beyond the confines of the palisaded training camp. In the meantime, the physical routine began to transition from physical conditioning to the basics of learning how to use a heavy training shield as both a defensive and offensive weapon. They were armed with a weighted wooden gladius also heavier than the metal sword they would eventually carry. Thanks to the training his father had subjected him to when most boys of his age were engaged in less martial activities, he quickly stood out from the others. Scevola's praise was genuine, prompting questions how he had become so proficient in the use of shield and sword. He responded with a vague account of having been given lessons some years before by an ex-legionnaire.

Brecius entered the tent and saluted Centurion Marinus sitting behind a table opposite the entrance. The optio saw the set jaw and glaring eyes of the officer and wondered what he was in for now. He couldn't think of anything to earn the wrath of his superior although he had quickly learned it didn't require much to get on the wrong side of the prickly centurion. He didn't have to wait long to find out.

"I saw Tertious on guard duty. Can you explain why he is instead of training with his contubernium?"

"Sir, he wasn't working out. After the latest incident, I felt I had no choice and I sent him to the guard detail. I brought in another veteran to replace him I thought would do better."

"What incident?"

"Two nights ago, he confronted Marcellus Strabo and found out he was no match for him. For me, it was enough. His replacement has already proven I should have gotten rid of him before now."

"Optio, I was the one who told you to assign Strabo to that particular contubernium because of Tertious. You should have informed me of the *incident,* and *I* would have decided what should be done. You've exceeded your authority. I'll not tolerate any such occurrence again, or you'll be back in the ranks where you probably should never have left. Now get out!"

White-faced, the optio saluted, and with all the restraint he could muster, turned and left the tent. Until now he had ignored the petty criticisms, but this was enough to convince him to seek Tulio's help in getting transferred to another century.

Marinus noted the optio's expressionless face and stiffened posture and wondered if he had gone too far. He had been criticized in the past for not controlling his temper, a failing which had caused him problems. General Strabo told him it was the reason he didn't select him as First Spear when by experience and length of service, he was more qualified than the man the general selected. The refusal was enough to quash any further consideration for the coveted position in the Tenth or any other legion including the *Claudia.* He would curse General Strabo with the last breath in his body. If he couldn't get revenge on the father, the son would have to do. Tertious may be more distant, then there were other ways the legionnaire could be useful with an incentive encouraged by a few sestercii and the possibility of restoring him to his former optio rank.

As watch officer, Marinus saw his opportunity for a private conversation with Tertious when he saw the legionnaires name listed for the third watch. Normally he would have had the optio of the guard check the guard posts during the late hours. Tonight, he intended to make the rounds instead of the optio.

Marinus was pleased to find Tertious fast asleep leaning against a parapet. The centurion struck the legionnaire across his exposed neck with enough force to send him sprawling and followed up with a vicious kick to the ribs.

"Tertious, have you forgotten how painful or even fatal the consequence is for sleeping on guard?" Unable to stand and struggling to breathe, the legionnaire didn't answer. "All right, let me remind you. The least that could happen to you is 500 lashes with a *flagellum*. Occasionally an individual lives to regret it, but it's a rare exception. I'm willing to overlook your dereliction and give you a chance to keep on living."

Resigned to hearing the worst, Tertious managed to regain his feet and come to attention.

"This is what I want from you. I understand Marcellus Strabo — yes, he's the son of General Lucillus Strabo — is the reason you're no longer in a contubernium and are serving guard duty. Well, I want you to do something to him to make up for it. Are you listening?"

"Yes, Sir, what do you want me to do and why?"

"Why is no concern of yours. You enjoy using a knife which is why you're no longer an optio..."

"The son of a bitch hit..."

"Shut up and listen. I don't care why you were demoted. Here's what I want. Do what I tell you, and you might have a chance to be an optio again. I want Strabo hurt and hurt bad. Not killed, mind you. Take an eye, maybe hamstring him, enough to send him back to Massilia as a civilian. Make it look like an accident. I'll leave it to you to figure how and when. Do this and all things are possible including you've never slept on guard. I'll be waiting to see you get it done."

Tertious watched the centurion disappear in the darkness with a mix of relief and shock. He smiled and thought a centurion had never told him to do something he would be more pleased to obey. It didn't take long to come up with a plan.

Strabo woke up and vaguely wondered why until he felt the urgent need to piss. He crawled out of the leather tent trying not to wake up his tentmates. The close confines made the effort impossible. He wound up waking several of them in the process of getting outside. Half asleep, he stumbled the short distance to the latrine trench dimly illuminated by a single torch and near where the cavalry and officers' horses were stabled. He pulled aside his under drawers barely in time, sighed with relief and closed his eyes already anticipating getting back to his pallet. He thought of the day when he no longer slept with seven other men and used a malodorous trench in the middle of the night. Half asleep, he felt an arm tight around his neck and the sharp prick of a dagger near his right eye, followed by a warm trickle running down his cheek. The raspy voice in his ear easily identified the assailant as Tertious.

"Keep holding your cock, you whoreson. One move, and I'll cut you more than this. I said you'd regret what you did to me. The gods woke me and told me to piss then I saw you. The gods have never been so good to me."

"You're even dumber than I thought. Whatever you do to me, a dozen men including Brecius and Marinus will know who did it."

"It will be my word against yours. They'll find you in the shit below and think you hurt yourself falling in..."

Strabo heard Tertious grunt, and the arm around his neck loosened. It was enough incentive to drive his right elbow into the legionnaire's side. He felt the dagger slide down across his cheek as Tertious released him. Ignoring the burning wound, he turned around in a crouch and saw Tertious on all fours with Quintillus on his back. The legionnaire abruptly stood up, reached behind him and easily tossed the smaller man over his shoulder. Stunned, Quintillus remained on the ground. Tertious quickly turned around, but he wasn't fast enough to avoid Strabo's knee to the groin.

Strabo looked down at the moaning legionnaire. "I think the gods only intended you to piss after all. Go back to your tent and give thanks

31

to the whore who dropped you that she gave you enough sense to do that rather than trying to finish what you can't."

Tertious picked up the dagger, hesitated and sheathed it. "I swear before the gods there will be another time and place when you won't be so lucky." Clutching his groin with both hands, the legionnaire stumbled toward the tents.

Strabo bent over Quintillus. "Are you hurt?"

"I'm all right. He just knocked the wind out of me."

"I'm glad you needed to piss; otherwise, he was about to do things I care not to think about."

"You woke me up when you left the tent. I thought as long as I was awake, I might as well visit the latrines. I happened to see Tertious going that way, too. When I got here, I saw him come up behind you. I forgot about the dagger he wore until he dropped it, or I wouldn't have done what I did."

"My friend, I'm glad you did. I'll find a way to pay you back."

"No need. You did us all a good turn when you were the reason Brecius had him assigned to guard duty. Are you going to report him?"

"No, but from now on I'll be more careful to keep him in front of me, particularly when I'm taking a piss."

The second week started with a long run to a small lake nearby. The sweaty legionnaires were delighted when the optiones told them as a reward for their efforts, they would be given a chance to cool off before returning to camp. They were led to a steep bank and told to jump in. Too late to realize the water was deep, those who couldn't swim were soon floundering and desperately trying to reach the bank. The laughing optiones used their knobbed rods to push back those who obviously could not swim. After a few minutes, the panicked non-swimmers were allowed to crawl up the bank and told they had survived their first swimming lesson. The second would begin in five minutes in the shallows, after which future lessons would be in deep water. The challenge was to learn to swim or risk drowning if they were unable to successfully complete a quarter mile swim at the end of training.

By the end of the additional week, the heavy wooden swords were replaced with blunted metal blades as the recruits were taught to integrate the use of shield and sword to fight effectively while protecting the legionnaire on the left in a shield-wall. It wasn't long before it was apparent to the dullest recruit the gladius was intended to be a stabbing movement rather than a hacking weapon that left the torso vulnerable with a raised arm.

In the third week, the recruits were issued two pila. Both javelins had wooden shafts containing soft, removable metal spear points. One was clearly heavier than the other. The initial demonstration by the optiones suggested this was going to be a physical reprieve from the arduous shield and gladius training. The demonstrators armed with two javelins apiece appeared to make it look easy when their first spears struck two of the four shields propped against hay bales fifty paces away. The two shields promptly fell forward. The demonstrators quickly had the second volley in the air almost before the first ones struck the remaining two shields. The shields remained propped against the hay bales.

Hands on hips, Brecius looked at the line of recruits. "Can anyone tell me why the first two shields fell and the other two didn't?" His question was met by silence. "All right, you pathetic bastards, I realize this requires a little more thought than bedding a whore when you're fumbling around depending on her help to get it done. I'll ask again, tell me what just happened." Strabo knew why and didn't respond, preferring to remain just another faceless recruit.

Finally, there was a tentative response. "Was it because the second javelins were lighter and pinned the shields to the bales?"

Brecius smiled. "Not a bad answer, and you're right about them being lighter, but that's not all of it. The points on all our javelins are too broad to pass through a heavy shield like a *scuta*. However, there is a difference between the metal shafts of the first spears and the second two. Anyone else want to try?" Again, there was silence.

"By Jupiter's sacred balls, is there not one of you who can figure it out?" When no one answered, the optio threw up his hands in mock exasperation. "Look, you shit-for-brains, I'll give you a hint. Take the metal spear shaft on the heavier of your two javelins and bend it." He waited while the recruits bent the metal shafts. "Now why do you think we give you javelins with metal shafts that bend so easily?"

Quintillus spoke up, "The first two spears had bending shafts which pulled the shields down, leaving the one holding it vulnerable to the next javelin."

"Praise the gods!" The optio responded in mock reverence. "At least one of you may be intelligent enough to become an optio one day."

A few days later, the trainees left the palisaded compound for a week in the field to concentrate on unit cohesion during the march and on the battlefield. They practiced different battle formations according to various situations described by the trainers. Each day ended with the requirement to dig an entrenched and palisaded camp before being permitted to eat.

The trainees were also instructed in the duties and responsibilities of the night guard detail. They were told a guard officer, the *Tessera*, was responsible for the password and that it was passed on to subsequent reliefs. The recruits were unaware their time on guard was nothing more than a training exercise. The cadre provided the real guard force beyond the limits of the closer-in perimeter for an external threat virtually non-existent in Provincia. In reality, the cadre was there to prevent desertion, which remained a much more practical concern.

Strabo thought there was finally an opportunity to escape when reliefs were established, and he found himself assigned the third watch on the second night, the least desirable of the watches as it required staying awake during the middle hours of the night. Far from being disappointed, he thought the opportunity to escape was a gift of the gods. He knew exactly where the marching camp was. Its proximity to where he kept his two horses in a stable nearby was an opportunity too great to resist the opportunity offered. He was certain he could be miles away west to Aquitania and farther south into Hispania well before any determined effort was organized to come after him. He doubted there would be any serious attempt to go after a ranker who was likely to be written off and easily replaced.

The moon was no more than a pale sliver and made darker with an intermittent cloud cover, perfect for moving silently toward the western perimeter. He hoped the sentinels would be more focused on an assumed attacker than anyone trying to escape the camp. Strabo thought he was well beyond the camp outposts and began to relax when he suddenly found himself on his back and struggling to breathe while feeling the sharp point of a blade at his neck.

"Marcellus, your attempt to leave was ill-conceived and unwise even had you succeeded."

Strabo saw two shadowy forms in the dim moonlight and recognized the voice of Centurion Valens. He suspected the other was Tulio. Valens confirmed the suspicion.

"Tulio had a hunch you would try something tonight as close as we are to where you stable your horses."

"I told you I would leave at the first opportunity, and this seemed the best chance so far. Whatever you do to me, I'll try again."

"This is your first and last mistake, and I'm willing to overlook it. If you try again, there will be no appeal, and the consequences will be severe enough to make you wish you hadn't. Tonight, I'll give you a choice to decide if Fortuna favors you and the life you've so far led, or if she intends you to be a legionnaire."

"I don't understand, what choice?"

"I'll make no attempt to stop you, nor will I inform Centurion Marinus or Brecius. We'll both see if the gods approve of the decision you make tonight."

"You're just going to let me walk away?"

"It's your choice to make — stay and endure the hardships of the campaigns ahead or leave now and go back to a purposeless existence."

"I never wanted any part of this. I'm not my father who spent his life in endless campaigns to the glory of Rome."

"Poor Marcellus Strabo who only wanted to spend his life in idleness at the expense of a father who provided the means to coddle you while serving Rome to an extent you cannot conceive. You had privilege and opportunities, yet so far, you've squandered it all. I've watched you since you were conscripted, and I saw much to believe you have promise, possibly more than you ever realized," there was slight hesitation before he added, "or deserved."

Without a word, Strabo turned and went back to camp resolving to bide his time and prove to the centurion and optio he was a model legionnaire who had accepted his fate and the will of Jupiter — at least until the next chance to escape a fate he had no intention of enduring one day longer than necessary. He would wait for the gods to show him the way back to winning the next race and enjoying the delights afterward in the arms of a pliant woman.

Tulio watched Strabo disappear in the darkness. "Why didn't he accept your offer to leave?"

"He didn't believe me," Valens paused, "and he was right not to. I said I wouldn't stop him, but I didn't say for how long."

"You think he'll try again?"

"Perhaps. If he does, he'd better do it soon. Ready or not, Setarius will obey Caesar's order to be at Ocelum when ordered which means we can expect to leave here in four or five days. Soon Marcellus Strabo will be more concerned about the Gauls and keeping his head on his shoulders than deserting."

Dumnorix leaned back and listened to the Helvetii emissary with a concerned expression while savoring the opportunity now before him. The opportunity would further his already growing influence, not only within the confederation of Aeduan tribes but with the other tribes in northern Gaul. He already had a good idea what the Helvetii wanted from him. He didn't want to reveal just how much he knew about the tribe's inability to get past the Romans south of Genava. With the significantly greater strength of the Helvetii, he was surprised Orgetorix had not yet crossed the Rhône River.

Dumnorix asked, "The Romans have only one legion with far fewer numbers than the Helvetii. Why haven't they crossed the river?"

"The Romans burned the bridge crossing the Rhône and built an earthen wall on the opposite bank of the river stretching all the way from the river to the Jura Mountains. The river is too swift to allow us to cross over in the few boats we have with sufficient warriors to defeat them."

"Then why do you come to me?"

"Lord, since Caesar will not allow the Helvetii to cross the river to enter the land they call Provincia, we will have to go over the Jura Mountains into the land of the Sequani and cross the Saône to journey west. You have great influence with the Sequani; therefore, we seek your assistance in getting their permission to pass through their land."

"It isn't just the Sequani who might object if you enter their land. Once you do, you'll need my permission to cross Aeduan lands."

"Lord, it is our second request in addition to assisting our passage."

"I do have some influence with Casticus, but he will want the same assurance I do — a guarantee you won't take our grain and horses as you pass through our lands."

"Casticus no longer lives."

37

Dumnorix stiffened and tried not to show his concern. "He seemed well enough when I saw him not long ago."

"Lord, it was because he met with you and Orgetorix that he lost the confidence of the Sequani. Orgetorix suffered the same fate for the same reason."

His throat tightened. The emissary's bemused smile was enough to indicate his agreement with Orgetorix and Casticus was too well known. They had conspired to help each other replace the confederation each tribe enjoyed with single kingdoms ruled separately by each of them. At the time, he thought the plan would not only benefit him but the Aedui as well. With his recent marriage to Morgane, Orgetorix's daughter, his private alliance foretold a bright future. With both Casticus and Orgetorix dead and Divico obviously aware of his arrangement with the two former leaders, his ambition to be king of the Aedui appeared to be no more than a dream.

It was clear the request to mediate with the Sequani was not the real intent of the emissary's visit. In fact, Dumnorix suspected the Sequani already had agreed to help the Helvetii flank the Romans after crossing the Jura Mountains. The emissary's mission was a not-so-subtle message for him to assist the Helvetii in whatever they required. The alternative was the pact he made with the dead tribal leaders would be revealed to the Aedui with fatal consequences.

"I will confer with the Sequani and see what can be done to assist the Helvetii."

"Does it also mean we have assurances from the Aedui?"

Dumnorix replied through clenched teeth with a single word, "Yes." He stood signaling the audience was over and waited for the emissary to leave. The Helvetian remained where he was. Irritated, Dumnorix said, "I don't believe there is anything more to discuss."

"Perhaps there is one more thing. We would like you to go back with us to intervene in our behalf with the Sequani. We intend to begin crossing the Jura Mountains in a few days; therefore, it will be beneficial to us and the Sequani not to waste any time getting their assistance."

Dumnorix felt a cold chill. The request was nothing more than a veiled order. The thought of placing his life in the hands of the Helvetii left him momentarily speechless. With difficulty, he recovered and managed to sound unconcerned when he responded. "I do not believe my physical presence will be necessary. I'll send one of my senior clansmen well-known to the Sequani who can speak for me."

"Lord, I do not think that is what the leadership of the Helvetii intended when I was sent here. If you are concerned you will suffer harm, you may be assured I will remain here as hostage until your safe return. I'll remain here tonight, and you may give me your answer tomorrow." The emissary bowed and left.

He heard the rustle of the hide screen closing off the room behind him and turned to see Morgane come in the room. Her face was composed.

"I can see you're grieving deeply for your father," Dumnorix said.

"I cannot grieve for someone I never knew. He understood the risk, and now you do as well, even if you didn't know before. Will you go with him?"

"I don't know."

"I think you have little choice if you want to spare the Sequani and the Aedui what I think will be inevitable."

"What do you mean?"

"The Helvetii will be locusts laying waste to your land, leaving nothing behind no matter what you do to help them."

"You mean *our* land?"

"If you say. Perhaps it's not too late to make amends with Diviciacus." Morgane referred to her husband's older, more reserved and less ambitious brother who by rights had been and should be tribe and clan leader. "He has great influence with the Romans through his daughter's marriage to the former general who once led the legion now fighting the Helvetii. You may recall he was also the former governor of Provincia."

"Strabo's no longer influential as he once was. He's neither a general nor a governor anymore, and Brigitte died years ago."

39

"You have more chance to achieve what you want with the Romans than the Helvetii who will never do anything for you or the Aedui."

"Now your father's dead, you may be right even though, unlike my brother, I hate the Romans. It's only a matter of time before the Romans take all of Gaul, and we'll be ruled by Roman governors who expect us to become like them."

"Husband, if Orgetorix was still alive, it would not matter. When he gave me as wife to you, it was a bribe and a hollow promise the Aedui would benefit and you would be king. Yes, you would have been a king, but one who owed allegiance to Orgetorix whose ambition was to be ruler of all the tribes in Gaul."

Dumnorix wanted to refute what she said. The lingering doubt he soon had after agreeing to Orgetorix's plan only confirmed the truth of what she said and what his unassuming brother had also warned him would happen. He felt his chest constrict, and it was with effort he concealed his anguish and indecision from Morgane.

When Orgetorix first offered Morgane to him, she was described as a young and beautiful woman. He initially thought it was nothing more than a political arrangement — that is until he saw her. In the two years since their marriage, his initial infatuation with the considerably younger woman had given way to a cold acceptance on her part and loveless coupling thereafter. It was also apparent either by design or nature there was no sign she was willing to provide another heir to the fortunes of the Aedui. Now, there was little between them, only a precarious political alliance now cold and dead as Orgetorix.

"I'll talk to Diviciacus and see what he has to say. Perhaps he'll consent to go in my place."

"I'll be surprised if he agrees considering how you've treated him. It would be better if he went to the Romans to seek their support which we will need to resist a reality you so far seem unable to grasp."

Dumnorix knew what she said was right. Her casual indifference to the peril he would face in the hands of the Helvetii nettled him.

"He dislikes confrontation and will do as I ask. I may have to cede power to him which will both surprise and please him."

"Why would you do that?"

"Expedience, my dear wife. I may require help from the Romans. He's well-liked and trusted by them in a way I'm not. The Romans are justified to think so."

Morgane nodded approval thinking her husband may have a deeper understanding of the situation than she'd observed so far.

"Husband, you choose to follow a road between the Romans and Helvetii, a road which will narrow quickly when your border is crossed. When that time comes, which side are you prepared to support?"

"Whichever I think will benefit the Aedui — and me." It was a practical response and suited her purpose and welfare as well. She didn't care who prevailed as long as she survived.

A few hours later after presenting what he believed was a well-reasoned, practical solution to Diviciacus, he was reeling from his brother's unbending refusal to accompany the Helvetii emissary. There was a subtle change in Diviciacus, a quiet resolve unlike the affable, indecisive dreamer he was more used to dealing with. More alarming, his refusal included an implied suggestion circumstances may warrant consideration for a change in tribal leadership. Morgane's half-smile and lift of her shoulders after his brother left was silent but eloquent confirmation, she had sensed a difference in Diviciacus before he had. With growing apprehension, he realized he had no choice. He would go north to the Helvetii.

Chapter 4 Ocelum six days later

Strabo looked up at the low hill they were passing and saw a group of men on horseback watching them. From the horsehair plumes on their helmets and the elaborate cuirass each wore, he gathered these were the generals and senior officers who would dictate their future. His attention was drawn to the mounted and bare-headed man wearing a red cloak and gold circlet instead of a helmet. He wondered who he was although it was an idle thought. He was occupied with the reality every step over the past five days took him farther away with fewer opportunities to escape.

The mind and body-numbing monotony of the march discouraged any thoughts of escaping in a largely open landscape offering little chance of evading the cavalry flanking the snaking two-mile marching column. For now, he accepted the reality he would have to be patient and keep on developing an idea he began to think might be the best way to see the last of the *Claudia* Legion.

Caesar watched the two legions straggling into the cantonment with misgivings and wondered if Crassus had got his money's worth. Both legions were little more than half the size of a veteran legion; however, given the time to muster and the need to meet the threat of the Helvetii, he thought Setarius had earned the reward he intended to give him. Briefly, he considered if it would be better to consolidate the two legions into one. He quickly dismissed the notion in favor of retaining the additional eagle standard and the psychological advantage it might have in countering the overwhelming numbers the legions would face when they reached Genava. Any thought of ordering the departure of the five-legion army the next day was quickly discarded as he watched the exhausted men marching past. He would give them two days to recover from the long march from Provincia. They would need it to face the far more arduous trek from the relative rolling foothills below the snow-capped alpine mountains they would have to cross to reach their destination.

He saw Tribune Setarius leave the column and gallop toward him. The tribune reined in, saluted and said with no hint of apology, "Caesar, under the circumstances, you have two more legions defined more by the standards they bear than by their capability to fight. The *Fulminata* Legion is more prepared with the majority consisting of seasoned legionnaires. The *Claudia* Legion consists of conscripts or volunteers with little or no experience. I put enough veterans in each century to give the legions a chance of surviving the first battle and the ones certain to follow."

"I couldn't have asked for more. You've achieved the objective I gave you. They will have two days to rest before we march. The generals who will command them are here now. Come to my headquarters after you've seen to their encampment, and you'll have the opportunity to brief them on the capabilities and limitations of their commands. Flavius, there's a place on my staff for you. I would have you join me where I can make use of your experience and counsel."

"I accept your offer, but I warn you age has only made me more willing to say how bad a turd smells when I see one."

Caesar laughed. "If I'm about to do something stupid, I need at least someone to tell me." He signaled to one of his orderlies who quickly came forward holding a leather bag. "You have served me well, Flavius, and I would have you accept my appreciation with more than words."

"My thanks, Caesar. I'll share this with others who have made these new legions possible."

Strabo looked at the rundown, weed-grown area designated as their quarters for the next two days and breathed a sigh of relief. Rough as the site was, it already had the remains of a defensive ditch and earthen walls. A minimal effort would be required to restore them to their original condition. There was almost a festive atmosphere permeating the preparations for the night encampment at the prospect of more time to relax and recover from the forced march since leaving the Massilia training camp.

The only one in the contubernium who appeared subdued was Scevola. During the last weeks of training and the five-day march to Ocelum, Strabo was increasingly drawn to the serious and strangely pensive older legionnaire who had proved such a welcome relief to the abusive Tertious.

"Scevola, you're quiet at the end of a day when we didn't have to prepare a night camp, and tomorrow we'll have time to rest and mend before resuming the march."

Scevola eyed the younger man and took his time responding. "I know where we're going, and it will be more difficult than perhaps you and the others have ever experienced. The last five days were nothing to what we will face in the days to come. I wager you've never experienced the ice and frigid cold you will soon endure in the high mountains we will cross to reach Genava. That isn't the worst of it. The tribes who live in those high mountains are used to such conditions in ways we are not, and they'll not permit an easy passing."

"Tell me about them."

"The mountain tribesmen are large and dressed in fur. They wear their hair long to their shoulders, and they grow facial hair above the upper lip hanging down well below the chin. Their weapons of choice are the axe, bow and arrow and spear rather than the sword. They strike at a distance except in narrow defiles where they bury themselves in the snow and wait for a longer time than you can suppose until the signal to attack is given. At close range, they favor an axe or a long, heavy spear. They also have the advantage of being used to the high range of the mountains we must cross where we'll have difficulty breathing. Marcellus, it will be a difficult march during which the weather and cold will be as much an adversary as the mountain tribes. Tomorrow, I'll show our messmates how to grease and wrap their feet and legs with an additional layer of linen beneath their *braccae* to reduce the chance of freezing."

Strabo considered what Scevola said and quietly accepted the more experienced legionnaire's assessment without question. It was a surprise when Scevola asked abruptly, "Marcellus, what happened between you and Tertious?"

Caught off guard with the sudden and unexpected question, Strabo hesitated before replying, wondering why Scevola was asking. His response was guarded, neutral. "It seemed he was there not to help and motivate but to bully. It wasn't only me he mistreated. The others suffered more. He finally made a mistake and pushed me too far."

"Tertious said you attacked him when he was asleep."

"That's not how it was."

"I suspected as much. Brecius didn't believe him either. He said you and Tertious had a confrontation in the bath house when he accused you of being only half Roman."

"It was the first but not the last." He briefly described the attack in the latrine. "If it hadn't been for Quintillus, I wouldn't be here to tell of this."

"Be careful of Tertious. I know him well. He's now your sworn enemy and will neither forgive nor forget you for being the reason he was replaced and shamed." Scevola paused and abruptly asked, "Marcellus, who are you, and why are you here?"

"I'm just another volunteer looking for a legion to look after me."

"Give me more credit than you seem ready to give. The way you talk and your skill with sword and spear tells me you're educated and from a class far higher than the usual legionnaire."

Strabo recalled what Setarius said about keeping his identity secret and considered making up something. Instead, he found himself ready to confide in the one individual he had come to admire and trust.

"In a way Tertious was right. My mother was Aeduan and high-born. My father is Lucillus Strabo."

"By the gods, General Lucillus Strabo and the former governor of Province."

Strabo responded with a wry smile. "Yes, I'm favored, or possibly more ill-favored, to be his only son. He's the reason I'm here, and by the way, I didn't volunteer. I'm perhaps the most unwilling legionnaire you'll ever know."

"Who else knows who you are?"

"Setarius, Valens and Tulio in addition to Centurion Marinus."

"Marcellus, you could be a centurion or, with your background, just about anything you wanted to be so why were you conscripted?"

"I suppose you're right. My father expected me to become an officer, and, for a time, I did as well."

"What changed your mind?"

"I'm not sure. My father and I were never close — he was gone most of the time I was growing up. The more he expected from me, the less I wanted to follow in his footsteps. I think it's often the case with boys and young men who rebel against the discipline and wishes of their fathers no matter how well-intentioned they may be. I'm here because I had become a complete disappointment to him."

Strabo paused and with a humorless laugh said, "My father was probably justified in his poor opinion of me although I'm not willing to forgive him for having me conscripted. I wish he and I could have found an easier way of getting me to change than serving in a legion. I suppose I credit him for the thought even though I have no intention of remaining here any longer than I have to."

"Listen to me, Marcellus. When the campaign season is over, you'll have a chance to muster out instead of doing what it sounds like you're planning to do. Perhaps it's the gods rather than your father's hand who decided your destiny. I'm sure some of the officers know who you are and will be keeping a close watch on you."

"You speak the truth. Centurion Valens and Rufus stopped me the first time I tried to leave before we left the training camp. I suspect I wasn't punished because they were concerned what my father may have done to them if I'd been dealt with harshly. If that was their reason, they don't know my father. He would see any punishment I receive as justified and probably less than I deserved. You asked me before why I stopped wanting to be a centurion. The answer isn't easy to explain.

"I didn't know my father very well. He was remote and absent most of the years I was growing up, except for one brief period when he took me to Rome; it was one of the happiest times I ever had. He seemed attentive friendly. After we left, he went back to being demanding and remote. Praise was seldom given no matter how hard I tried or succeeded. As I grew older, I had more and more difficulty relating to him which eventually caused me to rebel against a life in the legions he expected me to pursue."

"What were you planning to do with your life after turning your back on what most men will never have a chance to live?"

"It's a fair question and the same one my father asked the last time I saw him. I told him I wanted to do whatever I chose to do."

Scevola shook his head in disbelief. "I would have thrown my son out on his ass if he had ever told me anything as brainless."

"Well, you and my father are in agreement because it's close to what he said and did. My being here is proof of it. Fortunately, I bought land and a stable of horses a year ago. There's nothing I like better than riding a spirited horse. I'm good at it and have built a modest reputation for winning races. My plan is to breed and sell horses for the games and people rich enough to afford the best horseflesh anywhere in Italia. There's a trader in Massilia who imports horses from Alexandria, I contracted with him to get a dozen mares and two stallions to seed my stables; they should be arriving soon. I need to get back to Massilia, or I'll lose my investment."

"Your chances don't look good. The farther we get from Ocelum the less opportunity you'll have. There are no villages, only isolated huts until we cross the high mountains. Most of those you will encounter will not be friendly to a Roman."

"I'm half Gaul and speak the language very well. The Aedui Tribe where I'm known is not far west of Genava. I'll leave the legion on the other side of the mountains."

"I'll have a week or more to convince you not to do it."

"Save your breath. Only the gods will prevent me from getting to Massilia."

"What if they decide in favor of the *Claudia* Legion?"

"I'll offer sacrifices enough they'll weigh in my favor."

"I envy you, Marcellus. You're young enough to believe in dreams and to discount how fickle the gods are in helping you achieve them. I once had dreams, but I'm too old now to remember them."

Chapter 5

By the end of the first day northwest of Ocelum, the lower elevation and comparative comfort of the coastal plain remained nothing but a pleasant and fading memory as they marched with each step higher toward the snow-capped mountains ahead. Although the road they followed was narrow, the cohorts were able to march in columns six abreast. The long snaking line of legionnaires and baggage wagons stretched for miles. The usual twenty-mile march on even terrain and lower altitudes was reduced by a third with the increasing elevation and the uneven road, more game trail than road. The *Claudia* Legion was positioned behind the baggage wagons and ahead of one the veteran legions marching in the rear of the column. The other new legion marched in front of the baggage wagons with the other two veteran legions taking the lead.

The rocky soil in the narrow valley selected for the legion made preparation of the night camp more difficult than usual, bathing the legionnaires in their own sweat as they toiled. By the time the walls were complete and the tents pitched, the sun had disappeared over the snow-capped peaks ahead. The temperature quickly dropped, and the legionnaires who just a short time ago had been miserably hot in their exertions were now thankful for the heavy woolen cloaks they had cursed a few short days ago. Already chilled to the bone, Strabo recalled Scevola's description of what they were going to face in the days to come and regretted not accepting Centurion Valen's offer to let him leave the legion unopposed.

The encampment was rudely awakened in the early hours by horn blasts reverberating in the narrow confines of the valley. The haunting, eerie sounds began in a sustained deep-toned rumble gradually increasing until ending in a bone-chilling screech. Scevola identified the cause of the unworldly sound as a *carnyx*, a six-foot long horn the tribes often used to intimidate their enemies while encouraging their tribesmen before battle.

The legionnaires were ordered to the walls to repel an expected attack that never materialized. A random fusillade of arrows inflicted only a few minor wounds for those unlucky enough to be in the way. Soon after there was silence, no longer any indication another attack was imminent. A stand down was ordered, and the legionnaires stumbled back to their tents only to be awakened again soon after by the mournful sound of the horns. The noise was nearly impossible to ignore and continued intermittently through the rest of the night. Sleep was difficult even for the veterans who had heard the sounds before and near impossible for those hearing them for the first time. The morning formation at first light revealed officers and legionnaires alike bleary-eyed and looking forward even less to the steeper and increasingly colder march ahead.

The first attack occurred mid-morning in a foggy, narrow defile when visibility was reduced to little more than the distance a well-aimed javelin could be thrown. Marching in the outside rank, Strabo saw Enrius just ahead of him stumble and fall face forward with an arrow protruding from his neck. Moments later, Strabo felt and heard the impact of an arrow hitting his shield. Farther ahead in the vicinity of the supply wagons, loud cries arose over the metallic sound of metal striking metal and the hollow thump of shields being struck. In contrast, the noise of battle in the immediate vicinity was subdued and isolated. Strabo turned in time to see an indistinct form running downhill toward him. As it drew close, a leather-clad figure immerged carrying an ax in one hand and a small, round shield in the other. He drew his sword and leaned forward bracing himself for the impact and the momentum the attacker had in his favor. The collision nearly felled him. His larger and heavier shield helped him to maintain balance. The axe intended for his head struck the top of the shield with enough force to penetrate the iron rim deep into the wood below. The warrior was slow recovering the axe and exposed his upper body long enough for Strabo to shove his gladius deep into the other man's neck. The dying man fell backward desperately trying to staunch the torrent of blood spreading between his fingers. With the axe imbedded in his shield, Strabo looked around prepared to meet the next assailant. Except for a few shouted demands for a *medicus* to aid the wounded, there was silence. The inexperienced legionnaires continued to look about cautiously in case there was another attack.

Strabo bent down to look at Enrius laying on the rocky path beside him and realized the wide-eyed, sightless stare was focused on the next world. When he stood up, Brecius was standing next to the dead warrior.

"Marcellus, it seems you've learned something from the training you've had, although I think the next time luck may not be enough to save you."

Strabo was defensive. "What did luck have to do with it? I put the blade exactly where I intended and killed him. What else did you expect?"

"Fair enough. Next time aim for the gut, his chest or his balls. You were fortunate this time to strike such a small target. Better to inflict a crippling wound the rank behind can finish while you move forward to meet the next man."

The optio bent over the corpse and dabbed a finger on the dead man's bloody neck after which he stood up and swiped his finger down Strabo's cheek. "You're now blooded and know what it's like to kill a man who's trying to kill you." He pointed to the man closest to Strabo and gesturing to the dead legionnaire said, "Help Marcellus carry him to one of the wagons. We'll bury him tonight along with the others who were chosen by the gods today."

Strabo handed his shield to Quintillus. "Felix, give him your shield, too. We'll use Enrius' shield to carry him."

When the two men reached the line of supply wagons and saw how many were damaged or had been pushed off the road into the cavernous ravine below, it was obvious what the objective of the attack had been. During the next two hours the columns remained in place while recovery of supplies and repair of the wagons that could be salvaged took place. The rest of the day was uneventful with only the inclement weather to battle.

That night the legions were again subjected to the same disquieting nocturnal horn blasts. Expecting this would be the case with little chance an attack would occur, the guard was doubled, and the legionnaires were not required to fully man the walls as was done the previous night.

Except for Scevola whose snoring was evidence of untroubled sleep, the other five men in the contubernium were fitful, less from the sound of the dissonant horns than each one reflecting on the loss of Enrius and the possibility it could have been him.

"Marcellus, what was it like?" Felix asked in a low voice.

"What do you mean?" Strabo had a good idea what Felix was asking. He didn't really want to talk about it, too busy trying to understand how he felt or was supposed to react.

"To kill a man."

"I'm not sure." He paused and added, "My blade went into him easier than I would have imagined. It happened so fast I didn't have time to think. Maybe that was a good thing, and I reacted instinctively. If I hadn't, maybe I'd be under the ground with Enrius."

Apparently woken by the conversation, Scevola said, "Marcellus is right. That's why we train the way we do. If you have to think about what you're going to do, your adversary has the advantage. Fighting the way Marcellus did today, you will have a better chance to live to fight the next battle. One more thing, Felix. It's best not to think how you feel when the battle's over unless it's to understand what you did right or wrong to better prepare yourself for the next one. Now all of you get some sleep. It will be another long day tomorrow and probably much like the one today.

A short time later the only sound was Scevola's deep and measured breathing. For Strabo, sleep was a long time coming. He was bothered by what he didn't feel, wondering why he had no remorse for the dead warrior. But neither did he feel a sense of elation or a desire to boast about it. Long after the others had gone to sleep, he remained awake, oblivious of the mournful horns that continued to blast periodically throughout the night.

He wondered about the man he killed whose long moustaches, light-colored hair and size brought back memories of the occasions his mother had taken him back to Far Gaul and the domain of the Aedui. During his first visit, he was too young to appreciate his mother was the daughter of a ruling family. It wasn't until many years later when he was on the threshold of manhood he understood and appreciated his mother's heritage. The antagonism and rejection he experienced during his first visit was replaced in time with warm acceptance.

He credited the Aedui for his passionate love of horses and riding skill. Over the years since, he was as likely to evoke *Epona*, the Gallic goddess of horses, as Jupiter. Before they returned to Massilia, he was ritually accepted into his mother's clan which included receiving the tattoo he wore on his arm with pride despite the occasional ridicule he was subjected to in Massilia. The tattoos and the reality of what he experienced earlier in the day only emphasized his determination to escape, if only to prevent the possibility of ever facing the Aedui on a battlefield. In the meantime, he would do what he must to stay alive and think about the day he would be free.

The next day before reaching the snow level at mid-day, the column suffered two more interdictions not unlike the one the previous day with similar results — few casualties and much less than the tribesmen suffered. Except for a few individual warriors who apparently sought to win glory in individual contact, the others were content to maintain an arrow distance away, harrying the Romans from concealed and safe positions above. A few hours later, the tribal tactics changed. The increasingly narrow roadway forced the centuries to march in four files instead of six, and with frequent snow squalls reducing visibility, the tribesmen attacked in greater numbers and once in engaged, remained in contact longer than before. Typically, the tribesmen launched their attacks from an uphill position. The legionnaires quickly adapted to the unvarying tactics launched during periods of reduced visibility. The more organized Roman defense against a generally uncoordinated, individual attacks resulted in proportionately higher casualties for the tribesmen.

The attacks were fewer over the next three days perhaps reflecting tacit acceptance nothing could be done to stop the Roman advance. The more serious enemy facing the legionnaires was a combination of weather and elevation in which they sought to avoid freezing while trying to breathe the thinning air with every step they took. The road wound through narrow passes with steep inclines on one side and sheer cliffs on the other heightening the risk of slipping on the icy roadway and falling to a rocky, snow-covered depth hundreds of feet below.

By mid-afternoon of the fifth day, the column had reached the highest pass, and progress quickly became faster and easier. The last encampment a day later was in a valley with grass growing between isolated patches of snow overlooking the shimmering blue water of a large lake and the Jura Mountains farther north. At the southwest end of the lake, tendrils of smoke drifted lazily above the town of Genava. The bucolic scene gave no hint of the fierce battles that would be waged in the weeks ahead.

Chapter 6

Caesar looked at the haggard face of General Labienus. "Titus, I congratulate you for what you've accomplished. The nineteen-mile wall you finished along the west bank of the Rhône was brilliant."

"We prevented the Helvetii from getting across the river, but we couldn't prevent them crossing over the Jura Mountains. It's most likely they intend to cross the Saône somewhere north of its juncture with the Rhône."

"The Aedui believe they may be close to crossing the Saône River. I received a delegation from them two days ago. They're worried the Aedui will suffer the same treatment from the Helvetii the Sequani apparently have and are looking for Roman support to prevent it. In return, they're prepared to provide grain, forage and cavalry support as we need it. I accepted the offer. In the meantime, scouts are being sent to help guide us; they should be here by now."

General Labienus nodded. "The Aedui scouts arrived yesterday and are camped nearby. Preventing the Helvetii migration with only six legions will be a little less challenging if we have an alliance with the Aedui."

"Unfortunately, 'an understanding' may be closer to the truth than an *alliance*. While Diviciacus may be ready to help us fight the Helvetii, I'm not sure the feeling is widespread among the other Aedui tribes. We'll soon see just how much the Aedui are willing to help. We'll march the day after tomorrow toward the confluence of the Saône and Rhône Rivers. Titus, I wish I could give you and the Tenth more time to rest; the circumstances dictate otherwise."

Strabo's mind was not on the mundane tasks of helping fold the tent and load the wagon shared with three other contubernia for the day's march. He kept thinking of the previous afternoon and the familiar terrain features he saw in the distance. He had spent some of the happiest times of his life with the Aedui, riding, swimming and hunting;

most of all, he recalled the night when a young widow introduced him to an experience until then had only been something to fantasize.

He heard his name called and turned to see Brecius coming toward him. He had a feeling his day was going to be different than what he expected.

"Marcellus, get your personal kit, put your shield on the wagon and come with me. Centurion Marinus wants to see you."

The centurion was waiting in front of his tent tapping his vitis impatiently against his leg. Strabo saw little of him except when he was wielding the vine stick hard enough on occasion to leave a lasting reminder. He wondered why the centurion continued to single him out, a fact which had not gone unnoticed by his messmates. He worried the day would come when he would no longer curb his urge to grab the hated vine stick and give the bastard what he deserved.

Brecius saluted the centurion and stood silently aside.

"I wonder it's taken this long for you to take advantage of the Strabo name," Marinus said with a curled upper lip.

"Centurion, I don't understand..." He tried not to flinch when the vine stick struck his left upper arm with enough force to leave a reminder of their first conversation.

"Do not interrupt me. You speak only when I give you permission. Do it again and I'll have you flogged for disobeying my order. You are a privileged bastard, and I use the word accurately to describe the circumstances of your birth, for I doubt the general would have lowered himself in formal marriage with a native wench. Why he allows you to use his surname, if he does, is beyond me. You've been summoned to Caesar's headquarters for reasons I don't know. I suspect it's because of who your father is and not what you've earned or deserve. I fancy before the day is out, you'll be one of Caesar's idle orderlies. I'm certain you'll benefit, and I will, too, because you're gone. Brecius, take him to the *principia.*"

The optio saluted and gave a quiet order to Strabo to march on. Once out of earshot of the centurion, it was Brecius who spoke first. "Marcellus, what in the celestial clouds above was that all about?"

"I have no idea. I never saw him before the night I was conscripted. I think it's not about me, rather my father for reasons I can't explain."

"Whatever the reason, it appears he's ready to shove it to you whenever he can."

"Optio, do you know why I'm going to Caesar's headquarters?"

"No. If you have a chance to stay there, you should do it and not come back here. Jupiter knows, given the chance, I'd take it."

In front of the headquarters, Tribune Setarius was talking to General Arridius, the legion commander, and Centurion Valens. Standing nearby an orderly held the reins of two horses.

Strabo came to attention and saluted the General who casually waved his hand and looked at him curiously.

Setarius cocked his head to one side and said almost accusingly, "Marcellus, I'm told you can ride a horse, and you know the Gallic languages. Is this true?"

"Yes, both are true, Tribune, but there are some differences in the dialects the different tribes speak ..." He was about to elaborate when the Tribune impatiently cut him off.

Setarius responded with some irritation, "Are you able to communicate sufficiently to understand them?"

"I can, Tribune."

"Good, you're coming with me. Now, get on the horse over there. I'll see if you can mount and make it go where you want, or I should say, where I want to go."

Strabo walked toward the horse with mixed feelings. The joy of having a horse beneath him once again and the chance it could offer an even quicker opportunity to get away seemed too good to be true. He wondered if he was being tested or whether the gods were merely playing with him. He looped the strap of his kit over one of the rear pommels, took the reins from the orderly and with practiced ease vaulted into the saddle. In contrast to Strabo's effortless mounting, Setarius took advantage of the orderly's cupped hands to gain the saddle.

The tribune kicked his horse in the ribs and headed down the *Via Principia* to the southern entrance of the night camp. Without a backward look to see if Strabo was following, Setarius left the fort and turned northwest. Strabo considered if he had just been given the opportunity he'd been looking for, and yet he hesitated, wary all was not as it appeared. The road made an abrupt turn around a rocky outcropping revealing a detachment of Roman cavalry a short distance ahead, dismounted and waiting on the side of the road.

Strabo reined the horse to a stop. He was angry enough to consider drawing his sword and attacking the tribune. Setarius looked behind him and reined in when he saw Strabo looking defiantly at him. For a moment, the two men stared at each other with Setarius' neutral expression only fueling Strabo's building anger.

"You're wondering if this is the chance you've been waiting for. I think your odds of succeeding is a wager the gods would tell you not to make."

Strabo fleetingly considered taking the chance. Setarius was right. The older horse he rode was good enough for a canter or a short gallop, but it was no match for the younger cavalry horses he had just seen.

"Tribune, you speak of odds, what would Jupiter consider your chances are if I draw my sword, and we end this one way or the other before they," gesturing to the cavalry detachment, "can get here?"

"Your odds are less than I gave you before. I understand your anger and frustration for the circumstances you find yourself in. If you were anyone else, I'd draw my gladius, and you'd be food for the ravens for what you just said. You're young and have the advantage of being strong without the experience you think you have, but don't. Valens told me how well you wield a sword, and you're blooded; however, compared to what I've experienced the last forty years, you're no match. I wouldn't require any assistance from my escort."

"What do you want from me? If you're so resolved to see me in the ranks, why not leave me there, or is it by putting me on a horse, you taunt me with a hopeless chance to ride away for your own perverse satisfaction?"

Setarius frowned and paused before replying in a softer voice. "Fair enough, I deserve that. There's much more to it than what you know. I owe your father not just my advancement but my life as well, a tale for another time and place. It's enough to say there's nothing I would not do for him including trying to keep you from doing anything either discrediting his legacy or depriving him of his only son.

"I'll overlook your words and behavior this time, but not again. Next time, if there is one, I'll kill you or have you flogged within an inch of your life. Never presume to challenge me again or address me as an equal — you haven't earned the right. As it so happens, your capability to speak Gallic is useful. Early this morning a cavalry patrol from the Tenth Legion returned with three prisoners. So far, no one's been able to understand anything they say. I thought of you and the possibility you learned the language from your mother. Now you understand the situation, we've wasted enough time." Without waiting to see if Strabo would follow, Setarius turned his horse and cantered toward the escort. Strabo hesitated, then followed the tribune.

Soon after the two men and the escort detail drew rein inside the camp of the Tenth Legion. Setarius handed the reins of his horse to a nearby orderly and motioned for Strabo to do the same.

"Follow me." The tribune headed toward two large tents. In front of the nearest tent was the eagle standard of the Tenth Legion while in front of the other a white flag showing a gold olive wreath billowed in a fitful breeze.

"Marcellus, our auxilia cavalry consists of men from the far west of Gaul, and while they're skilled as cavalrymen, they don't speak the local languages, much less the dialects you spoke of. I want you to interrogate some prisoners and find out what they know about the Helvetii. Whatever you learn may determine what Caesar will do and when."

"Where are the prisoners?"

"You'll find them over there," Setarius pointed to the south end of the camp where four legionnaires were guarding three prisoners kneeling on the ground, heads down with their hands bound behind them. "I'll be in here," gesturing to the tent with the olive wreath flag in front. "Report to me when you're finished with them."

Two of the prisoners looked up as he approached, their unemotional expressions suggested they already accepted their fate. He didn't think there was anything they were going to say that would help the Romans no matter what was done to them.

The third prisoner's expression was different, hopeful. He wasted no time saying, "Roman, they think I'm Helvetii. I'm Sequani and neither am I an enemy of Rome. I escaped when the Helvetii attacked my village without warning and slaughtered everyone who couldn't get away."

"What do you mean they attacked without warning?"

"There was an understanding between the Sequani, the Aedui and Helvetii. In return for safe passage and forage through our lands, the Helvetii would leave us in peace and not take our horses and cattle. We believed them, but they lied. What they couldn't take, they burned and killed. I was in the fields watching over the horse herd, and it was the only reason I survived."

"What's your name?"

"Tasco."

"Tasco, you say the Aedui also made the same agreement as the Sequani?"

"It's what our village chief told us. The Helvetii outnumber the Sequani and Aedui by many times, and so it was thought an agreement with them would be enough to leave us in peace. We were wrong to think so. Now I only wish to go and help the Aedui by killing as many Helvetii as the gods will let me."

"Where are the Helvetii now?"

"I heard those two talking hours ago. I believe they are already about to cross the Saône on the way to the Aedui main settlement at Bibracte. If they get there, they will treat the Aedui the same as the Sequani."

Strabo turned to the two Helvetii prisoners and asked, "Does either one of you have anything to say?"

The larger and older of the two sneered and said, "Your mother coupled with dogs and you are the result. Tell these bastards to hurry up and kill us. We prefer to meet the gods than kneel under the Roman boot."

Strabo looked closer at the younger man and saw an expression less resolved. "Is it the same with you, or do you want the chance to live longer and see your gods another time?"

"What do you want?" He responded hesitantly, looking askance at his companion.

"You heard what the Sequani said. Do you have anything to add?"

The older man lunged forward and head-butted the younger captive, sending him sprawling face down. "Dosso, you son of a pig, keep your mouth shut and try to act like the warrior you never were, not the coward you've always been. If you say one more thing, I'll see the gods fill your mouth with shit and your balls given to the dogs, that is if they can find them."

Strabo reached down and pulled the half-conscious man away from the reaches of the other while the guards looked on with disinterest. "Dosso, tell me what you know, and I'll intercede on your behalf."

Bleary-eyed, bloody nose streaming down his tunic, the young man retched and tried to focus on what Strabo was saying. A few moments later, he recovered enough to say to the other man, "You call me coward, yet you were among the first to say we needed to leave our lands before the Germans forced us to go. I wanted to stay and resist while you and the other and older faint-hearted wanted to flee to the west and confront easier foes. I say to you, Tinus, you'll fare worse in the other world than I will." He hesitated, looked at Strabo and told him what the Helvetii intended.

Believing there was nothing left to be learned, Strabo walked to the tent where the tribune entered and told the guard who he wanted to see and why. The guard ducked into the tent and emerged a moment later motioning him to enter. He passed through a vestibule into a larger room where the tribune and two other men were sitting. He came to attention and saluted.

61

Setarius looked at the youngest of the two men and said, "Caesar, this is Marcellus, a legionnaire with the Claudia Legion. Because he understands the Gallic tongue, I directed him to learn what he could from the three prisoners the cavalry patrol brought in last night."

Strabo recalled seeing the same man wearing a red cloak watching the two new legions march into Ocelum. He assumed the other and older man wearing a silver cuirass was the general commanding the Tenth Legion.

Setarius asked, "Marcellus, what did the prisoners tell you?"

"Tribune, one of the prisoners is a Sequani, not a Helvetian. He described what he saw and heard concerning what the Helvetii did to the Sequani as they moved west. They laid waste to the Sequani before they started crossing the Saône yesterday. He thinks as slowly as they're moving, it will take them many days to get across. He also spoke of an agreement between the Helvetii and both the Sequani and Aedui. In return for unimpeded movement west, the Helvetii would not ravage the lands they crossed. Apparently, the agreement was hollow for the Helvetii, and the Sequani suffered. He believes the Aedui will suffer the same."

Caesar looked at General Labienus. "I think we're going to march sooner than I expected."

The general nodded and asked Strabo, "Did he say where they're crossing?"

"Northeast of the Aedui main settlement at Bibracte. How far he doesn't know."

"What about the two Helvetii? Did they have anything to say?"

"One of the captives refused to talk; the other was ready to confirm what was said in return for clemency."

Setarius motioned toward the entrance. "Marcellus, wait for me outside."

After Strabo left, Caesar spoke first. "It seems I've underestimated how quickly the Helvetii were able to advance. Titus, it also validates the concern of the representatives from Diviciacus about the Helvetii support of a federation favorable to all three tribes in return for unopposed movement west. They seemed to feel it was no more than a fart in the wind. Flavius, send for the legion commanders and tell them to prepare their legions to march at first light tomorrow. I want to convene a *consilium* here with the legion commanders and their senior centurions in two hours. There's nothing we can do for the Sequani. There's time to help the Aedui by keeping the Helvetii from moving any farther west."

Setarius stood up to leave then paused when Caesar asked, "The legionnaire who did the interrogation, who is he? He seems intelligent and has the bearing at odds with what to expect from a common legionary."

Setarius laughed. "He's no ordinary legionnaire. He's Marcellus Strabo, the son of General Strabo. He's assigned to the *Claudia* Legion."

"He seems more than what I expected. Perhaps I should bring him onto my staff as an orderly where he will not risk the dangers of a battlefield."

"Caesar, he may be safer in the ranks than next to you when the battle is joined. He did well in the mountains on the way here. I'm told by those who saw him, he quickly and skillfully killed a tribesman who attacked him with an axe." Setarius gave Caesar a quizzical look and asked, "Do you intend to deploy the two new legions with the others?"

"No, they'll secure the baggage train and remain behind the four veteran legions as a reserve in the event circumstances require them. You knew how I would use the two legions. I wonder why you asked."

"I have in mind keeping Strabo with me for a time or attach him to the cavalry as an *eques speculator*. He rides well, seems to know the country and proved useful as an interrogator. He may have more value as a scout in the days ahead guiding the legions than in the ranks guarding the baggage train."

"I'll leave it for you to decide. You risk when he's on a horse he'll decide to go in a different direction than you intended. I would rather tell his father he didn't survive a battle than his son deserted."

"I understand up to a point, although I'm willing to risk the possibility. Given time and opportunity, I think young Strabo may be more willing to serve than I first believed. I owe it to his father to do what I can to help his son make something of himself."

Caesar's expression was skeptical. "Do what you think best. If you're wrong, he'll suffer the consequences even if he is the son of Lucillus Strabo."

Chapter 7

Waiting outside the tent, Strabo presumed the three men were discussing when and where the legions would be deployed in the coming days. He walked over to where the horses he and Setarius had ridden were tethered. Over the past several months, he missed the smell, the feel of a horse beneath him. The animals also brought back distant memories of how he had come to have a kinship with horses that might never have happened except for his visits to Bibracte. He had Corius to thank for it.

It was Corius who had been the first to befriend him when his mother brought him there. Two years older, long hair so yellow it was almost white, Corius had done much to explain and help him understand the ways of his mother's tribe, including their bond with horses. Soon he, too, had learned to ride like the wind. Before he left for Massilia, he would find Corius and rekindle their friendship. He wondered if he was married and by now a responsible clan member contributing to the welfare of the tribe. He felt a momentary twinge when he considered how he had been spending his time over the past several years. He wondered how Elantia fared, Corius' gangly and much younger sister who continuously begged to go with them on their hunting trips. If Corius had become the brother he never had, Elantia was the sister he never had. He smiled, recalling the few occasions when they let her accompany them, conditioned on performing all the menial chores they wanted to avoid. He recalled waking up after a cold night to find her plastered next to him fast asleep. The last time he saw her, she was beginning to show rounded curves in contrast to the rangy, awkward little girl he was used to. She also had become noticeably different from the other girls, more interested in practicing with a sword or bow than engaging in traditional female activities.

The tranquil thoughts were quickly replaced with images of what the Aedui would be subjected to by the Helvetii. It was possible they were already facing similar depredations. He saw the lined and kindly face of his grandfather, the gregarious tribal chief who died a year before his mother did and the other...

"Marcellus!" the imperative sound of the tribune's husky voice brought him abruptly from idle thoughts to the present reality he was nothing more than a miniscule cog in the Roman war machine.

"Yes, Tribune?"

"You see the tent over there?" pointing to a smaller one pitched behind the larger tent of Caesar's. "Wait in there until I return."

"What is it you want of me?"

"Marcellus, do not question any order I give you. It's your lot in life the gods have given you to obey anyone serving above you. I neither have the time nor inclination to explain or justify the orders I give you. Despite your short time in the Roman Army, you should have at least learned that much. Now do as you're told!"

"Yes, Tribune," he responded neutrally, stifling the urge to say what he actually felt as he watched the heavy-set, aging man walk away.

It was late in the afternoon when Setarius returned to find Strabo standing at attention in the tent's vestibule. The Tribune hesitated, walked past him and said over his shoulder, "Come inside, I want to talk to you."

Setarius sat down on one of several camp stools grouped around a small table and indicated the one opposite him. With his elbows on the table, hands folded under his chin, he stared at the young legionnaire with an inscrutable expression. During a lengthy pause, Strabo felt increasingly uncomfortable. Finally, Setarius said, "Against my better judgment, I'm about to give you a chance to become more valuable to Rome, which depending on the outcome, may give your father a reason to reconsider the poor opinion he has of you."

Strabo bristled and resisted the impulse to say something he knew he would regret. He dreaded the patronizing lecture he was certain he was about to get. For now, he clenched his teeth and resolved to keep his mouth shut.

"Caesar was much taken with you and suggested you might be useful as one of his orderlies..."

"I prefer returning to my contubernium than—"

"If you interrupt me again, you'll be the most unfortunate legionnaire in the Roman Army. Now shut your mouth and listen." With visible effort, Setarius regained his composure. "I do not intend for you to be one of Caesar's fat-cat orderlies sitting on your ass with little to do except doing your best to look useful. And you're not going back to the *Claudia*, at least for now. As it so happens, your interrogation was enough for Caesar to order a march on the Helvetii tomorrow. The Aedui are concerned about what's happening to the Sequani and have asked for our support if the Helvetii enter their lands. According to what you learned from the prisoners, the Helvetii already have. Diviciacus has sent a small contingent of scouts now camped north of the Tenth as part of the mutual agreement of support. They're here to guide the legions as required. I've a mind to have you join them for two reasons, you speak the language, and you can be potentially more useful scouting than fighting in the ranks. It also appears you can ride a horse without falling off."

The last descriptor of his horsemanship ordinarily might have been enough to justify an angry response, but he was so astounded over what the centurion said he remained silent.

"Perhaps most important to you and your father, this could be the opportunity to earn the respect of your father as a Roman soldier. What do you have to say?"

"I never expected to be given a choice—"

"I'm not giving you a choice. When we're done here, you'll be issued a *spatha* to replace your gladius, the round shield and helmet of a cavalryman and a horse more suitable than the one you rode today. When you're outfitted, you'll ride to the Aedui camp three miles north of here."

"Why are you doing this when you know in a few days on a horse I can be 100 miles away from a life I don't want and never will?"

"Perhaps I'm making a mistake, thinking there's more to you than your father and others have so far not seen. I could be wrong as I've been too many times before. I'm about to risk giving you a chance you've been waiting for since you were conscripted. The difference now is I believe you won't go any farther than where the Aedui are because of the current Helvetii threat. Should you do that, I'll find you and bring you back to face the consequences. Since we're actively engaged with an enemy of Rome, you'll likely be sentenced to the *fustuarium*," referring to the ritual gauntlet and certain bludgeoning death of the accused.

"If you do manage to escape, you'll enter a nether world where you will regret your choice for the rest of your life. Whatever you choose to do is not something I'll lose sleep over."

Strabo looked away considering how to respond. He realized he was being offered an alternative few in the ranks could expect. He also thought it was his father's influence behind the proposal.

"I will do as you've ordered, mainly for the practical reason you described. I also admit I'm concerned what may happen to the Aedui in the days to come."

"Marcellus, I'm hopeful for your father's sake you won't disappoint him. As for me, I've no intention now or in the future of wasting time trying to convince you not to do something for which you will certainly pay a price. I do expect as long as you serve as a legionnaire, you'll do your part. Now I've spent all the time on you I care to. Report to the decurion commanding the cavalry *turma* for the Tenth Legion and draw the equipment you need; he's expecting you."

"He's expecting me? How did you know—?"

"As I said, you had no choice; you could not refuse my order. When you find the Aedui scouts, tell them the legions will march tomorrow at first light. They'll join the Roman cavalry of the Tenth Legion. The 32-man *turma* you're being assigned to is commanded by Decurion Tarquin, the senior decurion of the legion's ten-*turmae* cavalry. He also represents the other turmae when he attends a legionary *consilium* convened by General Labienus. You and the Aedui will take orders from him."

Strabo saluted and left. He was looking forward to seeing the Aeduan scouts and hoped he would see one or more familiar faces. He was also curious whether he would be welcomed and comfortable with them as he had been years ago.

Decurion Tarquin was talking to a young, bare-headed man whose cuirass and the respectful attention the decurion was according him suggested he was an officer. Strabo came to attention and waited until the two men finished their conversation and acknowledged him. He saluted and identified himself.

The decurion gave a sigh of resignation and said to the young officer next to him regarding Strabo, "Dux Crassus, Tribune Setarius apparently believes legionnaire Marcellus may have some use to the turma as an interpreter — evidently he speaks Aeduan. I'm told he can ride a horse, and we'll soon see if it's true." The decurion pointed to the spirited gray stallion tied to a stake separate from where the other horses were tethered. "Take that one. His name is Aquilo, and like the north wind he's named after, he's unpredictable but sound and fast. Legionnaire, I hope you can ride and you're favored by the gods because otherwise the grey bastard could be the worst thing you've ever met. If I never see the nag again, I'll give thanks to Epona for sparing the turma any more trouble than what he's already caused. Now if he's too much for you to handle, there's another one over there you can have instead; he's not much to look at, but just about anyone can handle him."

Strabo took one look at the drooping dun horse at the end of the picket line and shook his head. He picked up the pad and four-pommeled saddle. "Aquilo will do."

Several grinning cavalrymen stood nearby watching in anticipation as Strabo walked toward the prancing stallion whose bared teeth and flattened ears visibly verified the decurion's description of the animal's behavior. Strabo stopped a few paces away, dropped the saddle and pad and slowly approached the horse. Talking in low tones and holding his arms down, palms facing forward, he stepped closer. He waited until the stallion stood motionless, ears fanning forward, cautious, waiting to see what would happen next. He took another step forward, close enough to put a hand on the horse's flank. The horse flinched and snorted but didn't pull away. He moved his hand caressing the warm, smooth body so familiar to him, slowly moving toward the horse's neck. He waited a little longer, talking in low soothing tones until the horse quieted. He untied the reins and gently lifted them over the animal's head. He waited a few more minutes and moved in front of the horse, murmuring reassurances while continuing to stroke the horse's muzzle and neck. When the horse finally stood and whickered, Strabo knew it was time. Effortlessly he vaulted onto the animal's bare back and waited for the surge of adrenalin and rejection he reasonably expected to occur. Instead, the horse stood still. Strabo waited wondering what would happen next. To his relief and the awe of those watching, the horse snorted, shook its head and remained docile. Strabo flicked the reins and gave the stallion a gentle kick in the ribs. The cavalrymen, including Tarquin, looked on in open-mouthed astonishment as Strabo cantered down the via principia.

Strabo reined the horse in next to the decurion, dismounted and said, "I believe Aquilo and I have reached an understanding."

The young general approached him. "Marcellus, it's obvious you know horses. Where did you learn to ride like that?" After Strabo briefly summarized how the Aedui taught him to ride and his riding experience in Massilia, Crassus smiled and said, "I thought you looked familiar, I've seen you race in Massilia and profited when you won. Decurion, I think Marcellus will be an asset to the turma and one day quite possibly to me as well. I wish you good fortune, legionnaire."

The two officers walked away, leaving Strabo to wonder how a man not much older than he could be given the rank of dux, the title of a senior official equal to a general. By the time he mounted Aquilo, he was thinking of nothing else except the chance to achieve what he'd been dreaming of since leaving Massilia. As he neared the north entrance of the camp, he felt like shouting in exhilaration for the freedom it beckoned the closer he came to the guards stationed there. The guards waved him on with no more than a disinterested look from the optio posted there. For the first time in months, he felt in control.

He rode northwest with only a vague notion of where the Aedui scouts were. The sun was about to disappear over the distant hills when he saw a campfire around which a number of men were either standing or sitting. He turned the horse and walked it toward the flickering light. He barely left the road when a man stepped from behind a tree and ordered him to stop. "Who are you and what do you want?"

"I'm looking for the Aedui scouts sent to help find the Helvetii."

"You've found us."

"My name is Marcellus, and I've come to tell you the Romans will come this way at first light tomorrow. You'll join the contingent of Roman cavalry leading the march. The cavalry commander is led by Decurion Tarquin, and you'll take your orders from him."

"Marcellus? You're Roman, and yet you speak our language well enough."

"I once spoke it better. It's been more than five years since I was last here in the land of the Aedui."

"I knew a Roman by the name of Marcellus. For a Roman he was different, and over the years, he became a friend of mine in spite of being a Roman."

There was something about the man's voice and what he said that stripped away years gone by. Strabo dismounted and approached him with open arms.

"Corius, who could have imagined after so many years we would meet again like this?"

"Marcellus, the gods have never favored me so much." The two men embraced, at first neither one speaking, not trusting their emotions enough to say anything.

A moment later, Corius said, "Come to the fire, there are others who will remember you as well. We have much to talk about, and most of all what you're doing here."

As the two men walked toward the campfire, Strabo quickly summarized how and why he was a legionnaire in the Roman Army. Corius stopped and responded quickly. "If you're serving against your will, why not leave? You know these lands almost as well as I do, and there are places you can go the Romans will never find you."

"What you say is true and what I wanted and planned for the day I was conscripted. I changed my mind when I learned what the Helvetii are doing to the Sequani and could do to the Aedui. It may be in time I'll change my mind, and I'll do as you say."

"We'll talk of this again. Come now and we'll speak of better things and happier days before you return to the Romans."

Strabo laughed and put his hand on Corius's shoulder. "My friend, we'll spend much time together in the days ahead. I've been ordered to join you for the time being. Decurion Tarquin does not speak Gallic."

"Raven will be happy."

"Raven?"

"Elantia, she changed her name to Raven because *Doe* didn't suit her. She chose the name Raven when she became a woman — and the warrior she said she wanted to be but never believed she would. Marcellus, believe her now, for she's almost as good with a sword as I am, rides better than most of the men sitting there and no one can surpass her with a bow."

"Unfortunately, I'll not be permitted to go to Bibracte to see her."

"You won't have to. She's over there," gesturing toward a smaller figure sitting slightly apart from the rest and next to a man leaning attentively toward her.

"What's she doing here with you?"

"She's a scout like the rest of us. I'll tell everyone you're a messenger from the Romans here to tell us what they want from us. She'll be surprised and pleased to see you."

With mixed feelings, Strabo approached the campfire and stood silently while Corius identified him as a messenger from the Romans and finished by saying, "Raven, come take his mount and tether it with the other horses."

He saw her stand up and come toward him. At first, there was nothing to distinguish her from her masculine companions except her slightly smaller stature. As she came closer, he was amazed at the change in her. She was no longer the gangly, boyish little girl he remembered. She was both striking and beautiful with a confident bearing and self-assured expression more masculine than feminine; however, the leather jerkin and woolen trousers did not entirely conceal the lithe, shapely form of a mature woman. Her long black hair was tied at the neck and hung down to her waist. When she stopped and reached for the reins, she looked in his eyes, and her own widened slightly. She froze. Her expression reflected a combination of amazement and uncertainty.

"Elantia, I mean Raven, it's me, Marcellus." He heard Corius chuckling beside him.

The sound triggered a reaction neither man anticipated. She turned to her brother and slapped him hard across the face.

"I don't like surprises!" She moved a step closer to Marcellus and looked more closely at his face. She abruptly turned and quickly walked away without the horse.

The two men stood there, each one trying to understand what had just happened. Corius spoke first. "I don't think it's what I expected. I thought she would be pleased to see you."

"I'm not sure," Strabo responded, "I can't think of anything I said or did years ago which would explain it."

"Well, let's forget about it. Now, come and greet those you know, and I'll introduce you to the ones you don't."

Raven stumbled through the trees, blind to where she was going and overwhelmed by the cascading emotions washing over her. The sudden appearance of Marcellus caught her unprepared to revisit a past once full of pleasant memories and expectation, eventually ending in reality and a time that became too painful to recall. The marriage two years ago was a vain attempt to forget and move on, but it, too, ended in disappointment. She had just recently begun to think Talos might be someone with whom she could have a future, and the promise of laughter instead of facing each day with grim resolve. She had known his intentions for some time. It was only recently when she began to think of him in other ways. He was different than the others she rode with, awakening thoughts and desires she was almost resigned could never be kindled again. She was old enough to know her juvenile attachment to Marcellus Strabo years ago was just that — something that once burned bright, at least for her, in time turned to ashes. First it was his indifference then his failure to come back after the last time he visited Bibracte. Suddenly he appears, looking much like he did but mature and physically more desirable than before.

The hours lengthened, and after sharing the food and the heady wheat-brewed beverage favored by the Gallic tribes, Strabo began to feel the effects of a long day. He vaguely remembered bedding down near Corius and drifting off in a peaceful slumber. He roused briefly by the sensation of a warm body pressed close to him. He was too befuddled from the celebratory drinking to give it any thought and promptly went back to sleep. He woke up a few hours later more sober and found Raven clinging tightly to him. He spent a long time before falling asleep confused and strangely unsettled trying to make sense of it. He thought about what Setarius had said about the Helvetii threat, insinuating he wouldn't be able to turn his back on the Aedui when they were in threatened. He sighed in resignation, conceding the truth of the tribune's prediction. So much for distant memories coming forward in a way he never would have imagined only hours before.

Strabo woke to the familiar sounds of men waking farting, spitting, voices cursing and the restless stamping of horses nearby. Raven was gone, and he was relieved she was. He didn't know what he would say to her or how he should treat her. He wondered if she was thinking the same. He decided there was little point in dwelling on questions that for now had no answers. He resolved to concentrate on things he understood and needed doing such as first seeing to the welfare of Aquilo. He looked around with mixed emotions at the leather-clad figures moving in the early light attending to the common chores typical of any encampment. For years he had become accustomed to the privileged life of the upper strata of the Roman Republic thanks to the martial and public success of his father. Now sober, he saw the leather-skinned, hirsute-tattooed men wearing enough gold and copper amulets to make them objects of interest or perhaps ridicule in a Massilia marketplace. He felt both uncomfortable and defensive for thinking so.

Not surprising, most of the men were either heading toward the picketed horses or were already there tending to their mounts as if they were prized possessions which they were. He found Aquilo feeding on a small pile of oats, and Raven busy giving the horse a minute examination.

She turned to face him. He was struck by how naturally beautiful she was unlike the powdered and painted women he was more familiar with in Massilia.

"He's exceptional. How and where did you get him?"

"He is for certain. I wish he were mine. Regrettably, he belongs to the Roman cavalry. The decurion we will serve today and the days to come would be happy if he never saw him again. It seems no one could handle him."

"They do not know horses very well."

"Certainly not like the Aedui." He wondered what else to say and couldn't think of anything to break the awkwardness of a meaningless conversation and the lengthy silence that followed.

She turned to stroke the horse's neck and said over her shoulder with studied casualness, "I suppose you've been wondering about last night."

"I must admit it's been somewhat on my mind."

"I apologized to Corius for slapping him."

75

"Why did you?"

"I was the shock of seeing you. I thought Corius had played a cruel joke on me, and you may have been a part of it. I didn't realize he was just as surprised as I was when you arrived last night. I came to you last night to tell you why I behaved the way I did, but you were already asleep."

He waited to hear her say why she slept with him. When she remained silent, he started to ask her then noticed her shoulders were shaking. She turned around, and it was clear she was working hard to maintain her composure even as a tear rolled down her cheek. She started to walk away. Instead, she ran toward him and threw her arms around him, burying her face in his chest. Taken aback and not knowing what else to say or do, he held her until she leaned back and gave him a searching look.

"Marcellus, I think I loved you the first time I saw you. Eventually I came to realize you never felt the same for me. I waited and hoped in vain you'd come back until I finally quit hoping. Two years ago, I hand-fasted a man I thought I could love. I was wrong, and it didn't take long before he realized it and had the sense to find another woman. Until last night, I thought I had accepted my life the way it was. Now, I'm no longer sure."

"The last time we saw each other you were a little girl, and I had barely reached my manhood. I thought of you as a sister."

"And you still do. I can see it in your face."

"You didn't let me finish. I was going to say, now I'm not sure it's the way I feel. You've become a beautiful woman, different from what I knew and the child you were many years ago. Neither one of us is any longer what we were. Give me a chance to know you as you are now. Possibly you need to take the time to do the same with me. You may be disappointed to find I'm not the man you thought I would become."

She leaned back in his arms, smiled and said, "You're right. I'm behaving like a silly woman, and I hate it because I don't believe it says who I am at all. It won't happen again."

"Today will be a new beginning for both of us." It was the only thing he could think of to say in response. He watched her walk away and considered if he wouldn't be better off returning to the *Claudia* Legion.

Neither Raven nor Strabo saw the man standing in the shadow of a nearby tree who had been silently watching and listening to them with an expression quickly transitioning from disbelief to anger. Frozen, he didn't hear Corius approaching until he called out to him.

"Talos, you'll ride with me. If necessary, I'll use you to go back to tell Marcellus I need him."

Talos nodded and without speaking walked toward his horse. Corius noted the angry scowl on the man's face and wondered what was bothering him. He intended to ask him when he had time but soon forgot as the myriad demands of the day pushed the thought from his mind.

Chapter 8

The distant sound of drums and horns signaled the approaching legions. Strabo nudged Aquilo and followed Corius to the top of a hill near the campsite. The two men didn't speak as they watched the snaking ranks coming toward them led by a cavalry turma a mile ahead of the first column and fanned out an arrow shot on both sides of the road. The impressive formation stretched as far as the eye could see undulating slowly over the low hills. Polished helmets and the forest of golden standards preceding each legion, cohort and century flashed in the bright morning sunlight. In the intervals when the drums and horns were silent, they heard the faint but clear chanting of a familiar marching song to which Strabo unconsciously mouthed the words.

Corius said with a note of awe, "They seem invincible. I almost feel sorry for the Helvetii."

"Don't. If there's any truth in what the Helvetii prisoners I talked to said concerning their numbers, the Helvetii far outnumber the legions."

"Marcellus, you don't sound encouraging for our capability to stop them."

"It may well depend on the Aedui and their commitment to resist rather than appease." The look on his friend's face was enough for Strabo to soften the implied criticism. "I overheard some of the officers suggesting there was dissension within the Aedui leadership over how to deal with the migration, either by helping or preventing their passage west."

The expression on Corius's face was sufficient to confirm Roman concerns. "I can't deny the tribe is divided, and Because it is, our resistance may not be all it could be. Those legions may well be the salvation of the Aedui. As for me, I intend to fight the Helvetii until I can no longer do so." Corius paused before continuing, "Marcellus, tell

78

me what you would do if your mother had been Helvetii instead of Aedui? Which side would you take?"

"I don't know and thank the gods it's a decision I won't have to make. Unlike you, I'm only half Aedui, and I don't feel either more Roman or Aedui. I never intended to become a soldier as my father expected, but I also did not expect I would one day come back here as one. Once the Helvetii are defeated, I intend to leave the Roman Army for good and disappear somewhere to live the way I want. Unfortunately, it is reason enough to go far away to escape the stigma and punishment of desertion should I ever be found."

"I'm sorry to hear you say it for Raven's sake and mine. She came to me last night upset and repentant for what she did to me. I had no idea my sister had such feelings for you from what now seems such a long time ago."

"I was no less surprised. Did you know she spent much of the night with me?" Interpreting the sharp look Corius gave him, he hastened to explain. "Our time together was innocent. In truth, I didn't even know she was with me until I woke up hours later considerably more sober than when I turned in. I didn't know who it was at first until she turned toward me and I saw her face. In a way it reminded me during our early years how she would sneak into my blankets to get warm. We talked about it earlier this morning when she told me things I never knew or suspected."

"What are you going to do?"

"I don't know, and neither does she. We agreed to leave the past and dwell in the present to give both of us time and circumstances to determine the way ahead. I live in two worlds, and I'm starting to wonder if I fit in either one."

"In time you'll decide which one it will be or learn to accept both. Raven has also lived in two worlds. She finally chose the world of men instead. Did you know she was once hand-fastened?"

"Yes, she told me this morning."

"She also has had difficulties in recent years. She wasn't happy or comfortable doing the things women were expected to do, nor was she welcomed at first by the men until she proved she could do as well and often better than the men. I ask you to treat her well."

"I wouldn't consider doing otherwise."

"I'm sorry. I shouldn't have said what I did. Enough of questions without answers. It's time we finish breaking camp and get ready to see what the Romans want us to do."

Tarquin watched Strabo coming toward him riding next to an impressive man with long flaxen-colored hair hanging well below the neck and moustaches drooping down past his chin. He was dressed in leather breeches, soft boots rising above the knee and a sleeveless leather shirt. Both arms were tattooed and liberally festooned with gold and silver bands. He was struck by how naturally both the stranger and Marcellus seemed to be a part of the horses they rode. He wished he rode as well.

"Decurion, this is Corius. He leads the Aedui scouts. He wants to know your orders."

"I want his men far forward of my cavalry screen and report anything his scouts see that could threaten our advance. He can leave his pack horses in the baggage train immediately following the Tenth Legion behind me. Marcellus, you'll remain with me as interpreter for whatever the Aedui report."

While waiting for Strabo to finish translating, Tarquin noted the passive behavior of Strabo's mount and recalled Tribune Setarius mentioning Strabo was part Aedui. He heard from others serving in Farther Gaul about an equine bond the Gallic people seem to have. If so, Strabo must have inherited it which might explain why in minutes he was able to do what he and the rest of the turma were unable to accomplish with the troublesome horse.

Strabo turned to Tarquin. "Corius understands and will do as you say."

The two men watched as Corius rejoined the Aedui band keeping pace with the cavalry troop. Moments later, Corius galloped off down the road ahead followed by four men while the remaining scouts broke into several groups of comparable size and rode off on either side of the road. Strabo observed one of the contingents riding northwest and frowned when he noticed one of the riders was smaller than the others. He knew it was Raven. Instead of a shield, she had a bow across her back and a quiver of arrows tied to the right side of her saddle next to the long sword the other scouts also carried. Until now, he assumed she'd been included not as a scout but to look after the pack horses and spare mounts. He realized there was nothing about the young woman resembling the pesky little girl he once knew. He started to turn his horse to join the cavalrymen behind when the decurion restrained him.

"Wait, ride with me. I have questions for you. How well do you know the Aedui?"

Strabo hesitated before responding, knowing what the decurion was really asking. "What you really want to know is can they be trusted."

"That's certainly one of my concerns."

He thought the reply was disingenuous. He noted the decurion's expression when Corius reported, the condescension as he took in the long-haired, leather-clad figure with gold bands partially covering his tattooed arms. He forced himself to be objective without condemning either the decurion or feeling defensive for the way Corius and the Aedui appeared foreign to Roman eyes. Just as quickly, he wondered if he only imagined Tarquin's reaction, and he was the one with the Roman eyes.

"Were I in your position, I might be just as concerned. The answer is I trust them with my life. Corius would do anything for me, and so would his sister who is presently scouting on the left flank. I would do the same for them."

"How did you come to know them and speak their language?"

"My mother was Aeduan, and from the time I was out of the cradle, she took me with her when she visited her family. Over the years, the visits were frequent and long enough I became as much Aeduan as Roman."

"Marcellus, I mean no offence when I ask, do you consider yourself Roman or Aeduan?"

Strabo didn't have to think and answered quickly. "I think I am no more the one than the other. I have no more or less allegiance to Rome than I have for the Aedui."

"What if the day comes when you have to choose?"

"I pray that day never comes, for I don't know the answer. It will be either Jupiter or Epona, the principal god of the Aedui, who will help decide my fate."

The sun was hours away from setting when Strabo saw one of the Aeduan scouts riding toward them on a lathered horse. As the individual grew closer, he struggled to recall the man's name. By the time the scout reined in, he remembered.

After listening to Talos, Strabo said, "He reports the Helvetii are almost across the Saône a mile or so north of where it joins the Rhône. The confluence is about ten miles from here. He estimates most of the Helvetii force is already on the west side of the river."

"Marcellus, you and the scout come with me. General Labienus and Caesar need to know this."

The three men cantered past the eagle standard of the Tenth Legion and the long ranks of the first cohort to where General Labienus and Caesar rode surrounded by Caesar's personal staff including Publius Crassus.

While Tarquin turned his horse and drew close to General Labienus, Strabo and Talos remained off to the side waiting for whatever would be required of them. Tarquin saluted and wasted no time in preliminaries.

"Salve, Caesar, General Labienus. Most of the Helvetii have crossed the Saône a mile north of where the two rivers meet and are encamped on the west side of the river. The rivers join ten miles from where we are now. The Aeduan scout estimates a quarter of the Helvetii remained on the east bank."

Before the general could speak, Caesar said, "General, we'll ride to the hill over there out of earshot from the column. I want to hear more from the scout."

Once on top of the hill, Caesar paid no attention to the others summoned to join him. He looked thoughtfully at the surrounding terrain then the long line of legionnaires now sprawling along the road taking advantage of the unexpected reprieve.

Finally, Caesar said to Strabo, "Tell him to describe exactly what he and his scouts saw."

After telling Talos what had been asked, Strabo listened carefully to the scout without interruption. When he was finished, Strabo said, "The Helvetii are having difficulty crossing. The river is slow-moving and too deep and wide to cross easily. They built rafts and tied them together for horses and those on foot. There are a few boats they're using to ferry wagons across, but many of their supply wagons and horses remain on the eastern bank."

"How many does he thinks are on the eastern bank?"

"He believes there are about six or seven thousand warriors and a thousand, perhaps more, women and children present in a horseshoe shaped camp extending a half-mile from the river."

"Can he guide us if I decide to attack from the east?"

After Strabo translated the question, Talos lifted a shoulder and replied, "Of course, it's why we're here."

Strabo gave the answer, wondering if there was a lingering suspicion concerning the resolve of the Aedui to commit to the Roman offensive. Caesar nodded in dismissal. "Give him my thanks and tell him orders will soon follow."

Caesar waited until Tarquin and the two other men left. "Titus, we'll go no further. The legions will remain where they are and prepare to spend the night."

Uncharacteristically, Labienus reacted quickly and vehemently. "By Jupiter, we have a chance to press on now and bag one-quarter of the Helvetii force and possibly even more of their supplies. Why would we even consider pausing to give them time to finish crossing?"

Caesar laughed. "Titus, I've no intention of turning my back on the opportunity at hand. You have a few hours of daylight to confer with the other legion commanders and their senior centurions to develop a plan to attack the Helvetii on the east side of the Saône at dawn tomorrow. With their backs against the river and separated from the Helvetii on the west side, it will be our battle to lose. We'll remain here to rest and plan the attack before we march during the third watch for a dawn attack. I'll leave the details to you and the centurions to tell me how this will be done. I want the Tenth to be the vanguard with the other veteran legions behind. The untried legions will be our reserve and defend the rear and baggage train."

The sun was about to drop beyond the distant hills when Tarquin rode into the Aeduan camp and saw Strabo sitting beside a small fire next to an attractive young woman talking to Corius. The three individuals stood up and waited silently as he dismounted and walked toward them.

"Marcellus, I've come to tell you what the generals have decided and want the Aedui scouts to do. We leave here at midnight to guide four legions into position to attack the Helvetii rear at dawn tomorrow. It will be a silent march with no horns, drums or marching songs."

Tarquin picked up a stick and sketched a crude map showing the Saône River flowing south and where it joined the Rhône. He drew a half-circle extending from the river to show the Helvetii camp. He pointed to the confluence of the rivers and said, "The legion leading will march east from the confluence." He indicated the route with a sweeping motion of the stick around the camp to a position approximately a mile north of the camp with its right flank anchored on the river. "The second legion will follow the first legion and face the Saône a mile or so from the eastern side of the Helvetii camp. The third and fourth legions will take position a mile south of the camp with the left flank anchored on the river. My turma will be with the tenth Legion in the center legion and deployed to maintain contact with the legions on its flanks. Caesar will be with the Tenth Legion. When the legions reach their position, the Aedui scouts will move to the rear of the legion they guided and remain there. They will not participate in the battle to avoid any chance of being mistaken for Helvetii. The *cornicines* of the Tenth will signal the time to attack."

The decurion waited while Strabo finished translating. The two men talked for a few minutes after which Strabo said, "Corius says he understands what's expected of them but he's concerned his scouts will not like being told they will not be allowed to fight. They would rather take the risk of being mistaken for Helvetii than be accused of riding away when the fighting begins."

Tarquin responded. "It's their risk to take. One of my men will come here well before the end of the second watch to take the scouts to the legion they're assigned to. Marcellus, make sure they understand where each one is supposed to go."

Corius called for all the scouts to assemble to explain their role in the Roman attack the next day. The mood was subdued and there was no bluster or concerns until he informed them the Romans wanted them to withdraw when the fighting began. Angry shouts protesting the withdrawal caused Corius to throw up his hands and commend each to do as he or she thought best. Strabo was taken aback when he saw Raven expressing the same concern with just as much passion. The scouts' reactions seemed to him naïve, even reckless for ignoring the common-sense directive. Corius ended by pointing to the sketch Tarquin had drawn; he elected to guide the legion traveling to the farthest position north; Talos would lead the second legion where Raven would be; Damos was given the third legion; Garos, assigned the fourth legion, drew raucous cries of derision for the comparative easier and shorter march he and those riding with him would have.

The few hours of sleep before it was time to march were fitful regardless of rank for both Romans and Aedui. Under a half moon, nearly twenty-thousand legionnaires formed up on the narrow dirt tract passing as a road leading north. The legionnaires traveled light, each with his shield and personal weapons including three javelins and rations for one day. The only wagons following the four attacking legions carried the pontoons and planking necessary for crossing the

85

river. The rest of the noisy supply and equipment wagons would follow the legions two hours later. There was little talk except for the muted orders of the officers and optiones as the three legions began to move, one legion at a time with a half-mile separation between them. The stillness of the night was soon replaced with the muted tramp of booted feet, an occasional curse when a legionnaire stumbled and the muffled clinking of metal accouterments.

Two hours later, Strabo knew they must have reached the confluence of the two rivers. Corius turned around and pointed northeast.

"We leave the road here. The ground is clear ahead with only a few streams to cross and some lightly forested areas that will not slow us down. We'll reach our designated position well before dawn and with time enough for the legionnaires to rest before the attack."

Tarquin nodded after Strabo told him what the Aeduan scout said. The decurion rode back to inform Caesar and General Labienus. An hour later, the Aeduan turned his horse west, and Strabo knew they were close to where the legion would deploy. Talos soon drew to a halt and in a low voice told Strabo they had reached the position opposite the north side of the Helvetii camp as seen by the flicker of campfires a mile away. It took each well-trained legion only minutes to form four long lines in a semi-circle, with each line consisting of three cohorts abreast in eight ranks thirty feet deep across a front stretching 500 paces.

Following Caesar's example, all officers dismounted and had their horses taken to the rear of the last rank. Strabo and the Aeduan scouts dutifully did the same. Identified only by her smaller stature, Strabo recognized Raven coming toward him. Together, they threaded their way through the nearest gap between the first two centuries.

In a low voice, Raven spoke first. "Why don't the Romans attack now with cavalry? It is what the Aedui would do."

Feeling defensive and inexperienced except for the brief, inconsequential skirmishes during the mountain crossing, he was hesitant to answer. He resorted to his training at Massilia and the few occasions when his father had talked about his battle experiences.

"In battle, Romans rely principally on infantry and use cavalry to attack the enemy flanks. Since the flanks are secured by the river, the cavalry here will keep the gaps between the center and left and right wings protected. There is also the practical problem of riding in darkness through a crowded camp, and the danger the cavalry would face when the legionnaires begin launching their javelins."

She paused and remained silent until she asked, "Where is the honor in fighting in such a way? There's no glory in impersonal killing. We honor battle when warrior meets warrior in personal combat."

Strabo didn't know how to respond and considered what, if anything, he could say. The difference and philosophy between how and why the relentless, impersonal Roman war machine and the Aedui fought was so completely at odds. It caught him off guard. He compared his boyhood and maturing years spent in part with his Aedui kinsman and living in Massilia as a Roman. While Roman life was more restrictive, it was also a world much more sophisticated in contrast to his mother's tribe. Drawing comparisons between the two cultures made the Aedui in contrast look more primitive than he ever considered when he was younger.

He decided not to respond. This was not the time to challenge either his or Raven's beliefs in some philosophical discussion minutes before a battle was about to begin. Raven apparently thought so as well, and they waited silently until the piercing sound of bugles gave the signal to advance.

Accompanied by the sustained beat of drums, the legionnaires stepped forward. If the surprise attack was shocking, the ominous thunder created by the legionnaires rhythmically striking their shields with the flat of their sword blades was designed to further erode the morale of the Helvetii defenders.

Talos and the other Aeduan scouts immediately mounted and without a word cantered north leaving Strabo to wonder where they were going. Without any specific orders from Tarquin other than an assumption he would remain with the Aedui scouts, he mounted and followed them. A few minutes later, after passing the flank of the northern legion, they met Corius and his contingent waiting for them. Soon after, the rest of the scouts arrived.

In answer to Strabo's question, Corius smiled and said, "We're going hunting. The country you've seen so far is clear with few places the Helvetii can escape. Ahead all the way to the river is dense forest. It's my intent to see very few carrying a sword, spear or bow will live long enough to reach it. Now we'll wait until the battle is joined then the hunt begins."

Moments later the repeated guttural roars in the forward ranks told Strabo volleys of javelins were hurtling toward the enemy camp. Soon panic-stricken women and children could be seen running toward the distant trees. Corius motioned for the scouts to fan out while cautioning them to wait for the warriors and let the women and children go.

"There they come," one of the scouts shouted and kicked his horse into a trot which was enough for the rest to follow suit. The one or two warriors coming into sight were soon joined by dozens more and spreading out to increase their chances of making it to the trees.

Strabo drew his spatha and urged Aquilo nearer to Raven; however, before he reached her, she was off in full gallop after one of the fleeing men. As she rode past him, she brought her sword down in a scything movement across the side of his neck with enough force it nearly decapitated him. It was a maneuver he and Corius had spent endless hours watching and trying to replicate what the older boys were being taught to do. It was evident he and Corius had not been the only observers. She appeared to have mastered the maneuver where his experience had been until now merely a training exercise.

She galloped on looking for the next victim. She was riding past a cluster of bushes and trees when he saw the warrior she did not. The man stepped out from behind a tree as she came abreast and with a single stroke of his sword across the animal's neck, brought it down, catapulting Raven over the dying animal's head.

Strabo desperately kicked Aquilo in the ribs and rode toward the Helvetii warrior. With no time to reach her sword or the quiver of arrows laying nearby, Raven drew her dagger and faced the warrior running toward her. Intent on an easy kill, the man failed to hear the horse and rider bearing down on him. Too late, he turned around and made a desperate and hopeless run for the nearest tree. Strabo leaned forward and drove his sword through the warrior's back then used the horse's momentum to withdraw the blade.

He reined in and turned the horse toward Raven, who was bending over the dying horse, dagger in hand. By the time he reached her, she was wiping the blood off the blade. He dismounted and helped her unsaddle the dead animal, scrupulously avoiding looking at her and saying nothing as she regained her composure.

"Are you able to ride?"

She answered with a faint, "Yes."

"We need to find you a horse." He mounted and crooked his arm to pull her up behind him. In the direction of the river, the noise of battle continued loud and unabated. There seemed to be fewer people and children fleeing toward the trees than a short time ago. Strabo ignored the refugees including the few men among them as he rode slowly north looking for any stray horses. They soon caught up to Corius and the other Aedui scouts standing in a circle. The men were so preoccupied in looking at something on the ground they were unaware of their arrival. Corius looked up with a welcoming smile when he saw them. His smile quickly disappeared when he saw his sister riding behind Strabo.

"What happened?"

Raven said, "The only fortune I had today was when Marcellus killed the Helvetian about to kill me." She slid off Aquilo's back and said, "I need a horse."

Corius turned to the others and said while pulling off one of the gold armbands from his left arm, "You heard her. The first to bring Raven a decent horse will have this." The offer was met with an enthusiastic response more to do with the competition than the intrinsic value of the arm band.

Their quick departure revealed to Strabo what they had just been looking at. His jaw tightened in revulsion after he saw the severed heads, some with open or-half-opened eyes. He knew from the veterans the habit of the Gallic Tribes to take trophy heads, but until now it had only been a curious tale. Before judging the tribesmen, he recalled his father saying such a thing was not uncommon with the legions.

Misunderstanding Strabo's expression, Corius waved his hand at the grisly spectacle behind him and said with a pleased smile, "As you can see, we've been more fortunate than my sister." His smile slowly disappeared when Strabo didn't seem to be showing any appreciation. "What's the matter, Marcellus, is there something wrong?"

Strabo determined it wasn't his place to criticize the barbaric custom. After all, the Romans were always referring to the tribes as barbarians. He recalled a crucifixion he once witnessed after a Roman tribunal sentenced a man to die. Perhaps the tribesmen would consider such an execution was far more barbaric than decapitation in the aftermath of battle.

"Nothing, except what nearly happened to Raven. It was a near thing. The Helvetian wounded her horse, and she was thrown hard enough she was lucky to survive without serious injury. I managed to get to him before he got to her. Tonight, I'll give thanks to Epona for helping me."

"And I'll do the same as I've already done for bringing you back to the Aedui for whatever purpose she did."

The heart-given sentiment was sufficient to erase his earlier misgivings regarding the more primitive habits, the Aedui traditions he never took note of or would have thought to criticize in his early years. The two men looked where Raven was sitting underneath a tree, leaning against the trunk with her eyes closed.

Corius nudged him and said, "Go to her. She needs someone other than her brother right now."

Strabo watched Corius ride away and realized in comparison to what Corius and Raven had experienced in the intervening years, he had, as Setarius had made clear, lived a life far different to theirs. After tethering Aquilo, he sat down beside her.

She spoke first. "I wouldn't be here if you hadn't been riding behind me and saw what I didn't. My thanks seem too little for what you did."

He reached for her hand and held it without quite knowing how to respond or what to say. She stirred feelings he neither understood nor particularly welcomed. She was an unknown, vaguely reminiscent of a young girl years ago who by her own admission had a juvenile regard for him he never imagined. At the time and his age, it would have embarrassed him. She was now a mature woman who appeared more comfortable on a battlefield than attending to the affairs young girls and women traditionally followed. She was different from any woman he'd ever met in Provincia.

Gradually he realized the din of battle had begun to diminish indicating the battle was nearly over. He had no doubt concerning the outcome. He saw Tarquin riding along the tree line toward him leading a dozen or more of his turma, presumably in the process of consolidating the troop. The decurion slowed as he passed the severed heads. Strabo stood up and caught the attention of the decurion. With a sudden smile, the cavalry officer altered course and reined in a few paces away. He took no notice of Raven who remained where she was.

"Well, it seems the Aedui acquitted themselves well. I had a feeling they would not meekly stand aside when the battle was joined. Marcellus, the Helvetii camp is ours. Tell Corius to cross the river and follow the Helvetii. For the time being, you'll remain with the Aedui."

Strabo saluted and walked over to where Corius was busy sharpening his sword and told him what Tarquin wanted.

"It is what I intended to do anyway. Marcellus, if the Helvetii turn south toward Bibracte, I'll try to get there before they do. You must decide whether to go with me or remain with the Romans. I won't try to influence your decision."

"There's no choice to make. I've been ordered to stay with you."

To occupy the time until the scouts returned and feeling reluctant to go back to Raven, he busied himself inspecting Aquilo for any injuries the horse may have incurred. He finished as the scouts returned leading several horses.

"Raven," Corius called, "you have a choice to make."

Finally showing some animation, Raven walked toward the three grinning men, each one extolling the praises of the horse he offered. Strabo saw Talos was one of the men.

With a frown of concentration, she minutely examined each horse in turn. When she finished, she announced, "All three are excellent horses, and the choice is difficult. I'll ride each one before I decide."

There was an excited commotion as the men began betting on which horse she would choose. For the next several minutes, Strabo watched in amazement as Raven rode each horse bareback in a series of movements and quick turns which not only tested the capabilities of the horses, but also demonstrated skills surpassing his own. After putting the final dun-colored horse through its paces she trotted back with a smile on her face.

"This is the one for which my brother will sacrifice his arm band." The decision was greeted with a yell of approval from the winner and a good-natured jeer from one of the losers; Talos remained silent and scowling. Strabo thought it curious Talos was looking at him instead of Raven.

After Corius surrendered the arm band, he told the men where they were going and led them to the river.

Chapter 9

The aging Helvetii leader listened stoically as one of the bloody survivors fortunate enough to escape the slaughter of the camp east of the Saône described the brief and one-sided battle. The report started out bad and quickly got worse. The wounded man described how the Romans were crossing the river in contrast to the cumbersome rafts and boats the Helvetii had used.

"Divico, the bridge the Romans are building is almost complete. It's a marvel and wide enough for wagons to cross. They could begin their crossing tomorrow; already their scouts have crossed."

There was a profound silence while the wounded man was helped out of the tent. Divico massaged his forehead and thought of the time and effort it had taken to build the narrow, unstable contrivance to cross the river. The latter followed by the two weeks it took for most of the Helvetii to cross the primitive structure. He recollected the long, high wall of dirt and timber the Romans built requiring a detour across the Jura Mountains and a delay of several weeks. He shook his head in silent resignation for the stark reality the Romans were organized and capable of doing things well beyond what the Helvetii could do. He not only suffered the loss of many warriors and a quarter of his supplies and the immediate prospect of facing five more legions than the one legion at Genava.

Dumnorix looked at Divico's strained face and fought down the rising panic. He knew he had to return to Bibracte before the assistance he'd given to the Helvetii was known to the Aedui. But how? He was more hostage than the ambassador he was supposed to be, made obvious by the thin veneer of respect he had been accorded.

Finally, Divico broke the silence. "This is what we'll do. I don't wish to confront the Romans until I find terrain more favorable for battle than where we are; therefore, tomorrow we'll go north. In the meantime, I'll make overtures to the Roman leader whom I believe is Gaius Julius Caesar. I do not know him. I am aware, as young as he is, he's resourceful and proven by what he achieved today. I'll send an emissary to Caesar with a proposal to meet and try to reach an accord. In return for allowing us to proceed west, the Helvetii will pledge not to enter Provincia."

The proposal was met with an immediate repudiation by the subordinate leaders representing the other tribes in the Helvetii federation.

Not surprising, Lidonica, the bellicose leader of the Tigurni, the Helvetii's prominent tribe, was the first to object.

"Divico, you defeated the Romans many years ago, and I cannot understand why you are so ready now to seek terms before we meet them in battle. I say instead of fleeing north with our tail between our legs, we turn and meet them as they begin to cross and before the other legions can reinforce them." The declaration was met by a chorus of enthusiastic support from the other tribal leaders.

Divico waited until the passion of the moment began to subside. In measured tones, he acknowledged both the logic and the emotion prompting the proposal.

"Lidonica, hear me. You speak with a warrior's heart, but there is more to this than bravado and success of a battle fought long ago. Our objective is to go far from the threat of the Germanic tribes which each year have become more troublesome. With our losses today, I prefer a peaceful accommodation with the Romans to escape the continued depredations of the Germans."

He sat back and allowed the spirited debate to continue unabated. Gradually passion was replaced with a pragmatic, grudging acceptance of Divico's proposal.

Dumnorix stayed behind as the tribal leaders left the tent, silently rehearsing the rationale he hoped would persuade Divico to let him leave the Helvetii camp. The Helvetii leader interrupted his thoughts by saying in a voice and with an expression making clear his opinion of the Aeduan.

"Dumnorix, the others have left, and I wonder why you're still here."

"It's time I returned to Bibracte. If I stay here any longer, there will be concern I serve the interests of the Helvetii more than the Aedui."

Divico's smile was humorless. "The only interests you've ever served are your own. By now, there are few left in the Aedui Tribe who do not ask why you've spent so much time in the company of the Helvetii. Perhaps they think you remain with us at the urging of your wife who wishes to return to her tribe. In truth Dumnorix, the Helvetii don't want Morgane with us any more than we would welcome you. I think you and Morgane are well-suited for each other."

Dumnorix flushed and resisted the urge to say what he thought of the old man. "As you are well aware, I came here at the request of the Helvetii and with the approval of our *virgobret* as a gesture of good will to expedite the tribe's passage through both the Sequani and Aedui lands. I believe I've accomplished the reason I was sent here."

"We haven't crossed the Aedui lands yet, and given the present circumstances, this will not take place until we either defeat the Romans or negotiate passage to the west. Frankly, I see little value in allowing you to return. For now, it serves my purpose to keep you here, no matter how distasteful, as hostage for the support I'll require from the Aedui."

Dumnorix was quick to respond. "You and I know you cannot fight both the Romans and the Aedui in the event you demand too much of us."

The Helvetii tribal leader's response was blunt. "I will not demand anything. If necessary, I'll take what I need and treat the Aedui the same as the Sequani when and if I think the Aedui favor Rome more than the Helvetii."

"And you fail to see the Romans accomplished in one day what the Helvetii required almost two weeks. You also have lost a quarter of your numbers as well as most of your supplies." Dumnorix held up his hands in supplication. He continued in a more conciliatory tone. "This is not the time to argue; rather it's a time to plan how the Aedui, and I, can help the Helvetii."

"How?"

"The Romans have requested food and forage, and the Aedui have agreed to provide it. I have the means to control when and how much the Romans will be supplied. Without adequate support, the Romans will be limited in what they can do to you. I cannot make such arrangements and ensure they will be carried out while I remain here." Dumnorix was gratified to see a flicker of interest in the older man's expression.

"How do I know you will or can do what you say? Perhaps your words are empty, a pretext to release you."

"For the simple reason I don't want the Romans imposing their will on the Gallic tribes. Rather, I would see all the tribes united under one, even if it isn't the Aedui." He thought the speculative look on Divico's face was a good sign at the broad hint the Aedui would accept dominance of the Helvetii over the prospect of Roman domination.

"Tell me why you think you're able to control the supplies."

"I already do. We need each other. I'm willing to continue helping the Helvetii for the practical reason I may need your help. My brother has recently undermined my authority and my control; however, I have the influence to offset my brother's authority. I'll help you in order to increase my chances not only to secure my leadership of the largest Aedui Tribe but as permanent *virgobret* of the Aedui federation."

"I believe you mean king, not principal magistrate." Dumnorix only smiled. "Your argument is persuasive, and I'll see in time if your actions are equally so. All right, you can leave; however, I warn you it would not do you or the Aedui well should you disappoint me."

Dumnorix breathed a sigh of relief as he left the tent. He planned to do no more to help the Helvetii than the Romans, just enough for each to believe he was. His preferred outcome was for the Helvetii to defeat the Romans decisively then keep going west leaving behind an uncontested field to him with the opportunity to achieve his own objective.

Strabo looked at the battleground which only a few hours ago had been the Helvetii camp and was horrified at the carnage. Neither animals nor humans, whether warrior, woman or child had been spared. Mounted cavalrymen were dragging dead horses and oxen away from the river while Legionnaires loaded bodies onto the empty wagons that had carried the pontoons now about to be used by the *fabri* to construct the bridge. The steep banks on both sides of the river where the bridge would be placed had already been leveled. He looked at the abandoned boats and rafts the Helvetii had used and wondered how they were able to get wagons and carts across.

Corius dismounted and had a brief conversation with one of the engineers who seemed to be in charge. Strabo saw the two men appear to reach an understanding after which Corius beckoned for him and several other scouts to come forward.

"We've been given permission to use two of the pontoons to get our weapons and packs on the other side."

The pontoons were quickly loaded and wagers made for who would be the first to gain the other side. Strabo noted Raven was just as eager to accept the challenge as he was inclined not to participate. Their light-hearted banter was in contrast to his reaction for the indiscriminate slaughter in the Helvetii camp.

"Marcellus!" Corius shouted from across the river. "Are you coming with us, or have you decided a cold swim is too much for Roman blood and you're waiting until the bridge is finished? You've holding us up. It's time to see how far the Helvetii have gone."

The jocular challenge and his friend's infectious smile were enough to shake off his somber mood. With an embarrassed smile, he guided Aquilo into the water. When the horse began swimming, he rolled out of the saddle and held on to the girth strap while the horse pulled him effortlessly across the deep, sluggish river.

The wide trail of trampled brush and turned earth leading through the shallow valley would have been easy to follow even on a moonless night. The brutal signs the Helvetii left behind made it even easier to follow. Corrals were empty, most of the circular and steep thatch-roofed dwellings on either side of the wide swath were burned to the ground. Strabo was appalled at the senseless destruction of the isolated homesteads. Mutilated bodies tied to corral posts or left where they were killed were mute testimony of the futile effort to resist the Helvetii invasion. The few shocked, bewildered survivors they passed salvaging what little was left were too numb to take note of their passage. He was reminded of his interrogation of the Sequani captive and his description of what he witnessed. He was seeing firsthand what the man described.

Hours later, the abundance of smoke columns spiraling in the late afternoon sky beyond a range of low hills signaled they were close to the Helvetii camp. Corius and Strabo reined in and surveyed the immediate vicinity while waiting for the others to catch up

"Ahead is certain to be the Helvetii camp. We've come a long way, and the horses are tired. This is as close as we need to go." He pointed toward a line of trees less than a mile away. "Garos, somewhere over there should be water. Find it, and we'll camp where it is. While you look for a suitable campsite, Marcellus and I will ride on to verify it is the Helvetii camp."

The two men continued on for several miles until Corius said, "We'd better leave the horses here and go up there to take a look," gesturing to a hill ahead and taller than the others surrounding it. Near the crest of the hill, they dropped down and crawled the rest of the way.

For a moment, neither one spoke as they looked at the valley stretching below filled as far as they could see with a vast array of tents surrounded by wagons and animal herds. "By all the gods above," Marcellus said in wonder, "It's a city! I had no idea there were so many."

"I warrant all the Aedui tribes together would not number half as much," Corius said. "I doubt anything can stop them, even the legions. It may be better for the Aedui to let the Helvetii move on."

Strabo studied the valley more closely. "Corius, I remember this valley. I killed a deer down there."

"You wounded it. I was the one who had to ride it down and finish what you didn't."

"I suppose you're right. I do seem to recall you weren't pleased. I also remember Raven wasn't happy after we reminded her as payment for letting her come with us, she had to dress it out."

Corius smiled. "I think we took advantage of her."

After a moment of silence, Strabo said, "From the way they've surrounded the camp with the wagons and carts, they look as if they intend to stay where they are."

"I agree. They chose a good place to stop. The narrow valley and steep hills on either side would make it difficult to attack them here. Better to fight them when they move farther north where the ground is more open."

"Wherever they choose to fight, I'm confident the legions and the Aedui will cause the Helvetii to regret they ever left their lands." Strabo thought his words reflected more confidence than might be justified.

"I wish I shared your conviction. There were some who wanted to come to terms with the Helvetii soon after they crossed the Jura Mountains. It's possible after what happened to the Sequani and what we saw today, there will be more who will prefer to negotiate than fight. Let's go. I've seen enough to keep me awake tonight. Tomorrow it would best for you to ride back and tell your decurion where their main camp is. We'll stay nearby and keep an eye on the Helvetii. I'll send someone back if they start breaking camp."

The two made their way back to where they left their horses and mounted up. They had ridden less than a few hundred paces when Strabo felt a subtle and quickening change in Aquilo's gait. The horse snorted, and with ears fanned forward, turned its head toward a clearing on the left. Strabo saw three riders emerge from the trees walking their horses in the direction of the Helvetii camp. From their casual attitude, it was evident they were unaware anyone else was nearby. In a low voice, Strabo warned Corius, who looked where Strabo pointed. The smile on his friend's face was not the reaction Strabo expected. He had a feeling Corius was about to do something both of them were going to regret. Sure enough, Corius retrieved the shield tied to his saddle, drew his sword and without waiting to see if Strabo was doing the same, charged the riders with a blood-curdling war cry ending the slight advantage of surprise it might have given them. With no choice except to follow, Strabo drew his sword and followed a pace behind.

They were halfway across the clearing before they saw four more riders come in sight. Except for one rider without a shield and carrying a bow, the rest were variously armed with axe, spear or sword. The odds had now changed dramatically from acceptable to stupid. It was too late to turn around and avoid what looked to be a one-sided fight.

Strabo thought Aquilo was not helping when the spirited stallion surged past Corius, possibly for no other reason than refusing to allow another horse to get in front of him. It had been years since he and Corius had been taught how to fight on horseback, and he hoped his arm remembered better than his head the techniques and movements for a mounted defense and attack."

He steered the stallion toward the right side of the lead rider. Aquilo thought otherwise. and at the last minute swerved left, crashing headlong into another and smaller horse that put both animal and rider down. Out of the corner of his eye, Strabo saw the fallen rider struggling desperately to get out from under the thrashing horse. He managed to fend off a spear thrust with his shield from a rider passing on his left even as another warrior passing on the right leaned toward him with an upraised sword. With no time to shift his shield to protect his exposed flank, he brought his sword up, deflecting the oncoming blade. Both men turned their horses to renew the contact, but Aquilo was faster. Strabo reached the other man as he was half-turned and thrust the sword blade deep into the Helvetian's exposed side.

He reined Aquilo in and looked around to see where the next threat might be and glimpsed Corius with an arrow protruding from his left shoulder fending off two attackers. He started to go to him until he saw the Helvetian archer across the meadow drawing his bow for another shot at Corius. He appeared to hesitate for fear of hitting the wrong man. Focused on his target, the archer at first didn't see Strabo galloping toward him until his horse shied. The arrow intended for Corius was now speeding toward him. The missile came in low under his shield and struck him in the left thigh. Ignoring the sharp pain, Strabo rode on. The archer dropped the bow and started to draw his sword. Before he could, Strabo with a downward stroke, buried his sword deep in the archer's head.

He heard a horse coming from behind and managed to turn Aquilo around in time to raise his shield and stop the attacker's spear. He let go of the encumbered shield and concentrated on regaining his balance and controlling the prancing stallion. He felt a heavy blow between his shoulder blades followed by a sharp sting. He faced his assailant only to see him slipping sideways from the saddle with an arrow protruding from his chest. He hunched his shoulders and again felt the discomfort of something scratching beneath his ringed armor.

Strabo turned to where he'd last seen Corius and was relieved to see him being helped from the saddle by a trio of Aedui scouts. Holding her bow, Raven was in a heated exchange with Talos who also was holding a bow and listening with a tight-lipped frown. Other scouts were fanned out looking for any additional Helvetian threat and dispatching the few still alive.

Garos came out of the woods and rode up next to him laughing. "Marcellus, I think you had enough on your hands with the Helvetii without adding more from those who came to aid you."

"What do you mean? If you and the others hadn't come when you did, I think Corius and I would be kneeling before Epona."

"And she is now thinking you were fortunate you wore your Roman armor." Garos reached behind Strabo. He felt a tug, and the annoying scratching immediately stopped. Garos handed an arrow to Strabo. "This is what I mean." Chuckling, he added, "You'll have to ask whether it belonged to Raven or Talos."

Strabo knew now why Raven was angry with Talos. He guessed both had released their arrows simultaneously while his back was momentarily turned to his adversary. He was lucky he was wearing the Roman chain armor or he would have been as dead as the archer.

He walked Aquilo over to where Corius was lying on his side gritting his teeth with Raven occupied in carefully extracting the arrow from his shoulder. She didn't look up as he remained in the saddle and watched her. Two other scouts, one with a cut on the arm and the other with a bleeding cheek, were waiting their turn.

"Instead of watching, you could get down and help," she said with an edge to her voice.

"I was waiting until you finished. You did such a good job, now you can pull one out of my leg." She looked up in alarm when she saw the shaft protruding from a blood-soaked trouser leg and his right forearm bright red to his fist.

Corius rolled over on his back. "The one archer managed to do more than the other six. Maybe they should have stayed in the trees and waited until he finished."

Raven took a cursory look at the arrow imbedded just above Strabo's knee. "It can wait. You're lucky, the arrow didn't go deep enough to hit the bone. In fact, I'm surprised it even went through your breeches."

"Well, it hurts," Strabo said, put off by her trivializing the painful if not serious wound.

Clearly exasperated, Raven said, "You both deserve what happened to you. If either one of you had any sense, you would have thought twice before taking on so many."

"We didn't see the other four in the trees until it was too late to do anything else but fight." Strabo thought the response was lame and refrained from voicing his agreement with her. Corius made it worse by adding, "We could have handled a few more." She gave him a withering look without bothering to respond and walked over to help Strabo hobble to where Corius was now sitting up with a concerned expression.

"How bad is it?" Corius asked.

"It could have been a lot worse — the arrow could've hit my ..." he caught himself in time and substituted, "somewhere else and more critical." He heard Raven muffle a laugh and quickly changed the subject. "Raven, how did you happen to be here?"

"We saw them pass by a quarter mile from camp heading in your direction. I told Goros we ought to find you." With more than a trace of sarcasm, she said, "Obviously, considering your superior skills and how it turned out, we need not have bothered."

Neither man said another word.

After Corius described the Helvetii camp, the mood in the camp was subdued. There was little conversation and none of the characteristic banter Strabo had become accustomed to. Soon, those not on the first watch drifted away to attend to their own needs. Strabo looked for Raven, and when he didn't see her, accepted the probability she was cross and had found a place away from him and Corius. He was both relieved and disappointed for reasons too confusing to understand after such a long day.

When he finished tending Aquilo, he was too much awake to sleep and limped down to the creek to scrub off the grime accumulated over the past several days. The water was cold and felt soothing to his injured leg. The wound proved to be more superficial than he first thought, and apart from being a little stiff, he didn't think it would hinder the ride he would have to make the next day.

Teeth chattering while using his linen tunic to dry off, he retied the bandage Raven made. He stumbled back up the bank to where he thought he had left his woolen cloak. After reaching level ground, he stopped and looked around, uncertain in the darkness of a quarter moon where he was. He heard a soft, familiar voice a few steps away. "Marcellus, you're cold, and so am I. It's late. Come to me."

Faced with what he had been unconsciously thinking and more recently resisting, he hesitated. "Are you sure?"

"I am even if you're not."

He knelt down carefully, ignoring the pain it caused and lifted the cloak covering her. She was naked. Even in the dim light, she was a dream-like image reminding him of what he hadn't experienced since leaving Massilia. Whatever guilt he had or concern for the wound disappeared in a lingering kiss that stopped both the pain and a conversation neither wanted to have.

It was pitch dark with no hint of dawn when Strabo woke and discovered Raven was gone. He reflected on the first night she spent with him and was mystified why she had. He was even more so now they had moved beyond innocence. What happened a few hours ago was an experience very different from the impersonal couplings he had always known. While he had more tolerance than affection for her in past years, it was apparent it had been different for her. He felt uneasy he didn't feel the same and might never have similar feelings. By the time, the sky began to transition from black to gray, the only thing he'd resolved was to avoid talking to her about what happened, primarily because he didn't know what to say. Resolute, he got up and started preparing for the long ride back to the legions. He delayed only long enough to tell Corius he was heading south and thankful he hadn't seen Raven.

The expected twenty-mile ride turned out to be only half as much when Tarquin and his turma appeared riding toward him. He quickly summarized where the Helvetii main body was with no indication they were in a hurry to leave.

The decurion made no comment until Strabo finished. "The legions are encamped a few miles behind. General Labienus will want to hear what you have to say. When you've finished reporting, unless the general says otherwise, go back to the Aedui scouts."

Strabo saluted and continued south. Soon after, he crested a hill and saw the low walls of three rectangular forts with two legions occupying each one. He spotted the eagle standard of the Tenth Legion near the north entrance of the third fort and the Claudia Legion standard posted at the south end. After identifying himself and his mission to the the optio in charge of the guard detail, he was waved through. He dismounted in front of the headquarters tent of the Tenth legion and reported to the centurion standing near the entrance. The officer listened attentively until Strabo finished.

"General Labienus is with Caesar at the moment. I'll see if he'll hear your report now or after Caesar leaves."

While he waited, Strabo thought back to the first time he saw the two men inside. The information he provided had come from interrogating prisoners. The difference this time, he was reporting his own observations.

The centurion quickly appeared and motioned for him to enter. Caesar sat at a table with General Labienus seated across from him. Neither man commented on Strabo's limp and bandaged forearm. When Strabo finished describing what he'd seen and how close the Helvetii were, Caesar remained silent, thoughtful.

General Labienus said, "Tell me more about the camp and the surrounding terrain."

Both men listened intently as Strabo described in more detail the long narrow valley and the rugged countryside flanking the camp, concluding with an opinion the camp's defenses seemed well prepared as if they intended to remain where they were. Belatedly, he thought he might have gone too far by offering an unsolicited observation from an inexperienced legionnaire. He was relieved when neither man rebuked him.

Caesar asked, "Do you know what lies beyond the valley?" After Strabo finished describing the increasingly more open terrain, Caesar looked at General Labienus and said, "It appears the Helvetii may have decided to go on the defensive for the time being for reasons I can only conjecture. Where they are now, I've no intention of ordering an attack. Titus, we'll remain where we are until the Helvetii give some indication of what they intend to do. It's possible they'll seek an accommodation rather than risk what happened to them at the Saône. If I'm right, we can expect the Helvetii will send a delegation to negotiate some kind of settlement.

"If they decide to attack us here, the terrain is suitable enough for battle. If they go farther west or north, we'll pursue until there is ground more open and to our advantage. Marcellus, thank you for your timely and excellent report. I'll want your services as an interpreter should the Helvetii want to talk. Tell the centurion outside where you can be found. You should see a medicus about your wounds."

Accepting he had just been dismissed, Strabo saluted and left the tent thinking about Caesar's last words. Not only did Caesar remember him, he knew his name. He wondered if Setarius told him who he was. It seemed likely and might explain the centurion's passing comment about joining Caesar's staff as an orderly, an offer he wasn't willing to accept.

He followed Caesar's instruction and told the centurion he was rejoining Decurion Tarquin. He decided to ignore the suggestion to see a medicus, trusting Raven's ministrations as more than adequate. He limped over to Aquilo and started to mount until he saw Setarius walking toward him.

"Marcellus, I'm surprised to see you. Why are you limping?"

"The Aeduan scouts found some Helvetian scouts, and we engaged. The wound isn't serious, but riding is preferable to walking."

The centurion smiled. "What brings you here?"

He repeated what he had already summarized twice before, adding only what Caesar intended to do. Setarius listened without interruption until Strabo finished. "After what happened to them at the Saône, the Helvetii may have suffered more than the loss of a battle. Caesar may well be right, and they want to talk instead of fighting." Strabo didn't feel he had either the knowledge or experience with which to agree or disagree with the assessment and remained silent.

"Marcellus, would you prefer to remain with Tarquin or return to the *Claudia* Legion?"

The question came as a surprise, both for being offered an unexpected choice and because he wasn't sure how to answer. Before last night he wouldn't have hesitated to give his preference to stay with Tarquin and the opportunity to see Corius and the others. Now he wasn't sure it was something he wanted to do.

Seeing his hesitation, Setarius said, "Well, never mind. It isn't a question that needs an answer now. You've done well. Your actions and observations have done you credit. Your father would be pleased. Caesar has a favorable opinion of you. If offered a chance to join his personal staff, you should accept your good fortune. Few at such a young age are given the opportunity to advance so quickly."

Strabo considered the practical wisdom of the centurion's advice. His response was both respectful and measured.

"Tribune, I'm not unaware of the possibilities which would improve the circumstances you've been instrumental in arranging. I'm also not ungrateful for what you've done, but I'm here not by choice. I have changed to the extent I will not dishonor my father and disappear in the dark of night."

"For the sake of your father, I'm relieved to hear you say it. Why don't you accept an easier path to serve your time than as a legionnaire in the ranks?"

"I accept what my father wanted, not because I either agree or am content with the outcome. Given the chance, I'll choose what I want to do and when. Until then, I prefer to remain in the ranks." In response to the centurion's quizzical expression, he gave a partial answer without mentioning Raven. "During the past several days, I've learned something about me I didn't know before. I may be more like my father than I realized."

"What do you mean?"

"I'm good at what the army expects of me, particularly if someone is trying to kill me."

The centurion laughed. "I think Centurion Valens may be right. He saw something in you the night you were brought in puking and resisting. He thought you showed potential that I did not. It could be, even if you don't, the gods will let your father sleep better tonight."

Chapter 10

Strabo saw the turma close to where he had seen them hours before, dismounted and dispersed in pairs at some distance on either side of the road. Tarquin was sitting under a tree talking to his two *decuriones*: Costa was the *duplicarius* and second in command of the turma; Priscus, as *sesquiplicarius,* was third in command. Corius with another scout were standing by their horses nearby talking to a pair of Helvetians.

The decurion got up and waited until Strabo dismounted and gestured toward the Helvetians. "They showed up a few minutes ago. Whatever they want to tell me must be important because Corius wasn't too happy when you weren't here. I used enough sign language to make him understand you'd be along soon. Find out why they came here then you can tell me what General Labienus had to say."

As the three men walked over to Corius, Strabo saw the concerned expression on the Aeduan's face. "I can see you have something important to tell the decurion."

"I do, tell him the Helvetians are here with a request for a truce so their leader, Divico, can talk to Caesar. He said there's an open meadow three miles south of their encampment where the meeting can take place. Divico will be accompanied by twenty warriors and suggests the same number for Caesar. If agreed, he suggests the meeting take place at noon tomorrow in the center of the meadow. He proposes having both Roman and Helvetii scouts ensure there's no treachery by either side. I know the place he described. It's large with good visibility around it. They will remain here until there's an answer from Caesar."

After Strabo finished translating, Tarquin said, "Marcellus, tell him we'll inform Caesar. It should only take about an hour to find out whether or not he agrees. Costa, go back and tell Caesar and General Labienus what Divico wants"

Tarquin left Strabo to tell Corius what the decurion said and returned to where he was a few minutes before. Typically for a cavalryman used to constant patrol, it didn't take long before the decurion was fast asleep with no concerns for tomorrow.

Corius told the scout to go back and tell Divico the proposal has been given to the Romans and a response was expected soon. Strabo and Corius were left alone in a prolonged and awkward silence. Corius finally spoke.

"Before you left to tell the Romans where the Helvetii were, Raven woke me and told me she was leaving for Bibracte."

"Did she say why?"

"I asked. She said it was better for both of you if she left. Then she got on her horse and rode away. Do you know what she meant?"

Strabo hesitated, unwilling to talk about something neither he nor possibly Raven understood and was so personal. Reluctantly he knew he owed Corius an answer.

"We spent the night together, and it was different than before. It's possible she regrets what happened although I don't."

"I thought perhaps it was something like that."

"It wasn't planned, nor did I expect it. She evidently has a deeper feeling for me than I do for her. I have great affection for her, but I can't tell if I'll ever feel the same as she does for me. I think she understands this, and it could be the reason she left."

"You may not be familiar with how the Aedui look upon such as this. If she had been untouched or hand-fastened, there would have been severe consequences for both of you, and our friendship would be over. Since neither condition has been violated, it's a matter only for the two of you to decide the outcome. I hope whatever it is, you will both be content."

Strabo was relieved by Corius's reaction, and the time spent was relaxed until Costa returned and reported to Tarquin.

Tarquin came over to Strabo and wasted no time in preliminaries. "Tell your friend Caesar agrees to all the conditions and will be at the appointed place at noon tomorrow."

After Strabo finished the cryptic message, Corius mounted. "Tell the decurion I'll come back tomorrow in time to guide the Roman delegation to where the meeting will take place."

The decurion turned to Strabo. "By Caesar's order, you'll remain here tonight and join the delegation when it arrives tomorrow. General Labienus and Tribune Setarius will be part of the delegation. My orders are to scout ahead of the delegation. The legions will be ready to march if there's any indication of treachery. After the meeting is concluded, you're ordered to return to the *Claudia* Legion."

Strabo thought a day earlier he would have been saddened his interlude with the Aedui was coming to an end; instead, he felt relief. He would miss being on a horse again; it seemed a reasonable if more arduous solution to his current circumstances. He thought about Aquilo and was concerned for what might happen to him back under Tarquin's care.

"Decurion, I have a question. Since I'm to be a legionnaire again, what will become of Aquilo?"

Tarquin looked at Strabo with a trace of irritation. "He comes back to the turma where he'll be expected to behave, perhaps with a better chance of surviving than before considering how he seems to have improved under you."

"What if he doesn't? Then what happens to him?"

"If he doesn't behave, he'll be horsemeat and a hide for shields which I predict will be his lot. What does it matter to you?"

"I think he won't do well in the turma, and I think he has more value than you believe. Why not give him to Corius in thanks for what the scouts did for you and the legions?"

Tarquin frowned. "You seem much taken with the animal."

"I owe him for serving me well during the last two days. I'm part Aedui, and I have the same regard for Epona as my forbears, who believe a horse is more than food and leather for making shields or breeches."

The decurion regarded Strabo with an expression reflecting both exasperation and interest. He hesitated before saying, "He's been nothing but trouble for me and the troop; however, what you say has merit. I'll think on it and let you know tomorrow what I decide. In the meantime, see Costa for your watch assignment."

It was late morning, when the Roman delegation came in sight. Tarquin gave the order to mount up for the few scouts kept back to screen the immediate area. On a white horse with a calm, composed expression, Caesar rode at the head of his personal guard in full regalia, gold circlet on his forehead, signature red cloak draped across his shoulders and down the horse's withers. General Labienus rode to the right of Caesar with Tribune Setarius following behind the two men.

Corius leaned toward Strabo and said in a low voice, "He looks like a god." Strabo nodded without replying, certain he had never seen a more imposing man.

Tarquin rode forward and reported to Caesar. The decurion indicated Corius and said, "He's the Aedui scout who will guide the delegation to the meeting place."

Caesar nodded and asked, "How far?"

"Four miles, and he says the way is easy. We'll be there with time to spare."

"We will take our time. Marcellus, tell the Aedui scout I'll wait until Divico crosses to the center of the field before I ride to meet him." Strabo nodded and told Corius. "Decurion, lead the way."

Tarquin saluted and led the scouts at a gallop to a position a hundred paces ahead of the delegation and slowed to a canter.

Strabo estimated it was close to the mid-day hour when Corius said, "The meadow is not far off. Better to wait here and let me ride ahead to see if the Helvetii have arrived."

Tarquin nodded and rode back to inform Caesar while Corius headed in the opposite direction and disappeared in the trees ahead. He reappeared a few minutes later and beckoned for them to come forward. Corius told Strabo, "Divico and nineteen men are mounted and waiting in the field. Divico is the older man in front wearing a green robe and a long gold chain. My scouts see only a small number of

Helvetii scouts in the trees on the other side of the field. They've seen no indication of any other warriors between here and the Helvetii camp."

By the time Corius finished, Tarquin returned with the delegation, and Strabo quickly summarized what Corius reported.

Caesar nodded in satisfaction. "Decurion, keep the turma and the Aedui scouts in the trees."

"Caesar, the Helvetii delegation is larger than what you have."

"Of course, I intended it to be so. Divico will understand why, and he will not be pleased. Marcellus, ride with Tribune Setarius. Now, let's find out what Divico has in mind."

At a walk, Caesar led the delegation out of the trees toward the mounted green-robed figure slightly ahead of the other nineteen men grouped behind. As they drew closer, Strabo saw Divico was much older than he expected. From his haughty expression, he was a man used to getting his own way. His face was weathered and deeply lined with a prominent hooked nose reminding Strabo of an aging bird of prey. Similar to the Aedui, his moustache curled past his mouth and his long grey hair hung down well past his shoulders. Divico was the first to speak as Strabo quickly translated the following exchange.

"I am Divico, leader of the Helvetii and the other tribes who joined our migration. I am well-known to the Romans, particularly Cassius who I defeated long ago not far from this place."

"And I am Caesar who leads six legions. Have you asked to meet me to boast of things long ago, or do you have another purpose?"

Divico's jaw tightened at the rebuke and with visible effort restrained himself from responding in kind. "It is always better to seek peace than war, and I sent emissaries before we left Genava seeking a peaceful passage to the west."

"And permission was not given. I had no wish to see such a large migration passing through Provincia to do what you have done to the Sequani and now the Aedui."

"I no longer want to pass through Provincia. Even now my intention is to travel north away from Provincia before continuing west to the coast."

"It's too late. You've ravaged the lands of the Allobroges, the Sequani and appear to be ready to do the same to the Aedui. The Aedui is an ally of Rome that asked for my help to stop you from invading their land."

"Caesar, we had no choice but to leave our homeland. The Germans coveted our lands, and we tired of resisting them. If the Roman people would make peace with the Helvetii, we would go wherever Caesar chooses and remain there without threat to anyone. If on the other hand, you continue to invite war, you should remember what happened and the disaster the Romans suffered when you last fought the Helvetii. Caesar, you attacked one canton of my force at the Saône and won by subterfuge and defeat. We fight with courage without relying on cunning or stratagems. Do not let this place be remembered by the Romans as a place for another Roman disaster."

"Divico, I find your boast of a battle fought long ago both insolent and ignorant of what you face today. However, I'll overlook your intemperate remarks and offer peace. These are my terms. You asked where I should tell you to go, and this is my answer. You will return to your homeland in peace under the following conditions: first, you will compensate the Aedui and Sequani for the outrages you have done. Second, you will give hostages to ensure you return from where you came."

Tight-lipped, Divico's expression and words were defiant. "It has always been the custom for the Helvetii to demand hostages, not to give them. So be it. Once again Rome chooses war, and the Helvetii will willingly face you on the battlefield. Give sacrifices to your gods, for in the days to come you will need them to defeat us." Without giving Caesar a chance for rebuttal, Divico abruptly turned his horse and galloped away with his bodyguard thundering behind.

With a thoughtful expression, Caesar silently watched the Helvetii delegation disappear in the tree line. General Labienus was the first to break the silence.

"Did you expect he would accept your terms?"

"No, and had I been in his place, I wouldn't have either. He hoped to be allowed to continue but suspected I would not grant his wish."

"What then was his purpose?"

"To learn something about me and to test our resolve."

"Then there was never any doubt we would fight."

"There never was. He's probably right about the Germans, and perhaps had I been in his place, I might have migrated as he chose to do. He's in a dilemma. He cannot voluntarily go back, yet he's reluctant to fight. Even if he should defeat us, it will cost him more than he wants to risk."

"Is it any different for us?"

"Yes, because while he would avoid battle, I will not. I will defeat him and give him no choice but to accept the terms I offered today."

"The gods willing it should be so."

"I'm always ready to accept the help of the gods. I'm confident this time they need only to stand by and watch what a disciplined army can and will do. Titus, what do you think?"

"We are already well-positioned where we are if they decide to fight. As reported, the terrain north of the valley where they're located now is more open and favorable to their greater numbers; therefore, I think it more likely they'll go north."

"I agree, and if you're right, we'll follow behind until I find the place where I will fight them or Divico changes his mind and accepts my terms. It must be soon as our supplies are low, and the Aedui are late in supplying the food and forage they promised."

Caesar looked at Strabo. "Marcellus, you did well today, and you have my thanks. Tribune Setarius tells me you're returning to the Claudia Legion. I've no doubt there will be occasions ahead when I'll require your services. In the meantime, I expect you to do your duty as a legionnaire, although I'd be obliged if you would take care not to do so too excessively." The dry humor drew smiles from Setarius and Labienus.

Corius waited for the last of the scouts to appear before they departed for Bibracte following Tarquin's announcement they were no longer needed. Strabo had intended returning with the delegation when Corius suggested, "I'll ride with you as far as the Roman camp. It will give me more time to persuade you not to stop there but to go with us to Bibracte."

"As I said before, there may come a time when I will; however, it won't be today."

Corius frowned. "Why?"

Strabo hesitated because he wasn't sure how to answer. "Not long ago all I could think of was how to get away and live my life the way I wanted to. In a way, it's true. I've also come to realize after seeing you and the others fighting for your homeland, my ambitions seem small in comparison. I'll remain a legionnaire while there's an imminent danger to the Aedui, after which I'll find a way to leave the Roman Army one way or the other."

"It makes no sense. Stay with us and fight beside us." Corius saw Strabo shake his head and gave up in disgust. For several minutes, they rode in silence until Corius said, "Divico seemed willing enough for a settlement, but his last words told me Caesar did not accept his proposal. Does Caesar intend to fight, or will he eventually allow the Helvetii to go west?"

"The Helvetii will have to defeat Caesar before they go any farther, and I don't believe that will happen."

Corius's expression reflected his doubt. "Caesar's army is impressive, but it's greatly outnumbered. Those numbers could increase the longer the Helvetii remain here."

"Why?"

When he saw Strabo's puzzled reaction, Corius wished he hadn't hadn't said what he did. He was at a loss how to respond without giving offense. "I told you days ago the Aedui are divided, and it may have grown worse where factions have created distrust and animosity. It's also true in our relations with the tribes in neighboring lands which are no longer as peaceful as they once were."

"I don't understand."

Corius took a deep breath regretting more than ever his inadvertent invitation to an unintended discussion he shouldn't be having with a Roman, even Marcellus.

"There's a growing feeling throughout Gaul shared by many Aedui that Rome may be a greater threat than the Helvetii or the Germans."

"The Aedui have always been treated well by Rome, and my father maintained good relations when he was governor of Provincia, not to mention he took my mother for his wife."

"What you say is true. What you don't understand is Provincia and what you call Cisalpine Gaul now look very Roman, and the language spoken is primarily Latin. There's concern about a stronger Roman presence spreading into Gaul and the tribes there becoming much like Provincia and Cisalpine Gaul are today. Even the Romans refer to Cisalpine as 'Togate Gaul' because of how Romanized it's become."

"The Aedui and other tribes need only to look at what the Helvetii migration has caused so far to understand they will take what they want when they want. And they will without the help of Rome."

"I agree, but there is also the concern, if and when the Helvetii are defeated, what will Rome do then? Will the legions leave, or will they remain?"

"My father helped the Aedui, and afterward he did not make any advances beyond the boundary of Provincia."

"Yes, it is the reason he is respected and a special friend of the Aedui. There is much doubt Caesar will be like Lucillus Strabo."

"Caesar has only recently been appointed governor of Provincia and Cisalpine Gaul and came here just days ago. How can anyone know what he intends?"

"Marcellus, I think we may know more about Caesar and what happens in Rome than you realize. We have to keep informed. What's decided in Rome may well affect us. Caesar is known to be ambitious, and there is great concern not only what it will lead to but where. Ever since he left Provincia and came here the concern has only grown."

Taken aback by the stark view expressed, Strabo made no reply. He was not unaware of Caesar's meteoric rise to fame and fortune. Nor if the truth be known, had he thought much about Gaul in recent years except for the occasional fleeting boyhood memory. He suddenly felt guilty. The reality was in he hadn't cared much for anything except fast horses and inventive whores. The revelation was disquieting, tempered only by how his father was responsible for him being conscripted and depriving him from pursuing a life he enjoyed. He glanced at Corius and wondered if he and Raven would feel the same if they knew more about his life in Massilia. The thought was enough to make him feel guilty.

"Marcellus," Strabo was quickly drawn back from his internal musings when Corius asked, "I see three Roman forts ahead. Which one is your destination?"

"The farthest one south." A few minutes later, he stopped in front of the west entrance of the fort and dismounted. After untying his kit from the saddle, he led Aquilo over to Corius and handed him the reins. He saw the questioning look on his friend's face.

"Tarquin doesn't like Aquilo. I asked him what would become of him. I didn't like his answer and suggested he might consider giving him to the Aedui for what you and the scouts did guiding the legions to the Saône. He agreed. Corius, he's worthy of more than how he will fare with the Roman cavalry. Give him to Raven. She has a regard for him as do I. Perhaps Aquilo will remind her I care for her more than she might think."

Corius took the reins. "I'll tell her. I think she'll be pleased as I am." He hesitated and asked, "Aquilo, is there meaning in the name?"

"He's named after the Roman god of the north wind which as you know is troublesome, often unpredictable."

Corius smiled. "He's well-named and perhaps much like you. Marcellus, you're like a brother to me, and my wish is you will always be no matter what happens between Rome and the Aedui."

Strabo nodded, not trusting himself to speak, and walked away toward the fort's entrance. A trio of curious guards watched him coming toward them, and he understood their quizzical expressions as they took in the round cavalry shield on his back and a spatha hanging from a baldric at his side. He suspected they thought he was a curiosity. He wouldn't have disagreed.

Chapter 11 Bibracte

Leading Aquilo, Corius reined in next to the small beehive-shaped dwelling and called her name. There was no response. He knew Raven was inside because her horse was tethered nearby. He waited, and when there was no response, he dismounted and scratched on the leather hide hanging over the entrance and said her name again. This time he was rewarded by a quiet, composed voice without an invitation to enter.

"Corius, what do you want?"

"I have a gift for you."

"Leave it where you are."

"Well, it isn't something I can do, and if you'll come out here, you'll understand why."

He heard her mutter something ending with an irritated vulgar epithet he had never heard her say before. He thought perhaps his sister may have spent more time with the scouts than he realized. It was also obvious from the tone of her voice and unenthusiastic greeting, she was in a bad mood.

She pulled the curtain aside with an expression of resigned acceptance. She never looked at him, seeing only the stallion beside him looking at her.

"Aquilo," she said with a catch in her throat. "What's he doing here? Is Marcellus here?"

"He isn't, but he talked the Romans into giving the horse to the Aedui for what we did for them. When they agreed, he told me it was for you he made the request. He wanted you to have Aquilo. It seemed important to him..."

His voice trailed off as he watched her run to the stallion and throw her arms around the horse's neck, burying her face in the sweaty, dirt encrusted mane. Her response was so uncharacteristic that he was too astonished and at a loss for words to say anything. When she turned to face him, he understood there was much more to the gift than a token of gratitude and friendship in the giving and the acceptance. He was pleased, and his suspicion was confirmed there was something deeper between Marcellus and his sister than either had said. At the time, he felt a sense of foreboding as if a cloud had drifted across the sun. He shrugged it off.

"It appears you're pleased with the gift. I'll tell him so when I see him again."

Her response was sharp. "You will not. It's for me to thank him."

He thought it best to back away and say nothing more for fear it would be taken the wrong way. He was caught in a dilemma he hadn't foreseen when Marcellus unexpectedly came back into their lives. It wasn't long ago when Talos approached him to enlist his approval and support in gaining Raven's attention. He'd been agreeable not because of any concerns about Talos but the belief Talos was wasting his time in a fruitless conquest. He concluded long ago Raven was never going to be like other women. He wondered if he should, or had the right, to question her about Talos — and Marcellus. Reluctantly, he thought it might be better to ask her than risk a more unpleasant outcome later by remaining silent.

"Raven, what will you tell Talos? It's obvious to him and the others you've distanced yourself from him since Marcellus came here. Before, I. and others had come to believe there was an understanding between the two of you."

"Before Marcellus came back, I was aware of Talos's attentions and was beginning to think he might be someone who could become more than a friend. I did nothing to encourage his intentions, but I confess I did nothing to discourage his interest. I may have made a mistake when I didn't. I think he imagines and wishes a deeper friendship than I can give, particularly since Marcellus returned. Does it mean the opposite is true for Marcellus? It's a question I keep asking, and I have no answer. It's possible I never will." She saw his bewildered expression and smiled. "Marcellus was a girlhood dream and one, I admit, I embellished over the years. I'm trying now to separate fantasy from reality without any idea how this will be reconciled for me and for either Talos or Marcellus.

"I fear I will not be kind to either. I tried to be willing, subservient the way young girls are raised to believe when they become a wife. It took me almost no time to realize when I married Tanisia, I didn't want to be with him or possibly any man who cannot accept me the way I am. I will not be subservient to anyone including Marcellus."

"It's obvious to me and to Talos by now, Marcellus has affection for you."

"Yes, I believe in his own way he does."

"I don't understand what you mean."

"I too have feelings for him, and I think deeper than he has for me or ever will. Marcellus is caught between our world and Rome. He doesn't know yet where his place is. He's here in Gaul and a Roman legionnaire not by choice but because of circumstance and the will of his father who made the choice for him. It's not for me to tell him where he belongs even though I wish he would leave all that is Roman behind and remain here. I don't believe he can ever turn his back on what he's known as a Roman. The brief time his mother brought him to Bibracte and what he learned about the Aedui, the way we live and what we believe, did not make him one of us. He's lived most of his life in a world I do not know and don't believe I could live in. I think it might be the same if he chose the life of his Aeduan mother lived before going to Provincia."

"You seem too ready to judge what he believes and what he'll choose to do. Give him time. Circumstances may help him decide."

She looked away while considering her brother's last words and conceded he had a point.

"There's talk among the scouts the arrow Talos launched and struck Marcellus in the back may not have been an accident. What do you think?"

"I don't know. I thought at first it could have been intentional. The truth is there was little time to think and aim. Marcellus was in danger, and we acted quickly. We launched our arrows almost at the same

121

time. It could easily have been my arrow. I think Talos was too quick, and his aim suffered from a hasty release. I cursed him for being careless. After listening to his denial, and considering the situation, I decided to give him the benefit of the doubt. I also didn't think there was any reason Talos would want to harm Marcellus."

"Did he know you spent the night before with Marcellus in our camp near the Romans?"

"But it was innocent and no more than reliving a childhood memory."

"Did Talos know you were with him that night?"

The question unsettled her, and she hesitated before replying. "I don't know."

"Perhaps he went looking for you and found you with Marcellus."

"I suppose it's possible."

"Raven, there may be consequences you haven't considered."

She watched him ride away and realized he was right.

Chapter 12

The first one Strabo recognized was Brecius standing hands on hips watching him approach. Typically, there was no warmth in his greeting.

"Marcellus, I'm glad you're back not because I missed you but only because you are; consequently, Optio Tulio owes me a sesterce."

"Why?"

"He figured you were probably back in Massilia with your wine and whores. I was only a little less sure you were. I'm not going to ask why you didn't go for the simple reason I don't really give a shit. I heard you were riding around playing scout and living easy. Well, you're back to being the low-life ranker you are and the business of being a foot-soldier."

"One of these days when you're not carrying a knobbed-staff you're so fond of hitting me with, you and I are going somewhere private and have more than a conversation."

"By Jupiter, do you think to borrow his balls to face me? And if so, there's no time like now, and I don't need my staff to make you regret challenging me. Drop the shield and the sword belt, and I'll have some fun at your expense. You'll get a lesson I hope you'll remember for as long as you're a legionnaire."

Strabo saw the taunting expression on the optio's face, and it became the target of everything that happened to him since being conscripted. He dropped the shield, unfastened his sword belt and headed for the optio left fist reaching down automatically to steady his leg. Almost within arm's reach, Brecius held up a hand. "Stop right there. What's wrong with your leg?"

"Nothing to concern you or that will interfere with what I'll do to you."

Brecius took a closer look at Strabo's left thigh and the bloodstains surrounding the cut in his breeches. "Anything happening to one of my legionnaires concerns me if it interferes with his capability to do whatever and when he's ordered to do. Answer the question!"

"We had a skirmish with some Helvetian scouts. One of their archers put an arrow in my leg before I finished him. The wound isn't serious."

"I'll let the medicus be the judge. Go see him, and that's an order. On the way, turn the shield and spatha into the quartermaster then get your gear from the wagon and start looking more like a legionnaire you're still trying to become."

"You keep reminding me why I never wanted to be in the army. The next time I disappear, you'd better not bet against Optio Tulio."

Brecius watched Marcellus walk away, a smile curving his lips and thinking of the conversation he and Tulio had whether the legionnaire would come back. Neither one thought Marcellus would desert.

Strabo saw a dozen men lined up in front of a medical orderly recording the real or imagined injuries or maladies that could get them relieved of duty. Legionnaires often purposefully injured themselves to escape guard duty, training, the physical labor required to maintain the fort, or tasks designed only to keep a legionnaire busy. By the time it was his turn to describe his injury, Strabo concluded he was the only one so far who was there against his will.

"I don't think it's necessary to see the doctor, but my optio ordered me to come here."

The orderly looked up for the first time in astonishment. "I've been doing this for years, and you're the first one trying to go back to duty. Maybe you're sicker than the ones the medicus is looking at now."

Minutes later the rotund, porcine-faced civilian physician with a blue-veined nose told him to pull his breeches down and gave him a cursory, painful examination of the entry wound with a thick, stubby finger. He missed Raven's sympathetic and gentle attentions.

"If you were expecting slack time and no guard duty, you wasted your time and mine coming here." Strabo started to make a sarcastic reply and decided against making his life more miserable than it was already. He left the hospital tent with a fresh bandage and a wound far more painful from the pine-pitch ointment the orderly applied than when Raven pulled the arrow out.

He limped to where the cohort was quartered and saw Scevola coming out of their tent. Seeing Strabo, his face lit up with a welcome smile. For Strabo it was enough to ease his tension, and he found himself genuinely glad to see the veteran legionary.

"Welcome back. You've been missed. Brecius said you were back and told us to get your things from the wagon. He also said you were with the medicus because of an injury. I hope it isn't serious."

Strabo laughed and related what the doctor had to say about the wound. "My friend, it's sore but trivial. Apparently, I haven't lost my place in the contubernium, and I suppose I have Brecius to thank for it."

"You do. However, we have a replacement for Enrius. His name is Vinicius, and he, too, was recruited from Massilia. He says he knows you."

Strabo laughed. "This day is ending better than I could've imagined. I know him well. He and I have been friends and rivals for years. When we weren't competing for who had the fastest horse, we were trying to see who could drink the most wine and able to service a whore."

"And who won?"

"I'm not sure we ever decided. He lied as much as I did, and the whores never took sides. Now, where's the son of bitch?"

"Right behind you and ready to kick your ass for not admitting you always came in second. I was also the one who ended up seeing you always got back to your villa in one piece." The two men embraced, momentarily overcome by the unexpected meeting.

Strabo stepped back and said accusingly, "I don't recall anything of the sort."

"Marcellus, you just proved my point."

"I'll concede you may be right. Why on earth are you here?"

"Expedience, my friend, and a couple of muscles working for a Greek who didn't take kindly to a wager I lost on a horse I misjudged. Well, maybe it was more than one, and sestercii I didn't have. I thought perhaps it was time to leave Massilia. I heard what happened to you and without any options left, I thought the army might be looking for someone better than you. I found out which legion you were in and told them I'd volunteer if I could be assured of being in the *Claudia* Legion. And so here I am. For me, it was a choice of expedience. For you it appears it was much the opposite. Too bad you happened to be in the wrong place at the wrong time and didn't have a chance to tell them who you were."

"The reason I'm here is because of who I am."

Vinicius looked at Strabo in wide-eyed astonishment. "It seems there's more to this than I suspected."

"And it isn't one I intend to go into now. It would be better not to tell anyone I'm a general's son."

"Whatever it is, you seemed to have adapted well and already earned a reputation for holding your own when the vicious hordes are on the attack."

"Hardly. It's more about doing what you have to do when the time comes if you want to see the sunrise tomorrow."

Their conversation was cut short when Brecius appeared carrying a tablet and told Scevola, "You and your worthless tentmates have the second watch. Report to the centurion at the east gate, and he'll tell you in what section you'll be posted. The watch will include our occasional legionnaire — evidently the medicus deemed his wound too trivial to be excused from guard duty. One last thing, the rumor is we'll be moving out tomorrow. The Helvetii are on the move. Get ready tonight to leave early. I'll not be in a good mood if your lot is muddling around paying more attention to your cocks than getting your boots on when the trumpeter blows last call."

Vinicius turned to Strabo. "What's this about a wound?"

Embarrassed, Strabo responded, "It's not worth talking about."

"Marcellus, they say on the way across the mountains, you killed a warrior. Is it true? What was it like?"

Irritated at the question, Strabo was ready to give a caustic response then decided against it. He didn't quite know how to answer the question. "There have been others since, and I don't feel any different. The truth is I don't think about it at all, either because I don't care or more likely, because I don't want to. You do what you have to when the time comes, and I take no joy in it. I'd rather be in Massilia and spend my time with horses, decent food and a willing woman even if I have to pay for her. Maybe you should've gone south to Italia or across the sea to Alexandria instead of volunteering."

The glum expression on his friend's face caused him to soften his words. "Perhaps you didn't have much more of a choice than I did. The circumstances why we're here are different, but there's one thing we have in common. We don't have any way to change things now."

The first blast of a trumpet came well before the glow in the east foretold the coming of a new day. Predictably, Brecius celebrated by banging his knobbed stick against the leather sides of the tents and shouting, "Rise and shine, you sorry bastards. You've got thirty minutes to piss, shit, get packed and in ranks with full kit. Move it now or see me later to tell me why you didn't make ranks on time."

Strabo heard the familiar refrain repeated as the optio went up and down the century's tent lines.

Slowly at first the legionnaires stumbled into action with little comment except for the muted and usual cursing no different from a typical morning wakeup. He rolled over and tried to stand up groaning with the effort and wondering how long he could march in full kit.

"What's the matter, Marcellus?" Scevola asked.

"It's nothing. I'm just a little stiff." He reached down and gently massaged the wound and felt some relief in doing so.

"Tell Brecius you're in no condition to march. You should ride one of the wagons until your leg is better."

"I'll do no such thing. I'll crawl before I ask the bastard for anything."

"Marcellus, I think you have the wrong opinion of the optio. He means well and is concerned about you and the rest of us."

"My opinion is well earned. I've been the target of his staff too many times to think he cares anything about me except to look for another reason to hit me with it. I count the hours and days when I'm no longer treated like a mindless animal."

In the pre-dawn blackness, the legionnaires went about the myriad tasks in preparation to march with little talk and practiced efficiency.

As a concession to his aching thigh, Strabo accepted Scevola's offer to carry his share of the *tribuli*. When tied together in the center, the three long stakes sharpened at both ends would form a triangular barrier emplaced on top of a defensive wall. The latter added to the weight of his armor and weapons including two javelins, a scuta, a daily ration of water and biscuit and his personal kit. He started having misgivings how long he was going to be able to carry over sixty pounds with a leg already smarting before taking the first step.

It was the usual hurry up and wait for the priests drawn from both legions to inspect internal organs of the sacrificial bull to forecast the success of the day's endeavors. By the time the veteran Sixth Legion, *Ferrata* marched out of the fort, the eastern horizon was showing the first signs of dawn, and it was time for the *Claudia* to march. To the disgust of the legion's optiones and centurions, the legion's exodus resembled more a ragged shuffle than a resolute advance.

With gritted teeth, Strabo ignored his painful thigh by concentrating on putting one foot in front of the other and listening to Vinicius marching beside him talk almost non-stop about Massilia and his brief time so far in the army. He'd forgotten what a raconteur Vinicius was with his self-deprecating humor and optimistic outlook on life. At times in the past, his constant patter had irritated Strabo, but now it served him well by lifting both his morale and taking his mind off the wound.

When the first halt was called a few miles later, he was relieved to find his leg, although no better, felt no more painful than when they started. He saw Centurion Marinus ride past with a grim look and rein in next to Brecius standing by the roadside at the rear of the century. By the time Marinus rode on, the optio's expression was equally grim. Strabo thought no more of it when the order was given to form ranks, and the march resumed.

The sun had barely reached mid-day when the unexpected order was given to fall out and prepare camp. The legionnaires looked around in disbelief at the reprieve from what promised to be another long march. For Strabo it was a gift from the gods. By century, the legionnaires followed the optiones to their designated area and grounded equipment, pulled off their mail and helmets and proceeded to the section of the perimeter armed now with *dolabra*, basket and tribuli. There was almost a festive air and uncharacteristic energy in digging a wide, deep trench with the upcast used to build the defensive wall above.

Two hours later, the six-legion force was enclosed in three rectangular forts positioned close enough to provide mutual defense. Strabo stepped back and surveyed the finished construction and thought except for the moist, darkened spoil, it seemed as if the camps had always been there. There was ample time when the physical labor was over to erect the leather tents and allow the legionnaires by century to wash off the sweat and dirt from their labors in a small slow-moving river nearby.

With his eyes closed, Strabo was lying on the river bank feeling clean and thankful his leg was no worse from the short march when a shadow darkened the sun, and someone sat down next to him. He thought it might be Vinicius, then the harsh voice of Brecius quickly dispelled the thought. The tranquil mood of the warm afternoon was gone when the optio asked, "How's the leg?"

"It hurts, but I can manage."

"I watched you. You did well on the march. I thought within an hour you'd be asking for a wagon ride. I was wrong. Today was a short march, tomorrow could be longer. I'll be watching you, and if I think you're not keeping up, you'll be riding one of the wagons."

"I suppose I should thank you for your concerns, then again it could be you're only interested in keeping a ranker in place and in condition to throw a javelin or use a gladius when necessary for the glory of Rome."

"Marcellus, you may be smarter and better than I've given you credit. I'll admit from the time I laid eyes on your drunken ass in the Massilia bordello, I thought you were worth less than the sponge to clean my ass in the latrine. I'm beginning to think you're more like your father than I gave you credit. Tarquin and I took the *sacramentum* and shared a tent many years ago. When he decided he liked horses better than I did, we went our separate ways but we remained close. He has a regard for how you've interacted with the Aedui as well as how you acquitted yourself in battle. He told me you ride better than anyone in his turma but turned down the opportunity to be a cavalryman."

"I just thought it better, at least for now, to remain a legionnaire." Thinking of Raven, he added, "It's hard to explain. Besides if I had a horse under me all the time, it might tempt me to ride away."

"So, you're thinking about deserting?"

"Yes, except when I'm asleep then I dream about it."

"I swear to the glory of Athena's marvelous tits, you're about the only one in the *Claudia* Legion who volunteered or was conscripted in Massilia who's been blooded and proved yourself in battle. Maybe you're more suited for this shit than you realize."

"Lately I've been thinking the same, and it gives me another reason to leave as soon as I can before I begin to like it too much. Then the thought of risking a fustuarium is also enough to keep me where I am."

"You're right to keep it in mind. I've no doubt before this campaign is over, you'll have the opportunity to see just how bad the gauntlet is."

Brecius started to stand up and stopped when Strabo asked, "Optio, the day isn't even half done. Why did we stop here?"

"The Helvetii are encamped where they've been. According to Marinus, they're only about eight miles from here. Caesar sent out a large cavalry force of Aedui and their allies as a screen and to determine where the Helvetii were going. Apparently, the Aedui cavalry got routed by a considerably smaller cavalry force according to some who were witness to the debacle." Brecius shook his head in disgust. "The commander claimed the ground was unfavorable. If I'd gotten my ass kicked in similar circumstances, I would have fallen on my gladius more ready to face the gods than the men I led to such a defeat. What puzzles me is why Caesar hasn't already ordered an attack."

"I think I know the reason. I translated for Caesar when he and General Labienus met with the Helvetii delegation. Afterward when the Helvetii refused Caesar's terms, Caesar and the general talked about when and where the next battle would be. Caesar wants a battlefield favorable to him. I know the valley the Helvetii are in. It's narrow and flanked by steep high ground and easily defensible by a force smaller than the legions. If it's true the, Helvetii far outnumber us. Caesar will wait to meet them on more open, advantageous ground. I described to Caesar where their encampment was and how defensible it was compared to the terrain twenty miles farther north."

Brecius looked at Strabo in astonishment. "You've probably spent more time with Caesar than any of the centurions in any of the legions. Is it because he knows who your father is?"

"Perhaps not at first. I suspect Setarius told him because he now calls me by name."

Brecius stood up and said over his shoulder as he walked away, "By the gods, I'm surprised you're not already one of Caesar's orderlies instead of being down here in the *Claudia* legion, and only a legion because it has an iron bird and a name."

Strabo watched Brecius walk away and considered Scevola's defense of the optio and found he was beginning to agree. He was heavy-handed, but he was also fair and took care of his own. Just as soon as he conceded the thought, he chided himself. *Shit, before long I'll be thinking the same of Marinus — well, there's a thought to give the gods a laugh.*

Chapter 13 Caesar's Headquarters, fourteen days later

General Labienus nervously approached Caesar whose mood had become increasingly testy. The Helvetii's continuing slow movement north was a clear intention they intended to remain on the defensive and avoid a decisive battle. The Roman advance was about to stop not because of the Helvetii's greater strength or their valor, but the reality the legions were running out of food and fodder essential to keeping an army in the field. Even if Caesar had not mandated there would be no pillaging the countryside to maintain the army, there was little left in the wake of the Helvetii advance.

"Caesar, we must talk."

"Titus, I can tell by the look on your face, you're reluctant to tell me what I already know. If we keep on, we'll be eating the oxen and horses which we might as well do since there's no forage left for the animals."

"The legionnaires expect to be issued their grain ration in three days; what we have to issue will not be acceptable, and I fear the consequences when they learn the ration will only be half what they expect."

"Rest easy. This is as far as we go, at least for now. The Aedui pledged support, but with so little given thus far, I begin to wonder if the reason is motivated more to see us return to Provincia than concern about Helvetii depredations. I want to meet with Liskus, the *Virgobret* of all the Aedui-related tribes, and Diviciacus, who I understand has once again assumed leadership of the largest tribe. Dumnorix is apparently in disfavor. I have in mind meeting with Diviciacus tomorrow with only the time negotiable. I'll want Strabo here as well to translate. I met Diviciacus in Rome last year. He speaks some Latin, although not well enough to ensure he will understand what I want. Liskus, I'm told neither speaks nor understands Latin."

Standing at the entrance of Caesar's tent, Strabo and Setarius watched as the two Aedui senior leaders accompanied by a small entourage were given permission to pass through the west entrance. As the horsemen drew closer, Setarius said, "The smaller man on the roan horse is Liskus, the Virgobret, chief magistrate of the Aedui. The man riding on his left wearing the gold torque is the tribal leader of the largest tribe; his name is..."

"Diviciacus," Strabo said. "I know him well. He's one of my uncles. It's been many years since I last saw him, and I doubt he'll recognize me."

Setarius looked at Strabo in astonishment. "I had no idea you're so well connected to the Aedui leadership."

"I didn't know I was either. He wasn't the leader last time I visited Bibracte. My grandfather was tribal leader then. He died not long after my last visit. When my mother died a short time later, I had little reason to go back; consequently, I didn't know who succeeded him until recently."

"You must also know his younger brother, Dumnorix, riding behind him who, until recently, claimed tribal leadership."

"Not as well. I never liked him. He was gone most of the time I was in Bibracte visiting the other tribes. I heard my grandfather tell my mother Dumnorix was both arrogant and ambitious and counted the days until he had enough wealth and patronage to become Virgobret. Many suspected if he did, he would try to hold the elected position longer than the traditional one year."

"What you say may support suspicions Caesar has of him ever since the cavalry contingent he led against the outnumbered Helvetii was soundly defeated. You may not like some of the things Caesar intends to tell Liskus and your uncle. If I knew anyone else with your language skills, I'd replace you. Just to be sure you accurately translate what's said by all concerned. If Diviciacus and Dumnorix don't recognize you, it would be better for both you and Caesar not to tell them who you are, at least for now." The last was said in low tones as the two Aedui leaders drew rein and dismounted. Diviciacus glanced at him but gave no indication he was recognized while Dumnorix took no notice of him at all.

Strabo noted the serious expressions on the faces of Liskus and his two uncles. If what the centurion said was true, they had good cause to expect an unpleasant encounter. Dumnorix remained outside as Setarius led the two leaders and the six other representatives into the tent. With Liskus and Diviciacus standing in front, the other representatives formed a semi-circle behind. The absence of stools or any amenities was conspicuous. Expressionless, Caesar sat on his ivory curule chair in front of the fasces wearing both his red cape and gold circlet. General Labienus stood to the right of Caesar and General Crassus on the left. Strabo hurried to take a position standing a step away on the left and behind Caesar. Caesar wasted no time on pleasantries, and Strabo was challenged to give justice to Caesar's stern rapid exchanges.

"Noble leaders of the Aedui, I asked you here to explain to me why the pledge of food and forage to support my legions in your resistance to the Helvetii has been insufficient for my needs. I have had to reduce rations to maintain pursuit of the Helvetii. So far, I've refrained from what the Helvetii have done in pillaging what they need and paid for what little supplies we've been able to obtain from local villages. I wonder why this must be so when I'm here at the request of the Aedui."

Liskus stood with arms extended in appeal and said in a manner both hesitant and pleading, "Mighty Caesar, we are grateful for what you and your legions have done to thwart the Helvetii incursion, and I regret our delay in providing the supplies in sufficient quantity to satisfy your requirements. We will try to do better. There have been some difficulties among the tribes from some who are unwilling to provide more than has so far been collected."

"I presume you are going to explain why this is so and what you intend to do about it."

Liskus looked increasingly uncomfortable glancing nervously at Diviciacus and the other clan leaders.

When it became clear to Caesar the magistrate's hesitation signaled a more private conversation was called for, he said, "Marcellus, tell them I want to speak to Liskus alone." When Diviciacus and the others left, Caesar said, "Liskus, I think you have more to tell me than you're willing to say in front of the others."

For the first time looking both relieved and more relaxed, the magistrate said, "Mighty Caesar, you are correct. There is more to be said, but I could not say it in front of the others as it would not help you or me. I take great risk in telling you what must be said; however, I can no longer compromise my honor by remaining silent. Unfortunately, there are within the tribes many influential and wealthy men who are unwilling to provide the promised support. Their concern is it will encourage the Roman presence to remain in Gaul long after the Helvetii have been defeated and no longer a threat. Some fear the primacy of Gaul would be better served by Gauls than Romans even if it is claimed and secured by the Helvetii. For some that is preferred to having the legions remain here. Certain people have been actively helping the Helvetii by reporting your movements and intentions when known. I do not have the power to restrain them as they are too many and too powerful."

"So, you wish my help. It seems though, it's conditional I give promises to leave as soon as the Helvetii are no longer a threat. Well, this is a matter to consider after the Helvetii have been defeated. I'll decide to leave Gaul when I think there is no longer any reason to remain here from invasion by the Germans, the Belgae or any other tribe. Who is the one who has been the most influential and involved in all this?"

Liskus looked down and said in a low voice, "I do not wish to name him. I prefer to consider this an internal matter to be resolved by the Aedui."

Until now Caesar had spoken in somber tones, displaying no emotion or anger. Abruptly, he lost his temper. "I want you to answer the question! I've already lost legionnaires to this cause, and I will not have them kneel before the gods and be told they died for nothing. You need not tell me who is behind this. I suspect I already know. It's Dumnorix." The startled expression on the Virgobret's face confirmed the truth. "I thought as much."

"It is so. Dumnorix has for many years been extremely successful and wealthy in trade. He's used his riches generously to gain political influence. He gave his mother to the most powerful man of the Biturges in addition to doing the same with a half-sister and other female relations to men of other tribes. He married a daughter of Orgetorix who at the time was magistrate of the Helvetii. He also accompanied Divico during the Helvetii advance through the land of the Sequani. He has more power than I do, or at least he did until Diviciacus reclaimed the leadership of the Aedui. Dumnorix wasn't content to be tribal leader. He wanted to become king of the Aedui and eventually the other tribes comprising the Aedui federation."

Caesar sat back and considered the intricacies of the internal problems within the Aedui Tribe and the dilemma Liskus and Diviciacus were facing, all of which had decisive impact on the events in Gaul — and the interests of Rome. The question was should the Republic be more involved or remain neutral in whatever happens in Gaul. He knew the answer the senators in Rome would give if asked; therefore, why should he ask?

He began to see a greater purpose for the Roman incursion into Gaul than only preventing an invasion of Provincia. The thought made him wonder if Jupiter was tempting him or ordering him to seize the opportunity occasioned by the Helvetii migration. He assumed a more conciliatory demeanor when he addressed the magistrate.

"What you've told me explains things I've suspected including the defeat in the recent cavalry engagement with the Helvetii. We will talk again on the internal problems within the Aedui and the effect they may have on my campaign to defeat the Helvetii. In the meantime, I'll consult with my staff. Then Diviciacus and I will determine how to deal with his brother."

Once the Aeduan departed, Caesar turned to general Labienus. "Titus, what have you to say?"

"The Helvetii invasion has encouraged the likes of Dumnorix and others to change the political balance of power within the Aedui. It threatens our success not only in defeating the Helvetii, but also undermines what has been until now a relatively stable frontier that has served Rome well. I believe you need to make an example of Dumnorix to stop his efforts to destabilize the Aedui and the impact it could have on the other tribes in Gaul."

"Diviciacus is a friend of Rome, and I don't wish to antagonize him by treating Dumnorix too harshly in spite of his treachery to both Rome and the Aedui. Whatever I do, I must be certain it's acceptable to Diviciacus. If I'm not careful, I risk making things worse for him and the Aedui by treating Dumnorix with a heavy-hand. It's in Rome's interest to openly support Diviciacus by helping him unify the Aedui. We need a unified Aedui to achieve a decisive defeat of the Helvetii or any other tribes crossing into Gaul. In return, I expect Diviciacus to provide the support we need. Marcellus, invite Diviciacus to return."

Strabo left to carry out the summons and found his two uncles apart from the rest of the delegation in a heated discussion. His normally mild-mannered older uncle stood with eyes narrowed, angrily stabbing a forefinger in Dumnorix's chest.

He coughed to gain their attention and addressed Diviciacus, "Lord, Caesar would like you to return."

The grim-faced tribal leader nodded and followed Strabo back into the tent. There was a change in Caesar's former stone-faced demeanor when he indicated the stool now positioned in front of him. His brief smile and the presence of an orderly pouring wine from a pitcher into several cups suggested a more cordial tone.

Caesar extended one of the cups to Diviciacus and another to General Labienus, then took one for himself. "My friend, I wish we could spend the time talking of happier times when we were in Rome, but unfortunately circumstances demand more serious discussion. Tell me how all this trouble within the Aedui started."

"Caesar, I am perhaps more to blame than my brother. I overlooked his youth and the ambitions a young man often has and

137

indulged him in ways I finally came to see were not in the best interests of the tribe after I returned from Rome. I have since reclaimed tribal leadership given to me at birth. I was too indulgent of his behavior, neglectful of the damage he was doing to my authority and the divisions he was creating within the tribe. I have much work to do to bring the tribe together; therefore, I ask that you treat my brother leniently. I fear punishment perceived as dictated by Rome and deemed too severe will weaken my authority and make things worse than they already are."

"I understand and sympathize with your situation. A unified Aedui under your strong leadership is what I also desire. Tell Dumnorix I forgive him for what he's done. In the future, I expect him to give his full support to your governorship and to stop any further efforts to sow dissention among the local tribes. I will impose a close watch on his movements to monitor both his behavior and with whom he has contact. More importantly, I need food and forage."

"Caesar, I thank you for your wisdom and generosity. I will not disappoint. The supplies you seek are even now being consolidated at Bibracte."

"Good. It's my intention to leave for Bibracte tomorrow. I am in sore need of those supplies."

"I will leave now to ensure the supplies are ready when the legions arrive. Caesar, I ask only for one more indulgence."

Caesar's jaw tightened, and his smile froze. "What is it you want?"

"When circumstances allow, I ask permission for Marcellus to visit Bibracte. It has been many years since I've seen General Strabo's son, my nephew. It would please me greatly if we might have the pleasure of his company as circumstances permit. His mother, Brigitte, was a very dear sister."

Setarius was the only one present whose lips tugged in a smile while Caesar, General Labienus and Strabo looked at Diviciacus with unconcealed astonishment. Afterward Labienus and Setarius agreed it was the only time they had ever seen Caesar taken by surprise.

Quickly recovering his composure with a smile, Caesar said, "I know Marcellus is General Strabo's son. I wasn't aware he's related to you. As you say, when circumstances allow, I'll ensure Marcellus will be permitted to visit you. In the brief time he has been with us, he has shown great potential and personal courage, a tribute to both his father and his Aedui heritage. Marcellus, you have leave to spend time visiting with your uncles before they leave for Bibracte."

Diviciacus walked over to Strabo and gave him a warm embrace. "Marcellus, you've grown into a tall, handsome man no doubt thanks in large part to your mother who was much favored by all Aedui." With his arm across Strabo's shoulders, the two men left the tent. Dumnorix was nowhere in sight when they came out.

After Diviciacus left, Caesar said, "Sit down, gentlemen. I've been thinking now that I can no longer trust the Aedui cavalry since Dumnorix all but declared for Divico, I think we need to consider some changes in how our auxilia cavalry are used. Titus, Publius Crassus has given me an interesting idea to consider, and it may be time to explore the possibility further. I'll let Publius explain."

With the confidence and poise of a much older and experienced man, Crassus stood. "Caesar, in my opinion the less than earnest support by Dumnorix is only part of the problem. The auxilia cavalry is capable enough at the turma level, but it's comprised of different tribes from southern Gaul. There are differences which do not ensure a cohesive force. The result is we can't depend on it to deploy in a coordinated manner guaranteed to influence a favorable outcome. During the time I spent with them, I found no overall unifying leadership. Decisions tend to be made by consensus, a process taking too much time with some left dissatisfied and less enthusiasm for whatever follows. I suggest the latter can only be remedied by restructuring the auxilia under the umbrella of Roman leadership and responsive directly to you or in your absence, General Labienus in the manner the legion commanders do now. This approach would have the advantage of a single individual speaking for the auxilia thus avoiding a delegation comprised of the tribal leaders reporting to senior

139

leadership. I believe the result would be a more rapid and cohesive battle response."

"What do you think, Titus?"

"The concept has merit, although, I wonder how the tribal commanders would react. They may see this as a criticism they are inferior and do not have our trust."

"I agree it could be problematic and difficult to implement. Flavius, what say you?"

"It's a sound concept. It may be difficult to bring about for the reason given. I also think you've decided General Crassus should, as it were, put the meat on the bones." Setarius looked up in mock wonder. "Who do you suppose the gods will decide will be the commander?"

"Publius, as Flavius so aptly said, proceed to put the meat on the bones." Caesar's lips curled in a smile. "As for who will command the organization? I'll not burden the gods since I've already decided."

"How did you know who I was?" Strabo asked his uncle.

The tribal leader laughed. "I confess I had some help, and without it, I doubt I would have recognized you. Corius told me about you, and among other things, he said you were Caesar's translator. There was no doubt when I saw how much you remind me of your mother."

"Does Dumnorix know who I am?"

"He does not, and I do not intend he knows."

"Why?"

"You heard Caesar. He wants to keep a close eye on my brother; it suits my interests as well. If I were Caesar, I would use someone who speaks our language. Marcellus, it might be Caesar will think of you."

"I have no liking for such intrigues. I don't wish to be—"

"A spy," the tribal leader interjected, "If you're told to keep watch on him? I would not consider, nor would I ask you to act as such. Consider the possibility you might be able to prevent your uncle from doing anything more to cause his own destruction. He walks a fine line by giving both the Romans and me reason to distrust him. If the distrust deepens further, the result could prove fatal for him."

"I doubt I would be ordered to keep an eye on him." The quizzical look on his uncle's face obliged him to tell how he became a legionnaire. "Because of it, there will continue to be great care where I go out of concern I won't return."

"You had an opportunity to leave the army when you rode with Corius. Why didn't you take it?"

"I gave my word I would not while there is threat to the Aedui. Once the threat is no longer there, then I will choose to either leave or remain in the Roman Army."

"I don't understand. Your father was a highly respected soldier by Rome and the Aedui, and I would have thought you would follow in his footsteps. Caesar seems to favor you."

"Honored Uncle, one day it may be what happens, but it isn't what I wish. I was forced to become a legionnaire against my will. Eventually I will decide what I want to do, not my father nor the Roman Army."

"It so happens, it's in the mutual interest of Caesar and the Aedui, at least for now, to know if my brother is violating the trust I've pledged on his behalf. Caesar is depending on me to maintain a mutually beneficial status quo between the Aedui and Rome. I must do all I can to fulfill that trust. Now, I have a question for you. What happens if the day comes when Caesar determines the future of Gaul is exactly what Dumnorix and others, including me, fear will happen?"

"I haven't thought of it. It's my hope the day will never come, and if it does, I prefer to be in another place even in another land and far enough away not to care."

Chapter 14 Divico's Headquarters, early the next day

The cavalry commander burst into Divico's tent interrupting the council of tribal leaders. Divico looked up with an angry scowl. "How dare you come in here unannounced?"

"Lord Divico, a messenger from Dumnorix reports the Romans are turning back to get supplies in Bibracte. I didn't believe him until I saw them breaking camp at daybreak. One of the legions is already marching southeast, and the others by now may be on the way as well."

Divico smiled. "At last, the gods have given me the opportunity and the ground I've been planning and waiting for!" He looked at the tribal leaders of the Boii and Tulingi whose combined strength of 15,000 cavalry and infantry had formed the Helvetii advance. "I want you to attack their rearguard as soon as we are done here to avoid a prolonged battle. It will take a few hours to catch up to the Romans and launch the main attack at which time the Boii and Tulingi will withdraw to the rear to secure our baggage and be ready to join the battle as needed.

"We'll launch the main attack in the center of the Roman formation. I want to force the Romans to concentrate their efforts on the center while I look for the opportunity to sweep whatever flank looks the most vulnerable." He turned to the leader of the Latobrigi. "You will be on the right flank, and the Rauraci will be on the left flank. With our greater strength, it may be possible to envelop both of their flanks. If we're unable to turn either flank, I'll order the Boii to sweep around the Roman left flank while the Tulingi does the same on the right for a combined attack on their rear. Are there any questions?"

The tribal leader of the Boii stood and asked, "Lord Divico, what of the Roman Auxilia Cavalry? It far outnumbers ours and will likely be used to attack our flanks. How do we plan for this?"

"Don't worry, the last time our outnumbered cavalry fought them, we routed them even as they outnumbered us four-to-one. We had

Dumnorix, the tribal Leader of the Aedui, to thank for it and will have again. He hates the Romans more than he fears our passage west. Do not be concerned; their cavalry will be more help to us than the Romans. Enough, there's much to be done and little time to take the advantage the Romans have given us. Go now and ready your warriors for the battle soon to be fought. When the battle ends, we'll go west, and whatever is left of the Romans will go south and out of Gaul."

Caesar turned to General Labienus. "How much farther to Bibracte?"

"I estimate six miles, perhaps..." He was interrupted by the arrival of a cavalryman whose lathered horse and high-pitched voice punctuated the urgency of his message.

"Caesar, General Labienus, Helvetii cavalry are attacking the rear guard in force. Our scouts report their main force has turned south and are moving close behind."

"It seems after two weeks of trying to get Divico to engage, he's decided to oblige. Titus, go back and assess the situation and determine how serious the situation is. Assuming it is a credible threat, order the Hispania Legion to delay their advance to give us time to find a better place to engage than here. When we came this way before, I recall terrain more favorable lies only a few more miles ahead close to Bibracte. I'll ride ahead to confirm the location I have in mind. Flavius, inform the commanders of the *Claudia* and *Fulminata* Legions the *Claudia* will lead the two legions to the front of the column with the baggage train following behind."

There was a stir in the ranks of the legionnaires, and the usual chatter stilled as officers were seen riding past in both directions with a sense of urgency. Strabo glimpsed Setarius rein in next to the legion commander. After a brief exchange, the tribune galloped past heading toward the rear of the column. He heard Centurion Valens shout an order quickly relayed by the cohort commanders echoing back through the ranks calling for an oblique move to the right while the two veteran legions in the lead were given the order to halt in place. Good-natured jeers erupted between the veteran legions and the two untried legions challenging or defending the capability to take the lead. Strabo looked back and saw the baggage train lumbering along behind the *Fulminata* Legion.

Speculation within the ranks for the surprise shift continued and fueled by the frequency of couriers passing by on horses close to foundering. Gradually the level, open ground they'd been marching on became hilly, and conversation tapered off in silent accommodation to the heavy load the legionnaires carried and a faster pace than required before. Strabo felt rivulets of sweat running down his back and face. He was at least grateful the arrow wound had healed to the extent it no longer caused any serious discomfort.

Two hours later, the column topped a high hill overlooking a narrow valley stretching east and west. The valley sides sloped gently to the valley floor below and were generally open until halfway up when forest obscured the higher reaches. Strabo identified Caesar by his red cape surrounded by his security detail waiting on the treeless valley floor. The legionnaires were relieved when the order was given to rest in place halfway down the slope while the centurions from both legions converged on Caesar. The curiosity of the sweating legionnaires continued to rise along with nervous excitement.

It was Scevola standing next to Strabo who broke the unnatural silence. "Lads, I'm ready to lay bet Caesar is getting ready for a fight. Anyone want to wager before the centurions come back here and confirm it?"

Scevola's challenge caused an uneasy shifting in the ranks accompanied by quiet murmuring as private thoughts were given voice to the growing possibility Scevola was right. No one took the bet the seasoned veteran offered. Strabo looked more closely at the surrounding terrain and remembered Caesar saying he wanted to choose the terrain on which to fight the Helvetii. He was too inexperienced at the time to understand what it meant. If there was going to be a battle here, he would have a better perception.

Centurion Valens returned to the cohort and called the optiones forward. He was too far away for Strabo to hear, but the centurion's arm movements suggested the slope across the valley was their destination. Moments later, Brecius returned and confirmed it.

"Well, you sons of bitches, you've been waiting to give the bastards a nosebleed, and your wishes are about to be satisfied. For those who weren't looking forward to a fight, tough shit. Before the day is out, you'll wish you were back in Massilia. Now listen close, you untried shitheads, here's what we'll do. We're going down to the valley floor and part way up the opposite hill with the Twelfth Legion on our right flank. When we get tired of marching, the legions will form a half-crescent 1000 feet wide with the ends sloping up hill. Once we've had enough fun doing that, you'll ground equipment except dolabrae and baskets to do the only thing you people have so far proven reasonably good at — digging a trench four feet deep and four feet wide to protect the baggage train positioned above us.

"Now here's the really good news. We've got to do it fast because the Helvetii are on our ass. On my order, follow me in columns of three, and for the love of the gods, try to look like you know what you're doing. Centurion Marinus doesn't want to hear bad words from Caesar who will be watching. If you screw it up, you won't get words from me, you'll get a whole lot worse."

Strabo paused in his digging and looked up when he heard the clatter and rumble of the supply wagons starting to lumber downhill to pass around the two legions. The legionnaires were making visible progress in excavating the entrenched, curving barricade. It was obvious the lot of the two untried legions was to be passive guardians of the baggage and camp followers. The thought angered him in ways he couldn't have imagined weeks ago. It caused him to think he made a mistake in not accepting Tarquin's invitation to request reassignment to the cavalry. He took out his frustration with an energetic attack with the pickax that drew the attention of Quintillus.

"Why should we bother to dig? Instead, we should let Marcellus get on with his ambition to be an optio." The sarcastic comment brought additional remarks and snickers from others within earshot.

With less criticism than practical advice, Scevola said, "Marcellus, have a care and save some for the Helvetii. What are you in a fit about?"

"We'll be on guard duty here watching what happens below. Years from now we'll try to explain why we only *watched* the battle instead of being *in* the battle."

Scevola laughed. "Marcellus, have you already experienced so much fighting you want more? Bide your time, my young friend for what may yet come. If not today, there's always another opportunity to give you what you seem to want for reasons perhaps even the gods don't know."

Further conversation was interrupted by the sound of trumpets. Strabo looked up and saw the first veteran legion come into view on the opposite side of the valley. He watched the first of the six-file cohorts begin its descent reminiscent of a giant slow-moving caterpillar. There was a grandeur in the precision of the formations that would give any enemy watching second thoughts about what they were going to face. Soon the four legion standards were positioned equidistance, east to west in three ranks part way up the slope below the nearly completed crescent-shaped ditch. On some stretches, tribuli were already emplaced. Cohort by cohort the veteran legionnaires filed uphill to where the wagons were to secure their personal possessions and equipment not essential for the battle ahead.

Strabo climbed out of the excavation with a heavy sigh and aching muscles and watched as the last of the stakes were pounded on top of the defensive barrier. He was tired from the long, fast-paced march and the exertions of digging the defensive barricade but more concerned about the guard and spectator role they were about to play. He stopped, thinking about what Scevola said about fighting. Why he should he care one way or the other.

He was, after all, a resentful conscript with no choice for being in this place at this time with the possibility he might never leave it.

Perhaps being a guard and spectator is what the gods had in mind for him for the present? It was strange feeling resentment for being an onlooker in the battle soon to follow, whatever the outcome. He looked around at his tentmates and envied their unconditional loyalty to Rome in contrast to his divided heritage. In reality, he had as much cause to sympathize with the Gaulish tribes as Rome.

The veteran cohorts quickly moved below where the baggage train was assembled and formed up behind their legion standards in three lines, three cohorts deep across a front two thousand-feet long. The Roman cavalry took position on the right flank while the auxilia infantry screened the left flank. There was no sense of urgency or alarm, only a methodical execution borne of experience and battles fought before.

The distant throb of drums grew steadily louder reaching a crescendo when the Helvetii vanguard finally came over the crest of the opposite hill and halted midway down the slope. Not unlike a human tide, the rest of the Helvetii army swarmed over the crest and came down the slope to take position on either side of the vanguard. In stark contrast to the disciplined Roman columns, there was no precision or discernible organization to the Helvetii army milling restlessly about. What was lacking in traditional martial display was more than compensated by the overwhelming numbers facing the Romans.

The drums abruptly stopped, and the tribesmen began to chant, a menacing sound which chilled even the most hardened legionnaires. Strabo observed the intimidating force across the valley floor stretching well past the Roman flanks. Until now, he'd never doubted the might of Rome, however, the massive numbers arrayed before them gave him reason to think otherwise. In contrast to the noise and heaving, undisciplined movement of the Helvetii, the Roman columns remained ominously silent and motionless. Increasingly emboldened by the silent ranks, individual warriors ran forward with taunts and crude gestures. Some came close enough to hurl a spear easily avoided. Several came too close and died.

The sun was well past midday when Caesar dismounted behind the third line and handed the reins to an orderly who led the mount uphill.

147

Following Caesar's example, the tribunes and centurions throughout the four veteran legions did the same, and their mounts joined Caesar's in the baggage train.

It was as if the Helvetii had been waiting for the Roman officers to dismount for their drums to signal the attack accompanied by the hoarse cries of the warriors as they slowly advanced downhill. Once they reached the level valley floor, they broke into a run toward the Roman ranks. The legions remained motionless, waiting. Strabo heard the order given by the legion directly below to launch the first volley of javelins. Almost in unison across the four-legion front, the air was filled with javelins hurtling down hill and quickly followed by the second rank of legionnaires stepping forward to launch a second volley before the first had found targets. Warriors whose shields had been struck by one or more javelins were quickly made more vulnerable when the weight of the soft pointed missiles dragged the shields down. Successive volleys continued to wreak havoc as legionnaires moved forward through the files ahead to launch their missiles.

The momentum of the Helvetii advance stopped abruptly as the leading ranks fell like sheaves, halting the ranks behind in a successive, confused jumble. When tribesmen either wounded or who had enough began making their way back, they impeded the advance of those trying to get into the battle.

The javelins raining down on the Helvetii front ranks shifted farther out as the forward centuries were given the order to attack. With the momentum of a downhill run, the legionnaires slammed into the Helvetii line with a thunderous crash of shield against shield pushing the tribal advance several paces back. The legionnaires slowly drove the Helvetii warriors across the valley in a devastating, relentless stab and thrust. For every legionnaire that fell, multiple warriors were left dead or too badly wounded to move.

Strabo watched the ebb and flow of the battle below raging for more than hour as the first eight ranks in the first line of legionnaires pushed the Helvetii back to the base of the hill occupied by the tribesmen. The number of dead legionnaires lying on the valley floor and the wounded making their way back was sufficient to order the centuries in the second line forward to replace the tired and bloody legionnaires in the first line. The effect of the aggressive Roman attack was evident with the number of retiring Helvetii warriors making their way uphill, some crawling, others being helped by those with less severe wounds. The carnage unfolding below gave him a new perspective. What he'd experienced so far bore no resemblance to the fighting he was watching. He wondered when the time came for him to fight as the legionnaires below were now doing, would he be able to acquit himself as well?

The Roman progress uphill against the Helvetii continued unabated for another two hours with progress measured so little it became gradually evident the Roman drive was faltering. Slowly the Roman second line was no longer advancing but only trying to hold the ground it had achieved. The legionnaires gradually began a slow, controlled withdrawal downhill accompanied by the triumphant roar of the tribal warriors as they regained their confidence. The battle suddenly appeared to be changing in favor of the Helvetii.

Strabo saw movement uphill in the rear of the Helvetii position soon revealed to be a large combined force of infantry and cavalry sweeping around the Roman right flank. He thought Tarquin and the cavalry numbering only several hundred positioned there were too few to resist what they were about to face. The thought was echoed by Scevola.

"Lads, we're about to be more than spectators. In fact, I'd say we're about to find ourselves in the shitter. Best get ready for what's coming our way."

Moments later, Centurion Valens and Tulio raised the alarm for the growing threat to the right flank.

Tulio shouted, "All right, now's the time to do what you've been trained for. You will be remembered today for what you are about to do, and it better be for how well you fought."

Strabo looked at Scevola tying a thick leather band to his right forearm from his wrist to his elbow. The legionnaire looked up and noted Strabo's questioning expression. "It won't save losing my arm if I let my guard down, but it will keep me from adding more scars to the ones I already have."

Scevola's terse comment explained the network of scars on the veteran's forearm Strabo had noticed and never questioned how he got them. He had an idea he was about to find out. Downhill, he saw the Roman right flank begin to crumble. The out-numbered Roman cavalry screen was quickly swept aside followed by a slower but equally large body of shouting warriors scrambling uphill toward them. He heard the sound of retching and turned to see Quintillus bent over the tribuli vomiting into the ditch below. Strangely, the visceral response of his tentmate to the approaching enemy had a calming effect.

Moments later, the first wave of mounted warriors reached the ditch only to be thrown into confusion when many of the horses abruptly stopped, refusing the attempts of their riders to jump over the barrier. The momentum of the attack slowed. Strabo was among the first to take advantage of the enemy confusion by hurling one of his javelins into the chest of the nearest sword-waving rider. At such close range, the volley of javelins that followed had a devastating effect. Here and there, a rider successfully urged his mount to attempt the jump down and across the barrier only to slide back down after failing to top the four-foot defensive wall. Many horses falling backward, crushed their riders. One horse managed to gain the top only to be impaled on the sharpened stakes. The unlucky rider died faster than the horse.

The milling horsemen began to fall back and move farther uphill where the trench ended. Strabo heard the shouts and the centurion's orders above him shifting the ranks to meet the cavalry threat. He was more concerned with the mass of infantry advancing uphill. He hurled his remaining javelin at a bare-chested warrior wearing tight-fitting, checkered trousers and missed and hit another warrior running behind him. He drew his sword and waited while the rear ranks continued hurling javelins at the Helvetians so closely packed few missiles failed to find a target.

With surprising agility one warrior managed to gain the top of the wall. Strabo thrust his sword in the other man's belly then butted him backward with his shield to withdraw the blade. He didn't have to wait long for the next opponent as more warriors gained the top of the wall with others pressing close behind. The Helvetii warriors were tired from the physical effort of an uphill charge and the difficult climb out of a deep trench. The heavier and larger Roman shield than that the native tribesmen carried was a decided advantage, and the legionnaires used them as a weapon almost as deadly as a gladius to push them back into the trench. The slashing, long-edged swords and axes favored by the Helvetians were also no match in close combat against the short, stabbing gladius.

Strabo lost track of time during the sequence of rear ranks moving forward to relieve the first rank closely engaged. Slowly the legionnaires were forced to give ground until they no longer occupied the wall where the battle began. He glanced at Scevola on his right and the number of dead Helvetians in front of him in contrast to the fewer he and Vinicius on his right could claim. The veteran's deadly skill and experience gained from years of engagements kept him on the front line longer than the more inexperienced legionnaires.

Farther uphill, the Helvetian cavalry were being repulsed by the combined efforts of both legions and the auxilia infantry guarding the rear. Strabo saw fewer tribesmen coming forward to engage the Roman defense and more moving back downhill. The sun had long since disappeared over the mountains when the defenders of the baggage train realized the last of the tribesmen were in full retreat. The exhausted legionnaires allowed them to go, too tired to pursue. He looked around and was shocked to see how few legionnaires were left standing compared to the number lying motionless or unable to stand either from wounds or sheer exhaustion.

He looked across the valley and saw the veteran legions had regained much of the ground recently lost and were slowly advancing back up the hillside foot by foot. The frequency which the leading files on both sides were replaced by those behind was an indication of both the ferocity of the fight and the fatigue of the combatants continuously engaged for the past six hours. Strabo was shocked at the number of bodies lying motionless from where the first contact was made to the last rank of legionnaires edging up the opposite hill. He eyed the darkening sky and wondered how much longer the battle would continue before the issue was decided. It was too early to be certain. The number of tribesmen disappearing over the distant ridge seemed promising. The absence of any Helvetian cavalry suggested the organized and relentless Roman advance promised success although at terrible cost.

Strabo walked over to where Scevola and Quintillus, both grim-faced, were leaning against the side of a baggage cart watching a medical orderly kneeling on the ground next to Felix. The legionnaire's eyes were closed as he clutched his belly with both hands in an attempt to keep his intestines from spilling out. Strabo knelt down opposite the orderly, and gently squeezed his tentmate's shoulder. Felix opened his eyes, and managed a wan smile. The orderly stood up and shook his head already looking for the next wounded legionnaire in need of attention.

"Marcellus, I'll soon be kneeling before Jupiter, and he will ask if I fought well. I don't know how I'll answer."

Strabo hesitated, too choked to speak. He found his voice and managed to say, "You will tell him you fought well and bravely, and all here today will bear testimony you did." The young legionnaire's face relaxed, and he closed his eyes. Moments later Strabo knew his tentmate was standing before the god of war. He hoped Felix and Jupiter heard what he said.

An aging legionnaire from the quartermaster division was slowly passing by with a bucket and dipper. Strabo took the offered dipper and drank the tepid water. He thought it was better than the finest wine he'd ever tasted. Gradually he became aware of the aches and pains of muscles and tendons stressed beyond anything he'd ever experienced, including the training in Massilia. He felt a sharp pain in his right side and was surprised to see his leather tunic was torn and bloody from a wound he wasn't conscious of getting. His right forearm was also painful with multiple minor scratches and some deeper cuts he knew when heeled would resemble Scevola's scars. He was mentally devoid of any thought other than the desire to lay down and sleep.

Dimly, he heard Brecius, face bandaged, calling to form ranks for roll call. Marinus stood stoically behind the optio with his right arm extended while a medical orderly bound a bloody wound. Strabo considered the possibility the centurion would wield his vitis less painfully using his left hand. He joined the ranks slowly forming up, some unable to stand without the support of one or more of the legionnaires on either side. It didn't take long when names were called without a response to realize the number of casualties was alarming. After the formation was dismissed, Brecius ordered those physically able to pick up any dead legionnaires in the ditch and bring them behind the wall. The dead Helvetians were collected and thrown in the opposite direction to further impede the next attack if there were any found alive, they were quickly dispatched.

Strabo dragged the last dead Helvetian several feet downhill and had just enough energy left to crawl up out of the ditch and over the earthen wall. He saw Vinicius and Scevola standing nearby listening as General Arridius talked to Centurion Valens and the few centurions left in the first cohort. Tulio and the other remaining optiones were clustered nearby listening attentively. The general abruptly stopped and turned around when he heard the legionnaires farther downhill cheering. The cheering grew steadily louder. There was enough light in the day to see the cause. Alone, wearing his best cuirass, circlet and red cloak draped across his left shoulder, Caesar walked his horse uphill and acknowledged the response with a wave of his hand while warmly praising the legionnaires he passed.

Caesar reined in near the legion commander and dismounted. He gripped General Aridius's right forearm and said, "Salve, Marcus, the *Claudia* Legion has done well and proven worthy of being called a veteran legion. Do you know the cost?"

"I have at least 150 dead and three times the number wounded, many of which the medicus does not expect will see the sun tomorrow.

I estimate I have about 2,300 legionnaires including lightly wounded fit enough to fight."

"Worse than I hoped. The battle across the valley is proving to be more stubborn than expected. Marcus, I must call on whatever you can muster to cross over and move past the right flank of the *Equestris* Legion and envelop the Helvetii left flank. I've already ordered the *Fulminata* Legion to do the same by passing the *Augusta* Legion on the left flank. Since *Fulminata* is already forming, you will give the signal for both legions to march when you're ready. When your signal is given, torches will be lit on both flanks of the engaged legions to define their flanks. Keep far enough away from the torches so the Helvetii won't see you until it's too late for them to launch an effective counterattack. We are fortunate there will be little moonlight which will aid the surprise we'll give to the Helvetii. With help from Jupiter, the field will soon be ours."

"It will be done and considered an honor for the *Claudia*. I'll leave two cohorts behind to secure the baggage train."

"Thank you, Marcus, I knew I could count on you." Caesar mounted, turned to the centurions and optiones. "And I thank you all for what you've done so far. I'll ensure all Rome hears of what you've accomplished." Caesar returned the salute of the officers and optiones and without further comment walked his horse back the way he came.

General Arridius wasted no time issuing orders. "Rufus, send messengers to the other cohorts with the following orders. The first cohort will assemble below the wall with the second and third behind in that order. The fifth will take position on the right flank of the first cohort followed by the seventh and eighth cohorts. The fourth and tenth cohorts will remain to secure the baggage train. When we pass the Tenth at the top of the hill, I'll give the signal to attack."

Centurion Valens turned to the surviving centurions and optiones of the first cohort and said, "We've lost officers and optiones either dead or too badly injured to join ranks. Until such time as the injured recover and appointments made to replace those who are with the gods, the senior optio in each century without a centurion will assume command. Missing optiones will be replaced by seasoned legionnaires as necessary."

The following few minutes saw the remnants of the *Claudia* Legion stumbling downhill too tired and numb to complain except for Vinicius whose loud cursing caught the attention of Brecius. The optio used his hastile to end the complaints, leaving the legionnaire on his knees with no breath left to swear or complain.

Disgusted, Strabo pulled his friend up and with no sympathy said, "You volunteered for this. Now save your breath and get moving."

There was barely enough light left for the centurions and optiones to get the exhausted legionnaires into a semblance of an organized fighting force. By the time the columns were assembled, the hill opposite was no longer visible. General Arridius told the trumpeter to signal the advance. After the brassy sound was given, the nearly two thousand tired legionnaires began moving downhill then up the opposite slope.

Chapter 15

By the time the first cohort passed the second torch fifty paces to the left, the labored breathing of the legionnaires was noticeable even with the clamor of battle farther up the hill. Strabo was convinced his shield now weighed twice as much as it did before the column started. Compared to others in the surrounding ranks, he knew his wounds were slight. He wondered if he was having difficulty maintaining the pace how those more severely wounded were coping. He stiffened his resolve to ignore his physical discomfort and focus on the attack about to commence. He glanced left and saw they were passing the last torch, now unnecessary as the sound of close battle just ahead clearly indicated the line of battle.

He sensed a quickening in the ranks, and the pace began to pick up. The fatigue and pain of wounds began to fade in anticipation of the coming battle. The blaring, staccato notes of the trumpets brought the columns to a halt and the order to face left. Seconds later, swords drawn and with hoarse yells, the long ranks of legionnaires surged toward the darkened Helvetii stronghold.

From the startled response ahead, it was evident the defenders had been caught unaware. Over the shoulder of Scevola and the legionnaire immediately in front of him, Strabo saw shadowy forms running toward them. Behind the warriors coming toward them, he saw the silhouettes of wagons dimly illuminated by torches.

He stumbled over a body and barely recovered in time to meet the impact of a heavy body smashing into his shield. Instinctively, he raised his sword and caught the descending axe half way down the haft. He knew the heavier axe favored the warrior's attack and used it to his advantage. When the Helvetian forced his sword down to the level of his waist, Strabo quickly disengaged causing the momentum of the heavy axe to fall. He stepped aside to avoid the warrior's lateral swing and stabbed his assailant in the belly. He left the badly wounded Helvetian for the ranks behind to deal with as he continued to advance a pace behind Scevola. The veteran legionnaire was being pushed slowly back by two howling warriors convinced they were about to cut down a hated Roman. Strabo lunged forward and thrust his sword in the side of the attacker maneuvering to get behind Scevola. The warrior fell back dropping his shield and collapsed to his knees. Strabo paused only long enough to give the Helvetian a second thrust in the neck before moving on to catch up with Scevola.

Strabo soon caught up with Scevola. He was bent over gasping for breath. He paused to see if the aging veteran was wounded and relieved to find he was only exhausted. Suddenly, he dropped to his knees, too drained to take another step. He was more than content to have the ranks behind move on past him to engage the remnants of what was left of the Helvetii defenders. Above the noise of battle, he heard the screams of women and children as the legionnaires quickly overwhelmed the few remaining warriors and pressed on sparing no one.

"What's wrong, Marcellus?" Scevola asked when he saw Strabo kneeling after the last rank moved past them. "Are you badly wounded?"

"No. I just don't want any part of that," waving his sword toward the wagons and the sound of the butchery taking place there.

"It's the blood lust. It causes men to do things most won't remember afterward, and if reminded, they'll deny it. They don't ever want to admit they ever did. I know this, for I've done the same things happening now."

"Then why aren't you over there?" Strabo questioned, his anger and disgust apparent.

"In time, I came to feel as you do now. The difference is it took me longer than you. What say we go on and see if we can find a few Helvetians not ready to believe the battle's over?"

"I suppose if I don't, you and others will think I have no stomach for a fight."

"I think you've proved yourself enough no one would think so much less say it, and me least of all. I probably wouldn't be saying this if you hadn't taken care of the warrior who came up behind me. My thanks.

Could be I'm getting too old and should consider making this my last campaign."

"It won't be. The truth is you'll keep coming back to the legions every time there's a call-up until some centurion kicks you in the ass hard enough to convince you to stay home."

"You're probably right, but the centurion won't need to look for me. The legions are my real home." Scevola smiled and added, "And when the day comes, and I go back home for good, my wife will be even more unhappy than I'll be."

Strabo laughed and stood. "For the glory of the *Claudia* and Rome, by all means, let's go find more to fight before it's over."

The crescent moon was nearly overhead with the battle gradually and slowly shifting farther east as the Helvetii Army pulled back in surprisingly good order. Strabo looked to his left downslope and saw legionnaires he supposed belonged to the Tenth legion advancing along the left flank of the *Claudia*. In the dim light, the lines of both legions were becoming comingled and no longer moved in the organized lines as they did in the early stages of the battle. Proximity of his father's former legion made him feel the *Claudia* would benefit from the legion's proven battle experience.

He pressed on in a battle that seemed to have no end. He resisted the urge to stop and give into the urge to lay down. He slowed down and allowed a legionnaire behind to pass him, more than willing to ease his arms from the weight of sword and shield.

Vinicius stopped beside him and said, "Marcellus, if I live long enough after a Helvetian sticks me bad, I'll probably thank him for his kindness."

There were no blaring trumpets or shouts of triumph to signal the end of the battle. The exhausted legionnaires collapsed where they were with the tacit permission of the centurions. The eight-hour battle had even dampened Caesar's inclination to continue the pursuit in practical recognition there was no longer the capability to do so. With the

158

approaching dawn and the scouts reporting no indication of a counterattack, Caesar assembled the senior officers with a blaring trumpet call. The call had little effect on the exhausted legionnaires who remained where they were, most fast asleep. Strabo was no exception.

"Marcellus!" Dimly, he registered it was Brecius' voice he heard and punctuated by a vigorous jab with his knobbed stick. "Get your ass up, greet the sun and give thanks to the gods you survived to serve Rome and your legion, what's left of it, for another day."

Strabo's initial reaction was to roll over in the belief he was in the middle of a bad dream. The second and harder prod was enough to open his eyes and see the blurry outline of the optio standing over him. The dream just got worse.

"Brecius, you hit me one more time, and I'm going to shove that stick up your ass."

"Well, aren't you the feisty one, and after all the fun you've been having and getting paid for it, courtesy of all the fat-cat sons of bitches in Rome happy you're willing to do what they won't and can't. If I found you alive, I've been ordered to tell you to report within the hour to Tribune Setarius at Caesar's headquarters in the valley below."

"Why?"

"Do I look like someone who gives a shit why? Just do it, and before you report, clean yourself up. You look like something a dog wouldn't touch."

Befuddled, he sat up and looked around. At first, he didn't recognize where he was. A short distance away, Vinicius was urinating against the trunk of a tree, and Scevola was lying with his head on his shield, arms crossed over his chest. If it hadn't been for his snoring, he would have thought the aging legionnaire was waiting for a burial detail. Brecius paused long enough to kick Scevola awake before moving on to wake the next legionnaire. He paused from time to time to signal for a medical orderly or one of the teams busy collecting the dead.

Strabo realized he was holding on to his blood-encrusted sword. He used it to help him stand which only made him aware of how much his body ached and how thirsty he was. The final hour of the battle was already a blur. The last desperate Helvetii defense failed, and they melted away in the darkness. He looked behind him and saw the two hills where the battle began were almost a half mile away. Helvetian dead dotted the surrounding terrain. He saw several bodies nearby missing an arm or fingers hacked off to retrieve valuable armbands and rings. Vinicius, sound asleep, was still leaning against the tree.

Setarius regarded Strabo's exhausted, vacant look and curbed the rebuke he was about to give for the indifference bordering on insolence the legionnaire silently projected.

"Marcellus, I'm ordered to go to Bibracte to get the grain Diviciacus promised. You'll ride with me as my translator. We'll be gone two or three days at the most. Get yourself cleaned up and ready to leave in two hours."

Strabo saluted and slowly made his way uphill to the baggage train to find his personal effects and enough water to wash off the dirt and blood, both his and the Helvetii he'd fought. He was relieved to find the wound on his right side was not much more than a scratch, and the cuts to his right forearm were not as bad as he feared. He found the cart assigned to his contubernium and retrieved his personal kit then went to one of the quartermaster wagons to replace his badly dented sword and damaged shield.

He saw two cohorts coming from the direction of where the *Fulminata* Legion was camped. When the legionnaires headed toward a line of empty wagons and carts, he surmised they would be the escort for the journey to Bibracte.

He spotted Tarquin waiting near Caesar's tent and headed toward him. As he drew closer, Strabo noted the decurion's drawn face and bloody tunic.

"Marcellus, I'm glad you survived." Tarquin saw Strabo looking closely at his tunic and said with dry humor, "I made sacrifices to Jupiter last night. He was satisfied, but many Helvetians were less so.

We're fortunate to see the sun come up. There were times I didn't think I'd ever see it again."

"I could say the same. By the time the battle ended, I had long stopped thinking or caring about anything."

"It was about the worst I ever faced. I lost nearly half my turma either dead or too badly wounded to ride." He gestured toward the lead wagon where a turma of cavalry waited beside their mounts. "Most of the cavalry escort I'm leading is from the auxilia. I assumed you would be going to Bibracte and brought an extra horse, unless you'd rather walk or ride in one of the wagons."

For the first time in days, Strabo smiled. "Since you've gone to the trouble, I'll accept the offer."

Further conversation ended when the six grim-faced legion commanders emerged from the tent and silently walked past them to their horses, too intent to acknowledge their salutes. Soon after, Setarius came out looking equally solemn. The tribune didn't waste time in idle conversation and told them to mount up. When they drew ahead of the lead cohort, Tarquin continued on to deploy the rest of the cavalry escort ahead and on the flanks.

Strabo was aware the legionnaires marching behind were uncharacteristically quiet without any of the usual banter or songs intended to relieve the monotony of a march. The silence of the legionnaires, the rhythmic crunching of the boots behind and the walking gait of his horse began to have its effect. Just as he was about to drift off, the tribune spoke.

"Marcellus, get down. We'll walk a bit, and maybe we'll both wake up. Yesterday was long and last night was worse."

Embarrassed he was caught falling asleep, Strabo dismounted and did his best to look awake.

"Caesar meant what he told General Arridius. Compared to the *Fulminata,* the *Claudia* Legion suffered the most. It could have been worse if the legion had not held the ground. I'm not sure I ever saw an untried legion do as well as the *Claudia.*"

Strabo appreciated the accolade the centurion was crediting the legion. He wondered if the objective was to defeat the Helvetii, why were they being allowed to escape only to fight again.

"Tribune, why are we going to Bibracte instead of pursuing the Helvetii to finish them?"

"Two legion commanders asked Caesar the same question a short time ago. Caesar believes the Helvetii are finished and, given time, Divico will ask for terms. There are practical reasons for breaking off the engagement. Our losses were not insignificant, and we need time to reorganize and reprovision. We also need to take care of the wounded, bury the dead and give the legionnaires and officers able to fight a chance to recover." Setarius saw the doubt on Strabo's face and added, "Marcellus, the reality of battle is not what happens before and during the fight. It's what's decided after the last javelin is thrown and the last sword is bloody."

"What terms will Caesar accept?"

"Only those he already dictated to Divico. He intends for the Helvetii to return to their homeland."

"And if Divico refuses?"

"We'll fight them again until they do, and afterward there will be even fewer of them to turn back. Caesar will win this, and decisively, because he has to."

"Why?"

"You may recall what Diviciacus and Liskus told Caesar about the concerns among the tribes, including the Aedui, for a strong Roman presence in Gaul. Also keep in mind what they said about your other uncle. If it's true Dumnorix and perhaps others are sympathetic and have actively been helping the Helvetii, we are in a precarious position. Caesar will prevail against the Helvetii because he cannot afford to fail. Neither can he grant lenient terms to Divico for it will be seen as a weakness and embolden other tribes in Gaul to take up a cause the Helvetii couldn't finish. Your father commanded the only legion in Far Gaul. One legion was not a threat and accepted as an insignificant irritant. Caesar came here with six legions, and the consequences for

Rome and Gaul are in the balance. He intends to show the tribes Rome will not allow any threat to Provincia and the Transalpine which means we are going to be here longer than most of us thought or the Gauls want."

"Tribune, I don't pretend to know for certain what the Aedui or the other tribes will do if Caesar remains with six legions in Gaul indefinitely. The tribes are protective of their honor and will not easily bend to the will of Rome. It may be Caesar will give the tribes a reason to come together to fight Rome."

"It could happen and may be precisely what Caesar wants."

Strabo was both startled and dismayed at the possibility the tribune might be right.

Chapter 16 Bibracte Settlement

While the two cohorts prepared camp a half-mile from the outskirts of Bibracte, Strabo saw the number of rounded, straw-roofed dwellings outside the settlement's walls had grown considerably over the five years since his last visit. Once they passed through one of the settlement gates, he saw there was little change. It was all familiar, yet time and distance had distorted his memories of living, playing and maturing here. He was uncomfortable thinking of the tile-roofed, stone-walled villas he was used to compared to the more primitive Aeduan structures they passed.

There was an irritable note when the tribune said, "I expected to be met long before we got to the gates." Strabo didn't respond thinking the same. "Do you know where to find Diviciacus?"

"He lives next to the large hall ahead, or at least he did when I was last here."

The two men rode on in silence to the top of the hill, ignoring the hostile looks of many they passed who outnumbered the few who flashed a welcoming smile. Setarius saw a dozen carts coming toward the settlement and frowned at the small number.

"What's on those carts won't feed one legion more than a few days, perhaps two on short rations."

Strabo saw several riders leave the carts and ride up the hill and enter the settlement. As they came closer, he was relieved to see Diviciacus was one of the riders.

The tribal leader and clan chief greeted Setarius in understandable if stilted Latin drawing a look of surprise from the tribune who murmured to Strabo, "It seems I've brought you here without good reason."

"My apologies, Tribune. I rode out to ensure the supplies expected today were coming as promised. I intended to be here when you arrived. Unfortunately, there was an unexpected problem I needed to solve. Marcellus, it's good to see you again."

Setarius gestured to the dozen carts. "I hope the problem you solved had something to do about arranging a lot more provisions than what's on those carts,"

"I assure you, much more is on the way. Regrettably, there was a misunderstanding that as we speak, Dumnorix is resolving. Tomorrow and the next day the rest of what I promised Caesar will be here."

"Very well. If there is any further delay, Caesar will not be pleased. I'll send the provisions arriving now and what comes tomorrow on to the legions. Bring the rest to where the legions are camped. You no doubt heard of the battle with the Helvetii."

"Yes, and as a result I understand the Helvetii surrendered the field to Caesar."

"The battle was hard fought on both sides, but Divico has not admitted defeat. We've delayed pursuing them until we've been supplied." Setarius gave Strabo a meaningful look which he understood to mean he was not to say anything about the other reasons for delaying the pursuit.

"While you're with us, I invite you stay in the quarters reserved for senior visitors. Marcellus, you, too, are welcome to stay there; however, I suspect Corius may be disappointed to be deprived of your company."

"Thank you, uncle. Tribune Setarius will decide where I must be to serve him as he requires."

The tribune's nod was noncommittal. "Marcellus will have ample time to see those he wishes. In the meantime, Marcellus, guide the wagons to our camp and inform the two cohort commanders to transfer the provisions to our wagons without delay. Find my orderly and slaves and bring them to me."

Strabo saluted and kneed the horse down the hill. It wasn't until he came close enough to see the outriders ahead of the carts that he recognized Corius in the lead. He nudged his horse into a faster gait.

"Marcellus, I thank the gods you've been spared to see another day. Those of us who watched from afar when the battle began until night obscured the field wondered who would prevail. I prayed you would survive, and I will give sacrifices you did."

"I'm ordered to guide you to where our wagons and escort are located two miles east of the settlement. The provisions your carts carry will be loaded on the wagons the Romans have waiting there."

Keeping pace with the slow-moving wagons the two men discussed the recent battle. Mindful of the tribune's comment to Diviciacus, Strabo avoided any mention of the severity of the Roman losses. Gradually the conversation drifted to other topics during which there was no mention of Raven as if they were purposefully avoiding any reference to her. By the time they drew near to the Roman camp, their conversation began to languish until they no longer had anything to say. Finally, Strabo could no longer restrain himself.

"Corius, if given the chance, will Raven welcome me, or would she rather I not see her?"

Strabo saw the smile of relief on his friend's face. "When you didn't ask about her, I was afraid to say her name and risk treading on sensitive ground."

"And I was afraid to ask because of the answer I didn't want to hear."

"I'm certain she would never forgive you if you didn't. She hasn't been the same since you were together. She didn't go with me yesterday to see the battle — too afraid of what she might see. Even now she's waiting for me to take her to where the legions are camped to learn your fate. When we're done here, I'll take you to where she lives."

Strabo was both relieved and apprehensive at the offer, conflicted both for the unexpected feelings he had for her, and unsure how she felt about him.

Without dismounting, Corius pointed at the small dwelling near the exterior wall of the settlement. "This is where Raven lives. I know she's inside because the horse you gave her is here and not with the herd. She's seldom parted from it and spends much of her time riding or caring for the animal. I grant you, it's a fine horse, but I don't see it as something the gods have decreed is worthy of them."

Strabo tended to agree. Aquilo was a fine animal, then he was used to assessing, riding and betting on horses all showing exceptional qualities and prized only for the promise of getting first to the finish line.

By the time he dismounted, Corius had already turned his horse and cantered off. Hesitant, Strabo approached the skin draped across the entrance, unsure what to say, what he should do and at a loss why he felt the way he did.

He pulled aside the skin curtain and called her name. He heard no response and wondered if perhaps she wasn't here after all. He heard a stifled cry, and she was in his arms, pressed tightly against him. He felt her trembling and embraced her. He was relieved. She took the initiative by pulling his face down and kissing him passionately. He soon found he wasn't as tired as he thought he was. Looking back, he thought the gods had stilled any words he or she might have said and let silence give more meaning to the moment.

"I have to go. Tribune Setarius has been generous in giving me a few hours to spend renewing family ties, but his forbearance has limitations. I don't want to risk the possibility I'll be refused the chance to come back and see you."

"Why do you stay with your legion when you were given no choice to join it? You can disappear in Gaul where the Romans will never find you. Somewhere we can be away from all of this."

"You make it sound like it's an easy decision to make. It's more complicated than that. I've come to believe, as unwilling as I was to become a legionnaire, there may be a reason the gods dictated the path I now lead. Besides it may be the gods intended I see you again."

She thumped him on the chest. "Claiming the gods sent you here instead of deciding to come here on your own isn't very flattering. Marcellus, I love you, and I want us to go away from what is happening in Gaul. There is disagreement among the tribes, and I fear it will only get worse with Rome becoming more dominant than ever before. I see only war and greater hardship ahead with little benefit to the Aedui and none for us."

He listened and understood what she was saying. He wanted to comfort her, reassure her the future was not as bleak as she imagined. He leaned back and held her close, wondering how to explain why he had changed during the time he woke up in a Roman training camp.

"Nothing would please me more than to go away and let the gods decide the fate of Gaul. I wish I was either Roman or Aedui so I wouldn't have to choose which side to be on. I have a foot in both worlds, and I can't bring myself to turn my back on either. For now, Rome and the Aedui are closely allied, and by serving Rome now, I also serve my mother's tribe and you. For us to go away somewhere to escape what is happening here is not something either one of us can do. If we did, in time we would feel we turned our backs on who we are and what we are."

"I know I'm being selfish. I'll try to accept what you say, what you believe, even if at the moment I cannot. I promise I'll try not to speak of this again. I would not have you more troubled than you are. I think I love you even more for being loyal to both sides of your heritage." She sighed in resignation and said softly as she reached down between his legs, "I think for now we've talked enough."

Dumnorix was both enraged and humiliated. He never thought his elder brother had either the interest or the passion to assert himself the way he did when he ordered him to get the rest of the grain the Romans had been promised. It had been a long ride and a long day before he saw the palisades of Bibracte in the last light of day. Morgane's sardonic smile when he entered their private quarters only intensified his displeasure. Losing control of the Aedui to his brother in an unforeseen turn of events was something he never anticipated would happen. Equally unimaginable was the decisive victory the Romans achieved in what should have been a victory for the Helvetii.

"Dear husband, you look as if you've had a long and hard day. I'll have food and drink brought to you in your quarters, and if you're so inclined and able," she paused before continuing, "I'll have one of the slave girls ready to serve you."

"Bitch, don't try me. I'm in no mood to put up with you."

With an exaggerated uplifting of her brow and an insincere smile she replied, "For once you and I are in complete agreement. I, too, am not in the mood. Tonight is no different from the other nights I've had to endure since my father gave me to the Aedui. The results of the battle yesterday ended any hope Divico, and you, would profit from the Helvetii migration."

"As it did any chance for you to become a queen had Divico beaten the Romans. Did you know the Romans captured one of your sisters and your brother last night?"

"Who cares? I was never fond of any of my siblings, nor were they of me. We were not a happy family. I doubt whichever sister it is or my brother will be any more interested in seeing me than I am in greeting them."

"You're the most coldhearted woman I've ever known. In giving you to me, I think your father had more interest in getting rid of you than forging an alliance."

"Well, it's certainly a possibility. Of more interest to me is what Diviciacus will do with you after your latest failed attempt to thwart the Romans. Did you really think the legionnaires were going to revolt because they were denied their grain for a few days? What did you expect to gain?"

He surprised her by saying, "My brother will do nothing as usual. He doesn't want to risk showing there's friction between us at a time when the tribe is already showing signs of becoming more divided. You believe I gained nothing, but you're wrong. What I achieved was to emphasize my pledge to see the end of Rome's growing dominance and our dependency. By doing what I did, it demonstrated I'll do anything I can to resist Rome's conquest of Gaul. The resistance to Rome is strong among the tribes as it continues to grow with the Aedui. It's time to set aside tribal differences and come together to achieve a greater and common objective. One day, when the time is right there will be someone who will bring all the tribes together in a campaign that will send the legions back to Rome."

She responded with thinly veiled doubt bordering on contemptuous disbelief. "And who is this paragon who will save us from the perils of Rome?" She saw his enigmatic smile and rolled her eyes in disgust.

Chapter 17

By early afternoon the next day and the arrival of two more heavily
laden convoys, Setarius was satisfied the promised Aedui support was
nearly fulfilled and confident the rest of the supplies would soon follow.
He ordered an immediate departure.

Strabo had no chance to bid goodbye to Raven. Their short time
together was both pleasant and problematic. He thought Raven would
probably agree. He felt some guilt he didn't seem to have the depth of
feeling for her she apparently did for him. He wondered if he was using
the present situation in Gaul as an excuse to avoid an obligation he
didn't want to make and possibly never would.

Long before the convoy approached the valley where the legions and
Helvetii had fought a long and bloody battle, the thick plumes of smoke
spiraling into the sky marked the site. The closer they came to where
the plateau began to fall away to the valley below, the more pervasive
and cloying the stench of the Helvetian dead burning a half mile west of
the battlefield. Predictably, the unpleasant task had been assigned to the
two new legions. The smell was almost more than even the veteran
legionnaires could stand. In the time they had been gone, three
entrenched camps had been constructed in the widest part of the valley
floor. East of the entrenched camps, a series of trenches had been
excavated where the bodies of the dead legionnaires were being
interred.

Setarius dismissed Strabo with a curt reminder he would likely be
called to serve Caesar as a translator in the event the Helvetii were
ready to negotiate rather than fight another battle. He dismounted,
collected his travel bag and surrendered the reins of the horse he'd
been riding to one of Tarquin's cavalrymen. He was thinking about his
brief time with Raven as he walked toward the nearest entrance of the
camp where the *Claudia* Legion was again collocated with the Tenth
Legion. It was a mistake. He saw the insignia of the Tenth Legion on
the shields carried by the two guards; an optio stood a few paces
behind. He knew when the guards saw his shield marked with the

Claudia Legion, he was going to suffer the abuse the veteran legionnaires were always ready to give to the legionnaires from the newly formed legions.

"Well, look what we have here, Avinius. It's one of the worthless young pups from the Eleventh and good for nothing but guarding the baggage. Do we let this *mentula* pass through or make him go around to the other side where he belongs with the rest of the slackers?"

In an even voice the optio asked, "Legionnaire, were you with those who fought last night?"

"Yes, Optio."

"You could have been the one who saved my ass before the bastard I didn't see would've split my head with an axe. The Eleventh did good work on our right flank and showed it can do more than guard the baggage. Let him through."

Strabo grinned in relief. "Thank you, Optio." He returned the compliment by saying, "We're grateful the Tenth had already done most of the work before we got there."

He looked at the guard who tried to provoke him and walked past him into the camp with a self-satisfied smile. Moments later, the smile quickly disappeared when he saw Tertious talking to several other legionnaires in the second line of tents on the right side of the Via Principalis. He pulled the helmet cheek guards down to conceal his face, and hoped the late afternoon shadows would also help to prevent Tertious from recognizing him. It was a forlorn hope.

He heard Tertious call his name. "Salve, Marcellus Strabo. If you came looking for your old messmate, you're in luck. You found him." In a loud mocking voice, Tertious said to the other legionnaires standing or sitting nearby, "In case you don't recognize the name Strabo, I'll remind you. His father is General Strabo who was also the governor of Provincia, and his mother was some native whore. This snot-nosed turd enjoyed a life the rest of us can't even imagine. Apparently, he eventually lived a little too grand, and Father Strabo had him conscripted in Massilia. Poor Marcellus, one day privileged, the next day forced to live with rabble like us."

Resigned, Strabo stopped and faced Tertious walking toward him with several other legionnaires following a pace behind. It was futile to keep walking without the widespread risk of being ridiculed for avoiding a confrontation. He didn't need to speculate how the legionnaire learned who he was. Scevola would never have said anything which left either Brecius or Marinus; he was sure it was the centurion.

"Tertious, I recall you didn't fare too well when we were messmates or the last time when you threatened me with a dagger. I don't think it will be any better for you if you try it again."

The legionnaire's face darkened. "I promised you a tattoo, and it'll be a Roman tattoo, not one of those primitive designs you've got. I think an X for the Tenth Legion will suit me." Tertious pointed at Strabo. "Get the half-breed whore son!"

With Tertious lagging behind, all three men ran toward Strabo. The smallest of the three men on the left reached him first, and Strabo reacted instinctively. Just as the first man reached him, he leaned forward and shoved the shield into his assailant's face. The legionnaire collapsed, bleeding from the mouth and nose. Strabo dropped the shield, pulled off his helmet and pivoted to the nearest man running toward him. Just before the legionnaire reached him, he stepped to one side and brought the helmet down hard on the man's head, sending him sprawling. Tertious and the remaining legionnaire crashed into him. All three fell to the ground with Strabo on his back under the other two. The second legionnaire regained his feet and rushed over to increase the already uneven odds. He made the mistake of reaching for Strabo's legs and suffered a hard kick in the face for the effort. With both arms pinned and Tertious straddling him, Strabo was resigned to the possibility he was about to get a tattoo.

Tertious drew the dagger and said, "Breed, I'm going to enjoy this more than you will. Tell me which cheek is your Roman side, I'll leave..."

Strabo heard a thump, and Tertious was on his back and groaning next to him. The legionnaire who helped Tertious bring him down was standing at attention. Strabo raised his head and saw the optio who allowed him entry into the camp. He stood up and came to attention.

"What's going on here? You three on the ground, stand up." Tertious pushed himself up and faced the optio. "Tertious, I should have known it would be you causing trouble. Explain yourself."

"It's nothing, optio, just having a little sport with one of the *Claudia* legionnaires."

"Sport? You call sticking a dagger into a man's face sport? We'll have some sport when I see you at the stake getting the *castigato* for brawling in camp. You other three are going to get the same for helping this animal." The optio saw Strabo's shield and asked, "Are you the one who I admitted a few minutes ago?"

"Yes, Optio."

"I think if I hadn't heard the commotion, you would have suffered more. Do you two know each other?"

Tertious and Strabo chorused, "No, Optio!"

"All right, break it up. Tertious, I intend to report this to your optio and centurion. And you, legionnaire from the *Claudia*, get your shield and helmet and get over to your side of the camp."

Strabo glanced at Tertious then said to the optio, "Sir, permission to speak."

"What now?"

"I may have been partly at fault. He gave me a rude sign, and I called him a turd. It got out of hand. I wouldn't have them suffer for what I shouldn't have said."

"I'll be damned. If someone was about to cut me the way he was, I'd be saying something a lot different than you just did. Very well, I'll take what you said into consideration. I have a mind to find your optio and tell him what happened. He may not be as generous as I am in excusing this disturbance. Tertious, escort this legionnaire to his camp. I wouldn't want anyone else trying to have some sport at his expense."

Once out of earshot of the optio, Tertious said in a mocking voice, "Sir, I wouldn't have them suffer for what I said. Do you think that bullshit is going to save your ass when I get my hands on you?"

174

"I would have paid a sesterce to see you getting flogged by telling what really happened. I felt sorry for the poor bastards trying to help you. If it had been just you, you'd be back there on the ground the way you were the first time you tried to take me on. You're dumb enough to try something again, but not capable enough to do any better than you have so far."

Tertious stopped at the intersection of the camp streets. "This is as far as I go. You were lucky the optio came when he did. The next time I won't bother with a tattoo. I'll cut off your balls and send you to the gods!"

"I take it as fair warning to watch my back. Be sure the gods are ready to help you as they haven't so far, otherwise you'll be the one seeing them."

The fourth day after the battle, Caesar ordered the legions to break camp. By the time the sun appeared, the legions were marching east in pursuit of the Helvetii. In late afternoon, the scouts found the migrating tribe in the form of a delegation from Divico with a request for negotiations.

Caesar waited until the last legion commander, also accompanied by his primus pilus, rode up the knoll where the others were already assembled. Caesar wasted no time in preliminaries. "Divico must have come to the conclusion he lost and wants to talk. I'll meet with him and presumably his senior tribe members tomorrow at mid-day at which time I'll renew the demands I made the last time we met. He'll either accept them as they are, or we will fight again. Until he decides, we'll remain ready to continue the campaign. We'll camp here for the night and perhaps longer as necessary." He turned to Setarius. "Flavius, I want you to go back to Bibracte and inform Diviciacus of the meeting with Divico with an invitation to attend along with other senior tribesmen as he wishes. Take Marcellus with you. I'll use him again to translate when I meet with Divico."

In a clearing a mile from the Roman encampment, Divico and a small number of tribal leaders sat astride their horses holding sheathed swords and waited for Caesar and Diviciacus accompanied by General Labienus and a token security escort to stop a dozen paces away. Strabo noted Divico's drawn, sallow face and saw how different the Helvetii leader looked today in comparison to the combative, confident man ten days before. Divico and the other members of his delegation dismounted and advanced holding their sheathed swords by the hilt and tip until they were a few feet in front of Caesar. Without a word spoken, each man knelt and placed their sword in front of Caesar's horse. Divico straightened up and spoke while Strabo translated.

"Mighty Caesar, we are defeated and now ask what you wish from us."

"I accept your surrender, and now this is what you will do. You will return the way you came, back to the lands you came from where you will remain. During your return journey, you will not take from or harm those who occupy the lands you pass through. On the contrary, you will pay reparations for the tribes you ravaged on the way here. You will pay for any food or fodder you require during your march. You will surrender senior hostages to Diviciacus to guarantee the terms I have given are fulfilled. Diviciacus will send representatives with you to see my requirements are met. Failure to meet them will not only determine the fate of the hostages, it will require me to lead my legions north against you. My terms are lenient for you have suffered on the battlefield, and your lands are wasted by your own hands. The oncoming winter will be harsh for you. There will be no terms if we meet again in battle."

"Caesar, I have a request to make."

Caesar's jaw tightened. "Divico, do not try my patience. Rome has suffered losses because of you, and I will not be more generous than I already have."

"I do not ask for me. The Boi have petitioned me to speak on their behalf. The tribe does not wish to return with the Helvetii. They

176

request permission to remain in the lands of the Aedui for they have ties here."

Caesar looked at Diviciacus who nodded his assent. "It's true, and the Aedui will honor their request if they pledge their loyalty."

Divico turned to the tall, somber-faced tribal leader of the Boi standing to the right of Divico. "Do you so swear?"

The tribal leader brought his fist to his heart and bowed. "I give you my oath the destiny of the Boi will be as one with the Aedui."

Caesar said, "So be it. I'll leave it to the Aedui to ensure the pledge is fulfilled in good faith." Caesar paused and gave the Helvetian leader a cold look, "Divico, pray to your gods we never meet again."

Divico flinched, turned away and walked to his horse, his slumped shoulders silent testimony the Helvetii invasion of Gaul was over.

Before the Helvetian tribesmen disappeared in the trees ahead, Diviciacus coughed nervously and said, "Caesar, I, too, have a request to make. On behalf of the tribes occupying our domains in the north, I and the other senior clansmen of the Aedui and Auverni ask for an audience at your earliest convenience. The threat of a German invasion led by King Ariovistus of the Suebi Tribe is imminent. We need your assistance. As you may recall, it was the reason I went to Rome and met with you. I failed to persuade you our plight was real. Since then, King Ariovistus has increased his army to the extent a German invasion is no longer in doubt."

"I recall your visit well. You said Ariovistus had only 15,000 Germans under his leadership. You also admitted Ariovistus had been allowed by the Auverni and Sequani to settle in lands the Sequani volunteered for their settlement. It did not seem to me at the time, or to members of the Senate, Rome had any reason to intervene. What has changed?"

"Over 100,000 more Germans representing multiple tribes have since joined him. We have recently learned the Harudes Tribe numbering approximately 24,000 intends to join Ariovistus. He will have the strength to do as he will in Gaul."

Caesar looked at General Labienus with a frown of resignation then faced Diviciacus. "Very well, come to my camp tomorrow at this hour with any who can add to this matter. I would hear more of this before deciding what Rome can or will do."

The clan leader's taut face relaxed. "Thank you, Mighty Caesar. We will do as you wish."

After the Aedui tribesmen left, Caesar shook his head. "Titus, we just defeated the Helvetii at great cost, and now we're faced with another campaign before we are healed from the effects of this one. Perhaps it was a mistake when as senior consul in Rome, I failed to see any real threat 15,000 Germans would pose. It's different now. I can hardly risk having ten times that number settling west of the Rhine."

Chapter 18

Angry, Caesar silently watched as Diviciacus led the senior tribesmen into the tent. He noted their dour expressions and wondered why their concerns were more apparent than in previous meetings during the Helvetii threat. He was sure Diviciacus had delayed telling him of the additional threat to Gaul. Had he known, he might have considered other options in dealing with Divico before risking the losses he suffered. It was as if Diviciacus had read his mind when Strabo translated the tribal leader's introductory remarks.

"Caesar, what we speak here must be closely guarded. We have given hostages to Ariovistus to hold our promise not to attack or entreat Rome to help free us from the tyranny of the Germans. The growing strength of Ariovistus has made clear his objective is to rule Gaul as a vassal state of the Germans. We must either accept this reality or migrate as the Helvetii tried to do, for without the help of Rome, we cannot match their strength in numbers. The Sequani have already lost much of their lands now occupied by the Germans. Their occupation has become increasingly brutal. We think Ariovistus was waiting to see the outcome of the Helvetii migration before taking action to extend his border in Gaul. We believe the intervention of Rome is the only way to prevent more Germans from crossing the Rhine to help Ariovistus."

Caesar deliberately delayed his response as he looked at each tribal leader in turn as if searching for both truth and dedication to the potential task ahead.

"Very well, I'll send a deputation to Ariovistus to determine his intentions and the possibility of stopping further encroachment into Gaul. I remind you the presence of Ariovistus west of the Rhine was occasioned by invitation and no doubt favorable to the Sequani at the time. As senior consul of Rome, I sent King Ariovistus gifts as a testament to Rome's friendship when it appeared his presence in Gaul

179

was peaceful. It seems the outcome, if not foreseen by Rome, should have been considered more carefully by the Aedui and other tribes. I will let you know the progress of our diplomatic efforts to stop what could end in a futile effort, particularly without the support of the local tribes in Gaul." Caesar paused and with a penetrating look slowly engaged each tribal leader before continuing.

"Do I have both your resolve and pledge in this endeavor? I ask this because in the battle with the Helvetii, it was Rome that faced the brunt of battle and subsequently bore the losses."

Barely containing his anger, Caesar ended the conference by saying, "I will let you know the success or failure of my deputation. In the meantime, I serve notice to all of you to prepare for battle and defend what is yours. Only then can you count on Rome's help should battle be required to determine the outcome."

Diviciacus bowed and answered for the rest. "We hear you, Caesar. You will find we are a willing and able ally to Rome in resolving this crisis."

"Diviciacus, I'm reassured by your words. My expectation is whatever happens it will be more than words the tribes will provide on a battlefield should it come to that." The comment was not lost on the tribal representatives. Most, including Diviciacus, avoided looking Caesar in the eye.

As the last of the tribal leaders filed out, General Labienus no longer restrained himself and laughed.

"Caesar, I thought some of those tribal chiefs were going to shit their drawers when they thought you were going to refuse, when you said we would help, but their presence would be required if we fight."

Caesar smiled. "I thought as much and considered holding my nose in preparation for the stench to follow. Diviciacus, the wily son of a bitch, knew what I was going to say before he came in, even if the others didn't. He knows I can't stand aside and let Ariovistus get any stronger. To turn away from the German threat would make Rome look weak and invite Ariovistus to move ahead faster in his plans to dominate Gaul. Frankly, the best I may be able to do is gain time by achieving a status quo with Ariovistus until I'm in a better position to meet him in battle with any confidence of winning. Our losses here are not inconsequential, and in spite of my demand to see our tribal allies fighting at our side, the result, if they show up at all, will be token at best. When this campaign is over, as soon as I can get back to Provincia, I'll recruit two more legions to reinforce the six standards we now have — which in reality is six standards in front of the equivalent of four full-strength legions."

"Is it your intention to lead the deputation?" General Labienus asked.

"No, if I were to go, it would look as if I'm concerned. I want him to believe I'm confident there's time and assurance diplomacy will achieve a peaceful resolution which we both know, if it happens, will only be temporary. We will eventually have to fight the Germans. Before we do, I need to replace our losses and recruit the additional legions I need. In the meantime, we need to get our legionnaires rested and the wounded who were not badly injured recovered enough to get back to their centuries.

"Perhaps I'm the one who should lead the deputation."

"Titus, you're too senior. Flavius, that leaves you to tell Ariovistus, or most likely someone well below his station, he has an invitation to meet at a convenient location somewhere midway between us. The purpose is to discuss matters to come to a mutual understanding and acceptance of his and Rome's intentions regarding the future of Gaul. At the moment, and privately, I would prefer diplomacy rather than swords to achieve an interim solution until I can do more than talk.

"It should be a place where each party feels secure to ensure the discussions can proceed peacefully. Flavius, you will be my emissary. Decurion Tarquin will command the escort of no more than two turma. A larger delegation would be a signal I consider Ariovistus an equal and adversary to be feared. I know it will be difficult for an old, one-eyed former primus pilus to look friendly and persuasive. I'm sure you'll rise to the occasion for me and the interests of Rome."

"Such a small escort? Surely a former First Spear and one with such renown as me deserves something larger for such a momentous task."

"My dear Flavius, were you a mere untried tribune I would have you go at the head of a cohort, but with your experience, anything more than a token escort would be an insult to you."

Setarius smiled and said with dry humor, "Now that you've explained it, I'm reassured I'll go with the blessing of the gods and with the hope they promise a safe return."

Caesar's face creased in a smile at Setarius' somewhat irreverent response. Almost as an afterthought, Caesar said, "Flavius, take Strabo with you."

It was late in the day when one of the lead scouts rode back and informed Tarquin of a large settlement two miles ahead and reported the tribesmen weren't friendly. When the scout finished his report, the decurion nodded and spoke to Setarius.

"From what we know about the general location where King Ariovistus can be found, I doubt the one ahead is the main settlement."

"I agree. We're too far from the Rhine. Perhaps Marcellus can learn where it is."

When they arrived at the settlement, Setarius saw his scouts surrounded by a silent, hostile armed villagers far outnumbering the small detail Caesar mandated. He thought it would have been better had Caesar sent a cohort with his invitation to talk. He was struck by how large the Germans were in comparison to the Aedui and other Gaulish Tribes. Tall and burly, they would have easily been the equal in size of the typical legionnaire recruited for the first cohort in a legion in which men at least six feet in height were required.

"Marcellus, tell them who I am and why I'm here."

After Strabo finished, a wizened man with gaunt features and long white hair flowing from far back on an otherwise bald pate, shuffled forward and responded while Strabo translated.

"My name is Siward, I am sent here by King Ariovistus in expectation the Romans would soon come here to seek an audience with him. He does not hold Romans in high esteem. He has no wish to talk to your general who no doubt believes his success with the Helvetii emboldens him to challenge his authority over the lands he occupies. He prefers to deal with Romans with swords and other weapons of war than the honeyed-tongues of would-be conquerors who expect whomever they face will kneel meekly and accept a fate dictated by Rome. He will consent to speak to your delegation only with the understanding not to come any farther, or it will be considered an act of aggression.

"The lands beginning here and claimed by Ariovistus stretch eastward beyond where we now stand and farther than a swift rider can travel without ever reaching the place where the sun rises above the far mountains." As he translated, Strabo tried not smile at the lofty declaration of unlimited power by a man until a few hours ago he'd never heard of.

Setarius' response was brief and measured. "The name of Ariovistus is well-known and respected for his bravery on the battlefield..." he paused briefly to emphasize the next comment, "except for Caesar whose prowess and battlefield success is unmatched. Caesar's might is vested in the power of Rome and the unlimited authority given to him by the Roman Republic. His request to meet is extended as a courtesy and a gesture of peace to a noble king. War serves the interests of no one dwelling either east or west of the Rhine River."

Siward regarded Setarius with studied indifference, a demeanor he had mastered over decades in dealing with tribal disputes. He thought the scar-faced man with his veiled threats and obfuscation had the makings of a true negotiator, reminding him of his early days learning to say much without saying anything. Ambiguity was the art of diplomacy using words that could either be disclaimed or celebrated for whatever diplomatic problem was being considered.

"King Ariovistus is not disposed to enter into discussions when there seems little reason to do so. He's here on this side of the Rhine not by conquest, but rather by invitation from border tribes seeking protection from inter-tribal rivalry. In crossing the Rhine, King Ariovistus has brought peace to the region. Go back to your general and tell him there is no reason to meet as there is no reason or incentive for further advancement into Gaul. That is if there are no provocations to justify further expansion to protect the Suebi. He wishes only for his people to live in harmony with the other tribes and enjoy the prosperity gained in the years since he came here by invitation," the last said to reiterate why the Suebi were there.

Setarius arched an eyebrow, and Strabo translated, "It is always better to talk of peace and accommodation and win with words rather than waging a costly and bloody war resulting in more loss than gain. Tell King Ariovistus it would be better to reach an understanding through peaceful negotiation and treaty than through force. Caesar invites King Ariovistus to meet in peace or accept the inevitably of war. His preferred alternative is to resolve peacefully the concerns of the Aedui and Rome for the encroachment of the Germanic Tribes in Gaul.

After Strabo finished, Siward frowned and said, "I will so inform King Ariovistus, although he will not be pleased your invitation to talk is presented more as an ultimatum than a peaceful overture. Return in two days to this place at this time, and I will give his answer." Without waiting for a refusal or agreement, Siward turned his back and walked away.

Tarquin looked at the tribune and asked, "Do you think we'll wait here for two days only to find this so-called emissary has made us look like fools?"

"It's possible. Despite the bluster, Ariovistus would prefer to hold on to what he has without having to preserve it with a battle he could possibly lose. A concern he probably considers more real following the defeat of the Helvetii. Send a messenger back to Caesar informing him of what I've agreed to. We'll remain in the vicinity until we know the King's intentions."

That night, Strabo heard the scouts talking quietly among themselves with the subject focused mainly on the physical size of the Germans.

He gave it little thought for the significance of the conversation that would not be apparent until days to come.

Three days later Setarius reported to Caesar. "King Ariovistus won't meet with you. He says there's nothing he wants from Rome, and if he did, he would have gone to you. If, on the other hand, you wanted something from him, he believes you should have come to him to say whatever was on your mind. He wonders why Rome has come into Gaul unless it is to conquer this land, including where the King has settled by invitation of the Sequani and other tribes, including the Aedui. Treaties were signed, hostages exchanged and tributes pledged to maintain peace in the region. He claims the Germanic Tribes are there by invitation or achieved by the rightful outcome of success on the battlefield by those who sought to disrupt a peaceful occupation. The king emphasized his sole objective in Gaul is to maintain peace in a troubled land which did not exist until the Suebi crossed the Rhine. It appears to him Rome is the threat to the current peaceful coexistence of the Germans and Gauls. I think that sums up what the son of the bitch had to say."

Caesar laughed. "Well, he seems to have a pair of balls Taurus would envy." He noted the tribune's look and added, "I expected him to say something of the sort. He's bluffing, and he's not without some justification for doing so. Yes, we prevailed over the Helvetii, but he knows we paid dearly for the victory. We have a tenuous supply line dependent on the vagaries of the local tribes, each looking out for themselves and ready to repudiate any alliance forged yesterday."

General Labienus said, "Ariovistus would be very comfortable sitting in the Roman Senate."

"Well said, Titus. Unfortunately, the reality is there is some truth to what he says and implies. He has almost as much control over the southern tribes as he does over the tribes within the lands he physically occupies. The danger has increased since Flavius left on his embassage. The warning Diviciacus gave concerning the Harudes tribe possibly crossing the river to join Ariovistus is serious. Our recent victory over the Helvetii was impressive, but it came at a price and has emboldened Ariovistus to take the position he has. He's gambling his strength of numbers as well as a tight hold on the collective balls of the local tribes will win a larger slice of Gaul and later, all of it." Caesar scowled and, added, "Unfortunately, given our recent casualties, he might be able to achieve his objective."

General Labienus looked skeptical and asked, "What are our options?"

"Unfortunately, we don't have many. We're a long way from Rome in terms of supplies and more importantly replacement for our losses; therefore, we're dependent on the local tribes for both logistics and their willingness to side with Rome when, and if, we fight. The only question left to is will we fight to decide the outcome? In the meantime, I'll send another embassage to reconsider the mutual advantage of a peaceful solution to a building crisis in which the only resolution will be decided on a battlefield." Caesar looked at the baffled expressions on the faces of General Labienus and the other legion commanders. He understood their discomfort for a situation appearing to be nothing short of perilous for Rome.

"Let me be clear, I think we will have to fight, and when we do, the outcome may be more favorable to the Germans. I'll try to avoid battle until the odds look better for us. In the meantime, we keep our swords sharp, and if need be, use them to get the Aedui ready to stiffen their cocks and backbone to join in chasing Ariovistus back across the Rhine."

General Labienus, the only one who would have dared, was quick to say, "Caesar, we've won a noble and decisive victory against the Helvetii which demonstrates both the resolve and capability of Rome to prevail. This alone should be enough to defeat the Germans."

"I wish it was possible. It isn't for two main reasons. First, the losses we sustained weakened our fighting capability by almost two legions. Second, we lack the solidarity of our allies. The ambitions of tribal leaders, the hostility between the tribes in addition to their lack of a dependable, resolute defense of their own tribal lands favors the

Germans. The proof was obvious during the Helvetii campaign. The Aedui were willing to leave the fight to us with only token support, requiring threats and ultimatums to provide the logistical assistance promised before the first spear or arrow was launched. I will not let it happen again."

"What's our strategy? It seems to me the longer we wait to take up arms against the Germans, the more we forfeit the momentum we achieved in defeating the Helvetii."

"Again, reality must dictate our course of action. Yes, we defeated the Helvetii, but there was a cost. Flavius, go back to Ariovistus with another and more forceful invitation. Make it sound convincing I'm merely looking for a time and place to discuss mutual concerns."

Setarius controlled his exasperation at the prospect of making another futile trip. He looked at General Labienus hoping he would say something. The general merely nodded in agreement. Setarius asked the question he would have preferred the general had posed.

"Caesar, do you expect him to comply?"

"Of course not, and if I were Ariovistus, I would reply in kind."

"Then why bother?"

Caesar answered with a note of irritation. "Time, Flavius. I need more time, and I'm hoping Ariovistus will help me get it."

Six days later, Setarius entered the headquarters and soberly delivered the results of his second trip to the Suebi settlement. "The king's answer is as you predicted, both in his refusal and the language he uses."

Caesar frowned. "I confess to wishing for a pleasant surprise."

There was a rustling at the entryway. The centurion on duty appeared and announced, "Caesar, a delegation from the Aedui led by Diviciacus is here. I can't understand most of what he says, but he seems to be in a hurry to talk to you."

"Very well, send an orderly to the *Claudia* Legion and have a legionnaire by the name of Marcellus get here as quick as he can. Centurion Valens knows who he is."

General Labienus said, "You think for once Diviciacus has something important to say other than reminding us how great the alliance between Rome and the Aedui continues to be? Perhaps to announce the promised support will be timely and to the degree expected?"

"Your sarcasm is justified; however, I think this time may different. It isn't the way of Diviciacus to come here without scheduling a visit beforehand. Flavius, invite them in here while we wait for Strabo. He speaks enough Latin I can at least get the general idea of what he's talking about."

A moment later, Flavius ushered Diviciacus and three other men into the headquarters. Caesar took one look at the strained expression on the faces of the four men and had a premonition the stand-off with Ariovistus could be nearing an end. Fortunately, they had barely got through the tribal chief's stammering apology when a breathless, disheveled Marcellus Strabo in dirt-stained tunic and with an odor suggesting he had been summoned from drill was pushed inside the tent. Strabo quickly took up position slightly behind Caesar and waited expectantly.

Caesar wasted no time as he looked directly at Diviciacus and said, "You honor me by your presence, but I sense you're here with a purpose of some urgency."

"Noble Caesar, what you say is true. With the blessing and encouragement of King Ariovistus, the Harudes have crossed the Rhine in strength along the borders of the Aedui. They've ignored all our offers to talk including the exchange of hostages to achieve peaceful resolution. There is no longer any doubt Ariovistus is about to challenge the domain of the Aedui and the tribes aligned with us. We have reports he's planning to attack Vesontio, the main settlement of the Sequani. Vesontio is important for two reasons: it has a great store of supplies needed for war; and it is also believed to be virtually impregnable because it's encircled on three sides by the river Doubs and a high escarpment surrounding the settlement. A considerable force of the Suebi has also encamped on the eastern bank of the Rhine and could cross at any time. We believe the crossing will begin when Ariovistus launches his attack on the Sequani. We desperately need your help to stop the Germans."

Expressionless, Caesar listened without giving any sign of the concern he felt for what was transpiring and far worse than he'd calculated.

When Diviciacus finished, Caesar said, "Thank you for the information, my friend. I will meet with my generals and begin immediately to plan how to stop Ariovistus and any additional migration by the Germans. In the meantime, I charge you to prepare the tribes to assist our efforts. I depend on the tribes on this side of the Rhine to ready their warriors *when* I summon them." Diviciacus winced at Caesar's emphasis. "Food supplies must be prepared for immediate dispersal in the days to come to support my immediate deployment against Ariovistus." He paused and gave Diviciacus a hard look. "Your support must be better and more dependable than it has been so far."

The tribal leader flushed and nodded. "It shall be as you say. With your permission, I will leave now to prepare for the battle that appears inevitable and soon to follow."

Strabo assumed his presence was no longer required and followed his uncle outside.

Caesar waited until the Aedui tribesmen left before turning to General Labienus with a sigh of resignation. "Titus, I hoped, but did not really expect to get a treaty with Ariovistus. If peace, no matter how transitory, could have been arranged, we would have at least gained more time to prepare for another battle. So be it. Convene the other legion commanders and senior centurions for a consilium in three hours. We need to get to Vesontio without delay before Ariovistus does.

"If Diviciacus is right about the supplies there, occupying it would deny the Germans what we also need in case the Aedui fail to meet their promises. We march at first light tomorrow. This campaign may well prove more challenging than we faced with the Helvetii. They were burdened with protecting a large non-combatant population and an equally large baggage train to support it. The Germans are a warlike people, more so than most of the Gaulish Tribes, including the Aedui. Although from what I've been told, they are also more primitive, a weakness that to some extent may offset our numerical disadvantage."

The three-day forced march to Vesontio was grueling, and no one was more relieved than Caesar when the legions arrived at their destination to find they had reached the settlement before the Germans. The Sequani voiced more protest than armed resistance, and the settlement was quickly taken. After learning of the Suebi advance, the elders were more than willing to accept a cohort from the *Augusta* Legion to add to their defense when and if the other legions left

Assured the Sequani were compliant and willing to fight the Suebi, Caesar and the legions took advantage of the peaceful occupation to rest from the forced march

Strabo went down to the Doubs River to wash off the dust from the last day of hard marching. At first, he paid little attention to the conversation around him until it took on a louder and threatening tone. The comments seemed to dwell on the size and ferocity of the Germans. He listened more carefully and detected uncertainty over the wisdom of marching against such a formidable foe. Negotiations and a treaty could avoid a needless battle in which Roman blood would be shed in greater quantity than by the tribal allies. He heard his name called and turned around and saw it was Septimus, a legionnaire from the first century.

"Marcellus, you've been with the cavalry as a translator when you visited one of the German settlements. Is it true they're giants and so fierce-looking no man can look them in the face without wanting to back away?"

Strabo stared at the legionnaire in astonishment and wondered how to respond to such an outlandish question. "Where in Jupiter's name did you hear such nonsense?"

"Why everyone is talking about it. The people in Visontio said as much."

"And you had such conversations with the Sequani because you speak their language so well?"

The obvious sarcasm was not lost on Septimus who quickly became defensive. "It isn't just me. Last night when I was standing guard on the second watch at the east gate, I overheard one of the tribunes saying as much to the centurion in charge of the guard detail." Several other legionnaires quickly joined in an animated chorus of agreement.

"I know nothing of what you say about the Germans. I agree they're sizable. As far as being ferocious, I saw nothing about them the way you describe. They're more primitive in dress and manner than the Aedui; however, I saw nothing about them indicating they're more threatening than the Helvetii we faced — and defeated."

Apart from inaudible muttering by those within earshot, there were no more voiced concerns. Septimus left the wash area without another word leaving Strabo to think the issue and outlandish concerns surrounding the matter had been laid to rest. By the next morning, he realized nothing could be farther from the truth.

Caesar studied the map and looked around at the legion commanders. "Ariovistus' main settlement must be about 100 miles or so northeast of Visontio, somewhere in this vicinity," pointing to an area east of the Vosges Mountains. "If I'm right, the settlement is close to the Rhine River and his support from across the river. The additional German tribes already crossed or preparing to cross will be nearby waiting for King Ariovistus to move southwest. My guess, his objective is Bibracte where he expects us to be unless he knows we've taken Visontio. We need to be better positioned. There's a narrow valley closer to the Vosges Mountains which would be logical for him to move through to avoid crossing the mountains. I propose we begin our move there tomorrow to block his approach. I estimate it will take a three to four-day march. It's possible we may engage him before we get there."

General Arridius asked, "Is it your intention to continue occupying Visontio?"

"Absolutely, it's a natural fortress. Each legion will leave one cohort behind in addition to any legionnaires incapable of making the long and difficult march ahead. Although the route we take appears relatively flat, we'll have to move quickly to gain the advantage I want."

The order to break camp in preparation to march came as no surprise and at first proceeded in normal fashion with the issuing and preparation of the morning ration. Later, the expected bugle call to dismantle tents, prepare field packs and load baggage carts did not sound. At first the legionnaires didn't take notice and automatically began to perform the tasks expected to be accomplished before the call to assemble. Several minutes later there was no bugle call. The puzzled legionnaires gradually stopped what they were doing and stood looking at each other in bewilderment. The bugle finally sounded — it wasn't the call they were expecting; instead, it summoned all officers to headquarters. In the distance, Strabo heard the same call echoing from the other two camps.

Brecius passed by wearing a worried frown and Strabo called to him. "Optio, what's happening? Are we going to march today or not?"

"Maybe Jupiter knows. If he does, he hasn't told me or any of the officers. The senior officers are going to Caesar's headquarters perhaps to find out if we are. In the meantime, nobody said to stop packing so get on with it, or you'll be getting the hard end of my stick." The optio continued on with the same admonishment for the rest of the century.

Strabo turned to Scevola standing nearby and making no effort to follow the optio's orders. He looked around and saw bewildered legionnaires from other centuries had also stopped their preparations for departure and were standing around talking. Others were taking advantage of the confusion by stretching out on the ground with their eyes closed.

"Scevola, what do you make of this?"

"I'm not sure, but I've seen the like before. Most times it's because the priests didn't like what they saw in the guts of the bull after they sacrificed it, and a legion commander still ordered the legion to march. It always ended when the general realized the order wasn't going to be obeyed and was smart enough to wait another day for another bull to improve the auguries. Other times it was about pay or short rations. Mutiny is always a possibility, particularly when generals are too stupid to recognize the conditions causing it and do nothing before it gets out of hand. When it does, it's bad. I saw it happen once, and I don't ever want to be a part of it again."

With a thoughtful expression, Strabo said, "Last night when I was washing up, one of the legionnaires in the second century asked me about the Germans after hearing they were big and formidable. He was joined by others saying similar things. I didn't pay much attention to it and wonder if it has anything to do with what's happening now."

"There may be some truth to it. I heard a rumor some of the tribunes were having cold feet after the Helvetii campaign, believing it was going to be worse with the Germans. I only saw a few tribunes who ever turned out to be worth more than a fart in the wind. They come out here to put their time in the army necessary to satisfy political and financial advancement, hoping when they do, there's little chance of risking a hard campaign with a safe return to Rome. Maybe some of the centurions are paying too much attention to what the tribunes are pulling out of their asses."

"What's going to happen?"

"It probably already has. My guess is Caesar's not going to sit by and let a bunch of political pissants and a few centurions who have lost their nerve dictate what he'll do and when. I warrant we won't leave today. The centurions will come back with their chins dragging and their asses on fire ready with their vine sticks to take it out on any legionnaire who farts without permission."

A short time later, the officers returned with little fanfare. An announcement soon followed the legions would march tomorrow after the fourth watch. It didn't take long before knowledge of what had transpired was well known and embellished throughout the camp. From the terse summary passed on by Brecius, Strabo thought it matched closely to what Scevola speculated.

The sun's appearance over the horizon marked the time a priest plunged the knife into the bull's neck and followed by a quick evisceration to examine the entrails. Scevola predicted they would march even if the guts were as black as night and had the stink of death. Before the sun had yet to dispel the early morning shadows, the blaring horns and measured tread of hobnailed boots signaled the accuracy of the veteran legionnaire's prediction.

Chapter 19

Several days later following the incipient mutiny, the scouts reported Ariovistus' main force was encamped only twenty-four miles away. Caesar called an early halt to the march and ordered the legions to prepare the night camp. The legionnaires had barely dropped their packs and started digging the protective ditches when Tarquin escorted a trio of Germans to Caesar's headquarters. The Germans had approached the scouts holding a tree branch as a gesture of peaceful intention. Using pantomime and Gaulish, they finally managed to make clear they had a request from King Ariovistus to meet with Caesar.

Caesar summoned an orderly and instructed him to send for Strabo. After the orderly left, Caesar frowned, and complained to Setarius.

"I've a mind to promote Marcellus Strabo to optio or whatever. I want him here faster when I need him. I'm tired of waiting for the arrival of a ranker to tell me when and where I may have to take my legions. Flavius, promote him. He's too valuable and talented to waste him in the ranks. Besides, he's the nephew of Diviciacus, and by promoting him, it may be interpreted as further confidence in our friendship and trust in the Aedui."

With some misgivings, Setarius nodded. He silently predicted if Caesar confirmed the promotion, it would not be accepted with the appreciation Caesar expected it would be.

A short time later, Strabo arrived and quickly confirmed they were sent by King Ariovistus. He turned to Caesar and pointed to the older German. "His name is Ellanher. He's come here with an offer from King Ariovistus to meet and talk of matters which may be clarified and end with mutual satisfaction."

Caesar asked bluntly, "Why now and not when I offered a peaceful overture before?"

"Because Caesar is much closer, and there is less risk in talking to the Romans without the might of the Aedui to threaten the outcome of any discussions. King Ariovistus has concerns for Gaul and why Caesar has come here with a mighty force. He wants to better understand

Roman intentions concerning Gaul and the potential threat to our peaceful occupation here."

Caesar frowned and responded quickly. "Rome also has concerns for what is happening in Gaul, especially the continued migration of other German tribes reported crossing the Rhine to join the Suebi. It looks to Rome that King Ariovistus is planning to progress farther south from the border agreed upon between the Suebi and the tribes living in northern Gaul."

The emissary threw up his hands in protest and was just as quick to say, "You misunderstand the reason we came to Gaul. You believe we entered Gaul to expand Suebi influence and occupation. On the contrary, we came at the invitation of the Sequani to resist the expansion of the Aedui. Such are the misconceptions and the accusations fueling the belief we intend to conquer Gaul. With great respect, Noble Caesar, it seems in light of recent developments, Rome appears more a danger to the autonomy of Gaul than the Germans."

Caesar concealed his admiration for the astute observation voiced by the emissary and his intent to refocus the attention on the conditions required for a peaceful interaction. He believed there was the possibility Rome could except a status quo out of practical necessity to gain time, time to bring more legions into Gaul and dictate an outcome more favorable to Rome than possible now. The risk was the reports of the German buildup and the conclusion it was not *if* Ariovistus planned to seize more of Gaul but *when*. The waiting game had started with both sides were not ready to act — with the legions considerably less prepared.

"What does King Ariovistus expect to achieve if I agree to meet with him?"

Ellanher responded smoothly, "What does Caesar want from King Ariovistus?"

"A chance to say what must be said to prevent further misunderstandings. It's better to talk and settle differences than on a battlefield, an outcome that favors neither Rome nor the Suebi."

"Noble Caesar, let that be the reason and need to meet. King Ariovistus believes there is mutual benefit in meeting to prevent misunderstandings that serve neither the interest of Rome nor the Suebi. Thoughtful leaders should come together with mutual resolve to solve any disputes with words rather than swords. King Ariovistus proposes to meet at a place where both can talk under conditions where neither party will be concerned for their personal safety."

"Where and under what conditions does your king propose?"

"There is a wide plain not far from here where you and my lord can meet on neutral ground without the possibility of risking needless bloodshed to either party. My king believes, as he assumes you do, nothing will result from war except the lamentations of the survivors for the dead on both sides with little distinction between the anguished voices of the victor and the defeated."

"Very well, I agree to meet with King Ariovistus with the understanding we have similar reasons and expectations to serve both Roman and German interests."

"The meeting place he proposes is a large field with a small hill located in the center equidistant between here and where King Ariovistus is camped. He proposes to meet there in four days. The location is open and provides visibility for both to meet without concern for personal safety. To further ensure peaceful intentions, King Ariovistus suggests the meeting take place without infantry present and only cavalry to provide the security for both delegations."

"The stipulation seems strange to me. Would a hundred infantry and a similar number for cavalry be sufficient for each side to protect an earnest and purposeful dialogue?"

"Under normal circumstances this would be so, but the prowess of the Roman legionnaires is such King Ariovistus seeks a more equitable arrangement without favoring Rome."

"I see, and because King Ariovistus knows his cavalry far outnumbers mine, he's graciously offering terms more suitable to him than to me."

"King Ariovistus is aware of the size of your cavalry and would not wish to take unfair advantage; therefore, he is willing to limit the number to 3000 for each delegation. It is a number large enough to give importance to the meeting without threatening its peaceful purpose."

"Tell King Ariovistus I agree to the terms." Caesar saw Titus Labienus' scowl and tight jaw and shook his head to stop the angry protest the general was about to make.

General Labienus waited only long enough for the emissary and Strabo to leave the tent before saying, "By the gods, why would you agree to such a disadvantage? They outnumber us in ways I don't wish to think about. Then you make it worse by surrendering the one advantage we have with infantry second to none in Gaul. Now we'll have to rely on the Aeduan cavalry for protection."

Caesar's indulgent smile only intensified the veteran legion commander's volatile reaction.

"Titus, I've not lost my wits, nor have I conceded the field to Ariovistus. On the contrary, I will meet his terms on my terms; however, I have no intention of using Aeduan cavalry to safeguard us while Dumnorix commands or controls it. The only thing I want from Dumnorix is his horses. I don't trust the son of a bitch, but his horses are another matter."

"I don't understand."

"Ariovistus fears our infantry legions with good reason. My good friend, it's my intention to use the Tenth Legion as my escort. As I've agreed with the King's emissary, my escort will look like cavalry. Which means, Titus, I will ask Diviciacus for his brother's horses and the Tenth Legion will have no more than three days to learn to sit on a horse and look as if they know what they're doing."

Labienus regarded Caesar with astonishment that quickly transitioned to open admiration. The general threw back his head and laughed. "By the gods, Caesar, you have a devilish way of seeing a possibility when anyone else would see an impossibility. Get me the horses, and I'll have the Tenth Legion looking as if they were born to ride." He laughed again and added, "It might work if they don't have to go any faster than a walk."

Several hours after the delegation from King Ariovistus departed, Strabo wondered why Tribune Setarius summoned him. He thought it might have something to do with the planned meeting between Caesar and the German king. He was at least half right. He identified himself to the guard standing outside the tribune's tent and waited until he reappeared and waved him inside. Setarius stood behind his field desk, left hand resting on his hip. The grim look on the tribune's face was not a good sign.

The tribune wasted no time. "Marcellus, I'm going to tell you something you won't like. Before I do, so help me if you interrupt or say one word before you hear me out, you'll regret it. Effective immediately by order of Gaius Julius Caesar, you are promoted to decurion. Your centurion in the *Claudia* Legion has already been informed. When you're dismissed, you will go back to the legion, turn in your equipment and collect your personal effects.

"Caesar decided a short time ago he was no longer willing to wait for your services when he wants them. He's also of the opinion your relationship to Diviciacus is too important to keep you looking like a ranker in spite of your preference to remain one as you made clear on the occasion we talked before. I shouldn't have to remind you that Rome does not give pig shit for your personal preferences in what rank or where you serve, only the way you serve." Setarius paused and considered Strabo's neutral expression.

He was surprised the legionnaire so far had remained silent. He continued with dry sarcasm. "In expectation you just might resent being so ill-treated, I thought to soften your misfortune by appointing you as a decurion instead of an optio as Caesar originally suggested. I thought you might be more inclined to accept a promotion you didn't want by the chance to ride a horse again. As of now, you are assigned to Decurion Tarquin's turma. Since the turma already has three decurions you will not command until such time as one of the three decurion slots

199

becomes available. Now, what have you to say?" He held up a warning hand and quickly added, "Speak this once. After this, I'll hear no more from you." Strabo's neutral expression relaxed and he nodded.

The tribune's eyes quickly narrowed in suspicion. "I warn you, don't say anything I don't want to hear or by *Morta's* shriveled teats, I'll make sure you regret it until the time you meet her in the underworld."

"I'm grateful to Caesar and Fortuna for the opportunity being given to me."

"You are? And I thought you would have welcomed my sword in your belly instead of what you've just been given. What's changed your mind?"

Strabo decided to give a version of the truth and avoid any reference to his increased opportunity for visiting Bibracte and Raven. "I told you before. Serving Rome also helps the Aedui, both of which have claim to my loyalty."

Setarius hesitated before asking, "What if one day one or the other has a stronger claim if circumstances change, and the Aedui decide their future is no longer with Rome?"

"It may be, but it is also possible before it happens, I'll decide my future independent of what Rome or my Aeduan kinsmen want from me. It's a question I'm now more willing for the gods to decide whether I'm more Roman or Aeduan. For now, I'm content to leave the answer for another day and time."

Setarius looked at the young man standing in front of him and considered how much he had changed. He no longer resembled the privileged young man and rebellious conscript months ago. He thought General Strabo would be pleased.

"All right, there's no more to be said. The paymaster has been informed, and you will soon realize there will be more denarii in your purse. Decurion Tarquin is pleased to have you — he's been asking me to transfer you to the troop since he first met you. He'll outfit you with what you'll need. This is my personal gift to you." The tribune turned and reached for a crested helmet resting on a table behind him. He handed it to Strabo. "Do not disappoint Caesar and more importantly, your father. Make your farewells quickly in the *Claudia*. You'll soon find out why after you report to Tarquin. You're dismissed."

Strabo saluted and left the tent. As he made his way back to the *Claudia* Legion, he had mixed feelings. He was pleased more than he would have believed a short time ago. He also saw the possibilities in having earned the trust and confidence of Caesar. He wondered if he was turning into a *Janus*, the two-faced god representing beginnings and transitions and commonly looked upon as two-faced, someone other than who the individual appeared to be. Time and circumstance would dictate the need to decide whether he was more Roman or Aeduan. It was not a choice he needed to make now.

Chapter 20

Scevola saw the distinctive helmet of a decurion nestled under Strabo's arm and smiled. By the time Strabo reached Scevola, the other members of the contubernium had stopped whatever they were doing and looked on with puzzled expressions.

Self-conscious, Strabo wasn't sure what to say and said the first thing that came to mind. "It seems I've been promoted to decurion and assigned to the Tenth Legion's turma. I've come to get my things." He hoped his promotion would not be seen as an advancement perceived as inevitable because of his father. Almost apologetically, he added, "I had no idea this was going to happen until a few minutes ago."

Scevola broke the awkward silence with a hearty laugh. "Marcellus, the only mystery is why it's taken so long. Come, we'll rejoice and celebrate your good fortune."

"Unfortunately, I can't stay long as I'm ordered to report without delay. I believe I'm about to accompany a delegation..." He was interrupted by the arrival of Centurion Marinus accompanied by Brecius. In contrast to the optio's expressionless face, the centurion's scowl predicted the usual unpleasant encounter.

"I knew it was a matter of time before you took advantage of your father's name to get a promotion handed to you for the asking."

Strabo clenched his jaw and allowed himself a moment to collect himself before responding. "Sir, I did not ask for the promotion. In truth, I was given no choice by Caesar himself who ordered it. The first time I was encouraged by Tribune Setarius to join Caesar's staff some time ago, I told him I preferred to remain with the *Claudia* as a legionnaire. It seems Caesar made the decision without concern for any preference I might have."

"A likely story to cover up going behind my back. Now, if you're sincere in remaining with the century, I'll speak to Caesar and intercede on your behalf."

"Tribune, I prefer you do not for my reasons for refusing advancement before have changed, and I now look forward to moving upward." He stopped before adding, *and to get away from you.*

The centurion's face turned red. "It sounds to me like a personal insult I won't forget. Enjoy your present favor, but we'll both see if it lasts. If it doesn't, you may find yourself back here in the *Claudia* and the misfortune of returning to the second century as a legionnaire."

"It's for you to decide if you interpret what I said as an insult, although, it sounds very much like the truth to me and easily confirmed by talking to Tribune Setarius. Sir, if you'll excuse me, I've been ordered to report to the cavalry troop without delay."

"Strabo, I've never pretended to like or respect you. I've little use for anyone who takes advantage of influence to rise above their capability and station. I say good riddance to you. Brecius, remain here and see his equipment is turned in properly and any shortages are compensated."

Strabo knew the centurion's public use of his surname was intentional. There was no longer any doubt Marinus harbored a deep resentment that had to be caused by something relating to his father. He had become the unfortunate means to take revenge.

Brecius waited until the centurion had gone far enough away and out of sight to face the contubernium. "First of all, Marcellus, I congratulate you on your good fortune. You have more than proved you're qualified. For those of you who may not have known his cognomen until the centurion used it, Marcellus never once used it as the centurion accused to secure any favoritism or seek relief from the hardships of being a legionnaire. He will always have my respect and admiration for it." He paused and said with a laugh, "I hope you remember what I said if the day comes when I may have to call you Sir." The comment drew a hearty chorus of approval and agreement which left Strabo momentarily at a loss for words.

Vinicius stepped forward and said, "Marcellus, the main difference between the two of us is if my cognomen had been Strabo, Labienus or

Cicero instead of the one my pig-farming father gave me, I would have made sure I was a centurion." Brecius joined in the laugh that followed.

"My friends and messmates, I appreciate your good will — I won't forget it. I admit coming to the legion in unwilling circumstances, but in the time since, I've come to have a different perspective and one I would never have anticipated. I credit all of you and those who are no longer with us for making me better than I was." He smiled and added, "I particularly thank you for helping me to stay alive so that one day Optio Brecius will call me Sir."

The optio quickly responded saying, "You won't know what I'll call you behind your back."

"I will, because it's what we've all called you on many occasions."

The last to say his farewell was Brecius. "I never once shared Marinus' opinion of you. He has his faults, but I've served under worse than him. He seems to have something against you which probably has nothing to do with what you did or didn't do. I suspect it might have something to do with your father; he was a centurion in the Tenth when your father commanded it. There were rumors of something that happened and resulted in Marinus leaving the legion. Be careful what you say and how you treat him. He's a senior centurion and not without influence. Now get your personal things and don't worry about the rest. I'll see to it you'll owe nothing to the quartermaster."

When Strabo arrived at the Tenth Legion's cavalry stables, Tarquin and his two subordinate commanders, Costa and Priscus, and the troop's veterinarian holding the reins of two horses greeted him.

Tarquin smiled and said, "Marcellus, it appears Caesar managed to overcome your refusal to join us. Since you're smiling, it seems you're here finally willing to join us."

"Well, I do prefer the company of horses more than I do most men although I cannot say the same for women."

"Spoken like a true cavalryman. We're glad to have you. Your arrival is timely. Martinus has selected two horses for you to consider for the two mounts assigned to you. I think you can trust his judgment that the horses will be more than adequate to your needs."

"I have no doubt he's chosen well."

The comment drew a smile of appreciation from the bearded horse-keeper and a quick response, "Marcellus, considering how you handled Aquilo, I believe you'll do well with these two. Both of them are spirited."

Tarquin nodded to Martinus. "Take them back to the line. The decurion will have time later to try them out, but now I need to talk to my officers. There is much to be done and little time to do it. You can draw your equipment and try out your mounts when we return from our meeting with Tribune Setarius. He's expecting us."

Tarquin led the way toward the headquarters and signaled Strabo to walk beside him while the two other officers followed behind. "Marcellus, your position is, shall we say, unusual. You will be *Eques Alaris,* fourth in command and positioned in the command section. If misfortune finds either Costa or Priscus no longer able, you'll assume command of whichever decuria requires a leader. In the meantime, you will be responsible for coordinating and supervising any native cavalry assigned to the turma. It could be such an eventuality may never occur unless Caesar's concern for the reliability of the Aedui changes for the better. You will continue to do as you have before by way of giving us the benefit of your knowledge of Gaul and its tribes."

Strabo bristled and said, "The Aedui has been a longtime and reliable ally of Rome."

Tarquin took a deep breath before answering. "Marcellus, when we fought the Helvetii, do you recall seeing any Aeduan warriors actively participating in the battle?"

The question hit him harder than if he'd been stabbed in the gut. At first, he resisted the truth of something until now he hadn't noticed or considered. He had flashes of seeing Aedui warriors arraigned on the heights above the surrounding high ground overlooking the raging battle, but he was too engaged in trying to survive the battle to notice or speculate why the Aedui didn't participate. Tarquin saw the dawning realization on Marcellus's face and hastened to explain.

"I say this not to impugn the integrity and the intention of the Aedui to vacillate concerning their wish to maintain an alliance with Rome. The reality is there was more reason at the outset to believe the Helvetii would prevail which may justify why Diviciacus appeared to take a middle of the road approach in supporting us."

Strabo considered the decurion's observation and reluctantly concluded there may be more truth than he was willing to admit. It was an unwelcome revelation.

The four men were ushered into the tribune's tent and waited for the officer to put down the tablet he'd been reading. Strabo noticed the tribune's uncharacteristic worried expression and wondered what the turma would be ordered to do.

"Caesar has assigned us an unusual task and one requiring immediate attention. Marcellus is aware of the invitation from King Ariovistus to meet in four days midway between here and his camp. The king's offer to meet is conditional. Caesar cannot be accompanied by any infantry, only cavalry. Caesar has agreed, but has thought of a way to satisfy the stipulation and still involve infantry, which is why you're here. He plans to mount 3000 legionnaires from the Tenth Legion. We only have a few days to prepare legionnaires who have probably never ridden a horse or thought they ever would to become cavalrymen — or at least look like cavalrymen."

Strabo glanced at Tarquin's face and saw the decurion's expression of utter disbelief.

"I know what you're thinking, and I confess that was my first reaction as well. Let me say we neither have the time nor permission to argue. The task is not open for debate. This is what we'll do and how we're going to do it. I leave for Bibracte in an hour's time accompanied by Marcellus and an escort of no more than ten men. My purpose in going there is to arrange the loan of 3000 horses. Decurion Tarquin, while I'm gone, I expect you to work with the legion's centurions to find

206

how many legionnaires have at least sat on a horse and knew enough to get it to go and stop without falling off. The decuriae from the other legions will assist you. My hope is we'll find enough legionnaires in the Tenth who can do that much while we concentrate on those who can't. Assuming by late tomorrow I return with the horses, we'll have no more than a day and a half to achieve a miracle before we leave for the meeting site. Decurion, now you may say what you were thinking, but I think our time would be better spent in the details and actions essential for making the plan work."

Tarquin said with an encouraging smile, "Well, at least the legion's officers all know how to ride a horse."

Setarius gave the decurion a sharp look then laughed. "Tarquin, with their help and the sweat off your balls, Caesar will be credited for creating the first mounted legion in the Roman Army."

After Strabo finished, Diviciacus looked at Tribune Setarius and shook his head. "Three thousand saddled horses by tomorrow — impossible. Why, that's more than all the horses here in the settlement. I'll have to reach out to obtain that many. If I had twice the time, I'm not certain I can do it. I'll have to get my brother to help since he owns or controls the vast herds belonging to the Aedui."

"Lord Diviciacus, I know the request is bold, but there is much at stake. Caesar intends to stop further German migration by convincing King Ariovistus to send back to Germania those who have recently crossed into your lands. If he fails, you risk losing your domain the same as you would have if the Helvetii had been successful."

The clan leader listened attentively, and when the tribune finished, he remained silent, looking away as he considered how to respond. When he finally spoke, it was with fatalistic acceptance.

"What you say has too much truth to ignore. It seems the Aedui is at a crossroads when we must choose which master will claim our allegiance. If you will excuse me, I need to confer with Dumnorix. Somehow, we will satisfy Caesar's request."

Setarius realized this was the opportunity to make clear Caesar's concern about the clan leader's wayward brother. "Lord, there's one more thing Caesar wanted me to say to you. He's aware the extent Dumnorix has gained influence as a result of the authority you ceded to him. Regrettably, he used it to advance his own advantage and ambition. It's in the mutual interest of both the Aedui and Rome to say nothing to him concerning the purpose behind Caesar's request. Ariovistus must not know what the horses will be used for. As further insurance, Caesar requests Dumnorix be the one to bring the horses to the Roman camp and remain there as Caesar's guest until the need for them no longer exists. Then he can bring them back to the Aedui."

Diviciacus blanched and said, "Guest or hostage?"

"Caesar prefers guest as a better way to describe his invitation."

"I think hostage may be more accurate. Why is this necessary?"

Setarius cleared his throat. "It is not in the interests of either the Aedui or Rome if Dumnorix decides in his own interests to notify Ariovistus of Caesar's subterfuge. If you recall during the Helvetii campaign, Dumnorix appeared to support their cause more than Rome or the Aedui. On one occasion, he allowed a small Helvetii cavalry force to defeat him even though he had six times the number of Divico's cavalry. Lord, Caesar does not trust Dumnorix unless he is under the watchful eye of Rome and not whispering in the ear of those who seek to dominate Gaul at the expense of the Aedui and Rome."

"I understand. I regret Dumnorix is responsible for the doubt concerning his reliability. My brother fears Rome more than the influence from across our borders. His concerns are not without foundation and shared widely among the tribes in Gaul. Dumnorix and I are blood-related, although common blood does not necessarily mean we believe the same for the future of the Aedui. You may tell Caesar I am his willing ally and will do all I can to support his wishes without interference from my brother. I will convene the tribal council to get support of Caesar's request in the brief time we have to honor it. Tribune, it's late in the day to return to your camp. You are welcome to remain here as my guest."

Setarius stood. "You are most generous although under the circumstances, it might be best if I remain outside the settlement with my escort and less visible to the clan chiefs who may resent Caesar's request."

"Unfortunately, you may be right. Some will interpret the *request* as a *demand* and further evidence of subservience to Rome." Diviciacus stood, turned his attention to Strabo and smiled. "I see by your helmet you have advanced. I am pleased Rome has seen fit to recognize your abilities." He patted Strabo on the shoulder and silently watched the two men leave.

Strabo was surprised Setarius had no objection when he asked permission to return to the Aedui settlement for a few hours under the pretext of spending time with his uncle and other relatives. As he rode toward the main entrance of the settlement, it was apparent from the number of riders heading off in different directions, his uncle was wasting no time in supporting Caesar's request. He hoped Raven was not one of them.

He breathed a sigh of relief when he saw Raven in the small paddock behind her dwelling. She had her back to him as she curried Aquilo. The gray stallion whickered, and Raven turned around. Instead of a welcoming smile, there was a frown and a curious appraisal.

"Raven, I was afraid you wouldn't be here." Her eyes widened, but there was no change in her expression. He dismounted, confused at a welcome different than what he expected. He walked over to her and saw she seemed fixated on his helmet.

"I've been promoted," he said at a loss for anything else to say.

She nodded and tilted her head to one side. "Yes, I can see. I'm glad the Romans have rewarded your ability."

Concealing his irritation at the unenthusiastic response, he attempted to make light of it. "How do I look?"

"Like a Roman," she answered and turned to resume brushing the stallion.

The terse response explained her behavior. "I see, and this is not a look pleasing to you?"

She stopped and turned back to him with a concerned expression. "I'm sorry. I was surprised and almost didn't recognize you." He smiled recalling the last time he heard her say something about not liking surprises. "What do you find amusing?"

"Now I understand how Corius felt after you slapped him."

She looked bewildered until sudden comprehension relaxed her face. Her smile eased the tension between them. She dropped the brush and came close enough to thump him playfully on the chest before wrapping her arms around him. She buried her face in his chest, and said in muffled voice, "I'm sorry, Marcellus. You came here proud of your achievement expecting a joyous reception, and I disappointed you."

He held her tight and realized her comment was true. The promotion had been a surprise not so much because it was unexpected, but because it wasn't long ago, he'd rejected the offer.

She leaned back and said, "You're here about the horses Caesar wants?" He nodded as she added, "I'm told Dumnorix is angry at his brother for putting him in charge and for ordering him to take the horses to the Roman camp. He was furious when he was told to remain there as long as Caesar wants. Already there's speculation why this has happened with some saying he's being punished unfairly by Diviciacus."

"Are you of that mind?"

"It's not for me to judge either one of your uncles or question their decisions. How long can you stay?"

"Not long. The tribune expects me back in a few hours."

She reached up and lifted the helmet off his head. "Now you look like Marcellus, and I think there's time enough."

Strabo sat up, pushed the woolen blanket down and said with genuine regret, "Raven, I have to go, or Setarius will begin to think I'm not coming back."

She pulled him back down and rolled on top of him. "Let him wonder. I would have him spend the rest of his life waiting for you."

Her sensuous movements stilled any protest. He thought there was time left before he had to leave. Moments later, the voice outside calling her name was an unwelcome interruption. Raven cursed and stood up with grim resignation muttering, "It's Talos. I was supposed to ride with him and the others to get horses in the settlements west of here. I'd better talk to him."

In the flickering light of the clay lamp, he watched her walk naked to the table nearby where she had left her clothes. He marveled at her small-breasted figure, slim and muscular yet more sensual than the voluptuous women in Massilia who suffered in comparison. She pulled a woolen shift over her head then walked barefoot outside. Resigned to the reality the interlude was over, Strabo got up and started putting on his clothes while considering whether it was better to wait inside until

Talos left or go outside and face the possibility of an unpleasant confrontation.

He heard Talos ask in a tone somewhere between concern and irritation. "Why didn't you ride with us as you agreed? We waited until Corius said we had wasted enough time."

"I changed my mind and decided not to go."

"Why? You seemed willing enough when Corius told us what we had to do." There was a pause, and Strabo heard the Aeduan say, "I think the owner of the horse with the Roman saddle is the reason."

"Yes, Marcellus is here."

Strabo heard the tribesman curse followed by a soft thump as he dismounted. He decided there was no longer any point in remaining in the dwelling without making it look as if he and Raven were trying to hide the obvious. He put on his helmet and walked outside. He hoped Talos would accept the way it was and leave without causing a scene. An angry confrontation would serve no purpose other than turning an already awkward situation into something they would all regret.

He stepped outside and quickly realized it was not going to end well when Talos came toward him drawing his dagger.

Raven ran toward Talos, arms outstretched, "No, don't do this! There's never been anything between us to justify this."

"Have you been so blind you didn't see how I felt about you?"

"Talos, I swear I did not. I enjoyed your company, and I considered you a friend but no more than I did with the others. It was never my intention to encourage or mislead you."

"It isn't the way I remember during the nights we shared a blanket."

"Talos, it was no more than I did with others on a cold night including my brother when we were children. I never knew how you felt. I'm sorry for both of us and regret this more than you realize. Put the dagger away and leave."

With a stricken look, Talos said, "Whore! You're blind to the Romans' intention to turn Gaul into another province of Rome, and he is part of it. I curse you both. Marcellus, I look forward to the day when you and I meet again, and Raven isn't there to save you."

Standing apart, Strabo and Raven watched the distraught tribesman leap on the back of his horse and ride away.

Raven was the first to speak. "I had no idea he felt that way, and if I had, I would not have encouraged him. He was a friend, and now he calls me a whore. I never imagined something like this would ever happen."

"What about his accusation concerning Rome's intentions for Gaul? I've already learned since coming here, Dumnorix has the same concern. Do you also share the same belief?"

Raven looked away and took her time replying. Strabo thought her hesitation was telling, and it prepared him for the answer she gave.

"There are concerns and speculation why Rome has come in strength to Gaul. There is growing alarm the Romans are here to stay, and the Helvetii threat was an excuse to acquire another province for the glory and prosperity of Rome."

Nettled, he responded more harshly than he realized. "In spite of the losses Rome suffered and the Aedui and other neighboring tribes did not, you have reservations if the rescue was worth the perceived threat of Rome." Her silence was affirmation his conjecture hit close to the mark. "I see. Now the Helvetii threat is over at the cost of over 2,000 Romans killed and three times that wounded in battle, a battle in which no Aedui or other western tribes participated or bled, there is now remorse we're here. I wonder will it be the same after the legions face Ariovistus. He's done more to threaten the sovereignty of the tribes west of the Rhine River than Rome has."

"You talk more like a Roman."

"Perhaps at the moment, I am. As part Aeduan I can see both sides. I confess to a growing suspicion the tribes are using the Roman eagle to protect them at the cost of Roman blood. If I think this way, I wonder if Caesar has similar concerns. If so, will he leave Gaul and let the tribes worry about the Suebi and the other German tribes?"

"Marcellus, we're left to choose between subjugation by the northern tribes or the dominance of Rome. You don't consider there's another alternative. The tribes in Gaul may unite and reject either outcome.

Yes, there are rivalries among the tribes, yet those differences are nothing to the concern for foreign domination by Rome, the Germans or the Belgae. It's possible we would choose the Germans or Belgae over Rome."

Strabo was struck by her calm, practical summarization of the current dilemma facing the local tribes which he assumed until now the Aedui would continue to be closely aligned with Rome. He recalled the hesitant explanations by Corius concerning the dilemma of supporting either Rome or the Helvetii. The thought made him feel more alone.

"Raven, I live between two worlds in a place where I'm being asked to choose to be Roman or Aeduan, a choice that means turning my back on the other. The choice is not simple, and frankly, I'm tired of being expected to decide. I'm beginning to think I won't ever belong in either world."

For the first time, she understood his dilemma, and it softened what she said next. "It's not for me to tell you what you should do. I don't want to be responsible for a decision you will one day have to make with consequences I do not care to think about. I prefer to live in the moment without fear of a future we do not know. I love you, but don't expect more from me than I can give you or any man. Go now. You have your responsibilities, and so do I."

Chapter 22

Astride their horses, Setarius and Strabo looked toward the settlement of Bibracte a mile away and shadowed in the early dawn. Both men were silent, each lost in his own thoughts. The tribune's concern was to what extent the Aedui would deliver the horses, if at all. Strabo's thoughts had nothing to do with horses; it was the last conversation with Raven and the reason he hardly slept.

The silence was broken by the faint sound of activity beyond the settlement, the occasional muted sound of horses neighing, whickering. There was a sound not unlike the distant rumble of a gathering summer thunderstorm gradually growing louder. A shadowy, surging mass came toward them. It was too dark to estimate the size of the herd, but the loudness of the pounding hooves was encouraging.

Setarius was the first to speak. "It looks like Diviciacus has made good on his promise. Caesar will be pleased." He leaned forward and peered more closely beyond the horses and exclaimed, "There's a line of carts following behind. By Jupiter, I hope they're loaded with grain and forage. Until now, I wasn't confident we would get close to what we need."

"It seems we have." Strabo's noncommittal response caught the centurion's attention.

Setarius looked at Strabo and noted the distracted expression on the young man's face. He stifled the sharp rebuke he was about to give. He was reminded of General Strabo's domestic problems with Brigitte, his Aedui wife, who refused to turn her back on the Aedui heritage. The cultural differences between them occasionally erupted in confrontations that threatened an improbable but genuine love match. He saw the possibility the general's son was walking on similar ground. At the risk of interfering in a delicate matter, he took a neutral approach.

"Marcellus, I think your time in Bibracte wasn't what you expected."

Startled, Strabo resented the intrusion and the expectation he was obliged to answer in a personal matter he was trying to process. He had second thoughts and decided the tribune's remark was intended as a friendly overture. He relaxed and found he welcomed the chance to talk about the dilemma he found himself in.

"There's a young woman..."

"Raven?"

"How did you know?"

Setarius laughed. "I may have only one eye, but I see more than most with two. I confess Diviciacus did mention something about her including her name and the fact you've known her from childhood. I gather over the years your interest in her has changed."

"I confess it has. Until yesterday the fact I was a Roman soldier didn't seem to matter to her, or at least I wasn't aware it did. She said one day I would have to decide whether I'm a Roman or an Aedui which seems conditional to a choice I feel no obligation to accept. I cannot change the fact of my birth, and I'm beginning to resent anyone who expects me to be one or the other."

"I don't blame you for feeling that way. I probably would say the same if I had been born in similar circumstances. Perhaps I was, then I'll never know. In a way you're more fortunate than I was and perhaps better served. My mother never told me who my father was. In time, I quit asking when it became clear it no longer mattered, and I no longer cared.

"You mother and father had a deep regard for each other without either one trying to change who they were. You haven't asked for my advice so I'll not give you any. As for me, I'd accept it will be Fortuna who will decide what you will be, what you will do."

Further discussion ended with the arrival of Dumnorix. His disgruntled expression was sufficient to convey what he thought of the task Diviciacus had given him.

Without looking at Strabo, Dumnorix reined in opposite Setarius and said, "The herd numbers 100 more than the 3000 you asked for.

When Caesar no longer has need of them, I expect the same number returned. Any less or too wounded to be of further value will require compensation."

Strabo quickly told the centurion what his uncle said then translated the response.

"The discussion I had with Lord Diviciacus did not include any mention of compensation; therefore, I will leave it for Caesar to consider. You will have opportunity in the days ahead to discuss the matter with him should he be so inclined."

"Tribune, your words border on insolence which your rank does not give you the privilege."

"Lord Dumnorix, my words were not so intended. You are correct; my rank only gives me the authority granted by Caesar. I merely want to make clear it is for Lord Diviciacus and Caesar to determine those things I've neither been empowered to discuss nor given the authority to decide."

Dumnorix flushed and shifted his attention to Strabo. "Marcellus, you resemble your father."

"My Lord Uncle, others have said as much."

"Your likeness is a reminder most disagreeable since I never liked him. I always felt your mother, whom I admired very much, could have done better. I find our family relationship regrettable, more so as I see by your helmet, you've apparently found favor with the Romans and most unexpected. I was led to believe you did not become a Roman soldier by choice. I conclude that is no longer the case."

Speechless over the unexpected and dismissive comments, Strabo watched his uncle ride away and tried to rationalize what he said was prompted by bitterness for being a hostage.

"What did he say?"

"My uncle was making it clear he did not like my father, and it apparently includes me as well. He also thinks my Roman blood is beginning to show too much. I'll try not to lose any sleep over it."

It was mid-morning before Strabo glimpsed Corius and several other scouts helping to keep the herd together and rode toward them. The anxious look on his friend's face suggested Corius may have been avoiding him.

"Corius, I hoped I would see you, but I wasn't sure I would."

"The herd is large. I was on the far side. When I didn't see you, I made my way over here hoping you would be here."

Strabo decided to ignore the feeling Corius was not being entirely truthful. "Is Raven with you?"

"No, she didn't feel like coming."

"Do you know why?"

"She didn't feel like riding. It may be her monthly courses have started." Strabo hoped Corius' speculation was true rather than caused by their tense parting. "Talos told me about the clash between you. I was afraid something like that was eventually going to happen."

"I'm sorry it did. I don't think Raven had any reason to believe he had such strong feelings for her. After what he said, I can understand how he might have come to the belief she did."

Corius remained silent appearing reluctant to comment. Finally, choosing his words carefully he said, "I love my sister, but there could be more truth to what Talos expected than Raven may be willing to admit. I told you before, she has had difficult times caused by trying to decide whether she should be a wife or a warrior. She failed as a wife and chose instead to be a warrior. Raven may never change"

"What of Talos? Do I need to sleep lightly wondering if on a dark night he intends to carry out his threat to run a blade between my ribs?"

"No, I know him too well. He would never do anything like that. Besides he's no longer here."

"What do you mean?"

"Before you came back, he never had strong feelings about the Romans believing they posed no more threat than any foreign tribe. The rift with Raven has changed his mind about Romans, and he's gone to join the Belgae. He's not alone in his changing opinion about

Rome. There are many within the Aedui, including Dumnorix, who share the concern the legions are here to stay."

"I'm aware of how my uncle thinks about Romans." He quickly related how he had parted with his uncle. "Caesar doesn't trust him, and frankly, neither do I."

"Why has Caesar asked for the horses? If he needs more cavalry, why would he not also want the men to ride them?"

Strabo hesitated, careful to answer the questions without revealing Caesar's plan or suggesting there was doubt concerning the reliability of the Aedui. "Caesar intends to find out if legionnaires are as capable on a horse as on the ground."

Corius laughed. "I have great respect for the capability of the Roman infantry, but except for you who we taught how to ride, I think legionnaires will not prove as capable on the back of a horse. I wonder who I will feel sorrier for, the horses or those who will try to ride them."

Strabo nodded in agreement.

Strabo reined in next to Tarquin on top of a low hill observing the progress of 3000 legionnaires from the Tenth Legion separated into several groups according to the legionnaire's capability to ride. By far the largest group consisted of men who were learning how to saddle and mount a horse. From the angry shouts of the cavalry trainers in each group and the cursing of the frustrated legionnaires, he thought Caesar would have been better served with another plan perhaps even risking the reliability of tribal cavalry without Dumnorix's leadership.

Disgusted, Tarquin let loose a string of colorful expletives. "The only one enjoying this spectacle is Jupiter who is looking down and laughing out his godly guts. Have you ever seen anything or imagined anything so hopeless? We've got two days to perform a miracle before these bastards have to ride twenty miles trying not to look as miserable as they do now." The decurion sighed in resignation and pointed to the largest group and said, "Go down there and do what you can to help both the horses and the legionnaires survive this disaster."

219

Stifling a laugh, Strabo saluted and cantered downhill toward several men being roundly berated by a cavalryman for their clumsy attempts. One of the legionnaires stepped forward, gave the smaller trainer a vigorous shove and appeared about ready to do even more.

"Legionnaire, hold fast!" Strabo shouted as he reined in behind the legionnaire and dismounted. "Touch him again, and you'll answer to me in ways you'll have a long time to regret."

The angry legionnaire whirled around in a crouch with clenched fists. His angry look was quickly replaced with open-mouthed surprise when Tertious realized who had given the order. The legionnaire focused on the plumed helmet and managed to stammer, "Marcellus, what..."

"Decurion will do, and I meant what I said. There's no time for the shit you're always ready to give." In a more measured tone, Strabo said, "Look, it's not as difficult to mount as you think. It isn't strength as much as technique. I watched all of you, and now I want you to watch me."

Holding the reins in his left hand, Strabo stood on the left side of his mount facing toward the horse's tail. "While keeping the reins in your hand, grab the left front pommel and lean slightly forward. In one motion while pulling down on the pommel, jump up and twist your body to the left and swing the right leg over the saddle." Strabo dismounted and said, "I make it look easy because once you learn the movement, it is easy. Watch and help each other and see what mistakes are being made. Tertious, you first. I'm going to help you a couple of times to give you a sense of when to begin swinging your leg to get the momentum required for a successful mount."

By the second attempt with his help, Strabo could tell Tertious was on the cusp of getting it right and stepped aside for the third try. It was clumsy, but the legionnaire's relieved expression when he landed in the saddle suggested a confidence lacking earlier. Before long, the large group had been pared down to a few hopeless individuals who would have to depend on a hand-up. He saw Tertious bobbing uncomfortably and felt sorry for the bruising the horse was getting. Thinking more of the animal than the man, he drew rein next to him.

"Tertious, relax and tighten your legs, and you'll feel the rhythm of the horse. It will be better for you and the horse."

The response from the legionnaire was predictable. "You son of a bitch, do you think I care what this nag feels or thinks. I'd rather run my sword in its belly than spend another minute sitting on it. And I don't want any more suggestions from you. Just because you were willing to have Setarius or some other headquarters officer shove it in your backside for a promotion doesn't mean it changes anything between us. The first chance I get, I'm going to split your belly and piss on you while you beg me to finish you."

Strabo laughed. "Considering your past and failed efforts, I can't say I'm troubled."

The angry legionnaire twisted in the saddle to reply causing the horse to stop abruptly. Tertious fell forward over the animal's shoulder and landed hard. He stood up cursing, drew his dagger and headed for the horse standing patiently as it was trained to do. "I've had enough of this shit. I am going to put this blade exactly where I said I would."

Strabo heard and saw what Tertious intended and kneed his horse toward the legionnaire oblivious to anything except to protect the horse. Tertious had just grabbed the reins of the docile horse when Strabo rode into him with enough force to send the legionnaire sprawling on the ground. He dismounted and walked over to where the legionnaire was on his hands and knees struggling to stand up, and clutching the dagger. Livid, Strabo kicked him hard in the belly. Tertious collapsed on his face gasping for breath. He managed to push himself up to his knees before he vomited.

Strabo waited until the legionnaire was able to look up at him with some degree of comprehension before saying, "Consider what I did is nothing more than a gentle reminder for what I'll do to you if I ever see you try or do anything to harm a horse. I'm part Aedui and proud of it. We worship Epona, goddess of the horse. She'll tell me what I'll do to you if I ever see or hear you have offended her." Tertious looked up his dazed expression showing a trace of fear of the granite-faced man standing over him.

"Crawl or walk back to the fort. I'll tell your optio you'll never learn to ride and suggest you be given other duties instead." Strabo took the reins of the other horse and without a backward glance rode toward the encampment.

Chapter 23

The training for those in the Tenth Legion selected for Caesar's escort ended early the next day to prepare for departure two hours after dusk. While progress in the legionnaires' horsemanship was acceptable, General Labienus thought a night move would be less likely to show the Tenth Legion mounted was not the trained cavalry unit it appeared to be. To keep the ruse more credible, the legion would keep the horses at a walk rather than a faster pace and risk an uncontrolled disaster by the novice horsemen.

Strabo wondered how effective the legion would be after an eight-hour ride either mounted or on foot. He thought back to his early days when he was learning to ride and the aching in every part of his body. He knew how miserable the legionnaires were soon going to be.

Tarquin reined in at the edge of the open field at first light and said to Strabo, "The mound where the meeting will take place is just ahead. Ride back and tell Caesar and General Labienus. We made better time than I estimated. The men will have a chance to rest a few hours before the meeting takes place. In the meantime, I'll send scouts out to see if the Germans are planning any unwelcome surprises. Since you will most likely accompany Caesar when he meets with the king, remain with him."

Strabo saluted and cantered back to the legion and reported to Caesar and General Labienus.

General Labienus nodded and said, "As always, Tarquin has led us well, and his counsel is sound." He beckoned to a staff centurion. "Send orderlies to notify the cohort commanders to report here immediately. Once you've done that, ride back and inform General Quintas Atilius where we are. Tell him to position the five other legions three miles behind the Tenth prepared to advance on order."

"Titus, how do you intend to deploy the Tenth?" Caesar asked.

"The three cohorts with the legionnaires who look and ride almost like cavalrymen will take position in front of the tree line. The other cohorts will remain mounted in the trees until I give the order for all

cohorts to dismount. If we're attacked, I prefer we fight on foot as we've been trained to do. The trees will also give us an advantage the Germans won't have."

Caesar nodded in agreement. "Ariovistus wanted only cavalry and no infantry because his infantry is no match against ours. He's depending on his superiority in numbers to negotiate until his strength is even greater. I think our chances are better if we fight sooner rather than later."

Strabo walked his horse over to where Setarius was mounted looking preoccupied. "Salve, Tribune, it's been a long night, and may the gods decide the day will be shorter."

"Careful, Marcellus, what you wish for unless you intend it for the Germans. There's something about this I don't like, and I fear we've been lured into a place and under circumstances not favorable to us."

"What do you mean? Caesar appears to have the measure of Ariovistus and the capability to dictate the outcome."

"Perhaps, but we're on terrain the Germans know and we don't. There's also the fact we're outnumbered this far from the other legions. The vaunted Tenth Legion is not as formidable mounted. The poor bastards have had a bad night, and the day could be worse."

Strabo was shocked at the aging tribune's bleak outlook. "The Helvetii outnumbered us as well, and we prevailed."

"Aye, they did. They were afraid of being conquered by the Germans and the reason they left their lands. They were no match for those brutes. The priests better make their offerings to the gods and make them convincing. We need their help." He paused, looked up at the early dawn sky and shook his head. "I must be getting too old for this. It may be time to spend my nights far from the sound of drums and horns and in the arms of a soft woman who isn't too demanding. Marcellus, Caesar is not only skilled, he's favored by Fortuna, and may she forgive me for doubting him. Enough of that. I see some ground over there looking soft enough for some sleep before we rise to the glory of Rome." Strabo thought it was an excellent idea.

The sun was poised directly above when they heard the muffled sound of horses and the jangle of metal accouterments. Without warning, a large body of horsemen appeared in the distant trees. A murmur arose from the ranks behind him at the fast pace the horsemen were approaching. He heard the centurions and General Labienus calming the nervous legionnaires. The Germans reined in on both sides of the mound in a half circle and remained motionless and ominously silent.

Astride his groomed white stallion, Strabo thought Caesar was suitably impressive. His ornate metal cuirass of silver and bronze glistened in the bright sunshine. His left hand rested on an ivory hilted gladius, and his signature long red cloak was draped over his left shoulder. Strabo thought Jupiter could not have appeared more regal.

Caesar turned in the saddle and said quietly to his small escort, "Ariovistus has made an impressive entrance, and I expect we'll have to wait for him to be sure we've been sufficiently impressed. I'll let the son of a bitch blink and make the first move."

Strabo estimated it had been half past the hour when there was a dissonant blare of a carnyx on the far side of the clearing indicating the German king had waited long enough. Moments later, the stipulated ten-man entourage with King Ariovistus in the lead passed through the ranks of German cavalry and approached the mound at a sedate walk. Caesar waited until Ariovistus stopped at the summit of the low hill before moving forward at a confident, leisurely walk, right fist resting on his hip which was the signal for the *cornicines* and drums behind to begin an accompaniment maintained until Caesar reached the top of the mound.

Riding a pace behind on Caesar's left beside Setarius, Strabo was struck by the Suebian king's imposing presence. He was older than he expected him; his blonde hair cascading down his shoulders was shot with gray. His cruel features combined with a large, muscular build suggested he did not depend on the gold torque circling his neck to confirm and maintain his sovereignty. With a mocking smile, Ariovistus was the first to speak in a voice surprisingly soft with a traditional Roman greeting.

"Salve, Caesar," after which he continued in the Suebian language. "Since it was you who wished this meeting, it seemed you were reluctant to join me. Now that you have, I'm eager to learn the reason."

Strabo attempted to convey the feigned surprise of Caesar's response as he translated.

"King Ariovistus, it was you who requested this meeting. After my previous overtures to meet were rejected, I chose not to pursue the matter. I conclude you reconsidered after realizing the mutual advantages of a meeting. Possibly your emissaries failed to convey clearly the purpose. I am pleased to have the chance to better explain it.

"My Lord King, when you entered Gaul and claimed kingship of a province, Rome did not interfere knowing your presence was at the time acknowledged peacefully by the Aedui who have long been our close allies. As first consul of Rome, I sent you gifts and congratulations to encourage a peaceful relationship with the tribes in Gaul. Circumstances have changed since by the continued crossing of the German Tribes into Gaul. Such crossings without invitation from the local tribes can only be interpreted as a growing threat to a peaceful Gaul. We meet so I can make clear Rome will neither accept further German encroachment into Gaul nor aggression against the Aedui."

Ariovistus sat back in the saddle and pointed an accusing finger at Caesar to punctuate his quick reply. "You accuse me of encroaching in Gaul, yet it was the invitation of the Aedui for me to come here because of their troubles with the Sequani. We came to their assistance in return for tribute and a pledge to intercede in their behalf. Only after we came here and helped them did the Aedui decide our presence is no longer welcome. We were told to return the hostages we held in good faith, and the yearly tribute to pay for our help would no longer be given. These were conditions which were an insult to our pride and the losses we suffered in their behalf. I did not agree to these insulting demands. It is my intent not only to remain in Gaul but to expand our presence. It would seem by your presence here Rome has the same objective. And I say to you, by what right does Rome claim supremacy in Gaul superior to any other kingdom coming here either by right of treaty or battle?"

The animated gestures and the king's angry tirade caused a stir in the German ranks with individual tribesmen riding closer to the mound shouting insults and making threating motions with spear or sword. Some rode past the mound to hurl stones or foot-long weighted darts at the ranks of the mounted legionnaires. Strabo looked behind at the ranks of mounted legionnaires and saw several men on the ground injured by either stone or dart and the ranks threatening to break into disorganized chaos. By the quick actions of the centurions and other more capable horsemen within the formations, calm was gradually restored.

Strabo looked at the king and saw a surprised look flash across his face. He turned and spoke angrily to one of the escorts. Whatever the king said was too soft for him to hear. With a chastened expression, the escort galloped back to the German line. His initial thought the demonstration was planned was replaced with a growing possibility it was not, and the king was angry.

Caesar calmly surveyed the raucous demonstrations and told Ariovistus, "Your tribesmen seem to have spoken for you, and I conclude we are at an impasse; therefore, I see no reason to waste my time any longer." Without further comment, Caesar turned his horse and without looking back, returned to the ranks of the Tenth Legion which despite the threatening actions, remained remarkably calm. Strabo felt an icy feeling in his back waiting for the sudden impact of either an arrow or dart followed by charging cavalrymen.

After reaching the comparative safety of the legion's ranks, Caesar said to General Labienus, "It did not go quite as well as I expected or wanted. I think it will soon prove a lot worse for Ariovistus."

Two days later, Strabo was summoned to Caesar's headquarters. He was curious why. There had been a lull since the initial negotiations with Ariovistus. He didn't think anything had been accomplished by the meeting between the two leaders except to raise more questions concerning the German king's intentions.

Except for minor incidents of skirmishing between the Germanic tribes and patrols from the six legions now encamped near the meeting site, it appeared imminent the situation had become a war of nerves. Even Caesar was affected, and his usual calm demeanor occasionally cracked. His scowls and sharp rebukes for comparatively minor things were uncharacteristic.

Off to one side of the headquarters tent, Strabo saw several dismounted German horsemen each holding the reins of two horses while a dozen other cavalrymen remained in the saddle. He was struck by their docile appearance compared to the recent belligerence demonstrated at the meeting site two days ago.

Tarquin was waiting for him at the entrance to Caesar's tent and visibly relaxed with Strabo's arrival.

"Marcellus, from what we've been able to understand since these bastards approached one of my patrols, they want to talk. Best get on in there and find out what's on their mind."

The guard pulled the tent flap aside as Strabo stepped inside and saw a stone-faced Caesar listening to the two Suebi emissaries trying to make clear why they were there.

Caesar looked at Strabo. "Forget all the diplomatic pleasantries. I have neither the time nor the patience to deal with them. Just tell me what in Jupiter they want."

Strabo listened to the surprising request. When they finished, he summarized what they wanted. "King Ariovistus regrets the unseemly behavior of his men during the recent meeting with the esteemed and noble Caesar. He requests the opportunity to meet again on more friendly and constructive terms."

Strabo translated Caesar's quick response. "It was apparent to me, King Ariovistus was not interested in discussing the future of Gaul except as it was to be determined by him. I am not inclined to give him another opportunity to hear his boastful and false claims for the reason he came to Gaul. His actions regarding the Aedui have not been peaceful, and the manner in which the German presence in Gaul continues to grow does not bode well for Gaul. You may tell King Ariovistus what I told him during our meeting remains unchanged. Unless he agrees to the conditions for retaining a province populated only by the Suebi who came here originally, I consider there is no reason to meet except on a battlefield to decide what will be. He should consider carefully what is best for him and the Suebi. Go and tell your King I will not wait long for his answer."

The angry expressions of the two Suebi emissaries as they left the tent was an indication how Caesar's harsh demands would be received by King Ariovistus.

A visibly relaxed Caesar looked at General Labienus and smiled. "What do you think King Ariovistus is going to do when he hears my answer?"

"He'll make sacrifices to whatever gods he worships after which he's going to tell his clansmen it's time to save Gaul from the terrible Romans. Personally, I think he wants more time to prepare for a war he's apparently not quite ready to start. You've given him no choice. If he backs down, he risks losing the confidence of the Germans and the loss of his crown."

"You've summarized the situation well. To tell the truth, I'm surprised at this latest overture. I expected him to attack rather than ask for another meeting. If I'd been Ariovistus, and anyone told me what I said to him, I would have ordered an attack without delay. The reason he didn't, and why he wants to keep on talking is precisely the one you gave. He's not ready, but I am. Inform the legion commanders and General Crassus to report here with their senior centurions within the hour. Before long we may see how well our new cavalry general has improved the performance of the auxilia cavalry. Who knows, perhaps his concept for tighter Roman control of the auxilia may become a proven model."

Chapter 24

Two miles from Caesars's headquarters, Strabo and Tarquin watched one of the scouts coming toward them slowly and unsteadily on a lathered horse. Tarquin kneed his horse into a canter and reached the scout in time to catch him before he fell out of the saddle. Strabo saw the broken shaft of an arrow protruding from his back.

"Fabius, what happened?"

"The Germans have left their camp and are moving with their supply wagons in this direction. By now they're ten miles from here. We were on our way back to report when we were ambushed. Priscus is dead along with several others. It would have been much worse if Costa hadn't arrived when he did. The Germans withdrew but left many of their warriors behind. Costa sent me back to report while he continues to observe their progress."

Tarquin said, "It appears the fight Caesar was looking for is coming to him. Take him back to the medicus and tell General Labienus. I'm going to join Costa and the others. When you finish your report, come and find me as quickly as you can. I need you. With Priscus gone, you are now in command of what's left of the third decuria."

Tarquin galloped off without waiting for a response leaving Strabo to wonder and worry if he would be equal to the demands. He was painfully aware of his inexperience in leading men. The thought quickly followed it might be the cavalrymen he was soon to lead who have cause to be more worried. He looked at the wounded scout, realizing he was of more immediate concern than misgivings about his capabilities to lead.

Strabo handed his water flask to the wounded man and watched him take a sip. Fabius handed the flask back and said with renewed energy, "I think during the last few miles the thirst was worse than the piece of wood in me. Decurion, if you would do me one more service, give the rest of the flask to my horse. He deserves it for getting me this far." The scout took off his helmet and handed it to Strabo and watched him empty the flask in it. Moments later, the helmet was dry as the flask.

Looking dubiously at the horse, Strabo said, "I don't think he can manage anything more than a walk. Can you make your way back by yourself? I need to ride ahead and alert the legions."

"I agree. I'll take the rest of the way just as slow my four-legged friend wants to go."

Strabo stood waiting to be dismissed and listened as Caesar proposed what Ariovistus might be intending.

"I think he's closing the distance less with the intention of forcing battle than to intimidate. Despite his recent build-up in strength, he saw what happened to the Helvetii, and it's my guess he's not yet ready to risk a battle he's not sure he can win. We'll wait a little longer to see what he intends to do — fight or decide to reconsider my conditions for a peaceful resolution.

"If he chooses to fight, where we're located is suitable terrain. Titus, alert the other legion commanders to double the guard and prepare to march on order. Inform General Crassus what we know. I want to hear his recommendations for deploying the cavalry now and later if Ariovistus decides to fight. He can assume the battle will likely be here or near our present location. Marcellus, rejoin the turma and tell Decurion Tarquin to keep me informed."

Strabo left the headquarters and saw his uncle coming toward him with a welcome expression. Considering their last, unpleasant exchange at Bibracte the week before, he didn't expect anything but the same. He wondered if Dumnorix was going to see Caesar. His uncle answered the unspoken question.

"I saw you ride in, and I've been waiting for you to come out. I wanted to apologize for what I said to you the last time we saw each other. It was uncalled for. I was upset at having to become hostage to Rome, and I directed my anger at you. You are my nephew, and if I was not on good terms with your father, it has nothing to do with you."

Astonished at his uncle's changed behavior, Strabo's relief the rift between them might be mended was tempered by an underlying suspicion his uncle's smile and words were insincere. He resolved to accept the apology and remain wary there was more behind the gesture than affirming blood relationship.

"I'm relieved to hear you say it, Uncle. If you and my father were not friends, it's no concern of mine."

"Are you at liberty to tell me what Caesar has in mind? I'm aware the meeting he had with King Ariovistus did not end on a friendly note. I assume you were there. Is it true?"

Strabo sensed the reason for the friendly greeting was beginning to surface. Concerned his uncle's probing put him in an awkward position, he chose his words carefully. He wished the centurion standing near the entrance to the headquarters could understand Aeduan in the event he was suspected of talking about things beyond family ties.

"I think both Caesar and the king would agree with you."

"What are their intentions? Is there a possibility of a peaceful settlement, or will their differences be settled on a battlefield?"

"It's fair to say either outcome remains a possibility." He didn't add a battlefield was the greater possibility based on the movement of the Germans rapidly closing the distance between the two armies.

Dumnorix frowned and said as much to himself as Strabo, "I see. I'll be held hostage longer than I expected." His uncle slapped his leg in exasperation and said, "I'll speak to Caesar and seek an end to this unbearable bondage. Go and tell him I wish an audience."

"This I cannot do. You exaggerate my position here. I have no voice except when given one, and then it is to speak only the words I'm given. I cannot enter Caesar's tent unless invited. If I did attempt it, I would be refused entry, and any request I made would be ignored."

The Aeduan's eyes narrowed, and he responded in a tone quickly transitioning from cordial to cold. "It seems I assumed your importance was greater than reality. I'll not trouble you again, nephew," and started to turn away.

Strabo looked past his uncle and saw Setarius coming out of the headquarters and said, "Wait, I'll make your request known to someone who, if he wishes, can intercede in your behalf. Give me a moment, and I'll see what I can do." Strabo walked over to the tribune and quickly summarized why his uncle wanted to speak to Caesar.

Setarius rolled his eyes and swore under his breath prepared to say no and concluded it was for Caesar to decide.

"Wait here, I'll see if he's in the mood to deal with this." The tribune returned faster than Strabo anticipated with an order Caesar wanted to see him before he agreed to see Dumnorix.

Strabo cautioned his uncle to wait until he learned what Caesar intended even as he wondered why his uncle's request would be influenced by anything he had to say. He followed Setarius inside and immediately saw the irritated look on Caesar's face and regretted he was once again caught between two conflicting loyalties.

Caesar wasted no time in preliminaries, and the fact he addressed him by his rank underscored his displeasure. "Decurion, are you taking advantage of your position to intercede for your uncle, or is he the one taking advantage of you?"

"He thinks I have influence I do not. I told him I would not ask you to see him. I saw Tribune Setarius and relayed my uncle's request. I have no relationship with my uncle except as it was achieved through the marriage of my father and mother. Unlike my elder uncle and my father who had a mutual regard, the same cannot be said for Dumnorix and me. My father and grandfather evidently didn't trust him. They thought he was ambitious with less regard for the Aedui than his own welfare. I share my father's opinion."

Caesar nodded and appeared satisfied with the explanation. "Marcellus, it seems I have the same opinion of your uncle." He, frowned and reluctantly said, "Bring him here, and I'll hear what he has to say. I regret I cannot say or do what I'd like to because of what I pledged to his brother. Diviciacus is convinced his brother has great influence within the tribe. He's worried he may try and reclaim leadership of the Aedui. It's an outcome neither the Aedui nor Rome can afford to risk."

After Caesar made it politely clear the brief meeting was over, Strabo followed his fuming uncle outside. Gradually, Dumnorix calmed down, and when he spoke, it was with an icy calm.

"Marcellus, apparently I have no choice but to endure this humiliation. I look forward to the day when I see an end to Roman influence in Gaul. I would rejoice to be the one to kill the last Roman in these lands. Nephew, you've made very clear the differences between us. I will ask the gods that you be spared when the Romans are defeated."

Chapter 25

Strabo drove the horse hard concerned and apprehensive for what he faced when he caught up with the turma and took command of what was left of the third decuria. He didn't know any of the cavalrymen he was about to lead. Many of the cavalrymen were a decade older or more than he was and with experience in battle that made him feel even more inadequate. The latter was balanced by an exhilaration and an anticipation for the challenge ahead. He focused on the reality of the moment when he passed a string of tethered horses with the bodies of dead cavalrymen draped over their backs. There were more casualties than Fabius reported.

He drew rein next to Tarquin and said, "Caesar is aware of the situation and alerted the legions. He's not certain what Ariovistus intends to do. Our orders are to observe and report whatever the Germans do."

Tarquin nodded. "As you can see, Third Decuria suffered more losses than Fabius told us. Costa is up ahead keeping an eye — a distant eye on the Germans. I made it clear, he's not to engage unless absolutely unavoidable. The last thing we need right now is to risk another engagement like the last one. Caesar could be right about the Germans putting up a bluff, but given what they did to the turma, it doesn't look like bluffing to me. Take what's left of your decuria and replace the section Costa has scouting to the north and north west. His section will then rejoin the First Decuria patrolling in the south and southwest. I'll remain with you until we're both comfortable you're ready. There are things you haven't had much opportunity to learn. As the Germans allow, our time together will give me a chance to catch you up on the difference between being a cavalry leader and a legionnaire."

"I appreciate your help. The Germans are providing the incentive to learn quickly."

"I'm counting on Ursinus to help you make the transition. He's the senior ranker in the troop and will be the one you'll come to depend on. He takes care of the men but barely tolerates officers. He has his faults, and he's difficult to get along with. He'll give you reasons every day to discipline him. It's better for you, and me, to find ways to settle differences without formal disciplinary measures. There he is over there." Tarquin gestured to a burly, lantern-jawed man with simian features. He caught the attention of the cavalryman and waved him over.

"Ursinus, this is Decurion Strabo. He now commands the Third Decuria. I want you..."

Giving Strabo an intense look, Ursinus bluntly interrupted the decurion and asked a question without prefacing it with a respectful *Sir.* "There's talk you're General Lucillus Strabo's son. Is it true?"

Strabo saw no reason to deny what apparently was fast becoming common knowledge. "Yes, it is."

"Thought as much. You look like him. I served with him in the Tenth. He gave me five lashes for assaulting an optio." To Strabo's surprise, the cavalryman laughed before continuing. "The general said if I'd killed the cowardly son of a bitch and saved him the trouble of having to deal with it, he would've given me a medal instead. Any other general would've sentenced me to the castigato and a discharge for hitting the bastard. For an officer, particularly a general, he wasn't half bad."

Out of the corner of his eye, Strabo saw Tarquin's resigned expression and with effort restrained the urge to laugh.

"Ursinus, I'll consider your opinion of my father most complimentary, and I hope in the days to come I'll live up to any expectations you may have of me. Decurion Tarquin told me you're an asset to the troop and to depend on your experience in the time ahead. This I will gladly do. I want the decuria assembled before we move out. There are a few things I want to say to them."

Ursinus nodded and said before leaving, "Good, the men need a few words. Keep it short. They aren't in the mood for a long speech."

Strabo waited until the cavalryman was far enough away to say, "I think you prepared me very well. I believe Ursinus and I will get along just fine."

"I hope so. Listen and pay attention to what he has to say, and you'll be a better officer for it. By the way, when we have time when we're not fighting Germans, we need to make up for our losses. There may be some legionnaires in the Tenth Legion whose experience in the last few days might encourage some who can ride to volunteer. Higher pay and a chance to ride instead of marching into battle might get us a few replacements."

Strabo smiled when he thought there was one individual in the *Claudia* Legion who would jump at the chance to get off his feet and on the back of a horse. Would Vinicius be ready to follow his orders without preferential treatment? If not, he would remain a legionnaire.

Late in the day six miles from the Roman encampment, the Germans stopped and prepared defensive positions for the night. At dawn the next day, they resumed the march. Tarquin left to take his position midway between the two other decuriae, an indication he was satisfied with how the Third Decuria was functioning under new leadership.

Standing on a knoll observing the German scouts, Strabo frowned as he saw them a mile away begin to turn southeast. He turned to Ursinus and said, "Send a rider to Decurion Tarquin and inform him the Germans are changing course, and if they maintain it, they'll pass west of the legions."

Ursinus grunted in what sounded like an acknowledgement, and moments later, a rider was galloping off in the direction where Tarquin was positioned. The sudden change in the direction the Germans were going was unexpected. Until now, the logical assumption was Ariovistus was taking a direct approach to the Roman encampment with the intention to fight. Strabo thought what seemed obvious hours ago was now open to question. Ursinus interrupted further speculation by pointing at horsemen in the trees a few hundred yards to the north and closing fast.

Strabo turned to the horn-blower and was about to order the call to rally to the standard when he recognized the distinctive facial paint and shield designs favored by the Aedui. Corius was in the lead. He quickly scanned the ranks and saw Raven was among them. He rode ahead to meet the Aeduan scouts ready to give a welcome greeting. The serious expression on his friend's face indicated there was more to this than a chance encounter. Corius wasted no time in preliminaries.

"A huge combined cavalry and infantry force is following far behind the German advance of five or six thousand cavalry that passed by an hour ago. I think they're intent is to make you believe their advance is all they have. There's more. Diviciacus believes they are changing direction and moving to the southwest to cut off any support the Aedui can provide from Bibracte. We will continue to watch and report what they do. Diviciacus wants Caesar to know the Aedui are ready to join him on the battlefield when the time comes. He has 5000 cavalrymen camped southwest of here where the legions camped before moving to where they are now. He will remain there until told when and where to take them."

Strabo turned and shouted for Ursinus. When he arrived, he quickly summarized the situation and told him to inform Tarquin of the development.

"Corius, I think you and my uncle are serving Caesar well."

"I wish you good fortune both for Rome and the Aedui." Strabo watched them ride off. He glimpsed Raven who acknowledged him with only a quick wave.

When Ursinus returned, Strabo said, "The day's getting long, and I think the Germans will soon prepare a night camp. We'll do the same and see what the Germans will do tomorrow."

Caesar watched the scout leave after reporting the Germans were making camp three miles to the southwest. The location confirmed his suspicion Ariovistus was there to prevent Aedui support he was dependent upon. He thought Ariovistus was doing exactly what he would be doing if their roles were reversed. He was satisfied Diviciacus' pledge apparently was sincere and a welcome sign of a steadfastness that had so far been more artfully promised than delivered. He had started to doubt the value of the Aedui to Rome based on the deep divisions within the tribe exemplified by the political difference between Diviciacus and his brother.

So far, maintaining a close watch on Dumnorix appeared to have accomplished the objective of helping Diviciacus to keep the Aedui favorable to Rome. The delicate political alignment within the tribe was a risk he needed to consider carefully for whatever circumstances Rome might face. He hoped Diviciacus remained strong, or in addition to the Germans, he could be threatened by Aeduans more loyal to Dumnorix than his brother. It was better to prepare for such an eventuality than regret later he didn't.

"Otho, send a messenger to the legion commanders and General Crassus. I want them and their senior centurions here for a consilium at first watch."

After summarizing what was known considering the current location and presumed German intentions, Caesar concluded by saying, "We'll prepare for battle tomorrow by remaining where we are even though I don't believe he's ready to fight. If he does, the terrain here is suitable. Considering his greater strength, my offense will be a strong defense. I'll let him make the first move. The legions will form three battle lines forward of our camp. Each legion will leave at least one cohort behind inside the fort to secure the baggage. Titus, work out the details with the other legion commanders.

"General Crassus, the auxilia cavalry will screen the flanks and east toward the Rhine River to ensure Ariovistus is not reinforced. Gentlemen, give me your thoughts and recommendations to better prepare and meet what Ariovistus plans for tomorrow and the days to come."

For the next half-hour, Caesar listened attentively to what they had to say. He gave an opportunity for each attendee to comment and voice an opinion. It was no surprise to him that the way he had described the situation, little dissent was voiced in the course of action he described earlier. Experience had taught him a plan had more chance of being successfully followed if the participants felt they had been given a chance to have their say. He gave particular attention to General Crassus who had remained comparatively silent; his furrowed brow indicated there was something bothering him. Caesar had a good idea what it was, and if he was right, it would be the same concern he also had. He purposely remained vague concerning the involvement of the Aedui to see how the young general would react to the potential risk of the tribe's support.

"General Crassus, I sense you have concerns. You are new to our council, but you're here because of the role the Auxilia will play when and how we fight the Germans."

Crassus nodded, relieved at the invitation to speak his mind. "You suggested the Aedui is ready with a cavalry force of 5000 to screen and defend our northwestern flank. My clear understanding was the auxilia cavalry under my command would be responsible for that mission as well as the northeastern flank. I'm also confused when you used the word *ready*. Do we have confidence they'll be *ready* to fight for us and not the Germans?"

"Publius, by your question, you've come to the crux of the matter. We have a dilemma. Until recently, the Aedui have been a staunch, loyal ally of Rome for many years. Diviciacus, the former and once again current tribal chieftain, has a tenuous hold on maintaining a reliable alliance with Rome. I criticized Diviciacus for his less than significant support during the Helvetii campaign. He's acknowledged as much, and I believe his present overture is an attempt to overcome my doubts for the reliability of the Aedui."

"By your leave, I want to send one of my centurions to meet with Diviciacus or whoever he appoints to command his cavalry. I want to ensure his cavalry deploys in coordination with my auxilia. We must make certain we're working together and not at cross purposes out of ignorance of what the other is going to do and where they will be."

"I agree and approve your request for precisely the reasons you've given." Caesar surveyed the generals. "The Germans are the adversary we face now, and one I'm confident we will defeat. My concern is less for what happens tomorrow or the next few days or any doubt we will prevail, but for the longer outcome of Rome's influence. Control of Gaul is dependent on maintaining reliable alliances with key tribes such as the Aedui. We depend on the Aedui to counter a growing hostility to Rome for which Dumnorix is much to blame. While I trust Diviciacus, I cannot say the same for many of the other Aedui tribal leaders. Therein lies my dilemma.

"I can't afford to risk further erosion of the Roman-Aedui alliance by denying the assistance of Diviciacus. Neither can I accept assistance that has the possibility it will hinder our efforts to defeat the Germans as Publius so clearly pointed out. The Aedui support may be token and less than we require in the belief an outcome favorable to Ariovistus may be more advantageous to them. I hope not.

"I want to pursue this matter in more detail with General Labienus, General Crassus and Tribune Setarius. The rest of you may leave to prepare your commands."

Caesar, energized and focused, went straight to the point.

"While I would have welcomed Aedui support with pleasure a few days earlier on the eve of a possible battle, my concern is not it will fail to appear, but that it will result in uncoordinated support Publius highlighted that could do more harm than good. Even worse is if the Aedui decide to depose Diviciacus in favor of Dumnorix and support Ariovistus instead. Publius, I won't restrict your planning nor your decisions how to deal with an Aedui contingent. You might consider giving the Aedui cavalry the responsibility for the far northwest flank and along the Rhine River in the event Ariovistus has additional reinforcements waiting to cross. Deployed in such manner will allow you to concentrate your cavalry closer to the legions." Caesar frowned and asked, "Have you had any interaction with Diviciacus since you assumed command of the Auxilia cavalry?"

"I have not. Apart from being present on occasion when he visited the headquarters, I've exchanged no more than polite conversation concerning his time in Rome and his time spent with my father."

"I thought as much. If I'm correct, Ariovistus is not ready to commit for reasons I can only speculate. There may be time for you, or one of your officers, to assess his intentions and coordinate any support he may contribute in a manner that benefits rather than interferes. Although he speaks Latin well enough, he'll have councilors who do not. In which case, whomever you send would not have the benefit of understanding any discussions he may have with them. Do you have anyone in the Auxilia who speaks and understands Aedui?"

"It's possible I do, but I would have to confirm it."

"Flavius, send word to Decurion Tarquin that I want Decurion Strabo to report here early tomorrow to accompany General Crassus or whomever he chooses to send to meet with Diviciacus. Publius, you may have seen the decurion here on occasion serving as translator; however, you may not know his father is General Lucillus Strabo and Diviciacus his uncle. His familial connections make him doubly useful to our needs."

Strabo arrived at the headquarters disappointed at once again being relegated to translator instead of leading his decuria. He reluctantly conceded the men might be better served under the more experienced Ursinus in the event the Germans decided to do more than march. The one positive for going to the headquarters was the possibility of seeing Vinicius and encourage him to request a transfer.

He saw an auxilia cavalry escort waiting nearby. He drew rein and dismounted close to where Tribune Setarius was talking to General Crassus. As he walked his horse toward the three men, he noted the tribune's creased brow. Standing next to the general was a centurion who appeared to be about the same age as Crassus. The centurion watched him approach with a bemused expression. He saluted and waited silently for one of the senior officers to acknowledge him. Setarius finally paused to make the introductions.

"General Crassus, I believe you may already know Decurion Strabo. Centurion Drusus, Decurion Strabo will be your guide and translator. Caesar has come to rely on his experience and capabilities."

General Crassus nodded. "Decurion Strabo, I remember you very well, especially how well you can ride. I appreciate your assistance."

General Crassus and the centurion walked away toward the escort where the two were quickly engaged in animated conversation. He saw the general's perplexed expression quickly transition to a smile followed by an outburst of laughter.

In a quiet voice, Setarius said in disgust, "Marcellus, I'm depending on you to see the newly-made centurion carries out his mission. Until now, I had more confidence in our young general of cavalry. To entrust a man so obviously inexperienced to accomplish the purpose of the meeting with Diviciacus is troubling. I hope there are hidden qualities the general knows about Drusus I don't see."

"How long has he been in Gaul?" Strabo asked.

"He arrived here a few days ago and has yet to see the Germans much less engage them."

"On the brief occasions I've seen and talked with General Crassus, I was impressed with him. It's difficult for me to believe he would select someone not capable."

"I hope you're right. It's a thirty-mile ride to Diviciacus' camp. Best you remind them."

Strabo saluted and approached the two men to tactfully suggest it was time to leave.

A mile from the fort, the centurion turned to Strabo and said, "Decurion, we've met before, but apparently you don't remember."

Thoroughly embarrassed, Strabo replied, "If we have, I regret my poor memory."

"I'm not surprised. It was a long time ago, and we were both young — and you were much younger than I was. I must confess I wouldn't have recognized you either. It was only after Tribune Setarius mentioned your name before you arrived then confirmed you're

General Strabo's son. It was a long time ago at my father's villa outside Rome. You and your father were guests, as was Marcus Crassus and his sons Publius and younger brother, Marcus."

Suddenly, he remembered. It had been during the only occasion he ever visited Rome. As a surprise, his father took him there to show him a far more affluent and influential Roman society than existed in Massilia.

"By Jupiter, it was the race."

"Yes, how could you forget something which to this day I would rather not recall for the way it ended. Publius Crassus didn't remember either until I reminded him just before we left the fort."

"I was about seven at the time, skinny and half the size you and the Crassus brothers were."

"The three of us were preparing to race our horses when your father suggested you be allowed to participate and bet my father fifty denarii you'd win. We all laughed except you and your father. I felt sorry for you and thought it was cruel of him to subject you to both the risk and ridicule sure to follow. When my father realized General Strabo was serious, he no longer thought the idea was amusing and tried to stop the race. The general smiled and assured him there was nothing to worry about unless the wager was too much to lose. Your father took off the saddle already on the horse provided and lifted you up on its back. At first, we held back to give you a chance to keep from being completely humiliated. Too late, we realized you really could ride. By then, you were too far in front to catch. I can still see the look of disbelief on father's face when he handed over the purse."

With a wide grin, Strabo said, "Centurion, I've been riding bareback almost before I could walk. If I'd been in a saddle, I probably would've fallen off."

There was a momentary silence between them, each thinking about the episode a long time ago.

It was the centurion who was the first to speak. "Tribune Setarius seems to have a very high opinion of you. I wonder, given who your father is, why you aren't a centurion, not suggesting the rank of decurion isn't important."

"A few days ago, I was no more than a legionnaire in the ranks of the *Claudia* Legion, conscripted against my will with the help of my father." Strabo briefly described the circumstances.

"And were you the wastrel he thought you were?"

"Looking at it from the perspective of my father, I suppose I gave him enough reason to believe it. Our relationship has not been good since my mother died. After I refused to entertain the possibility of a military or political career, it got worse."

"Apparently you've done well in spite of coming into the army the hard way."

"I suppose although at first all I wanted to do was find a way to leave without caring what consequences I might face if I was unsuccessful."

"It sounds as if you've changed your mind."

"Not entirely, but it's crossed my mind perhaps I made a mistake in refusing to take advantage of my father's influence to become a centurion rather than a conscript." Strabo thought about what he just said and added quickly, "I did not mean to give offense by inferring why you're a centurion."

Drusus laughed. "None taken because it's the truth. I put it off as long as I could until Publius asked me to come out here, and father insisted I accept. Frankly, I didn't have a good reason to say no without others, including me, thinking I was reluctant to face the reality of a battlefield." He gave Strabo a searching look and asked, "Setarius told me — his words — you've been blooded. What's it like?"

"I'm not sure I know the answer yet. The first time isn't as bad as the next probably because you don't know exactly what's going to happen or how you will react. Fortunately, fear comes mainly before and after the battle, not during when there's no time for deep thinking, only quick reactions."

Strabo noticed the dust cloud several miles ahead and the faint blaring of horns and thought it might be time to change the subject. "Sir, unless I'm mistaken, ahead is the German vanguard moving southwest to put themselves between Bibracte and where the legions are camped. I suggest we leave the road here," pointing south, "and head toward those hills. We can wait there until they pass. From there, it will take longer to get to our destination, the alternative is to risk running into the Germans."

"I agree." Drusus gave the order to the turma commander. "I trust you know the way."

Strabo smiled. "I believe I do. Too bad the road here is straight and even. If circumstances were different, I'd challenge you to a race to those trees up ahead."

"Careful, Decurion, I may have improved since the last time we raced. You're also in a saddle and a lot bigger than you were then."

They were close to the hills when they saw a wide stretch of broken ground and trampled grass indicating where the Germans had passed. Prompted by what Corius had told him the day before, Strabo said, "There's a chance not all the Germans have passed." He pointed to a dense grove of trees on a hill nearby. "I suggest we wait in those trees to make certain they have."

"What makes you think they haven't?"

"Yesterday, one of the Aeduan scouts reported a large combined infantry and cavalry force is following an advance of 15,000 Germans. I think that's what just passed by. If the Germans are maintaining the same distance between the advance and the main force, the German army has yet to come this far. We'll wait to make sure."

"Did the scout estimate the size of the main force?"

"He didn't get close enough to see clearly. He said it was *huge*. Caesar estimates Ariovistus has between 60 and 70,000 infantry and cavalry. The number may have increased half again if the report is true one of the larger German tribes has joined Ariovistus."

Drusus cursed and said as much to himself as to Strabo, "They number a lot more than our legions and auxilia."

"We faced about similar odds with the Helvetii and beat them."

"Perhaps, but I'm told our legions and cavalry suffered significant casualties."

Strabo knew the centurion was right. "All the more reason to have the help my uncle can provide and use it effectively."

For several minutes the two officers remained silent lost in their own thoughts. Strabo thought back to the morning just before the battle at the Saône River crossing when Raven criticized the Roman organized approach to the battle so different to the Aedui. This was a good time to tell the centurion something about the Aedui and how they fought in comparison to the Roman Army.

"Centurion, to better prepare how to deal with the Aedui, it might help if I explain how the Gauls, including the Aedui, fight. It's very different from the Roman way. For a Gaul, his focus is a personal matter, fought less for a large purpose than to gain and maintain honor and prove how brave he is. The latter makes him a formidable individual adversary. But this approach undermines their capability to fight as an organized unit in the way Roman legions are trained to do. They are quick to initiate battle and just as quick to leave it when individual objectives are satisfied, particularly if the opposing force is relentless and organized. The difficulty you face is to accept the fact they will listen carefully and agree to whatever you have to say. You must understand, they will not change the way they fight. In short, tell them what you want them to do but be careful how you tell them. They are quick to take offense"

"What you say is helpful, and it is much what General Crassus told me in dealing with the auxilia. Fortunately, the main purpose of the meeting is to avoid close contact with our auxilia cavalry to minimize the risk of confusing the Aedui with the Germans. Crassus has in mind a mission for them both helpful to us and an opportunity to avoid such a problem."

"I'm relieved to hear it."

Their conversation was interrupted when both heard the familiar sound of pounding hooves.

Strabo said. "It could be the German main force the Aedui scouts reported,"

From their concealed position in the trees, the two men watched in amazement at the long, wide column of mounted horsemen with a warrior running along beside each horse, clutching either the rider's right leg or the horse's mane.

"Look at the size of those bastards on foot," Drusus said. "I'd been told they were big, but I thought the description of them was exaggerated. You were right to come this way. We wouldn't have had a chance if they caught us in the open country in the direction we were going."

They waited for almost half an hour until the last contingent passed by to mount up and continue their journey. Strabo motioned to the hills ahead. "Those are the foothills of the Jura Mountains. If we go on the way we are, we won't reach the Aedui camp until after nightfall. I suggest we return to the original route I intended and risk the possibility all of the German rear body hasn't passed."

"I agree time is critical. The quicker we get there the better."

A few miles beyond where the Germans had passed, they reached the crest of a low hill and saw the point scouts frantically galloping back toward them. Strabo saw the reason. A group of horsemen appeared on the opposite hill. The centurion commanded the turma to halt and form line in preparation for a battle there was no chance to win or avoid. He looked at Drusus and was impressed with his calm reaction to what seemed a potentially hopeless situation. A moment later, Strabo breathed a sigh of relief when he identified a familiar standard.

"Centurion, we've been spared a long journey. The rider in the lead is Corius, a close friend from long ago." Far behind both men, he saw Raven's distinctive black hair so different from the blond and red-hair, prevalent with the men. "Diviciacus is the rider just ahead of the large green standard with the branching oak tree. My uncle is a druid, and the oak tree has great meaning for them."

"I thought druids were priests."

"They are. They can also occupy high positions including clan and tribal leadership as Diviciacus does."

Strabo greeted Corius warmly when he and those behind drew rein opposite the line of auxilia cavalry.

"Centurion Drusus," motioning to Corius, "this is Corius, senior scout of the Aedui." As Diviciacus came forward and stopped a length ahead of the scout, he introduced Drusus to the tribal leader.

"Centurion Quintus Drusus is Caesar's senior representative here to speak with you concerning your offer to support Caesar."

Diviciacus, always gracious and ready with a smile, said in clear but accented Latin, "I recall the name Drusus. Would you by chance be related to Senator Cornelius Drusus whom I was privileged to know when I went to Rome two years ago?"

The response came as a complete surprise to the centurion who managed to recover his aplomb and respond, "I'm his eldest son. I had no idea there was anyone this far from Rome who would know the name Drusus."

"The might of Rome and those who have been instrumental in making it so are known even this far from the Tiber." With self-deprecating humor, Diviciacus added, "Of course, there's also the practical advantage of securing friendship and assistance when needed. I believe our present situation with the Germans is reason enough to have justified a long, arduous trip to Rome. I assume you're here for the same reason I am, to provide support without risking misunderstandings regarding how this will be accomplished."

Strabo saw the centurion visibly relax reassured there was a mutual understanding for the reason they were there.

Diviciacus continued. "As tribal leader and at my age, I confess I'm now better qualified to settle matters more of a political nature than martial; therefore, I will rely on Corius to consider what you have to say and speak with authority on my behalf for whatever is necessary to defeat the Germans."

Strabo was pleased at how quickly concerns on both sides were resolved with Diviciacus in agreement to go northeast around the left of the Germans to prevent any reinforcements crossing the Rhine. Secondary to the mission was to attack the German rear as circumstances and opportunity warranted. Once the details to include simple recognition signals were settled, there was no longer reason to delay returning to report the outcome to General Crassus. They parted soon after on diverging routes.

As they turned back the way they had come, Strabo was puzzled Raven hadn't taken the opportunity to talk to him. It was almost as if she was avoiding him. He considered the last time they were together, and what he remembered most was her subdued reaction when she saw his plumed helmet. He wondered if in a subtle way she was putting distance between past, present and a future that didn't include him. If true, he was almost as relieved as disappointed.

Several hours later a few miles from the Roman encampment, Strabo spotted horsemen in the trees ahead and recognized Costa and his decuria when they came into view. The decurion looked back when he heard Strabo's shout and changed direction.

"Centurion, Decurion Costa is with the turma I'm assigned to. Since we're so close to the encampment, I request permission to join them."

"I see no reason why you can't. I'm quite certain we can find our way from here without too much difficulty. Go with my thanks. I look forward to an opportunity to know you better." Drusus smiled and added, "I also think you owe me and Publius Crassus a chance to redeem ourselves."

"I'm afraid I don't have the *denarii* my father had to bet on the outcome of our last race. I think, however, my father would willingly back my end of the wager."

"Then it's settled and only to await the more pressing business of defeating the Germans."

Strabo saluted and rode away already wondering if Raven would consider loaning him Aquilo if and when the opportunity came.

Chapter 26

Sitting on a log eating a hard biscuit and washing the tasteless ration down with equally stale water, Tarquin was exhausted as he watched Strabo riding toward him. He had no resentment for the young decurion advancing faster than he had and undoubtedly destined for more than he had any hope to achieve. He felt vaguely uncomfortable he was the one who pressed Setarius into getting the legionnaire transferred to his turma, not just because he thought Strabo had the qualities to be decurion, but the Strabo name for the potential influence it might have to help him go higher. Currently, his prospects for b higher rank were remote unless Fortuna intervened. The thought struck him maybe she already had when Strabo joined the turma.

He greeted Strabo with a tired smile and a caustic greeting he immediately regretted. "Salve, Marcellus, are you able to assure us the Aedui are willing to provide tangible support, or will they remain on the sidelines offering only prayers?"

Strabo curbed his anger and the urge to say something he was bound to regret. He knew Tarquin was just as tired as he was and nothing would be gained by a sharp and pointless exchange. He settled for a quick summary of the results of the meeting with Diviciacus before saying, "Costa told me the Germans are camped three miles southeast."

The decurion nodded. "Ariovistus ignored the legions all lined up and Caesar's invitation to see who can piss the farthest. Considering how many Germans there are compared to what we have, I can't understand why the German son of a bitch didn't pull out his cock and settle it right there. Caesar, possibly more than Ariovistus, may be sleeping better tonight hoping there's a chance to settle things with a parley. If so, could be better for us — what I saw going past us today tells me the odds don't look too friendly for the Roman gilded bird."

"What are the orders for tomorrow?"

Tarquin lifted his shoulders and yawned before answering, "Not much change from what we did today. Caesar's going to have the legions stand to as they did today in case the Germans get more interested in having a pissing contest. For us, no change. We keep on scouting the flanks and rear. Costa may have told you the few German scouts they saw turned tail. We'll see how things are tomorrow."

The decurion thumbed over his shoulder and said, "You'll find Ursinus about a hundred yards back. He'll have things under control. Get some sleep. We'll be busy tomorrow, maybe more than we were today." He hesitated and added, "Shit, I hope so."

Leading his horse, Strabo stumbled through the trees under the dim light of a waning moon. He heard a horse whicker. A shadowy form stepped in front of him, and he recognized Ursinus's guttural voice.

"Decurion, I didn't expect to see you back tonight."

"Neither did I. It's been a long day, perhaps longer for you more than me. Turn in. I'll take the first and second watch. I need to see to my horse, and I have some thinking to do. Show me where you'll be so I can wake you."

There was an unintelligible grunt from the cavalryman Strabo interpreted as acceptance followed by, "I'm over there." He pointed to a large tree a few feet away.

Strabo unsaddled the horse and reached for the water bladder balancing his personal baggage on the opposite side of the saddle. After removing his helmet, he poured a substantial amount into it and waited patiently for the horse to satisfy its thirst. Hours later, he was wide awake when Ursinus relieved him. He was no closer to deciding his future which was becoming more complex and undecided since his first day in the Massilia training camp.

Slowly shaking his head, Caesar looked at General Labienus and the others. "It's been five days, and every day I've offered him the chance to fight. The bastard only sits in his camp and sends out some cavalry to chase our scouts around without any serious effort to engage. Titus, it makes no sense. If I were in his position with the strength he has, what was left of the Roman Army in Gaul would be halfway to Genava by now. Maybe it's time to quit waiting for him to make the first move and do something he can't back away from. I welcome any ideas."

The following discussion was brisk and included recommendations to assault the German camp in multiple ways to using the same tactics the Germans were using by disrupting their supply line. Caesar grew increasingly impatient with launching reckless attacks or a prolonged siege which allowed the Germans a better chance to win the stalemate. He finally spoke up and ended what was fast becoming an inconclusive debate.

"This is what we'll do. Tomorrow, all six legions less enough cohorts to defend this camp, will march to a place close to the German camp. Four legions will lead with arms only and rations for one day. The two other legions, in addition to arms and rations, will take four light *ballistae* and equipment to construct a fort within *ballista* range of the German camp. While the fort is being built, the other four legions will remain under arms in three defensive lines. General Crassus, the auxilia will provide protection of both flanks. The purpose for building the fort is to provoke an attack. Ariovistus can't refuse to fight without making him look like a coward. Now, I invite your comments."

Caesar's offer was met with an uncomfortable silence. It was left for General Labienus to respond tactfully. "The plan is bold with perhaps some risk without already entrenched forts to move into should it become necessary."

"It's a risk I'm willing to accept. The entrenching will cease if Ariovistus attacks in force; the outcome will be ours to win and the Germans to lose."

The general swallowed and asked, "Is it your intent to occupy the fort if the Germans choose not to fight?"

"I'll decide when the time comes. The main reason for the fort is to goose Ariovistus in the ass enough to make him fight." There were no more questions. "General Labienus, I'll take position in the center with the Tenth. I'll leave you to attend to the details." Caesar left the tent for his quarters with a smile when he heard the sudden clamor erupt behind him.

Strabo watched the legions march off with trumpets blaring and standards glistening in the early morning sunlight. He had mixed feelings concerning what the legionnaires were going to face in the bloody battle sure to follow. He was uncomfortable that he and the other legionary turmae were going to risk far less by being ordered to scout farther out on the flanks. Tarquin gave the order, and the two turmae assigned to scout the right flank cantered off in the direction Drusus sent the Aeduan cavalry.

They were barely out of sight of the fort when Ursinus shouted and pointed ahead toward a large gathering of dismounted horsemen far outnumbering them. Their distinctive knotted hair identified them as Germans. What was puzzling was when the Germans saw them, they mounted in haste and galloped away instead of attacking. Over the next several hours and several similar occurrences, they had yet to bloody their swords except for when Costa's decuria fought a brief skirmish that left at least one German escaping with a minor wound.

It was late in the afternoon when Tarquin called a halt at a small creek and told them to water the horses. No sooner had they dismounted than they heard hoof beats growing increasingly louder. Strabo breathed a sigh of relief when he saw Corius and shouted to Tarquin, "It's all right. They're Aeduans."

Corius drew rein and laughed. "Marcellus, now you're the one who is saving me a long ride to the Roman camp."

"What do you mean?"

Corius indicated two disgruntled German cavalrymen with their hands tied behind them and their ankles tied together under the horses' bellies. "They told us things Caesar will want to know." After hearing what the prisoners revealed, Tarquin wasted no time leading the turma back the way they came at a pace much faster than before.

Scevola stopped digging and let the wooden handle of the dolabra slip down to rest on the bottom of the wide ditch they were excavating. He looked at the arrow in the dirt a few feet in front of him and wished he was holding a scuta and in the ranks standing behind him facing the enemy camp. The two-legion-sized fort under construction was located on a low hill a ballista shot from the German defensive wagon barricade. German cavalrymen, each accompanied by a lightly armed foot soldier, were making repeated but ineffectual attacks on the Roman front rank only to be repulsed time after time. He thought it was odd the attacks were not followed by heavy infantry. Periodically, there was the ratcheting sound of the ballistae being wound followed by a thump as the spear-like missiles were released. Occasionally there was a cheer from the ranks when a bolt found a horseman or archer venturing too far forward of the German barricade. He wondered why the legions were building a fort or standing in ranks instead of attacking the Germans. Moments later, Vinicius, digging next to him, asked the same question.

"Scevola, you've been with the legions for a long time. Why don't we attack instead of hiding behind shields or digging trenches? Besides, we're building a fort far too small for six legions to occupy. It makes no sense when we're probably going back to camp in a few hours.

"Have you noticed the *Claudia* and *Fulminata Legions* were the only two legions marching with equipment? The fact we're building a fort for only two legions tells me which legions may not be leaving here. Shit, we're already outnumbered with six legions. What kind of chance are we going to have out here when the others leave? I'll tell you what it is, about the same odds Venus will come down here looking for my cock."

Scevola laughed at the irreverent comment. "I think we might have better odds than that. The bastards keep backing off instead of taking advantage of their numbers. I've got a notion the Germans are avoiding a real battle for reasons they know and we don't." The veteran legionnaire hawked and spat before continuing. "Right now, I hate the idea I've got my back to them and the possibility I've got to explain to the gods why I got an arrow in my backend instead of my chest."

Brecius, walking on top of the growing palisade, heard the legionnaire's comment and laughed. "Scevola, you old fart, my guess is you'll be kneeling a long time trying to answer the other questions they'll have for you before asking about the arrow."

Scevola looked up and gave the optio a rude gesture. "Well, at least I won't have to tell them I was an optio with puckered lips putting a smile on every centurion you ever served." The comment brought a laugh or smile to those near enough to hear it including Brecius.

The optio looked down no longer smiling and said, "Only the gods, Caesar and maybe one or two generals know what the shit we're doing. For certain, I don't know any more than you do. The way those Germans are running around making a lot of noise without getting anywhere makes me wonder if they do either." The optio started to move on, stopped and said, "Vinicius, the centurion turned down your request for transfer to the Tenth cavalry turma. Looks like you're going to have to keep on marching and digging for the *Claudia*."

As the optio walked away, the legionnaire cursed and swung the pickaxe hard enough into the bank to split the wooden handle. He looked at Scevola and said in an undertone, "I guess I'm not surprised. Whatever that *mentula* has against Marcellus, it seems Marinus now includes me. One of these days, something's going to happen to send him to the gods before he's ready."

"Be careful, Vinicius, such talk can get you into more trouble than the worst bad dream you had or ever will have."

"I don't have bad dreams; they're always about women and horses."

"Go get another dolabra. We're not done, and we may need this fort in case Caesar says good night, goes back to the camp and Germans finally decide to fight."

Caesar angrily tore off his red cloak and tossed it on the table scattering cups and almost overturning a pitcher of wine Otho barely saved in time. Next was the gold circlet he pulled off his head and threw on top of the cloak. He waited impatiently for the orderly to finish unfastening his cuirass and greaves. Otho rarely saw Caesar give into his emotions. One of the few who had was General Labienus pacing back and forth with his jaw clenched.

Caesar shook his head in wonderment. "I was there, and I don't believe it. I was sure soon after we got there and started to build the fort, he'd either fight or talk. By the gods, he did nothing except pretend he might with cavalry charges in which he didn't accomplish anything more than raising dust. Now I have two legions back there I can only hope are going to be there tomorrow. I've a mind to countermarch and bring them back before Ariovistus finally grows some balls. What do you think? Have I made a mistake and risk losing two legions in the bargain?"

"It's possible. As you know and expected, there was some concern before we marched. It was a gamble, but the game may not be over yet. The fact he didn't fight today gives reason he won't engage tonight. A countermarch would be prudent and give us all more sleep tonight than staying awake worrying about it."

"If I do, I'd look more the fool sneaking back to retrieve the *Claudia* and *Fulminata* by the dark of what little is left of the moon."

"Julius, this is no time to let one mistake beget another. I think the potential loss of two legions is too much price to pay to keep you from the criticism you may have erred. I believe a countermarch is prudent and preferable to what I believe is an unacceptable risk."

"So be it. We'll march in one hour to take position with a legion on each side of the fort. Orderly, get the cuirass back on me and..."

Otho interrupted, "Caesar, Tribune Setarius and Decurion Tarquin wish to see you on a matter they claim is urgent."

Irritated at the intrusion, Caesar was brusque. "It had better be important — I'm in no mood for trifles. Send them in and tell them to be quick."

The smile on the tribune's face when he entered the tent, far from reassuring the news was good, only increased his anger and frustration.

"Tribune, I don't see a smile has any place in this headquarters tonight. What have you got?"

The cold welcome failed to erase the tribune's smile; if anything, it became broader. "The Aedui turned over two prisoners they captured a few hours ago. They told why Ariovistus hasn't attacked and has no immediate plans to do so. Apparently, the Germans have women they call matrons who make prophecies for events ahead not unlike our priests do. They told Ariovistus the gods have cautioned against fighting the Romans before the New Moon appears, and if he did, the Germans would not be victorious. This seems to explain why the Germans have remained defensive over the past ten days."

"Anybody!" Caesar yelled. "When is the moon at its darkest?"

Otho was the first to answer. "Here in Gaul, the New Moon will be the night after next."

"Praise to Jupiter for giving the prisoners to the Aedui even if I would have wished knowing about this days ago. Whether he wants to or not, I'm going to force Ariovistus to fight tomorrow. With the help of the German gods, he will be my prisoner or swimming across the Rhine to get back to Germania. Tarquin, when this is over, find those matrons. If any are alive after the battle is over, I've a mind to kiss them and give them Roman citizenship. Titus, there will be no countermarch tonight. The plan stays as is. Send a messenger to the fort and tell them what we've learned. The news could make for an easier night for the *Claudia* and *Fulminata*."

"General Labienus, I'd like to be the messenger," Setarius said. "And Caesar, with your permission I'll remain the night there just in case the Germans decide not to wait for the New Moon. I stood those two legions up, and if Ariovistus does have a change of heart, I'd like to be with them."

General Labienus looked at Caesar and nodded his approval. "Flavius, I suppose you've earned the right, go ahead. Better take Tarquin and his turma for an escort to be sure in case your one eye can't see well enough to find the fort. Before you go, join me in a cup. I'm thirsty. I think Bacchus would approve and Jupiter wouldn't mind if Otho poured us a cup to toast the New Moon and a better day ahead."

Chapter 27

The legions began forming up just before dawn. The priests were ready at the first glimpse of the sun to slit a bull's belly to examine the entrails for favorable signs for determining the outcome of the day. Waiting for whatever the priests decided, Caesar thought there was little difference between how the Germans and the Romans approached a battle, often relying more on superstition than a cold appraisal of the chance for victory and the confidence to make it certain. He had paid for the bull with much more than was usual and made it unambiguously clear he believed the gods were going to give the sign it was time to march. He considered the possibility if the senior priest failed to understand the message and reported finding a tumor or some equally bad omen, the bull might not be the only thing sacrificed today. Tradition and ritual had their place, but necessity occasionally dictated a practical solution for winning a battle.

The sun had just cleared the horizon, and the priest proceeded with the ceremony in accordance with Caesar's directive to speed-up the usually lengthy ceremony. More importantly, he understood the unambiguous demand the gods were going to be satisfied the bull's entrails would be satisfactory regardless of how they looked. Caesar wasted no time after a cursory examination of the entrails to give the order to march. Caesar was confident in spite of the one-sided advantage the Germans had in numbers.

The silence in the valley was broken by blaring trumpets, booming drums and the loud chanting of the legionnaires. The noisy departure was intended to intimidate the Germans and reassure the two legions camped opposite the German encampment.

The two legions across from the German camp had spent a restless, tense night caused by random arrows or rocks hurled over the ramparts. Therefore, the sound of the approaching four legions was a welcome relief to the rank and file standing on the ramparts.

In contrast, flanked by Setarius on one side and Centurion Valens on the other, General Arridius viewed the activity and noisy clamor breaking out in the German camp with a bleak expression.

Strabo heard the general say in quiet understatement, "I would have preferred a quieter approach than what Caesar decided. Rufus, send a runner to General Paulus and tell him when the Auxilia takes position to form the left flank, the *Claudia,* followed by the *Fulminata,* will leave the fort and take position on the Auxilia's right. Until then, we'll remain inside in case the Germans decide not to wait for the Full Moon and Caesar's arrival."

Soon after the messenger left, columns of German cavalry appeared from both sides of the wagon barricade with archers following behind. The two columns quickly joined and began to spread out in a wide front. Strabo was reminded of a widening river as the Germans came toward the fort. In minutes, the fort was surrounded. Individual riders with spears couched under their arms urged their horses down into the wide six-foot deep trench in an attempt to breach the ramparts. Most soon found it was a mistake when their mounts were unable to gain the top leaving the riders vulnerable to spears that at such close range were lethal to man and horse. Darts, spears and arrows thudded on shields. Occasionally, he heard a sharp cry when a missile found a target. Worse was the shrill whinny of an injured horse. There was little they could do to shield the animals; two had already been hit during the night seriously enough to be mercifully put down. He thought the longer this was going to go on, the turma would be fighting dismounted. He was sure by now Tarquin was already regretting his decision to keep the turma in the fort instead of returning to the main camp.

Ursinus came up behind him and said, "Decurion, most of the horses are gone, either dead or too wounded to be of any use. What are your orders?"

He didn't have to think and answered quickly. "We'll follow the legionnaires and fight on foot. Tell them if they see a wounded legionnaire too disabled to leave the fort, exchange their spatha and shield for a legionnaire's gladius and scuta. Long cavalry swords and our smaller shields will do no good where we're going. Bring whoever is able to fight, and I'll show them how to use a gladius."

Moments later when Ursinus returned with seven men, Tarquin and Costa followed with what was left of his *decuria*. With only a little time left before leaving the relative safety of the fort, Strabo demonstrated the advantage of a thrusting and shorter gladius and the protection a larger scuta provided for fighting on the ground at close quarters. He prayed the brief lesson would be enough for them to survive.

Tarquin, obviously uncomfortably resigned to an unfamiliar way of fighting, reluctantly said, "Marcellus, it might be best if you take the lead. You know how to fight on the ground better than me. Where should we take position?"

"We'll follow the *Claudia* Legion and take position behind the legion's third cohort. If we defeat the Germans fast enough, the third line of cohorts in reserve may not be deployed. Who knows, you may only have to watch how a legionnaire on the ground does what we do on the back of a horse."

The German cavalry attack abruptly stopped when the standard of the Tenth Legion came into view a quarter mile away. The Germans fled the field. With precision and measured movement, the four legions moved across the field looking as if they were on parade. As soon as the Auxilia took position on the far-left flank, the Claudia and Fulminata legions marched out and formed up in the gap between the Auxilia and the Eighth Legion on the right. The Roman Army quickly dominated the field in three long lines, three cohorts deep with the smaller Roman cavalry slightly to the rear of each flank. Silence descended as the ranks of 20,000 legionnaires stood motionless with only the muted sound of rattling shields and the low cursing or ribald comments by nervous legionnaires breaking the stillness. They were ready to face an enemy nearly three times greater with stoic resolve except for the few who nervously leaned over and spewed the porridge eaten a short time ago.

The German infantry ran through the gaps in the primitive barricade of felled trees and wagons opposite the Roman ranks and assembled in seven loosely formed group with no discernible order. Each group represented one of the tribes comprising the German Army.

Strabo spotted Ariovistus astride a black stallion and easily recognizable by the same elaborate winged helmet he had seen when the king and Caesar met. The German women standing on the barricade wagons, hands outstretched, started an eerie keening. Strabo had the impression whatever they were wailing about was directed at the German host and not the Romans. He stopped thinking about the strange implications when the entire German infantry began rushing toward the Roman ranks.

The two opposing lines came together so quickly the legionnaires had no time to launch their javelins and simply dropped them, drawing their swords instead as they closed in a thunderous clap of colliding shields. What followed was the familiar cacophony of battle, the clang of metal on metal, shouted orders, the hoarse grunts of straining men and cries of the wounded.

Strabo looked left when he heard the sound of a galloping horse and saw General Crassus ride toward the front of the cavalrymen waiting to be deployed. He regretted being on the ground instead of sitting on a horse. He hoped his horse picketed in the fort was alive or not too badly wounded. He didn't look forward to the brutal push and thrust of shield and sword that in minutes left you exhausted until you either collapsed or were wounded badly enough the legionnaire behind stepped forward to take your place. It wouldn't be long before the first cohort already in contact move back line by line through the lines of the cohort behind. If the battle lasted long enough, as it most often did, a legionnaire in the first cohort might have as much as an hour to rest after leaving the battle line before gradually rotating back to the front.

Soon after the battle started, exhausted and wounded legionnaires in the first line were making their way back through the ranks for the fabri to look after. Although the fabri were not qualified physicians, the engineers were often used to help with the wounded when there was no immediate requirement for their technical skills.

The tempo of the battle was escalating rapidly shown by the increasing number of wounded coming to the rear. Strabo knew it wouldn't be long before the *Claudia* Legion's tired and bloody first cohort would be replaced by the one immediately behind. Rotation was already taking place in the Auxilia on the left and accelerating within the centuries in the first cohort in front. The fast progress of the rotation underscored both the tenacity of the Germans and their superior strength.

The Roman cavalry farther to the left was engaged in a furious melee with their German counterpart. He was gratified to see the Roman horsemen, more organized, were starting to prevail and push the Germans back toward their barricade. The hopeful sign proved ephemeral as a large German force of mixed cavalry and warriors on foot appeared and quickly changed the odds. A steady fusillade of ballista darts was not enough to stop a growing disaster on the Roman far left. Strabo heard the triumphal shouting of the Germans as the second cohort began moving ahead to replace the first cohort.

Strabo looked at Tarquin and said, "It doesn't look good. I hope things are going better in the center and on the right flank."

The two men watched General Crassus gallop over to the centurion commanding the third cohort and pointed toward the Auxilia's crumbling ranks. The centurion quickly ordered the cohort to turn left and led it at a trot toward the front of the Auxilia.

Already breathless after only a short distance, Strabo heard Tarquin running behind say, "Marcellus, if we manage to survive this, it will remind me why I became a cavalryman."

Strabo said over his shoulder, "I was awake a good part of the night thinking the same."

There was no reply. He thought the decurion's heavy breathing was the reason.

Followed by the two other cohorts in the third line, the centurion led them in a curving line forward of the Auxilia to stop the Germans beginning to sweep around what remained of the *Claudia* legion's left flank.

Strabo was quickly confronted by a German cavalryman trying his best to spear him while the warrior hanging on to the horse's mane came toward him. The bare-chested attacker on foot was raising his sword up and vulnerable when he shoved his gladius into the warrior's belly. The cavalryman realized too late a spear in close quarters was a hindrance and dropped the spear. He tried to draw his sword and failed. Strabo pushed his shield into the horse's face and slapped the animal's flank with the flat of his sword when it reared. The unfortunate rider fell backward and struggling to draw his sword; he died before he could.

Strabo turned in time to raise his shield and stop the sword about to split his head with the edge of his shield. In the process of trying to dislodge it, the warrior yanked it from his hand. Unable to free his sword stuck in the shield, the German dropped it and grabbed the axe tucked inside his leather belt. The German eyed the gladius Strabo was holding and came toward him with a confident smile. Later, Strabo was certain the German was still smiling when he buried his sword in the warrior's neck.

He glanced to his right and saw Ursinus holding a bloody spatha and already moving on to the next German. He bent to pick up an oval shield laying across a dead German and felt a sharp painful blow across his shoulders hard enough he fell to his knees. He saw the legs of his attacker standing over him and swung his sword to the side, hitting the German across the shins. The German fell backward screaming. Strabo left the wounded man for whoever was behind to finish him and moved on.

Minutes passed so slowly they seemed like hours and Strabo, lungs heaving, wondered how much longer he could remain standing or lift his sword. His shoulders ached where the sword had cut him. Fortunately, blunted by the armor, the wound probably wasn't as deep as it felt. He hoped the trickle down his back was more sweat than blood. He took a moment to wipe the blood off his hand and sword hilt. Feeling the sting of the numerous cuts on his right forearm, he knew not all the blood was German. He recalled Scevola's leather forearm guard and resolved to make one for himself assuming he survived the day and had the opportunity before the next battle.

Strabo looked downhill and saw the thinning and wavering line across the Roman front. He wondered how much longer the Romans could hold or the Germans would fight. It appeared when the fighting started for every German falling to a Roman sword, two more were there to take his place. The disciplined legionnaire ranks had become less precise, nevertheless they were more disciplined than the milling mass of warriors. He sensed rather than saw signs the Germans seemed less aggressive and their battle cries more muted than before.

He took another look at the Tenth Legion in the center of the line and saw the legion's eagle standard remained in place. The dot of red near the standard could only be Caesar's distinctive red cloak. The legion was moving step by step closer to the German barricade. The Germans began slowly falling back. It wasn't long before the entire German line disintegrated as the warriors turned and left the field at the run, some casting away their weapons and shields in their haste.

At first the legionnaires stood in stunned disbelief then with renewed energy and confidence, the ranks moved forward at a run. The massacre began. Unlike his reaction when the Helvetii camp was stormed where he'd been revolted at the carnage that followed, he felt nothing except relief he'd been spared. Objectively, he considered his reaction was a result of more experience in battle and a need to insulate emotion from the awful consequences of battle.

There was a stillness on the field at stark odds to the fierce battle raging a short time ago. The silence was broken only by a subdued murmur as legionnaires moved across the field with practiced efficiency helping the wounded, collecting the dead and retrieving all equipment usable or repairable. The fabri were busy salvaging wagons from the German barricade to carry the dead and wounded. Strabo saw what was left of the turma's horses being used to pull the wagons. With indifference, the majority of the dead being thrown off the wagons were women and children. The fabri cleared the wagons in a hurry to get the wounded to the main camp. Soon trumpets would signal the time for centurions and optiones to form ranks.

Standing between Ursinus and Tarquin, Strabo surveyed what was left of the turma lining up behind the third cohort. Of the survivors, there wasn't a single cavalryman without wounds; eight had been seriously wounded and another more fortunate dozen would rejoin the turma soon. Five were already being loaded on the wagons with the rest of the dead. He supposed the victory today would be more celebrated among the generals tonight than in the rank and file thankful only to get some sleep and the chance to wake up in morning. He looked down at Ursinus sitting on the ground clumsily trying to tie a bandage on his leg as blood dripped down his arm from another wound on his shoulder. He knelt down and finished tying the bandage.

"Ursinus, you'll ride in one of the wagons with the other wounded."

"No, I can get on a horse, and it'll be a lot more comfortable than riding in one of those wagons." The cavalryman stood up, his eyes rolled back and Strabo caught him before he fell and gently lowered him on the ground. He pointed at the nearest two men in his decuria with minor wounds and said, "Take him to the fabri. When they're done with him, make sure he gets on a wagon."

Otho motioned to the slave to fill Caesar's cup for the second time. General Titus Labienus didn't recall ever seeing him so relaxed, casual. This was not the common demeanor of the calm persona he normally projected. The second cup of wine suggested the possibility Caesar, who had seemed so sure of success, harbored the same doubts he had for an outcome far from assured. He suspected Caesar's ebullient mood reflected relief more than joy over the victory. He gave great credit to him for the outcome, but he would give more to the gods. Days ago, he thought Caesar had made a mistake in not being more persistent in seeking a resolution with terms than arms. Caesar was convinced their only choice was fight or be starved into making concessions tantamount to a defeat. Caesar had been proven right. Labienus also knew his mood would be more somber when the rest of the casualty reports came in. The few he'd seen so far did not suggest the others would be any better.

"Publius, I congratulate and thank you for your quick intervention. Had you not acted in bringing the third line into the battle when you did, we might still be fighting." Labienus had wondered if he would recognize the young cavalry general's initiative for solving a developing problem Caesar should have seen first. Time would tell if there would be consequences; Caesar wasn't known to be kind to anyone who did anything that might leave him open to criticism.

Setarius came into to the headquarters carrying several tablets with the preliminary casualty reports including prisoners captured and an estimate of German casualties. By tomorrow and over the next few days, the number of Roman dead would continue to rise as more wounded were summoned by the gods.

Caesar put down the wine cup and frowned, his celebratory mood quickly dissipating as he reviewed the grim numbers. When he finished, he handed the tablets to General Labienus.

"It's much worse than I expected, more than we suffered against the Helvetii. Titus, we need replacements as quickly as they can get here. I'll be leaving within a few days for Provincia to conduct the annual Assizes. My first priority is to recruit replacements there and in my other two provinces for our losses here. Those without any training will be given just enough to get them to Gaul in some semblance of order. We'll finish their training when they get out here. Based on what I'm hearing about the Belgae, I intend to raise two more legions. I hope the Belgae don't do any more than talk and bluster until we can get the army in better shape to meet any threat from them — or any other tribes thinking we're vulnerable enough to chance a fight."

General Titus glanced at the last tablet Caesar had not bothered to read and said, "The Aedui says Ariovistus was able to get across the

Rhine. Diviciacus also reports the Germans on the other side of the river are leaving and heading northwest. I think we can safely conclude the border with Germania is secure at least for the foreseeable future." The general read further. "Evidently, the king's two wives were among those killed when the camp was overrun. I wonder while Ariovistus is looking to replace his wives, the Germans may be looking for a new king."

Caesar laughed. "I do believe Ariovistus will have difficulty finding any woman willing to marry a man who left his wives behind, and as you say, particularly when his prospects for retaining a crown are not good. On a more serious note, it's early to put the legions into winter quarters. We've had a challenging campaign. The men need to rest. I've been thinking Vesontio would be ideal for the main camp with smaller cohort-sized camps from each legion for active patrolling. Titus, you'll command the legions in my absence. I'll leave it to you to make the final decisions where the legions will winter."

Strabo, Ursinus and two other men from the decuria waited for the last of the wagons carrying the wounded to arrive. He looked at the long line of legionnaires sitting or lying down along the tent where the more seriously wounded were being taken care of. Nearby, there was a growing line of legionnaires stretched out on the ground who had lived only long enough to make it back to camp. The more fortunate already cared for, as much as the primitive conditions allowed, were being helped by or waiting for tentmates to get them back to their century.

Another smaller group separated from the rest waited listlessly under the watchful eye of a medical orderly. One legionnaire sitting apart had a bloody bandage where his right hand used to be and another one covering his right eye. He started to turn away and took a second and closer look. It was Tertious. All the animus he had for the legionnaire abruptly vanished. The once large, blustery legionnaire looked diminished. He wanted to walk away but didn't and reluctantly walked toward him, thinking there was nothing left in the legionnaire's future except begging for coins on a city street.

"Tertious, Fortuna hasn't served you well this day."

The legionnaire turned enough see Strabo walking toward him and his empty expression quickly changed to an angry scowl.

"Until now, I didn't think the gods could shit on me more than they already have. You come along, and I realize they're not through yet. What's the matter, Decurion..." emphasizing the title pejoratively, "don't you have anything else to do than help the gods dump more shit on me?"

Strabo wanted to turn around, angry his sympathetic gesture had been rebuffed. He was also at a loss for what else to say. A moment later, the legionnaire's angry bravado disappeared replaced by hopeless misery.

He sat down across from Tertious and said, "It's not the way of it. I would see no man treated so ill."

In a choked voice, Tertious asked, "Even someone who planned to gut you at the first chance?"

"It seems a thing better to leave in the past. Why we didn't get along, I don't know. I wonder if I only made it worse."

There was a long pause before Tertious replied, "Blame it on Marinus. He was the one who told me to go after you. He paid me the day you got conscripted to come down on you and make your life so miserable you'd quit or desert. After what you did to me, Brecius transferred me to the guard detail. Marinus caught me asleep one night. He said he would overlook it and give me a chance to get back my optio rank if I took care of you. He wanted me to carve you up, even maimed enough you'd have to go back to Massilia as a reject. I don't think he wanted you dead as much as disgraced or reduced to nothing. By then I was ready to kill you and maybe would have at the latrine."

"Did he ever tell you why he wanted this?"

"No, and I never asked because I didn't care. You were General Strabo's son and privileged, and it made it easier for me to do what the centurion asked."

"He told you who I was?"

"Yes, and he wanted your name known, maybe so others would treat you the way I was being paid to do."

Strabo remembered what Brecius had warned him about and the possibility it had something to do with his father. It was obvious Tertious had told him only part of the story. Perhaps one day his father could shed some light — considering his present strained relationship with him, it was unlikely he would ever know.

"Marcellus, best be careful. I wager Marinus isn't through with you. He'll find someone else like me to finish what I couldn't. He's worse than me; he won't do the job himself."

"Would you tell Tribune Setarius what you told me?"

"No, I don't have time to do anymore talking here. I'll save it for where I'm going." The legionnaire raised his arm and bit down on the hilt of the small dagger in the sheath strapped to his forearm. After letting the dagger drop, he quickly picked it up with his left hand and said with a malicious smile, "I hope Marinus gets done what I didn't. One day when Marinus joins me, I'll remember to ask him why." Without any hesitation, Tertious plunged the blade into his neck.

Strabo stood up and watched the dying man fall backward and give a final convulsive shudder. He walked away thinking the gods weren't going to be any more kind to him than when he was alive.

Chapter 28 October, Winter quarters southwest of Vesontio

It was late afternoon when Strabo led his decuria into the west entrance of the small fort. The *Claudia* Legion's second cohort was spending a month there before being replaced by another cohort from the main Roman Army wintering in Vesontio. The fort was one of four such camps dispersed around the main encampment. Century-size patrols accompanied by a cavalry decuria were sent out two or three days at a time both to keep the legionnaires busy during the winter months and to maintain surveillance of the nearby tribes. The cavalrymen and legionnaires were all looking forward to their rotation back to Vesontio in two days where the whorehouses were always open, and wine was available to get through a dreary fall and a fast-approaching winter.

The fort was near enough to Bibracte that if he asked the centurion commanding the fort permission to visit the settlement, it would have been promptly approved — unless the cohort commander was anyone other than Marinus. Strabo had no desire for an inevitable and another pointless confrontation with the centurion. He would soon be in Vesontio and confident Tarquin and Tribune Setarius would allow him a few days in Bibracte. Lately he was somewhat concerned about the reception Raven would give him based on her apparent indifference on the two brief occasions they last saw each other.

They were passing the cohort's log-constructed headquarters when he recognized the familiar face of Tribune Setarius' senior orderly. He kept going toward the part of the fort where the decuria was billeted when the orderly motioned to stop.

"Decurion, Tribune Setarius just arrived and is inside the headquarters talking with Centurion Marinus. He asked me to watch for you and request your presence as soon as you returned."

"Very well." Strabo dismounted and handed his spear, shield and the reins of his mount to the nearest cavalryman and said to Ursinus, "I doubt we'll be going back out on patrol before we return to Vesontio. When the horses are looked after, have the men start cleaning up their kit. We all look like we've been in the saddle for the last month which is about the way it's been."

Strabo followed the orderly and waited at the tent entrance until given permission to enter. The tribune's back was to him with the centurion sitting across from him. Marinus for a change was attempting to be cordial indicated by a rare smile albeit somewhat strained. Strabo fixated on the smile never imagining the bastard was capable of mustering anything resembling a friendly expression, faint as it was.

Setarius stood and greeted Strabo warmly obliging the centurion to stand up as well. When he did, there was no longer a trace of a smile.

"Marcellus, I received a message from Diviciacus yesterday inviting me to Bibracte. He asked if you would be able to accompany me. In my reply, I assured him I would and Centurion Marinus has agreed to support the request. We'll leave tomorrow."

Strabo had difficulty remaining composed at the welcome prospect of going to the settlement much sooner than expected.

"Tribune, I look forward to joining you." Assuming there was nothing more to be said, he started to leave but stopped when the tribune continued to speak.

"Centurion Marinus tells me you have done a commendable job scouting for the patrols and earned the praise of the other centurions you've escorted."

With effort, Strabo refrained from looking at Marinus whom he imagined was inwardly recoiling from having said anything complimentary to anyone, least of all Marcellus Strabo. He suspected the centurion felt he had no choice when Setarius undoubtedly asked how the new decurion was performing. He remembered what Tertious told him and ever since he had been sleeping lightly.

He did the only thing he could do and said to the centurion, "Thank you, Centurion. I have good men in my decuria, and they've helped me to become a better leader."

He quickly saluted and left before he was tempted to ask the centurion why only a few days ago, he berated him for the decuria's disheveled appearance after returning from a rain-soaked patrol. The incident was only the latest of similar occasions when the centurion went out of his way to single him out for criticism.

They left the fort soon after the sun topped the mountains. The night before, the tribune declined the offer of an escort befitting his rank reassuring Marinus that with Strabo and Patrin, his young muscular orderly, he would get to Bibracte safely. Before they mounted, Strabo noticed the tribune's silent and subdued behavior and wondered at the change so different from the day before.

His attempts at light conversation over the next two hours were met by curt, absent-minded responses. He finally gave up after it was apparent Setarius was too preoccupied with other matters.

His mind drifted to thoughts of Raven and their last time together. The passionate images were quickly displaced by the concern something had changed. Perhaps she realized her childhood infatuation for him had vanished even as his feelings for her had transformed from a tolerant, childhood affection to feelings he'd never experienced and wasn't sure months ago he was capable of — or perhaps didn't care if he ever did. His father may have been more right which, until now, he was not willing to admit. Whores were safe, and the only investment was a handful of coins without the concern of any emotional attachment. His memories of Helena, the Greek whore he'd been with when he was taken, remained vivid. He was starting to recall the details of their last encounter when the tribune's voice intruded.

"We'll rest the horses over there." Strabo wondered why. The ride had been easy, and there were only a few more miles left to reach their destination.

Before dismounting, Setarius told the orderly, "Patrin, I want a private word with the decurion." The orderly nodded and moved to the other side of the clearing out of earshot. "I need to tell you why we're going to Bibracte in case you want to stop here and return to the fort. It wasn't an invitation from Diviciacus. It was a request from your father. He's in the settlement waiting for us."

Too angry to speak, Strabo grabbed the saddle pommel and started to mount. Setarius snatched the reins and said, "Marcellus, you can leave after I've said what I need to. When I'm finished, you can go back to the fort or anywhere else you choose. I think you've earned the right to hear the truth and choose afterward what you do with it."

Strabo stopped, intrigued by the suggestion of something momentous even the faint possibility he might be offered a choice to leave the army a free man. He faced Setarius and waited for him to say more. He was both skeptical and hopeful the tribune was about to say anything he wanted to hear.

"Marcellus, I was in the next room the last time you saw your father. I heard the heated argument the two of you had. The reason I was there was to ask for his assistance in obtaining the men I needed for the two legions Caesar asked me to form. After you left. I listened to your father for hours telling me how often he paid the bills for the wine and whores you couldn't. I thought the young boy I watched growing up had more backbone and promise than the spoiled, ranting drunk I heard shouting and cursing in the next room. Unlike your father who only threatened to disinherit you, had you been my son, I would have thrown you out the door years before.

"I felt sorry for him and angry at you. I was the one who suggested service in a legion might stop you from spiraling farther downward, and conscription could be the way to make it happen since it was unlikely you would volunteer. At first, he was against it." He held up a hand to forestall the heated protest Strabo was about to make. "I'm not talking about following your father's footsteps. It was intended to give you a chance to make something of yourself. So, in some ways, I'm more responsible for what happened to you than your father."

Rigid with anger, Strabo rejected the unflattering description refusing to believe the truth of it. Dimly he recalled Vinicius once warning him to be careful. At the time, given his friend's wanton behavior, he seemed the last one to be giving advice. Reluctantly, he accepted there might be more truth to the tribune's characterization than he was willing to admit. Setarius noted the subtle change, and his voice softened.

"My words are unkind, but there are times when the truth is, too. The general finally agreed. I dictated the letter sent to Caesar requesting a favor to take you on as a centurion. The way I worded it, Caesar would never have agreed to appoint you to a rank which you didn't deserve and were unqualified to have. For better or worse, I intended you to be a ranker just as your father and I began."

Surprised, Strabo interrupted. "I thought he was a centurion when he first took the *sacramentum*."

"That only proves how little you know about your father. We spent years serving in the legions. Your father rose faster than I did. During a battle in Cappadocia, the officer commanding the century in which your father was an optio was killed. He took command of the century with results that caught the attention of General Marius. After the battle, he was appointed to the Centurniate. Not long after, in a subsequent battle we faced an overwhelming force. Because of my size, I was appointed Aquilfer to carry the legion's standard. It's heavy and requires two hands to keep it upright and visible. It also requires protection for the bearer to ensure the eagle standard never falls or is captured. The position can easily be a death sentence depending on the protection provided.

"During the battle, the legionnaires protecting me were killed or so badly wounded they left me to try and keep the standard upright with one hand while fighting with the other. I was wounded in several places, including losing my eye. Although badly wounded himself, Centurion Strabo saw what was happening and saved both my life and the standard. I tell you this to explain why I would do anything for him, even if it means subjecting his only son to the hardship of legionary service."

Strabo visualized the battle the tribune described, and from his experience so far, he was able to visualize and confirm the awful reality Setarius and his father had faced long before he took his first breath. He resented that his father or no one else had ever told him. Until now, he believed his father had also enjoyed privilege and opportunity.

"Tribune, what did you mean when you said I would choose what to do with the truth?"

"Before Caesar left, I asked him to release you from the army if you wished it. When your father returns to Provincia, you may go with him or anywhere as a free citizen or remain with the legions if you choose. If you leave the army, I'll be satisfied you lived up to all my expectations and more importantly your father's. Will you go on to Bibracte with me? If not, I'll go on without you."

There was no hesitation in his answer. "I'll go."

Both men said nothing during the short ride remaining to reach the settlement. Strabo began to dread the arrival and resisted the urge to turn back. He was angry at what the tribune had persuaded his father to do, and a part of him might never forgive it. Yet, what the tribune said about his behavior had more truth than not and recognizing it made it difficult and painful to face his father. He tried to think of what he would or should say, but his mind was a blank.

Too soon the principal gate of Bibracte was there and so was the desire not to enter. By comparison, facing the Helvetii and the Germans was less intimidating. He forced himself to relax and think about being free again to choose what he wanted to do and where to do it. The chance to remain in Bibracte with Raven was tempting as was the strong possibility of never seeing Marinus again.

He saw his father talking with Diviciacus in front of the tribal leader's spacious residence. He looked older, smaller than Strabo remembered since the last time they were together. The thought of their last meeting and how he behaved and the acrimonious things he said because he was drunk were too painful to recall. Unfortunately, he was beginning to remember too many other previous occasions when he had behaved badly. Setarius was right. He deserved to be cast out.

The two men saw them approaching. Diviciacus was smiling. His father was not. Strabo dismounted and tried to walk calmly toward him afraid his anxiety would be obvious. He stopped a pace away and tried to smile.

"Salve, Father, I have much to say to you, and I'll begin by saying I'm sorry."

"Marcellus, I will ask whatever else you have to say, let it be about today and the future and not things best forgotten."

They clasped arms and Strabo, his eyes watering, unable to speak only nodded.

Epilogue

Raven watched the reunion of father and son with curiosity and wondered how they would be able to overcome a stormy past. With mounting dread, she saw their initial stiffness quickly replaced by a warmth she knew was unexpected by either man. As a child she had never been comfortable with Lucillus Strabo on the few occasions he visited Bibracte. He seldom smiled and seemed austere although it may have been because his capability with the Aeduan language was limited. He wore a cuirass or tunic when he was a general and later after becoming governor of Provincia, a long white robe the Romans called a toga. She really didn't understand why her mother's close friend agreed to become his wife, particularly later on the yearly visits she came back to Bibracte and complained of living in Roman Massilia. She was glad Marcellus was different, not stern, seldom smiling like his father.

More asleep than awake, Marcellus reached over and pulled her closer. A moment later, his rhythmic breathing told her he was asleep

He told her what the tribune had said to him on their way the settlement. There was no hint of what he intended to do. She listened to him as he described how happy he was to see his father and grateful a past and unpleasant interlude had been replaced with reconciliation. He admitted he was surprised at the promise of a brighter, warmer father-son relationship ahead. She wondered if the same would be true for her and Marcellus. The fact she was awake after their passionate lovemaking simply underscored an uncertain future and a decision she hoped would never be required.

Talos returned occasionally and kept her informed of developments in the north. She knew he held out more than friendship with her. Had Marcellus not come when he did, it could well have been Talos next to her. He deserved better than she had given him, and she would always feel some guilt. Talos seemed more content to be with the northern

Aeduan and Belgae tribes where the Roman presence was distant. He sounded very much like many of the younger men here who would have preferred Dumnorix was tribal leader.

The winter encampment at Vesontio had not endeared the Romans and added to the fear it was a prelude to a Roman Gaul. The idea of Roman dress, the Latin language and customs becoming dominant was abhorrent. Particularly so with the Belgae who according to Talos were stoking the unrest among the tribes including the Aedui tribes in the north. Before she saw the five more legions enter Gaul, she never had any strong feelings one way or the other about Romans and any potential threat they posed for Gaul. In truth, she was grateful they had come to stop first the Helvetii and then the German tribes. Now gratitude was slowly being replaced with dread.

She reached down and felt the slight swelling of her belly and wondered when she should tell Marcellus. She had planned on telling him tonight when she saw him ride in. The way he greeted his father, and afterward when he appeared undecided about his future gave her pause. She would wait.

His decision would determine what she would do and where she would go.

Author's Notes

I believe every reader of historical fiction wants to know when and where the author departs from fact and relies on imagination to tell the tale and possibly to compensate for less than rigorous research. I spend almost as much time researching as writing in an effort to get time, place and events close to historical truth without subjecting the reader to details both disruptive and annoying.

The Strabo series follows closely Caesar's ten-book *Commentaries* with Book 1 providing the backdrop for the first volume; the next adventures of Marcellus Strabo rely on the events and places in books 2 and 3. The remarkable thing about the *Commentaries* is they provide a contemporaneous view of the Roman conquest of Gaul rather than relying on later historians to report what happened. However, Caesar's purpose was not to give an account to posterity as much as it was to tell the folks in Rome, "I may be gone, but this is where I am, and look at what I'm accomplishing." Does that mean Caesar stretches the truth? Based on the investigations of professional historians and archaeological evidence, most historians conclude he did. If I've made any mistakes in historical accuracy, I'm more than willing to concede they are in some part because of my reliance on Caesar's version of the truth.

The Legion: A legion was commanded by the *Legatus Legionis*, usually a senator, who held the post for several years. Second in command was the *Tribunus Laticlavius*, who was the senior of the other four tribunes. The name was derived from the broad stripe he wore on his tunic or toga. Tribunes were staff officers and normally did not command except under unusual circumstances, and this applied to the Laticlavius who could be put aside in battle conditions in favor of an older, more experienced individual such as the *Praefectus Castrorum*, camp prefect and third in command of the legion. The Praefectus would probably have been a former primus pilus, First Spear.

The strength of a legion was plus or minus 5000 men, about the size of a modern-day army brigade, consisting of ten cohorts with each cohort divided into 3 maniples. You will not find "maniple" mentioned in the narrative for two reasons. I wanted to simplify the structure for the reader, and Caesar makes no reference to the term. The unit was used during the Republic and later during the Empire. The maniple consisted of 6 eighty-man centuries. The first cohort had a strength of 1000 men with 9 centuries instead of 6 for the other cohorts. The first cohort was commanded by the primus pilus who was the senior centurion of the legion. The other 9 cohorts were commanded by the senior of the 6 centurions assigned to it. A century was organized into 10 eight-man contubernia. The Centurion (59 in a legion) commanded the principal maneuver unit in the Roman army. I strongly recommend looking in the glossary below for a description of the centurion. Each legion also had a cavalry troop of 130 men. It's fair to say the typical legion in the field seldom had the strength matching the organizational chart as my own army career can attest where from company to division units were fortunate if they had 80-90% strength in the field.

The Battles: All the battles in the narrative follow closely how and under what circumstances they were fought. The first battle with the Helvetii at the Saóne river crossing is called "The Battle of the Arar," which was what the river was called then. I never could pinpoint exactly where the crossing occurred. After crosschecking other sources, I'm confident I was within a mile of the location.

The second battle, "The Battle of Bibracte" was fought a few miles away from the settlement and northwest of the Saóne. The site is well known in part thanks to a French Lieutenant in the 19th century who found the crescent-shaped trench behind which Caesar's baggage train and the two new legions and part of the Auxilia were positioned. I did take one liberty in the narrative when I had the *Claudia* Legion more involved than they were to keep Strabo in the action.

The next battle Visontio, marked "3" on the map, was not really a battle at all. I believe it was more of a takeover of the tribal settlement with little resistance, if any because Caesar got there before Ariovistus. The third battle, "The Battle of Vosges" east of the Vosges Mountains was fought a few miles south of the modern French city of Colmar and approximately 15 miles west of the Rhine River. I credit Google Earth for helping supplement the terrain map of the region with getting a better perspective of the battlegrounds. The latter is especially true of the distinctive city of Besançon (Visontio) located within a U-shaped bend of the Doubs River.

Battle Numbers: Caesar never stops his emphasis on proclaiming the overwhelming numbers of his opponents. The tribal numbers often included the entire population of the migrating or attacking force. He can be alibied in part for the exaggeration because women did often fight alongside the men, and if they didn't fight, they were often present at the battle giving vocal and physical support (aiding the wounded). The six legions, if full strength would have had 30,000 legionnaires plus another 5000 auxilia (mixed cavalry and infantry), the legions alone had less than that, possibly by as much as several thousand. Discounting the women and children and tribesmen no longer able to fight, Caesar's adversaries outnumbered him by roughly three to one.

Logistics: I included Caesar's continued concern about grain for the legionnaires and forage for the livestock. It was a genuine concern for it frequently influenced where a battle was fought (Bibracte and Vosges) or postponed. The legions were not able to carry large amounts of supplies; consequently, they were extremely dependent on what could be obtained locally by paying for it, obtaining it by reason of helping a tribe (The Aedui) or by conquest. Roman army rations seldom included meat – wheat (corn) or when it wasn't available barley was the preferred ration. Barley was issued instead of wheat to a unit that by their actions or inactions did not deserve the food of choice.

Glossary of Terms and Place Names

Terms

Aquila (a qwee la): The legion standard represented by an eagle gilded in silver clutching gold thunderbolts

Aquilfer (a qweel fer): Legion's senior standard bearer ranking just below a centurion

Auxilia (owks eel e ah): Auxiliary refers to the non-Roman forces that frequently manned the frontiers or reinforced the legion, particularly with cavalry. It was also common practice to relocate indigenous troops to locations along the Roman frontiers in other than their own tribal lands. The latter provided further assurance against internal rebellion. During the time of Julius Caesar and the republic, the Roman Army depended on foreign cavalry, placing its emphasis more on heavy and light infantry to win battles. Caesar's battle experience in Gaul taught him the importance of cavalry, and gradually the Romans began to place more importance in their capabilities for reconnaissance patrols, skirmishing, and flanking maneuvers. By the second and third centuries, the Roman army completely embraced the use of cavalry and had become proficient in its use. The cavalry was the highest paid in comparison to the infantry units attesting to their increased value.

Auxilia cavalryman wore boots with spurs, a lighter cuirass and carried a longer sword. Their shields were considerably smaller and round instead of the rectangular, curved scutum of the foot soldier. In addition to the sword that all cavalry wore, some were armed with small javelins or darts carried in a quiver attached to the saddle. Other cavalrymen carried longer spears that were not thrown but were used as a lance to jab downward.

The saddle during the period had four pommels which helped to maintain a firm seat since there were no stirrups. Stirrups weren't used until sometime in the fourth or fifth century. Accordingly, it would have been very difficult if not impossible for a rider to remain securely in the saddle if the spear was used as a lance as was the case by cavalry and mounted men in later centuries.

Balteus (bal tay oose): The Roman military belt that more than any other item distinguished the legionary. Divestiture of the belt was considered a severe punishment and a disgrace.

Breccae: The leather trousers reaching below the knee worn primarily in winter. Apparently, they were uncomfortable and grudgingly accepted only in cold weather.

Caligae: The hobnailed boot-sandal all Roman officers and legionaries wore. They varied in thickness if not in basic design according to the weather and terrain. Somewhat open around the upper foot they were laced to mid-calf or higher, depending on the weather. In winter and cold regions, legionaries wore socks and wrapped their legs in felt or wool cloth for additional warmth. The Emperor Caligula derived his name from the time he was a small boy and spent much of his time in uniform around legionary barracks. Because of that, he was given the nickname *Little Boots.*

Carnyx: A type of tapered trumpet used in battle by the celtic tribes. It was almost six feet long and held vertically when played to allow the sound to carry farther, and presumably above the battlefield. Only pieces from the top (animal or dragon heads) of the instruments have been found. Depictions on Roman coins and decorative objects give some idea of the size and shape. Modern reconstructions have been included in Celtic music ensembles. The sound, mournfully rich and not unpleasant, ranges from a deep bass to a high-pitched blast. The notes would have traveled a great distance and made them both effective for signaling as well as inspiring warriors to give it their best. Sample audios can be heard by Googling 'Carnyx' on the internet.

Castigato: For major offenses, punishment was administered by a whip consisting of multiple of leather lashes with or without lead balls attached to each lash. See fustuarium below.

Centurion: The rank of centurion was both prestigious and highly coveted. The role of centurion in the Roman Army has no direct counterpart in the U.S. Army today. It is fair to say, the centurion performed the duties with the commensurate responsibility of a modern-day commissioned officer, warrant officer or senior non-commissioned officer depending upon the centurion's seniority and specific position in the Roman military hierarchy. For example, the most senior centurion in a legion of typically 5000 strong could be legitimately compared to a battalion commander and normally in the grade of lieutenant colonel, while the most junior centurion was assigned duties more in line with a first sergeant or sergeant major. The centurion above all represented the senior, combat-tested leadership of the legion, which represented the primary fighting unit of the Roman Army. Unlike the tribunes and even the legion commanders who normally served only brief periods in the army, the centurions were the professional backbone upon which legion and field commanders absolutely depended upon to maintain discipline and win battles.

Entry into the centurionate was achieved in diverse ways. He could receive a direct appointment if the candidate enjoyed sufficient political clout or served in various positions below centurion considered to be possible steppingstones but not necessarily within the legion. Being the son of a centurion was a decided advantage. Coming up through the ranks, where after about 12 years a legionary would become eligible, was undoubtedly the more traditional and preferred means of access as it allowed the selection process to focus on proven ability. Literacy was essential and may have been the greatest determinant for preventing a ranker from being appointed to the centurionate. Eligibility might be accelerated by extraordinary conduct in battle. Military governors of a Roman province had the authority to make appointments to the centurionate. The senior centurion was the primus pilus, First Spear, a reference to the pilum or javelin that with the gladius, or short sword, was the premier weapon of the Republican and Imperial Roman Army. As the senior centurion of the legion, he led the first and largest of ten cohorts in the legion. Each cohort was assigned 480 men in six centuries except for the first cohort, which was nearly double the size of the others. The duties and responsibilities of the primus pilus were considerably greater than that of the other centurions. By tradition, the position was held for only one year after which transfer as *primus pilus* to another legion was possible. Just as likely, it was a significant steppingstone to promotion to procurator in the civil service or as a *praefectus castrorum* (see below).

Century: A unit of 80 men commanded by a centurion; 60 centuries to a legion. The century was divided into ten *contubernia* with eight men assigned to each *contubernium*.

Cohort (Cohors pl): A unit of 480 men; ten cohorts to a legion. The exception was the first cohort nearly double in strength and led by the senior centurion, the primus pilus.

Consilium: Military council.

Contubernium (contubernia pl) An eight-man unit. Each contubernium shared a mule, with or without a cart, to carry their baggage, a tent in the field, a room or rooms in garrison and were allocated rations as a small unified mess See Century above.

Cornicin (ies): Horn blower(s).

Dignitas: The literal meaning meant dignity; however, the term conveyed much more than the modern literal definition. It represented the sum total of a man's stature gained from military and service to the state. Romans placed more importance and emphasis on maintaining dignitas than we do in modern times. In particular, Roman nobility and officers would seek death before the loss of dignitas, a loss of stature that could only be redeemed by suicide.

Decuria (e) A ten-man cavalry unit.

Decurion (aes): An officer commanding a 33-man turma or cavalry troop as well as his own decuria and banner carrier. A turma had two additional decurions; the duplicarius was second in command and the sesquiplicarius was third in command with each also leading a ten-man decuria.

Denarius (denarii plural) The denarius was the largest Roman coinage denomination.

Dolabra (e) (doe la brey): Combined pick and axe the legionary used to dig trenches and fell trees for constructing fortifications, obstacles and roads.

Draco: The dragon standard signifying a cavalry unit and carried by the *draconarius*. A tubular cloth sleeve, fashioned serpent-like, was attached to a metal dragon, wolf or snake head. A noise device in the jaws was activated by the wind that also filled the body of the sleeve. The wind-filled body and the accompanying noise must have been impressive to see and hear when carried on parade or in battle. Apart from the psychological impression the standard was intended to convey, it may have had a practical use for indicating the wind direction to the mounted archers. The use and design of the draconarius was not original to the Roman cavalry but was copied from the Dacians (see Dacia above). By the third century, the standard was in widespread use by the Roman cavalry.

Dux: Leader. The equivalent rank of a general without a leadership position and usually assigned to the staff of a Roman legion or army. Over the centuries, the title eventually became precursor to the title duke.

Epona: The horse goddess worshipped widely by Celtic tribes throughout Gaul and Britannia.

Fabri: Craftsmen: The fabri were similar to the modern-day military engineers responsible for technical supervision and construction of projects such as roads, bridges, even aqueducts. The legionnaire provided the bulk of the workforce as necessary. During the Roman Republic, there were no physicians (medici) except occasionally when a civilian doctor might be available to tend the sick and wounded. Most often the wounded were looked after by the fabri, likely because they were not required to fight as legionnaires and were available and possibly viewed as technically more skillful. The Roman practice at the time was to place the wounded in nearby villages with more medically qualified personnel. It was not until later during the Roman Empire when the army brought physicians and medical orderlies into the army structure

Fasces: A bundle of tied birch rods around an axe that symbolized the *imperium* (authority) of a high official including the emperor and province governors. The fasces were carried by *lictors* walking in front of the official when he attended a public event. The fasces continue to be used in modern day and are represented on U.S. coinage and as part of the formal seal of the U.S. Congress.

Ferrata: Legion name meaning iron

Flagrum: Also, *flagellum.* A whip consisting of three leather thongs and sometimes tipped with lead. Lighter whips without the lead were used for less severe punishment while the heavier version was reserved for major punishments and to scourge a victim prior to crucifixion.

Fustuarium: A harsh sentence reserved for particularly serious offenses such as sleeping on guard, cowardice or desertion during periods of active engagement with the enemy. The condemned man was set upon with cudgels, usually the wooden portion of the pilum with the metal shaft removed, by members of the individual's own unit, probably his century. The punishment was occasionally administered to an entire unit including a legion when the charge was cowardice. In such cases, lots were drawn and every tenth man was condemned. The term 'decimated' refers to this practice. In most cases, the individual or individuals died from the brutal beating. If an individual somehow managed to survive which was probably rare, he was summarily dismissed from the army in disgrace.

Gladius (glah dee oose): The short sword carried by officers and legionaries.

Gravitas: A derivation of 'gravis,' yet the word connoted much more than a 'grave' or dignified demeanor. To possess gravitas was to have not just the appearance of substance but the reality of it as well. Much like the oriental concept of 'face,' the individual who had gravitas commanded respect and authority far beyond the prestige accorded only by title or position.

Legatus: (le gah toose): Legate, a province governor and or a general.

Medicus: (medi coose) (medici pl): Medical doctor.

Mentula: Vulgar reference to the penis

Optio (nes): A rank just below centurion equivalent to a junior officer or senior sergeant. The *optio* wore a crest on his helmet smaller than a centurion's and carried a long, knobbed staff (hastile). Unlike a centurion, he wore his gladius on the right hip as did the common legionnaire. The optio was generally positioned in the rear rank to prod legionaries who appeared to be ready to break ranks.

Phalorae: Military decorations

Pilum (pee loom), Pila (pee la pl): Spear. It's common for most to believe the short sword (Spanish sword, or gladius, was the weapon that most characterized the Roman legionary. The argument can be made it was the heavy javelin which defined the Roman Army. Slightly over six feet in length, it had a long pyramidal shaped point that took up almost a third of the total length of the weapon. The opposite end was encased in a short metal sleeve. The Roman Army depended on volleys of pila to deliver a punishing barrage before the front ranks charged. The metal shafts of each pilum were not tempered and bent easily on contact. The latter was an intended consequence and resulted in weighing down the shields of the opposing ranks allowing more lethal opportunity to wield the gladius at short range.

Principia (prin sip e ah): The headquarters building or tent in a Roman fort.

Primipilatus (pre me pee lah toose): Former senior centurion.

Primus pilus (pre moos pee loose): It literally means "first spear" and was the form of address and title of the senior centurion commanding the first cohort in a Roman Legion. Prestigious and coveted, the position was the apex of the centurion's career. The position was usually held for only one campaign season before it was surrendered. There was no limit on the number of times an individual might hold the position. It was not unusual for a centurion to be so privileged multiple times. Once a centurion attained the position, he was automatically accepted into the equestrian class, a distinct step up in the social hierarchy of the Roman Republic and Empire. The vast majority of centurions never achieved the rank. See Primipilatus.

Pugio (poo gee oh): The dagger each legionary wore on the balteus on the opposite side from the *gladius.* Centurions wore the dagger on the right side while the legionary wore his on the left.

Sacramentum (sahc rah men toom): The oath each legionary took to the emperor after recruitment and later during the empire to the legion commander to assure personal loyalty

Sagum (sah goom): Military cloak made of rough spun wool worn by the common legionary

Salve: Hail. Used as a greeting.

Scutum (Scuta) (skoo toom; skoo tah)): Shield; (plural)

Sesterce (ses ter chee) (pl- sestertii): A coin worth approximately a quarter of a denarius (see above) and two and a half 'asses,' the smallest of the three denominations.

Spatha: Cavalry sword much longer than the gladius

Testudo: A tight defensive formation named for the tortoise in which the inside ranks placed their shields over their heads while the outside ranks kept their shield facing outward. The formation provided protection from arrows and other missiles from above and the sides.

Torque (tor kwee): Military or tribal decoration worn around the neck.

Tribuli: (thistles) Thick stakes 5-6 feet long and sharpened at both ends used as part of the defense of a Roman fort or marching camp. Three stakes were lashed together at the center to form a large caltrop which were embedded in the upcast obtained from the forward defensive ditch below the low rampart walls. The stakes would have been a deterrent to any foot or mounted attack. When the camp was moved, the stakes were pulled up, untied, and loaded on mules or carried by the legionaries for use in building the next camp.

Turma (ae): Cavalry troop consisting of 32 men and led by a decurion. (See decurion above). There were 10 turma assigned to a legion during the time of Caesar. The number of turmae varied considerably depending on battlefield requirements and the availability of cavalrymen.

Via Principalis: One of the two main streets that crossed in the center of a Roman fortress at a right angle with the *via praetoria*. Near the intersection of these two roads is where the headquarters or principia would be located.

Vicus (vee coose): Settlement, village

Vitis (vee tis): The distinctive twisted 'vine' stick a centurion carried symbolizing his rank. It was also frequently used as an instrument for administering corporal punishment.

Place Names and Geographical Features

Aquileia: Northeast of Genoa, Italy

Genava: Geneva, Switzerland

Ocelum: Approximately six miles northwest of Turin, Italy

Hispania: Spain

Massilia: The port of Marseilles, France

Visontio: Besaçon, France approximately 50 miles southeast of Dijon and 60 miles west of the Swiss border